THE
FOUNDRY

www.jfitzpatrickmauldin.com

To my wife and daughters,

for always believing I am more than the sum of my parts.

You make it possible to dream, to love, to touch stars.

FOUNDRY INTENT - CONTACT AND SAVE EARTH
UEI
F.I.C.S.E.

FROM: THE UNITED EXPLORATION INITIATIVE

TO: JACKSON AND ADRIANNA HUGHES

WE REGRET TO INFORM YOU, THAT DESPITE YOUR
TECHNICAL SKILLS, KNOWLEDGE, AND STELLAR
PERFORMANCE IN YOUR RESPECTIVE SCIENTIFIC
FIELDS, YOUR REQUEST TO JOIN THE F.I.C.S.E.
FLEET HAS BEEN DENIED DUE TO MEDICAL CONCERNS.

IF YOU WOULD LIKE TO DISPUTE THIS DECISION,
PLEASE CONTACT THE U.E.I. CENTRAL OFFICE
IN WASHINGTON, DC.

SINCERELY,
UNITED EXPLORATION INITIATIVE PLANNING COUNCIL

ATTACHMENT: MEDICAL RESULTS, JACKSON HUGHES

PART I

CHAPTER 1

"Have you ever dreamed of touching stars?" Mom whispered from across the kitchen table, its surface crosshatched in shadow, Dad standing by her side.

I blinked at her, not understanding.

From the tone of her voice, I knew this wasn't just more star talk. Even in the dim light I could see that her expression was mixed, excited and contemplative, as well as resolute. Something was up. Something was different.

Our dark kitchen stank of pepperoni pizza and stale coffee. The sink was full of dishes, and I could see that one of my toys had gotten kicked under the stove. The clock over the microwave ticked over, 12:45 AM. It was way past my bedtime.

I considered her words. It was such a small question, innocuous, common for her, yet I had a feeling it would change my life forever. I had no idea what to say, how to respond. In all honesty, my biggest concerns at the moment were if I had enough markers and crayons in my art box. If I would be allowed to play at the park when I came home from school tomorrow. I was highly concerned that the box of snacks in the kitchen was getting low, and that my Aunt Carol restricted internet access when I stayed at her place in the afternoons. I can bet *minha avó* wouldn't care, grandmothers and all, but she lived too far away for me to see her every day, so that meant I spent my afternoons with Dad's sister, which was fine.

I sat there for a moment in silence, telling myself Mom had to be messing with me. It was just another game she and Dad had come up with to teach me a science lesson. At a time when kids at kindergarten were talking to my parents about distant relatives setting foot on the Martian plains beneath Olympus Mons, I just wanted to dig in the dirt for worms. Space was too big for me to wrap my little head around.

Maybe we were about to go stargazing? Take the telescope out into a field on a clear night? Hot cocoa and a big furry blanket. That was fun, right?

"Touching stars?" I asked. "Is that like going to the moon?"

Mom smiled down at me, dark eyes gleaming. She was tired, withdrawn, and yet…

"Far beyond the moon, Milo," she said. "So very far, *meu lindinho filho.*"

And with that I knew to take her seriously. Mom only spoke Portuguese, her family's language, when the matter at hand was near and dear to her heart. She was a second-generation immigrant; her mom's mom having left the favelas in Rio in the 2040s to live in the Nevada sticks, then Colorado. Every syllable she had uttered was like spell work. I didn't understand half of it, most days.

Ferdie, our orange tabby, rubbed against my leg. I stroked her soft back and took a small comfort in her presence.

"That's right!" Dad added, a widening smile on his round face. He put a hand on his hips and swung an outstretched finger through the air. "The moon is but a breath away… But us, yes… us… We will live far beyond. The chance of a lifetime."

The great unknown was no new topic in the Hughes house. My parents both worked in fields that involved space exploration. Mom in a lab as a biologist, studying the effects of micro-gravity and cosmic radiation upon the human body, while Dad pored over data from half a dozen telescopes ranging from the Hubbell to the James Webb, to the Star Reach Constellation. Space exploration was their life, their passion. They lived and breathed all that involved the final frontier.

Yet none of this helped me understand why Dad was setting Ferdie on the back porch wishing her a good life, while Mom tossed our clothes into suitcases and set them by the door.

We were not going stargazing.

"Pick one toy, sweetie," Mom said, pointing to a pile on the living room couch. "Be quick about it."

My options were limited; the choice, hard. Did I take a die-cast motorcycle? A set of playing cards? A classic Buzz Lightyear action figure? No. All these were left behind. What I wanted in that moment, all the toys in my room, and what I needed, to feel secure in my uncertainty—were not the same. Only one thing would do in that frail moment, a plush anchor for my emotions. I squeezed Jasper in my arms, the ears of the soft doggy nuzzling against my neck.

I had made my choice, and it was a good one, but like any choice, this one was terminal for its counterparts. I mourned the loss of other possibilities, anxious sniffles held under my breath, but was not given long to remain in this place of sorrow.

Mom belted me into the back seat of our Tesla, our neighbors' houses dark, a pale half-moon hanging overhead. I couldn't see much from my car seat, but I saw enough.

The front door of the house beside us burst open, casting a pillar of light onto freshly cut grass. My Aunt Carol came bolting after us in a nightgown, waving her arms, screams issuing from her throat. I'd spent most days of recent months at her house, playing while Mom and Dad were absorbed by their work, our kitchen table covered in papers and laptops, counter covered in frozen meal boxes, crumbs and bits of food on the floor. Carol and I had fun most of the time. We did puzzles and watched classic television. She made me grilled cheese sandwiches and let me have as much chocolate as I wanted, so long as I took a break from my tablet.

Mom and Dad glanced at one another from the front seats, and a silent decision was committed to. The motors of our Tesla whined as we sped out of the driveway. My Aunt shrunk in the rearview. Everything in that moment went hazy as we thundered off into places unknown, rushing headlong into a void as complete as space itself.

But why?

Dad's phone rang. He held the button on the side and turned it off. Moms did the same an instant later. She tossed hers out the window and watched in the sideview mirror as it shattered on the highway, her raven corkscrews blowing back into her face before she could close the window. My heart found a seat in my throat. I clutched Jasper and kept my mouth shut.

Riding in the backseat at night was like falling into an abyss. I had little sense of true direction, no concept of where we were going. There wasn't much to see out the windows, not that it mattered. All that shot past were the occasional broken streetlamps or gas stations, abandoned buildings and empty lots, none of which told me where we were.

Mom and Dad cycled through unusual phases of utter quiet and manic conversation as they chugged can after can of energy drinks. One moment they would laugh, then engage in an intense discussion, then fall into anger, then apologize. I did my best to follow their exchanges, but after a while the exertion of decoding their rapid-fire debates exhausted me. I hadn't gone to first grade yet. I was in way over my head. The only snippets I was able to understand involved what they said was a journey into deep space aboard a starship, the *Vasco Da Gama* of the UEI, some fixy mission to follow a signal of greeting from something calling itself the Foundry. More space stuff.

I'd heard them discuss the UEI before, though I was too young to truly understand. The United Exploration Initiative was some sort of multi-national organization whose mission was to help humans settle on other worlds. Most talk of it had come in the form of Dad complaining about paying more in taxes to fund stupid projects, and Mom saying there was no other way to save humanity. Two distinct groups of people had emerged on our world, and they were each determined to save humanity from the other; those who lived in a world of automated decadence, and those who suffered and starved. It was just more babble that gave me stress.

Jasper nuzzled against me, and I closed my eyes, his velvety fur brushing against my neck.

I drifted in and out of consciousness, our car screaming into the darkest depths of night.

I dreamed throughout our entire trip but couldn't make total sense of the story that played out in my mind. Comprehension came and went, understanding beyond my years, then ignorance. In truth, I think it was a defense, a means to keep myself from thinking about the fact that my parents had snatched me up in the middle of the night, stuffed the car full of all our things, and took off without much more than a few cryptic words of explanation.

Endless fields of dead land appeared in that half-conscious state, the result of conversational snippets. What had once been fertile soil flanking the highway, capable of feeding millions, was now cracked dirt and desert, a dusty expanse of wasteland devoid of life. People had moved on to survive, left this place once filled with opportunity and piled themselves into cities, one on top of the next till all the work and resources had run out. Jobs had been sparse to nonexistent, leaving those in exodus to scratch by, to fight over scraps.

"The Earth was not meant for eleven billion people," Mom whispered. "Cascade failure is near. We have to stop it."

"The Foundry will help us," Dad replied. "It will help us."

Soldiers marched over a black hill, rifles in hand, bombs going off in the distance. Without abundance in their own country, these people had rallied together and went into battle. The world did not need their oil any longer, this energy source replaced by another, and so they opted to take what they needed from the world.

The shallow reaches of the ocean, once colorful and full of life, were now bleached and dead. People in rags stood along its shores, stabbing at the water with spears hoping to catch something to eat, but nothing lived beneath its surface that would qualify as dinner.

A pile of fried insects lay at the center of a table in a cramped apartment, the room smelling of onions and spices, nine sets of eyes fixed on it. It was all that was left, all that was available. Better to be bizarre than hungry. No veggies this time, son.

None of this was right. This was not how it was supposed to be.

Despite the madness, a few had found a way into luxury, living in their remote homes off of long-acquired wealth, precious food delivered by drone as they sat in their castles of homes. Had that been us? Was my neighborhood, Whispering Pines, a suburban bastion against this disparity?

I'd never missed a meal in my life. I'd always had what I wanted. What was this feeling?

People streamed in from the countryside. The cities swelled like water balloons, filling and filling and filling with sweaty, hungry bodies, their faces locked onto screens, single-minded, afraid, forcing a thin membrane of sanity to the cusp of bursting. More and more and more. The flow did not cease even if it had no place to go. It made me want to scream, I knew what would happen if it burst. All the pain, the fighting. How much more could it take?

The car hit a bump and Jasper tumbled from my arms. Distressed, I started to cry, grasping for him wildly, unable to move for the harness of the car seat. The dog was within sight but out of reach on the floorboard.

My heart pounded. Dreams. Just dreams.

"Are we lost?" Mom demanded of Dad, and out of instinct reached around and handed Jasper back to me. "I think we might have missed our exit."

"No, no." Dad shook his head. "According to the map they gave me it's up ahead. You see, right here. Service road, five miles down. They know their stuff. We're almost there."

The horizon brightened as night drew to a close, giving way to dawn. I scrubbed the rheum from my eyes and yawned.

"*Filho da mãe.* If we miss our window…" Mom let the words hang.

"I know, Adriana. I know. We'll make it in time, don't worry."

Jasper glared at me with his oversized eyes and we both gave a sigh. He was thinking what I was thinking. Morning or not, I was sleepy. About the time I drifted off again the car came to a halt. Mom unbuckled me from my car seat and helped me get out.

We were parked in a field of sand and dirt, a distant mesa the color of rust silhouetted by the rising sun on our right. I shivered in the brisk air. Dad handed me my jacket and I shrugged it on.

"Desert can be chilly at night and in the morning," he said, hugging himself with his arms, elbows rested on the tip top of his round belly. "Come on. This way."

We dragged our luggage through hard packed sand and powdery dirt, leaving the Tesla behind. For as much as Dad complained that "the damn thing" cost, it felt weird leaving it in the middle of a field unattended, not a parking lot in sight.

"Won't somebody steal it?" I asked.

"Where we're going, we won't need it," Dad replied. "I doubt they can collect on me, either. Like to see them try."

Mom glanced over her shoulder and sighed. "Are you sure this will work, Jackson? If it doesn't, we're going away for a long time."

"Yes, I'm sure it will work. We hired the right team. You know it's the only option, and the regrets… they far outweigh the punishment. *Desenmerda-*

te." Dad's accent was terrible when he tried to speak Portuguese, always had been.

"Did you just tell me to get my shit together? Right… It's just…" She paused for a moment and sucked in a breath of cold air, collecting her will. The raw excitement in Mom's expression had been replaced with resignation, determination, the focused look of a woman with an immovable goal, a true mission, a just cause. "Okay. You're right. *We're still an effective team.*"

Dad let out a nervous chuckle. "Damn right we are."

We rounded a set of rocks, eased around some prickly scrub, some cacti, and stepped past a cluster of shoulder-high succulents, before coming upon a chain-link fence. Dad peeled back a roll of severed links and Mom and I squeezed through. The sleeve of my jacket caught on one of its sharp ends and the fabric ripped. I snatched my hand back before it could cut me.

"*Toma cuidado, viu?*" Mom asked, turning my palm over to inspect the skin. "You okay? The end didn't catch you, did it?"

I shook my head and drew Jasper tight against my chest. "No."

"Good."

"Look at it, Adriana." Dad raised a hand to shield his eyes from the coming dawn. "Just look at it. It's magnificent."

There are a few moments in life that no matter what happens after them, good or bad, no matter how much time passes, you never forget the way they made you feel. For me, one such moment was when I looked upon the launch craft for the first time, the vehicle that would cement my fate and steal all choice from my future. The explosive spear stood before us in the deserts of Arizona, a white and black rocket tall as a skyscraper with the words SpaceX written down its length, its scale imposing upon my five-year-old existence like a timeless monolith. Thick plumes of white vapor billowed from the dozens of connections and umbilicals along its length, cryogenic fuel relief valves hissing as they regulated pressure.

I set foot onto the platform and could feel the ground beneath us vibrating, machines eagerly awaiting takeoff. The soles of my red Chuck Taylors slipped on a section of clear fluid, and I fell forward, my right knee catching on the pavement. Cool, ozone-scented air prickled at the back of my neck and my skinned knee. We were so close to this rocket, so close I could hardly see the tip of the explosive spear set to hurl my family and I out of the planet's gravity well.

Jasper and I were so small, so insignificant compared to this towering creation. This craft had swelled to encompass all comprehension. It was my entire world, my reality. My fate.

My heart gave a start and my feet locked into place. Standing became impossible, my legs having turned to jelly. I put a hand on my skinned knee and winced. Mom hurried over and scooped me up in her arms.

"Mommy?" I whispered in her ear.

"Yes, baby."

"Is that how we are going to touch stars?"

She gave a smile that crinkled her whole face. Even the tired lines at the corners of her eyes, hidden away most days beneath thick layers of mahogany foundation, were clear in that unfiltered expression. "Yes, Milo. We are going to touch stars."

Dad waved at us from up ahead. "Come on. This way. We have to hurry. Only a few minutes before they do a sweep of the area."

He led us down a series of paths hemmed by stacks of tubing and concrete walls. We rushed up several flights of stairs down to a tunnel with a locked door at its end. Dad punched a series of numbers into a box and the door opened.

At the end of a wide hall I could see the entrance to an elevator that led up the platform tower to the peak of the launch craft. A white box was traveling upward, pausing, and traveling back down. To the left and right of the access door, two uniformed guards stood conversing with another family, machine guns held loose in their hands.

Dad fumbled in his bag to produce a set of plastic, iridescent badges, one for each of us. He placed them over our necks and took a deep breath.

"Let me do the talking," he said.

Mom gave a swallow and set me down. "Will it work?"

"I'm tired of being asked this every two seconds."

"Fine."

"Sure paid enough."

We did as we were instructed and worked our way towards the queue. I watched as a mother and father, about the age of my parents, boarded the elevator with a little girl in red pigtails. The girl stared at me and gave a wave, her expression as serious as a funeral. She wasn't the only one feeling as if she'd been dragged to the slaughterhouse.

I lost sight of her as the elevator doors closed.

"ID badges, please," the guard on the right called, shouldering his rifle and holding out his hand.

"Right here, right here!" Dad held his up. "All here. All official."

"Name?"

"Yes, of course." Dad gave a mock bow, the gesture meant to hide the tremors of his nervous hands. "I am Jackson Hughes, astrophysicist. This is my wife Adriana, biologist, and our son, Milo, age five. We are bound for the *Vasco Da Gama.* This is the correct launch is it not? I would hate to have stumbled onto the wrong pad. Happens to me all the time, you know, absent-minded professor and whatnot."

The guard glared at Dad and inspected the badge. My lip quivered and I withdrew behind Mom's legs, Jasper held in front of my eyes.

I can't say how, but in that moment, I knew I had a choice. Mom had been tempted by the last-minute option to run, yet she had renewed her resolve. Even though I was only five, I knew I had one as well. If I screamed loud enough, hard enough, I could convince these uniformed men I wasn't supposed to be here. I could convince them my parents were doing something wrong and we could leave this rocket and go home. By that afternoon I'd be at my Aunt's house, playing on my tablet and eating chocolate, having fled uncertainty for safety. Then again, I knew my parents would be in big trouble if I spoke up. The choice was easy.

All I wanted was to be a good son.

"Nervous, little guy?" the other guard bent down and asked me. "First time on a rocket?"

I nodded, keeping my lips sealed.

"You'll be okay. There's a lot of noise and shaking but it's fun. Promise. It's like a roller coaster ride. I've been up a few times. But you, man you're lucky. By the time you turn my age you'll be an old hat when it comes to space. This is first contact, little guy. First contact! Your name will go down in history."

The first guard shook his head and scanned our badges with a handheld box. The box chirped and turned green.

"Alright, you guys check out." He pointed ahead. "Proceed to the elevator. You'll change into jumpsuits and give your luggage to the cargo technician. Have a safe liftoff. Good luck at the Foundry."

We followed the guard's instructions, and before I knew it, we were sitting in a capsule at the apex of the massive rocket. A middle-aged technician in a white jumpsuit buckled me into my seat. He could see my apprehension and gave both a smile and a nod that said, 'You got this, buddy."

"Just hang on to that doggo of yours." He gave me a pat on the shoulder and went to help the next person.

We were not alone on the launch craft. A dozen seats were filled with other families. Two parents, one kid, never more. All were now in white jumpsuits, a look of apprehension on everyone's face but for Dad. The space was dim and small. Almost every surface was covered in a dazzling array of lights and switches, displays crammed full of data and views from outside the craft. At the head of our seated rows sat three people, what could only be legitimate astronauts, our pilots.

"Oh baby, this is gonna be great," Dad growled in excitement. "Come on. Big money, big money, no whammies."

Mom took a clarifying breath and reached out to squeeze my hand before returning it to her side.

The girl in pigtails locked eyes with me. She raised her stuffed octopus and its tentacles jiggled. Jasper waved back.

"Attention, everyone aboard Launch Craft Zed Four Nine," a deep, baritone voice called over the intercom. *"This is your pilot, Henry Brittan of NASA and the United Exploration Initiative, our vehicle is done fueling and the skies over Arizona are free from commercial traffic. We are clear for takeoff. Support crew, please make your final check and vacate the capsule. We're ready to light this puppy up."*

The final crew member stepped through the external hatch and closed it behind him. A digital clock appeared on the wall above and to the right of me.

The voice on the intercom returned. *"Falcon 15D transfer to internal power complete. M1D fuel bleed complete. Prop GSE securing. Self-align verification. Final engine chill down. Cryo helium loading."* I gave a swallow and took a deep breath. Jasper did the same. He was nervous. I could tell. *"Pad deck water deluge system activation. Merlin engine ignition…"*

My seat began to vibrate, the intensity redoubling by the second. Everyone in the capsule went silent in anticipation of liftoff but for my Dad. He mumbled excited words under his breath in rapid succession.

I clutched Jasper against my chest and felt my stomach bottom out as the vibrations soon transferred into upward motion. I was slammed into the back of my seat as if someone had shoved their foot down on the gas pedal. My plush toy remain fixed to my chest. He might as well have been glued in place. Every part of my body had become as heavy as a neutron star, as if Earth was waving goodbye, showing me triple fold what its gravity was like before leaving its bonds forever.

I watched a video on my right that showed the base of the rocket as it distanced itself from the platform. Numbers at the bottom increased, giving feedback as to our current relative velocity. We were moving upward, screaming into the fading blue sky on a pillar of light hot as the sun's chromosphere.

Dad began to hoot. "Hell yeah! I'm goin' to space. Wooooohoo!"

From the front of the capsule one of the pilots shouted back at him over the noise. "Sir, please be quiet."

"How can I? This is the most exciting day of my life!"

"Try your best or I'll have to seal your lips with epoxy."

There was no going back. Whatever this was I'd been forced into was my life from here on out. I only wished I'd been given a choice in the matter. A real choice.

We hit orbit and the vacuum engines engaged for one last burn, jostling me in my seat, putting our capsule on a trajectory to intercept with a starship. Gravity vanished and I felt weight flee my body.

The blip grew larger on the tracking display, becoming a graphic of a slender cylinder with massive engine nozzles at one end, a great sphere at the other. Around its middle rotated a flat ring, half a dozen spokes connecting it to the main body of the ship like the hub of a bicycle wheel. Though the picture was small, as I let my eyes adjust, I could see fine details, the clusters of geodesic tanks along the cylinder, the spurs of instrumentation, the expandable docking areas for capsules just like ours.

I looked to Jasper for advice. He stared back with his shiny plastic eyes and kept silent. Typical.

Mom reached over and squeezed my hand again. "Welcome home, son."

"Home?" The word felt foreign on my lips, incongruous with what I could see and feel in that moment.

"*Bem vindo àto Vasco Da Gama.* Your home for the next forty years."

CHAPTER 2

Within a few short hours, we were given the all-clear to unbuckle from our seats and make for the exit. The pilot had brought the capsule up to the docking clamps of the *Vasco Da Gama* with little more than a bump. Mom and Dad gave each other a furtive glance as the support crew helped us get ready to disembark.

We were just about to vacate the capsule, having been the last in line, when a pair of men in white and orange jumpsuits blocked the hatch. They had angry looks on their faces, their eyes narrow and dark. They took the most menacing stance possible in zero-G, bodies spidered out over the exit, blocking most of the light from the docking extension. Even as a kid, the thought crossed my mind that if they withdrew into the hall, they could close the hatch and trap us in here. There would be no way to escape. There was no going back. We either went through them or remained here forever.

"Identify youself," said a thickly muscled man with a Spanish accent and straight, dark hair gone wild in null gravity. He was dressed in a white jumpsuit, the ship's emblem stitched on one side of his chest, his name and title stitched on the other. *Esteban Lopez – Quartermaster – UEI.*

"Hello, Mr. emm, Lopez." Dad lifted his ID badge and pretended to act calm. "Jackson Hughes, astrophysicist."

The slender man beside him, Deidrick Jones, shook his head. "Cut the shit, sir." Deidrick's feet were rested on the base of the hatch making him appear like a spring ready to deploy. "It took longer than normal, since you were already cleared to get on this can, but we just got word from UEI ground control. Your credentials are bogus."

"I—well—" Dad raised a finger and began to chew at his bottom lip. "I am Jackson Hughes. And this, this is my wife Adriana, and my son Milo. He is five years old, just as the mission requires. She is a biologist. One of the best in her field." He chuckled nervously.

Mom cut in, "We're a whole family. A whole smart family."

"We know all about you," Esteban said. "We been sent to escort you to the bridge. Don't make a fuss, ya?"

"Me?" Dad's expression became incredulous. "I never."

"Might be fun if they did," Deidrick added.

Esteban shook his head. "Too much clean up. Let's be tryin' to keep their blood on the insides."

I reached for Mom's hand. Jasper had a lot to say about the situation, but he was afraid to speak up. He didn't want to be left in the capsule any more than I did.

Esteban and Deidrick moved out of the way and waved us through.

The docking extension the capsule connected with was a long white tunnel, its walls a zigzagging pattern that resembled the inside of the expandable bellows of a narrow accordion. Where the space was wide at this end, it appeared to taper as it neared the ship.

"Have you ever moved around in micro-gravity?" Deidrick asked us. "Would have been part of your training if you were here legitimately."

Dad shook his head, and for a moment his face turned the slightest hint of green. "No. This is our first time."

"Alright then. Take it slow, no sudden movements. Especially you, kid. Most of the chambers are padded, but we don't want any broken arms or legs." He leaned towards Dad. "And if you feel sick to your stomach, sir, swallow it down."

"What does that mean?"

Esteban gave Dad a withering glare.

"Oh… Understood. Swallowing down."

Dad went first. At a nudge from Mom, I followed after, my body gliding through the seemingly frictionless air. Jasper's ears floated up and smacked me in the chin.

I followed the example of our guides as they led us through the null gravity environment, clasping the occasional handholds along the way, using the bars to both steady and propel myself ahead. We neared the end of the tunnel and a low hum intensified, the drone of well-tuned machinery hard at work.

We entered the main hub of the ship and a door closed behind us. A wall was painted with a picture of this starship hurdling through a ring towards a red star, the letters FICSE at the bottom, the words Foundry Intent - Contact and Save Earth curved around the outer edge.

They led us through another series of halls connecting to a lift of sorts, yet without true weight it was hard to say if we were traveling up or down. Jasper didn't like the sensation. If anyone was going to get sick, it would be him. I put my hand over Jasper's mouth and consoled him.

Our escorts said little, and my parents said even less. It was clear, even for a kid, they'd been busted doing something they shouldn't have. Now they would be forced to throw themselves at the mercy of the court.

We entered a spherical room lined with displays and controls with a dozen acceleration chairs similar to what we used in the capsule. At the center was a massive display that peered out into space, instrument feedback showing the location of stars and trajectories, lines of detailed stellar information.

A wide-shouldered man in a light blue jumpsuit with a UEI patch on his shoulder turned to face us. He rubbed his palm across his pale, baby smooth jaw, then over his slick bald head. His sharp eyes flickered, and the threads of his embroidered name tag, Captain Tobias Williams, glimmered in the instrument light.

At his side floated a short woman with umber skin like Mom's, her curly hair pulled into a ponytail, her face soft lines and angles, a tablet in one hand with a colorful collection of anime stickers on its back, a set of Chinese Baoding balls in the other. Stitched on the left chest of her jumpsuit was a black rod with snakes wrapped around it, open wings at the top. *Dr. Holly Reed - M.D. - UEI.*

Opposite her were a man and woman with the same last name and similar features, jumpsuits covered in pockets, tools dangling from belts at their waists. *Perry Stablecamp. Mary Stablecamp. Mechanical Engineer – NASA / UEI.* Were they brother and sister? Sure didn't act like husband and wife. I found myself staring at Mary's bright lavender hair, its color like that of cotton candy. I'd never seen hair like it, did she inherit this from her grandmother like everyone else?

"It really is you," Captain Williams said, his expression sagging. "When Deidrick called to tell me, Jackson Hughes was aboard the capsule I thought he was making things up. FICSE, this mission, has been a long time coming, decades in the making, mountains of multi-national political will gathered and pushed off into the sea to get us to this point. Our nerves are pretty stretched at this point, so, you know, a bit of humor never goes amiss. Right? You gotta be shittin' me Deidrick, I said. But here he is in the flesh. You got something to say for yourself, Hughes?"

Dad wrung his hands and offered a nervous smile. "Ready for duty, sir?"

Captain Williams turned to the woman at his right, while fiddling absent-mindedly with a silver pin of a cartoon dog with floppy ears that was stuck to his jumpsuit's chest. I recognized it. This was a Silver Snoopy, a special award in the astronauts' world that Dad had always hoped to earn for himself. Only the best of the best earned one of these little metal doggos. "Where are the Lancasters, Holly? Surely you didn't kick them out for medical review. They were supposed to be on the capsule in place of the Hugheses. It was a condition of the Canadian Space Agency."

Dr. Reed paused her rotating Baoding balls for an instant, then resumed. She was about to speak before Dad cut in.

"I can answer that for you."

"I'm sure you can, Mr. Hughes. Doctor Reed, would you be so kind as to give us the official word?"

The doctor pocketed the balance balls and gave a nod. "Yes, sir." She swiped her finger across her tablet and frowned. "Looks like they're stranded in Arizona."

"Stranded in Arizona?" Captain Williams raised an open palm to his mouth and acted surprised. "That's a long damn way from the Lagrange point. I wonder how this happened. Did someone send them the wrong evite? They did RSVP, yes?"

Mom took this moment to speak up, "Look, Tobias, we can explain."

"Does everyone know why we are here? Why we are on this ship?" The captain pointed to the display behind us. A black and orange signal wave appeared, its peaks and valleys jagged like a saw. He tapped a button on the wall, and it began to play, a vertical line starting at the left end and moving to the right. The sound that issued from the bridge's loudspeakers was unlike anything I had ever heard before. It was uniform and high pitched, like the cry of a baby seal that followed a complex, meandering sequence of dots and dashes. The sound lasted only a few seconds, yet it was burned into my memory forever. Something about it was infectious on a near genetic level. I felt as if I was on the edge of understanding things someone my age, possibly even my species, had no right to.

For a brief moment the world inside my mind flashed pink, and a sense of awe, a sense of calm washed over me. The flash of color told me everything would be okay. That my problems, our problems, a world overpopulated, short on food, an unbalanced environment, failing economics, death and war, were all mere obstacles to be overcome. That with help, help that would be provided, that they could be solved and put to rest.

I was not alone in my experience. Everyone on the bridge was moved by the signal. Influenced in some way. They had seen something, though I couldn't be sure we had all seen the same thing.

Had an alien talked to me?

"This is why we are here, people." He pointed again at the screen. "We have been sent a signal from beyond the edges of the Kuiper belt, far beyond the Oort cloud, and through the black gulf that lay between stars. This might sound like a bunch of scrambled nonsense, but what it says is, *'Hello, humanity. We are the Foundry, come see us soon'*. This is the primary mission of the United Exploration Initiative. We must give humanity a future no matter what the path, colonize new worlds, create more efficient technologies, find help beyond the stars. Humanity must become a multi-planet species or fall into darkness. The Foundry's signal is part of this plan. That message calls to us, but it is not all, and you all know it. The rest, the feeling… Everyone experiences it.

"This signal has originated from several locations over particle bands we never considered practical for communication until now. These neutrino streams, as you all know, are unhindered by most matter, meaning that the signal when it reached us came in clear as day. And of these mysterious signals to chase, ours is the closest.

"Humanity is at a tipping point. We've reached out into the solar system to colonize new worlds, but it might not be enough. A case of too little, too late. It doesn't take a PhD to see our planet is at a crisis point, even those Fifth Great Awakening yahoos know, despite saying it's God's wrath and Man's sins. Our ecosystem can't take much more. Too many humans, too little regard for sustainability, economic growth at all costs.

"In the next fifty years, we'll need to grow more food than the first ten thousand years of human existence. Our energy demands have increased twenty-fold in the past ten years. Corn and beans are going extinct. Have you seen Chicago lately? Southern California? Any border town with Mexico? Between flooding and drought, people are packing into those cities like sardines. Their local economies were not meant for that kind of pressure. People are fighting and dying. It's even worse in the Middle East, around the Mediterranean. How many more years till we either nuke one another out of desperation, or kill the soil where it won't grow anything else? The Foundry offers us help, offers to rescue us from ourselves. Does anyone not get how important this mission is? Does anyone here question its validity? The fate of humanity may very well rest on the shoulders of the five Foundry ships."

The room remained silent.

"This is exactly where we were meant to be," Mom cut in before he could continue his monologue. She squared her shoulders, and her voice took on an edge. "There are only five ships leaving the system, each bound for a different source. Five. This is a once in a lifetime opportunity, and we, Jackson and I, have the experience and ability to fill the necessary roles. You needed three things for this mission, an astrophysicist, a biologist, and a family with a five-year-old child. I see all three criteria floating before you."

"Experience? Ability?" The captain gave a chuckle. "Never in question. You know damn well why I did not accept your family's application. It wasn't because of that. Both of you, Mrs. Hughes, are talented scientists. Graduated with PhDs in your respective fields, each spending a summer at the newly reconstructed Arecibo Observatory in Puerto Rico at which you kicked it off and soon after married." He waggled a finger. "I remember those days, Adrianna. Jackson. Warm nights getting wrecked on *pitorro*. You were persons of influence and accolade within many of NASA, the ESA, and the United Exploration Initiative's projects on deep space, including this one, both in star charting and the long-term effects of micro-gravity on the human body. As far as benchmarks, there are none who could have fit them better.”

This history lesson made many of those gathered relax. Was that why he had said these things? Esteban gave Deidrick a look, who then shrugged in reply.

“And yet you turned us down,” Mom said, her hands balling into fists. ‘You sent us home.”

“Because FICSE is not an experiment in a lab. Not in a controlled environment. Because this is a journey that will last at least forty years. This is why we chose families, not individuals. This is why we have exactly four hundred and fifty souls aboard this ship, each with specialized roles and experience, complimentary personality profiles and genes.”

“Sara Lancaster can’t solve the atrophy issue in time,” Mom said. “Five years, tops, and the entire crew is looking at irreparable health issues from this environment. Humans did not evolve to live in variable levels of micro gravity. Without a solution, you have no chance to make it twenty years, let alone forty.”

Mom’s words seemed to make everyone uncomfortable. What was she talking about? I had heard her use that word before, atrophy, but I didn’t know what it meant.

The captain sighed. “Sara and her husband are accomplished biologists. Besides, there are four others ships with biologists working towards the same goal.”

“But none of them are me. I can do this, Tobias. You know I can.”

“So why not us?” Dad crossed his arms. “Hmm?”

“I’ve already told you. It was in the rejection letter. You didn’t pass the medical exam. It’s not your fault.”

“But I’ve dreamed of being up here all my life!” Dad’s voice began to raise, exasperation creeping into his forced calm. “From the time I was a boy staring at the sky to this very moment, I’ve been poring over books and data, looking through tiny lenses into space. I have dedicated my life to understanding what’s up here. Now, I’m here.”

Esteban and Deidrick exchanged a look, their eyes plotting. I began to pet Jasper slow on the head.

Captain Williams scratched at an eyebrow. “And that is a noble pursuit, one I can respect. That said, it doesn’t change the fact that you have a heart murmur. The doctors reviewed your physical and medical records. Their recommendation was that you should not undergo the stresses of take-off.”

“Well then, that’s behind us now, isn’t it?”

“Don’t get smart with me, Mr. Hughes. There were other issues as well. You are manic depressive, given to bipolar mood-swings.”

Dad shook a bottle of pills in the air. “I brought my meds.”

“But for how long?”

"We can do a lot here," Doctor Reed cut in, "but I'm not so sure we can synthesize what you need to remain stable."

"What about trust?" Deidrick asked.

Esteban agreed. "I'm no sure we can trust. Already lied to us, ya?"

"I certainly don't trust them," Doctor Reed said, and her eyes settled on me for an instant. I shrunk inside myself and wished for somewhere else to put my attention.

"Or I," Perry added.

Mary seconded with a nod and crossed her arms.

Captain Williams waved his colleagues off. "Look, Mr. Hughes, you've put me in a tough spot. Out here, the UEI desk jockeys have little control over what we do. I can choose to allow certain things so long as I deem them necessary for the mission. No one on Earth, loud as they scream, has jurisdiction in my world, and make no doubt, the *Vasco Da Gama* is my world. All that changes if you go back down the well. If I return you to Earth, there's no question—you'll face jail time. Years. Potentially the rest of your life. By the time we return to save Earth, you'll be an old man hoping for death as he sips tapioca in a home upstate."

The captain let his statement hang for a moment before continuing. No one dared speak a word of comment, especially Dad.

"Now this is only conjecture," he went on, "but I believe your current story goes as follows. After you received the rejection letter you spent a couple weeks processing it. It's quite possible you went through the seven stages of grief in that time. About the time you reached deliberation you said, forget this, and started to science out the problem. *I'm not going to lie down and take it*, you might have said. Not sure who made the move, but one of you went onto the dark web and spent your family's life savings, maybe even racked up a bit of unsecured debt, contracting the assistance of, let's say, Serbian hackers—"

Dad raised a hand the tiniest bit. "Chinese, actually." He put it back down. "With the economy and all. They're more affordable."

"These *hackers*," the captain growled, "permitted you access to alter the records of the UEI's database so that you could be allowed to board the launch craft with false identification. Once you arrived at the pad, you broke into a federally protected facility wherein you bullshitted past the guards and onto the launch. Does this sound accurate?"

To my surprise, even under such intense scrutiny by the captain and crew, Dad smiled, flashing the kind of look a kid might show who was clever enough to pull off a prank, just not clever enough not to get caught. "It's like you read my mind, Tobias. What a beautiful plan."

"If I send you back, I'll have to live with the fact that even though it was your decision, I'll be sending a genius to prison for the rest of his life. Not only that, I would be separating a man from his wife and child, breaking up a family." He gave a groan. "It was hard for my wife and I to make the decision to be here, to bring our little Shelly with us. But make no mistake, this mission will never come again. Humanity will never make first contact twice. What a better way for us to make a legacy than to have their names written in the annals of exploration?"

"What you plan for me to do with them?" Esteban asked, cracking his knuckles. "Do we escort back to the capsule?"

"Perry." Captain Williams pointed to the main display. At the bottom right a number was climbing. "How's the window looking?"

"Closing pretty quick at present." Perry activated his tablet and the display responded, showing a line as it tracked its way through the solar system, velocity in one corner, time in the other. "We have a narrow gap in orbital alignment to keep us on course and swing off Jupiter. The flight plan hasn't changed, if that's what you're asking. Barnard's Star, here we come."

"Are we already under thrust?" I could tell the captain hadn't asked the question for his own benefit. It was for us. He was drawing our attention to the information at hand.

"Ions only," Mary spoke up. "But yes. Yes, we're moving and ready to put my fusion drive to the test. She's hot and ready to mingle."

Captain Williams gave a sigh of resignation. I knew it wasn't genuine. He was playing with us. He was saving face with the crew, putting up a front so that they could play the hand that had been dealt without any guilt. Mom and Dad had plotted to get us here. The path was set.

"Well then, looks like we're past the point of no return," he said. "I can't in good conscience send you back. So either I have to make you part of the crew to fill the roles the Lancasters had, or, I have to put the three of you in a capsule and hope someone can give you a ride home before you asphyxiate."

"Thank you, Tobias." Dad extended a hand. "Thank you. Thank you."

Captain Williams stared at it for a long moment, appraising the cost of this action. He shook his head and took hold. "Don't make me regret this."

"This could put all of us at risk. Our mission has a long tail," Deidrick protested. "What about genetic matching? Personality integration?"

"What's a system if it can't be tested? Science is alive. We'll just be ever more purposeful." Captain Williams turned his attention for the first time to me, shutting the rest of his people out for a moment. He gave me a smile and extended a hand full of candy. I plucked one of the wrapped chocolates from his palm, fingers fumbling to grip it. "Besides, my daughter Shelly could use a good friend."

So could I.

Mom urged, "Say thank you, Milo."

"Thank you, sir."

"Milo. What a great name. Can you do me a favor, buddy?"

I gave a nod.

"We have limited supplies on board, and so I need you to make a critical decision before we move on. It will affect your life for years to come."

"Yes?"

The captain turned and fished in a compartment. "Red or blue?" He extended a pair of electronic tablets, one the color of ripe cherries, the other...

"Cerulean," I said.

He cocked his head and handed me the blue tablet. "Blue then."

"No. It's cerulean." And Mom spoke the rest of the words with me. "*The color of the sky.*"

The choice was easy. Mom's echo only affirmed it. She smiled down and gave my shoulder a squeeze. It's often the little things, like the songs we sing in the car ride to school, that mean the most. I needed something, anything familiar, and I'd take this little reminder of good times.

"Fair enough, vocabulary kid. It's yours. Take care of it."

"I would have taken red, vroom vroom," Dad mumbled. "What? Fine, fine. Ignore me."

Perry's hardened expression cracked for an instant and he chuckled under his breath. Mary glowered at him and slapped him on the shoulder with the back of her hand.

I clutched the tablet against my chest and grinned. Was wi-fi fast out here?

"Alright everyone." The captain let out a breath, all issues having been put to bed. "Time to strap in, crew. Let's get this ship underway. Ramp up the fusion drive, it's time to start piling on kph. We have a date with an alien megastructure, and I intend to keep it."

CHAPTER 3

Though Mom and Dad's little chats about the Foundry had primed me, the buzz aboard the ship was undeniable. This facility, as they called it, was central to our mission, and so the word soon became something immutable and divine, akin to a lesser god, an idea for which we devoted everything. We were one of five such vessels bound for similar Foundry signals spread out around the galactic neighborhood. Whatever this thing was, it was clear it was intended to pique our interest. Humanity had reached some sort of tipping point in technological development as to merit attention. Was this common for intelligent life? The mere existence of the Foundry suggested that our species and its level of development was more common than previously thought. But how common? Were we climbing our way up the Kardashev scale? How many were above us?

At a range of six light years, even the highest resolution telescopes could not gift us a clear picture of what we were headed towards. We knew it was circling the third planet around Barnard's Star, a red dwarf, and that the planet fell within the habitable zone, the orbital distance around a star at which liquid water could form, but the rest was pure speculation. Would this turn out to be their home world? Was it a staging location? Had we somehow come across a massive communications relay? The last seemed the most likely, given the additional signals. Yet the truth remained. We just didn't know.

We desperately needed to find the answer to two questions. Would they help us? Or were we hurling ourselves into a trap?

These discussions and more were had in hallways and conference rooms, over late-night beverages and while digging in the dirt of the ship's gardens. It was our life, our existence. Our reality. Our mission. I understood so little of it, and yet that did not matter.

As it turned out, just because I was millions of miles away from my elementary school, I wasn't absolved from going to class. I had changed districts without any preparation or approval. I found myself in a class both smaller than my previous one, the community of Whispering Pines, overcrowded from inland migration due to rising sea levels; and yet far larger than I had thought possible on a starship, given what I had seen of space travel online. The *Vasco Da Gama* was a new class of spacecraft, the largest ever made. Capsules, flyers, and ascent vehicles could not fill the shoes of a multi-light year journey, and so the ape people of Earth had built something far bigger and better.

My classmates were about the same age as me, give or take a few months. There were 450 people aboard. One hundred and seven of them were five years old. I asked Mom why this was, and she gave me an off-hand comment about us kids not being elderly when we returned to Earth. I wouldn't come to understand what that meant until I was older. Adults say a lot of things, yet as children we lack the context for true understanding. Such is all in the universe, and such would be the Foundry to the child race of humankind.

Kindergarten wasn't much different from back home. We worked on our numbers and letters. We practiced sight words and worked through obedience exercises masked as rhymes and games. Sure, there were subtle differences. Whispering Pines Elementary had fire and tornado drills, instead of decompression and radiation storm preparation. Whispering Pines Elementary also didn't serve endless varieties of protein substrates with fruits and vegetables presented as delicacies.

I was a shy kid before launch, and the trip on the ascent vehicle hadn't changed that. The other students were nice enough, but I was quiet. It took me several weeks to settle in, to make eye contact with more than just our teacher, Mrs. Lawson. The other kids acted as if they already knew each other, having attended birthday parties, played before at the park, casual cliques and groups cemented for a season that did not include Milo Hughes. I spent most days sitting in the corner beneath a set of colorful letter memorization posters, not saying a word, wishing I had been allowed to bring Jasper with me to class for company.

"One of the other kids might take him home and we can't get another," Mom had said more than once, her words resonating in my chest.

Jasper always kept me company. Always made me feel safe. In class I was alone. An island.

All that changed the day a girl in curly pigtails with pink hair ties sat down at my table and said, "Hi, want to color with me?"

I blinked at her, unsure what to do. Had someone spoken to me? How did I respond?

"Yeah?" I replied, the word strange on my lips.

"Here. You'll need something to draw on." She handed me a crisp white sheet of letter size paper. "And crayons. Can't color without crayons."

We scribbled over the blank sheets, drawing houses and people. She drew spaceships in the skies overhead. They were really good.

"Remember kids," Mrs. Lawson started. "Make good use of the paper. We only have so much. Use every bit you can! Make a pretty picture that your Mom and Dad can hang in your quarters for years to come."

The pigtailed girl leaned close to me, her breath sweet with the smell of sugar. "My name is Shelly," she whispered as if we were entering into a conspiracy.

"I'm Milo," I replied.

"I know you are." She gave me a smile, and I swore for an instant I had seen an angel. "Want to be my friend?"

I felt my crayon pick up speed, the picture in my head suddenly easier to translate onto the page.

"Okay," I told her. "I'll be your friend."

After school Shelly walked me home. I knew this would become my routine, or at the very least hoped. While our great-great-grandparents might have discussed walking both ways through snow to go back and forth from school, all we had to do was traverse the curve of the habitation ring.

After waving goodbye to my new friend, I went inside and presented the picture I'd drawn to Mom. She was seated in the dining room, her work laid out before her. She took the corner of the paper, gave a grunt, and set it on the table, her eyes not leaving her computer.

"Do you like it?" I asked, excited at what her answer might be. It was so good. A picture of our old house, green, green grass, our cat Ferdie a blob on the front steps, Mom and Dad smiling wide, a crescent moon and a full sun hanging overhead at opposite ends of the page, colors from every crayon filling in what space was left. I had used every bit of my imagination on this one. I hoped I had some left.

She said nothing in response, continuing to read what she was on.

Dad strolled into the room with a tablet in one hand, the other scratching his backside, then his head.

"Dad?" I pointed to the picture.

"Yes?"

"I made a picture in class. Want to see?"

"Of course." He took the picture and yet kept reading what was on his screen, backlight reflecting in his eyes. "There's plenty on the counter. Make yourself at home."

I cocked my head and looked to where he had motioned. Dinner was sitting out, protein cakes and bulbs of juice. I let out a sigh, grabbed some food, and went to the corner of the room to play. Jasper took a seat and snuggled against me as I ate.

"There's so much backlog," Dad said after pacing for a while. "The Lawsons were doing nothing, Adriana. It looks like they hadn't even gone through the prep work for this trek. I honestly think they were going to do it en route."

"Hmmhmm." Mom kept typing.

"Adriana!"

"What?"

"Are you even listening to me?"

"Yes, dear." She spun in her chair.

They stared at each other for a moment.

Mom spoke first, "Jackson, I am just as stressed as you are. We have the weight of the world on our shoulders. And while I agree with what we did, we have a long journey and a lot of work to prove. You know I wasn't kidding about five years. My best projections show that is all the time we have to solve this, or people are going to be very ill, us included. We will be weak, unable to walk, have heart attacks and blood clots, have an inability to bear gravity in its fullness again, and become thin, ragged sacks of meat stretched over toothpicks."

"Yeah yeah. But does it not piss you off that they were lazy? It will take us months to catch up on the back-log."

"No, it doesn't," Mom replied, rubbing her eyes. "What pisses me off is your bitching. It might take normal folks a couple months to go back through all this, but we are not normal. We'll just buckle down, nose to the grindstone, get it done. *Minha mãe* left a bit of creative survival in my blood, and I intend to use every bit of it."

"More favela talk?"

"Those people make a lot out of a little. It's an inspiration."

"You're right."

"We have to do the same."

"We really do have to prove ourselves, don't we?" Dad lowered his head. "They weren't kidding."

"They were not. Experts in our field or no, we have to show we are valuable to this crew. If I can solve the atrophy crisis, we'll not only be valuable to them, but all of humanity. Think of it. Think of all it could change. It would open up exploration even more. No mission time caps and safety limits."

"We got this. We'll solve the atrophy crisis."

"No. I got this. I don't need you anywhere near biology. You keep doing what you do best. Read the stars, help the captain keep this fusion candle pointed in the right direction."

Dad nodded and went back to his work. I recovered my picture and stuck it to the fridge with a magnet.

Maybe there they might see my perfect scene when they were done.

A new normal began to settle in. Jasper and I spent most evenings together, playing games in my bed, exploring imaginary worlds or interacting as I watched cartoons on my cerulean tablet. After a while even that felt two dimensional. I wanted someone to talk to, flesh and blood.

It occurred to me one night, Shelly had shown me where her quarters were on our walk home from school yesterday. I was confident I could find my way there, after all, the habitat ring was just a loop. It would take only a few minutes to arrive. Then me and her could have all the fun in the world.

I gathered up a handful of plastic, 3D printed toys from my room— tiny figures no bigger than the end of my finger—and stuffed them in the various pockets of my jumpsuit. I had a fixation for tiny things, little people and miniature vehicles, fine details and minutiae. I often watched videos for hours on end of people making tiny pancakes, playing with figures in pocket-size houses, stop motion scenes recorded on desktops that appeared like great deserts. It fascinated me to see the world scaled down, communities and stories that could fit in the palm of my hand.

Mom and Dad were in the living room, engaged in their work, the two of them furiously debating red dwarf emissions and orthostatic hypotension. There was no sense in bothering them. They were busy.

I stood by the door and watched them for a while, one foot turned towards my bedroom, one hand on the exit controls. For Dad, this sort of behavior had always been a thing, pacing around the house thinking out loud, his sole focus on his work and little attention on me. But for Mom this was new. She had always been a scientist, long as I had been alive, but she'd made time for me. She stayed home my first few years of life, and we did everything together, went to the park, shared meals, built things with Play-Doh. Sang songs about the color of the sky. All that had changed shortly after my last birthday. Life had found Mom again.

I let myself out into the main hall, my parents not even noticing the door had opened. There was no reason not to go see Shelly. I got this.

In the main passage I whispered to the wall, "Shelly Williams."

A flicker of green light appeared and dashed ahead of me across the floor. I followed the trail as it worked around the habitat ring, illumination guiding me to my destination. Since the halls of the *Vasco Da Gama* were uniform and mostly unadorned, it was easy to get lost if you didn't have a guide.

"Can it be blue?" I asked, and the ship obliged, transitioning the color of my navigational trail.

I rounded a corner and made a start. My path was blocked.

"Where you goin' little buddy? School let out a few hours ago, no?"

"I'm going to my friend's house," I said, raising my eyes to see the Spaniard, Esteban Lopez, towering over me. He had a towel thrown over his shoulder, his dark hair slick with sweat.

"All by yourself?" He looked around. "Your *mami* and *papi* say that's okay?"

"Maybe?"

He paused for a moment and let out a tired sigh. "Alright then, who's your friend?"

"Shelly."

"Ahh. Tobias's little girl. Come on, I'll walk with yous."

What could I do? I couldn't say no. He was an adult, and I would follow his instructions even if I was afraid he'd tell my parents before I had the chance.

We reached the captain's quarters and he pressed a button on the wall. The hatch swooshed open and Mrs. Williams appeared.

"Ma'am," Esteban said, tipping his head. "Found this fella wanting to see his friend."

"Hello, son," she said, her round, angelic face warm and bright. She was just like her daughter, and that gave me peace. "How are you tonight?"

"Good."

"What's your name?"

"I'm Milo."

"Milo? Oh, yes, a pleasure to meet you. I've heard all about you." She extended a hand and gave Esteban's shoulder a squeeze. "Thank you."

"Ma'am," he said and strolled off.

"Milo, come on in. Shelly is playing in the living room."

Shelly hopped up and threw her arms around me, nearly knocking me onto the floor. I recovered and let out a laugh, my pattering heart accelerating into overdrive.

"Milo!" she shouted. "Come on. I *haaave* to show you this." And she took me by the hand, leading me over to her toys.

"Want to see my guys?" I asked, pulling a tiny wizard from my pocket.

"Yes!"

Mrs. Williams brought us a spread of snacks, a kind of cheese crackers and a set of juice bulbs. Shelly and I ate while we played with dolls and my tiny guys. She had toy spaceships, big and small, all the major agencies—ESA, NASA, UEI.. Captain Williams even joined us on the floor for a few minutes, sitting crossed legged as he dealt cards.

"You see the daily Astro Update?" he asked, shuffling the deck. "We're passing Jupiter. We've got an instrument package bound for orbit, should last a few years, get some additional data Juno might not have. I'm sure your dad has been busy working on that. All in all, we're glad to have him."

"Yeah," I replied, not sure what else to say. Sarcasm was not yet one of my skills, yet I somehow knew I desperately needed it. "He works hard."

"Good man."

Mrs. Williams stepped up beside her husband and patted him on the back. "Who wants to play Simon Says?" she asked.

Shelly and Captain Williams threw a hand up in the air.

"Throw your arm up!" Shelly told me, taking hold of my right arm. "He wants to play too!"

"What's Simon Says?" I asked, dumfounded.

I was at ease in the Williams' home. There was laughter, the scent of cleanliness, peace. There were cheese crackers and chocolate, plenty enough to stuff my face till I was messy. Most of all, there was Shelly. When I was around her, I was important. When she looked at me, she saw me. She listened. She looked at my pictures.

"It's too bad Margaret," the captain said, then took a sip of his drink.

"What is?"

"They get along so well and they're not a match."

"Are you seriously talking about this now? They're right here."

"What, they're kids? They don't yet understand complemental genotyping. I just wish they were a match, that's all."

Shelly's mom rolled her eyes. "You've always been a touch romantic, haven't you?"

He took a sip of his drink and smiled. "Wouldn't be here if I wasn't."

I spent the next few hours with Shelly before returning home, this time without an escort. Even though I didn't need the ship to guide me back, it was fun, and so I used the navigation lights anyways.

The door to my quarters opened without a sound and I slipped back into my room. I picked up where I'd left off in my cartoons and readied for bed, slipping on my pajamas as I watched.

"Hey Milo, what you doing?" Mom stuck her head in my room, a cup of steaming coffee in her hand. Her eyes were red and dry, hair a mess on one side as if she'd taken a nap on it. "You've been quiet tonight."

"Playing." I told her and put my attention back on my tablet.

"Alright then." She gave a yawn and left the room. "Well good night."

"Night, Mommy."

I can't say it was surprising I hadn't been missed. There were more important things for two of the *Vasco Da Gama's* best scientists to be concerned with. Too bad pictures and playtime weren't among them.

CHAPTER 4

I flew a copy of the Orion spacecraft, a grey piece of plastic no bigger than my palm, around the living room while Mom worked, and Dad watched the news. The astronaut inside my ship, Francolato, was on a mission to the planet Jasper, which was just on the other side of the couch. Strange that this planet looked much like a doggie, made of plush with dark eyes and floppy ears, little atmosphere and uneven gravity. That was where the rest of my people had gone. The aliens had taken them, and they needed to be rescued.

As the Orion crashed onto the surface of Jasper, I made the sound of a quiet explosion with my mouth. Francolato, played by my tiny wizard figurine, hopped out of the ship onto the surface. I looked at the spaceship for a moment before continuing and smiled. Shelly, my friend from school, had given me this ship in trade for a knight on horseback. I had gotten the better deal. She disagreed.

I took a deep breath and Francolato forged up the mountainous fur of Jasper in search of his lost friends.

"Can you believe what these protestors are doing?" Dad asked no one in particular, standing in front of the main display, hands on his hips. The news feed was loud, a bunch of people walking down a crowded street with signs in their hands screaming something together.

Mom took a sip of her coffee from where she sat at the dining room table. She was working, as always, her laptop's display casting blue light on her face. "What protestors?"

"It's those right-wing people following James Carlisle, this whole Fifth Great Awakening movement. They are worse than the Flag Soldiers, America Once, and the Patriot Men combined. Looks like they're marching on Washington to protest the separation of church and state. Again... What a bunch of morons. This is a founding principle of our nation, not something new."

"They're just expressing themselves, dear." Mom's response was soft and kind. "Humans have a need to express themselves."

"Expressing themselves?" Dad's eyes bulged. "They are spreading false information that climate change is the result of God being pissed at them. You know as well as I do that this isn't true. It's science, not pillars of salt in a set of books that have been edited so many times there's no real canon."

Mom paused in her work and rubbed her eyes. "That may be, Jackson, but the truth is, people tend to fall back on traditions and beliefs that they are comfortable with when fear dominates the public conversation. This is either the result of the aforementioned crisis, or that asshole. What did you say his name was?"

"Carlisle. James Carlisle."

"How plain." She took another sip of her coffee, glanced down at me on the floor, then back at her work. "It's not their fault, they are just looking to make sense of all this."

By now I had circled my guys around a single character, a grey man with a gun that looked like a soldier. He was the bad guy.

Dad grumbled and plopped down on the couch. "Read a damn book and make sense of it. Geez. Even if it's not this century that everything happens, it will be the next. We messed up."

"And that is why we are on the *Vasco*, love."

The crowd on TV started to scream. Fires were everywhere, some white mansion with huge windows behind a tall fence their backdrop, men with guns on the other side.

Dad threw his hands up in the air. "Holy crap, seriously, now what are they doing? How is flipping over police cars in front of the White House, and breaking shop-front windows accomplishing anything?"

"Social pressure," Mom said, her voice quiet. "The unheard are easily goaded into violence and property destruction."

The main display let out a chirp and the video feed paused. Mom swiveled in her chair and grinned.

"Saved by the bell," she said. "Display, *play message*."

A warm, familiar face with dark skin and smile lines appeared on the display. It was the paused face of my mother's mother, Eneida Sousa. *Minha avó.*

"Timed message," the display said. *"Sent, twenty hours ago, encryption-Q5. Do you wish to play?"*

"Yes."

The video began. I couldn't understand but every third word.

Avó was speaking in Portuguese, as she often preferred. Her face was serious, then delighted, then rueful. I wanted to know what she was saying.

Mom was eating it up, nodding as she watched, while Dad and I stared at one another, confused.

"Pause," Mom said. "Rewind, play with English subtitles."

"*Done*," the display replied.

The video began again, but this time it had words at the bottom in English. I wasn't great at reading yet, especially this fast, but Dad mumbled under his breath as he read.

"Good evening, my hearts," the captions read. "Maybe morning. I have no idea. I miss you already. I should have known that some day you would disappear on me and shoot off into the stars. I hope it's not because of my company. There's a lot of talk on the news about how bad the two of you are. Broke the law and all. The others scientists that supposed to be on that ship have a case against you in court. They are taking it to the federal level, but what can they do about it? Like to see them try and catch that spaceship of yours. They might end up getting the house and whatever you got left in the bank.

"I am so proud of you. I know what this means, and it makes my heart swell, as well as a bit sad. You never coming back, not before I am gone. Still doesn't mean we can't talk. You have followed what you believe to be true. Always saving the world, my beautiful child. And that husband of yours, he's okay too."

Dad chuckled to himself.

"How is Milo? You feeding him enough on that tin can? He's a growing boy, needs plenty to eat. Get him some *feijão tropeiro, camarão ao coco*, some *sonhos*. Have him send me a video back and talk about school, they have that on the ship? Of course they do.

"Anyways, I am rambling. We are fine in Boulder. The family is missing you and smiles when they see you on the news. The only one who is sore is Jackson's sister Carol. If she would stop calling me six times daily, I might get some sleep. Kisses. Kisses. May God be with you. Bye."

The video ended.

Mom let out a long sigh. Dad stood up and went to her side.

"It's forever, isn't it," she whispered.

"It is," Dad agreed. "May not be a one-way trip for us, but it is for them. You going to be okay?"

She nodded. "We talked about this enough. We knew what the cost was." Mom turned to me and reached out a hand. I sat down my toys and came to her side, taking hold of it. "A life of possibility, paid to give others hope."

"You won't let them down," Dad said. "You never do."

"We believe in you," I whispered.

Mom smirked at us, but in that moment, I could tell she wasn't so sure.

CHAPTER 5

When it came to the big things, shipboard life was quite different from living back home on Earth. There was far less freedom and many more rules. Real estate was at a premium, cramped, with no opportunity to go out and get some sun, a bit of fresh air, which is probably why many people were very private. The only stand-ins we had were the VEs, Virtual Environments, which allowed us to explore any place we had on file with varying levels of realism. These were part of the school day as well as physical education, meant to keep us healthy in both mind and body. Besides the VEs, there were two gyms aboard the ship, one in the habitation ring with equipment such as stationary bikes and weight machines, and another along the spine they called the NullGym, where we played a zero-gravity game called NetBall.

We had a set of social rules to follow, designed to keep us safe and at peace. They were assigned graduated degrees of punishment for an infraction, from as little as VE restriction of a few days, to the withholding of food rations. The trouble was, many of these rules had not been so clearly outlined to the Hughes family.

I became aware of a few of these so-called rules at one of the first communal dinners, the only time large groups interacted on board. Three times a week, the crew of the *Vasco Da Gama* would gather in segments to enjoy a meal together. They converted part of the main hallways of the habitation ring to accommodate long tables and would setup a buffet covered in synthetic meats and a dozen different vegetables as well as breads and cakes and dips. The best treats always came out during the communal dinner, sweets and savories held back just for the occasion.

Mom and Dad always found us a spot near the end where it was less crowded. They weren't much for large groups to begin with, and so this was a touch sensory overload at times. All I cared about was that there were other kids to play with, and Shelly was usually one of them.

She and I chased each other up and down the hall with a half-dozen other kids, telling jokes about things we didn't understand and laughing at nothing. Mom called me over after a few minutes and I begrudgingly obliged.

"Have a seat and I'll make you a plate," she said before joining the buffet line.

I took a seat next to Dad, bored as I watched my friends have fun without me.

"At least there's no kids' table," he said offhanded. I wasn't sure what that was. "Hey, Mr. Lopez."

Esteban settled in across from us and to the left, his plate piled with food. He raised dark eyebrows at Dad. "Sir?"

"Tried to get on the virtual environments and play some shoot 'em ups. All seemed blocked, or just not available. There a reason for that? Figured, you being a quartermaster and all, you might have some insight. While I do love a good puzzle in my spare blocks, there are times I just want to blow shit up."

Esteban looked left, then right, as if making sure it was safe to speak. "Yous might have skipped orientation," he said. "Is prohibited, ya? Makes kids violent an' that. Best to keep content restricted."

Dad put a hand over his face. "We've blocked violent video games to keep our kids safe? That a UEI rule, or a Williams rule?"

"Who can say? Games an' streams, shows and that."

"This is going to be a long trip, isn't it?"

Esteban stabbed a slice of brown meat with his fork and shook it in the air at Dad. "Yes, sir. Might be places on board to find entertainment, ya? Don' get caught."

"We might need to talk later," Dad said, pointing to his eyes with two fingers then at Esteban's.

Mom returned with two plates, one filled primarily with vegetables, asparagus, beans, and cheese bread; the other, loaded with fried chicken tenders, or what passed for them, with a honey mustard-like dip on the side.

"Food on board has turned out to be far more diverse than I had expected," she said, her tone pleased. "We can produce synthetic meats which taste very much like the real thing, just in small quantities. Enjoy it while you can, Milo."

"Thanks, Mom."

The empty seats across from us and to our right were taken by Mary and what had turned out to be her brother Perry, two of our engineers. They gave us a greeting before taking in what all they had put on their plate.

"*Bom dia*," I said to them, trying to be weird and clever and like my extended family. I didn't know a lot of Portuguese, but I at least knew how to say good day.

"Excuse me?" Perry said, raising an eyebrow.

Mom patted me on the head. "What I wouldn't do for some coconut rice and *pae de queijo*," she said to Dad.

He paused, bite halfway to his mouth. "Like your *Mãe* makes?"

"I can make it just fine myself."

"Not as good as *Mãe*. No idea what her magic touch is, but damn."

A few of those standing in the buffet line began to laugh. Conversation broke out, making it difficult to keep track of who was talking about what. My little brain was on full overload. I scanned the crowd for Shelly but couldn't find her. What was she up to?

"Dear Lord, we are grateful for this food," Mary began, hands clasped together, her bright blue hair covering the sides of her face.

Her brother shook his head. "The captain would be disappointed in you. Fifth Great Awakening, and all. You know he doesn't like them, or religion for that matter."

"But those idiots are not Catholic. We are."

"Don't think that matters, Sis. There are things you don't talk about here. Religion or the Fifth Great Awakening."

"Someone say something about Carlisle's crazy religious movement?" Captain Williams said, taking a seat a few spots down, his plate piled high with strips of beef and buttered potatoes, a small bastion of green veggies at the edge surrounded by a moat of gravy. "The Fifth Great Awakening is just a bunch of backwoods religious zealots who let science go along with their common sense, don't know the difference between carbon emissions and sins. That what you were on about?"

Mary raised her head and smiled, hiding whatever it was she had been about to do. "No. Nothing, sir. Nothing."

"Alright then."

"Tobias," Mom started, "are you really going to eat all that?"

Dad gave her a quizzical look and dug into his own pile.

"It's okay to treat yourself once in a while," the captain replied. "I've been cutting back on our off days. The whole intermittent fasting. This is one of the approved diets for crew members."

"I'll tell Dr. Reed," Mom said.

"I dare you."

"I am just saying, Tobias. There are rules about overeating."

He narrowed his eyes at Mom. "And I'm just saying, there are rules against those who don't contribute."

This made Dad groan. "You saying we need to hitch a ride back?"

"I'm just saying, those who don't put in the work can let inertia deliver them to the Foundry."

"It's really a UEI rule," Esteban put in. "Orientation, Mr. Hughes."

"Yeah," he groaned. "So when are they having it again? Didn't see it on the schedule."

Shelly and her mother appeared a moment later, taking seats beside the captain. She raised her eyebrows at me, signaling that mischief was afoot, then disappeared under the table. I slipped beneath the white cloth before Mom or Dad could snatch me, my plate of half-eaten chicken tenders forgotten.

When we got home that evening, the display in our quarters was blinking. A message waiting. Mom and Dad tossed their things down. I was dog tired after playing with Shelly and the other kids. I laid down on the couch with Jasper in my hands and felt my eyes get heavy.

"*Play message*," Mom said, and the display began.

Minha avó appeared, her camera view from out on the porch of her house in Boulder, Colorado where she lived with six of my cousins. It was raining, a steady downpour, and yet her hand terminal was able to filter out most of the noise so that we could hear her clearly.

The message began, captions appearing, while Dad rubbed his eyes and mumbled the words.

"You see this rain? Never thought I'd see so much in my life. Winters here get cold, okay? Not rain like this. I got your last message. Milo is growing up like a weed. It's killing me we don't get to talk every day. This lightspeed lag you say, makes me sad we can't talk live. Just videos, videos, videos.

"By the way, those Lancaster people, they won in court and you lost the house. Not sure how that works since they are Canadian. Guess you'll need a new one when you get back. Hope they don't find a way to take the money you earn on this trip. Thieves. Your cousin André said he be happy to give them a visit, all you have to do is ask.

"Have Milo record me a video. I want to hear about what he's doing in class and all 'bout his friends. He got a little girlfriend, doesn't he?

She paused for a long moment, rain falling onto the tin roof of her home. It seemed as if there was something she wanted to say, but she couldn't find the words.

"I make some *brigadeiro*, send you the recipe to make on the ship, your neighbors will thank you. We talk soon. Kisses. Kisses. Bye."

The screen went black.

"Everything okay?" Dad asked Mom.

Mom stared for a while off into space. "Yeah, sure. Everything is fine."

CHAPTER 6

Sometime in the middle of the night the doors to our quarters began to chirp. In my groggy half-asleep, half-awake state, I could hear Dad scramble out of bed cussing under his breath.

"God damn it," he said. "Who in the hell is bugging us at this hour?"

I rubbed my eyes and took hold of Jasper, slid out from under my sheets and tip toed to my door. From where I stood, I could see light pouring into our living room from out in the hallway.

Perry was standing there, arms crossed, his face pale and distressed. "Sorry, Jackson. I know it's late. I just didn't want you to be the last to find out."

"Find out what?"

"You'll want to get Adrianna."

Dad's frame sagged and he scurried off to wake Mom. I stayed where I was, frozen by the doorway.

"What is it, Perry?" Mom asked.

"May I come in?"

She nodded, and waved him in. Dad called to the lights and brought a few lamps to life, not making the room bright, but giving them something to see by.

"I don't know if you've been following the weather on Earth the past few days," Perry started, taking a seat on the end of the couch, Mom and Dad on his right. "First there was a polar vortex that crawled its way over the southwest. Even the launch site we all left from is frozen solid. Near zero in a place that never hardly goes under seventy. The whole region has been disrupted."

"To be expected," Mom said. "With the climate crisis."

I snuck into the room and crawled below the dining table, Jasper's body against my face.

"Yeah. It's true," Perry went on. "Protesters are out again en force, 'time to pray, time to hold our leaders accountable.' All that again. But that's not where the story ends. A little further north, the weather warmed up fast and a series of storms converged into a supercell. It was roaring its way across the west until it ran out of steam and parked over Colorado. Everyone had expected heavy snow, as cold as it had been, but that's not what happened."

Dad cocked his head. "What are you saying?"

"Boulder, Colorado is underwater. They have had flooding before, but this is the worst we've ever seen. What with the crisis and all, I, well, we as a group, my sister Mary and Gareth and a couple others, have been keeping track of family members back home in case of emergencies. Not that we can do much. I am so sorry, Adrianna, your mother's home was destroyed by the storms. Best we can tell, she was taken with it."

"What?" Mom gasped.

"I'm sorry, Mrs. Hughes. I wish I had better news."

Mom stood, shrugging free of Dad's consoling touch. "She's gone?" She paced around the room then shook her hands and retreated to the bedroom, palms against her face.

"Adrianna," Dad said, chasing after her. The door swooshed shut, and Perry was left alone in the living room.

He turned in his seat to go when he saw me hiding. "Hey buddy."

I raised on of Jasper's arms to wave.

"You okay?"

I said nothing.

"Can I get you anything?"

I shook my head.

Perry made his way for the exit. "Try and get some sleep. Your mommy is going to need you. Okay?"

The door closed and I was left by myself under the dining room table, clutching Jasper, not sure what to think or how to feel. Never before had the word *gone* seemed so final.

"She's gone," I mumbled, seeing how the words felt on my lips. I didn't like this sour taste, no, not at all.

CHAPTER 7

For all that was different, the little things hadn't changed. People were still people, and school, still school. 3rd grade was the year I discovered test taking wasn't my strong suit. Math, a subject both my parents were strong in, was steadily getting harder. The tests were longer and the problems more difficult. Unlike school back home, on the *Vasco Da Gama* we attended year-round. As a result, the powers that be assumed that we were more advanced. This was not the case for me. Multiplication, division, two and three numbers deep, countless sheets of homework finished with mixed success, even with Mrs. Lawson's tutelage. Here we were, test number one for the year. My mind went blank.

Maybe I was distracted. The loss of *Minha avó* had been hard on Mom. She still didn't talk about it. The authorities had never found the body, or those of my six cousins. The flood had washed half of Boulder away.

The other kids hurried through their work, especially George and Kieran and Brandilyn, clicking numbers on their tablets in a fury, raising their hands an instant later saying, "Done."

All I could do was stare at the blank screen, not a single answer coming to mind. I felt a cold shiver down my spine, sweat bead on my forehead, my heart thundering against my ribcage. 243 x 426? Or does it say 234 x 624? Failure was paralyzing. If Dad said it once, he said it a thousand times, being off a digit meant it won't work. Rovers had crashed on Mars because of tiny figures being off, millions of public dollars turned to dust in a flash. People could slip beyond the veil in surgery, never to wake again, all because of miscalculations in anesthesia. Not to mention autonomous cars. How many lives did those formulas and algorithms hold in their hands? This math stuff was serious business, and so I had to get it right every time. No failure could be accepted. Failure meant that people died.

"Psst," I heard from my right, breaking me free of my nightmarish reverie. "Milo." Shelly tossed a folded piece of paper onto the floor beside my desk.

"Mrs. Lawson?" She raised her hand. "May I talk to you for a moment?"

"Of course, Shelly." The teacher tucked a length of wavy hair behind her right ear and gave a gesture towards the door. "Let's step in the hall so we don't disturb the rest of the class."

Shelly glanced back at me and gave a wink before exiting the room.

While the other students were busy, eyes focused on their tests, I recovered Shelly's message and unfolded it.

Here's most of the answers. I'll help you study.

I smiled at the paper, folded it into a neat square and slipped it into my pocket without reading the answers. It was kind of her to help. Good to have a friend. In good conscience I could not use her answers. I had to go this alone, for good or ill.

Needless to say, I royally bombed the test and my parents weren't happy.

I got better.

With Mom and Dad's long work hours, they began to earn the social credit they desperately needed. Early school graduations came and went, and they were there, cheering me on, shaking hands with colleagues and congratulating my progress. We had a school play, a variation on the *Wizard of Oz*, for which I played the Scarecrow. They were there for the show, but afterwards, our quarters were empty, nothing but a note they'd be home late.

They were in demand on and off the ship, a world of scientists at the other end of a neutrino stream vying for their time and abilities. They were in the unique position to provide data and insight that so many scientists back on Earth could only dream of. They were special, respected, on a path to historical achievement.

Good for them.

"Have you seen the recent reports?" Mom asked Dad one evening, both seated at the dining room table, her dinner going cold, my dish already in the sink. I was doing my homework laid back on the couch, wondering what Shelly was up to and if it would be possible to sneak out and play.

"The ice shelf is down another thirty percent," she went on. "NOAA is projecting a steep climb over the next few years. By the time we get home there might not be any left."

"They should have listened," Dad said, offhanded.

"That's the thing. Too much money involved. Too many politicians and special interests. Getting out of Dodge is our only viable bet if the Foundry turns out to be a bust. We'll be looking at a dead rock in a few hundred years."

"It's true."

"Where will that leave Milo's kids?" She stood and stretched, went into the kitchen and started a fresh pot of coffee. "I miss *Mãe.*"

"I know, I know. We all miss her."

Mom took a shuddering breath and cleared her composure. "I have to prepare them. I have to be sure that people can survive this trip and still be human on the other end."

"You will, dear."

She started to pace the room as the pot burbled. I put my books away. Jasper and I played quietly by the main display in our living room, colorful, fast-paced cartoons running as background more than anything else.

"No. There's no time," Mom went on. "The protein Dr. Reed and I have stumbled on might be a positive step, sure, but some of these models will take years to sift through. We don't know all the effects. What do changes in gravity have to do with fetal growth? We'll be extinct in less than a generation."

Dad shut his computer and let out a huff. "Dr. Yuri evaluated all the children on board for genetic matches. To the best of our knowledge, it should be fine."

"*Merda*, Jackson. I'm not talking about genetic matches!" She threw her hands up in exasperation. "I'm talking about environmental conditions. The cardiovascular system slows, the body produces less red blood cells in micro-gravity, it can cause issues with eyesight and suppress the immune system. Imagine what that can do to a child in utero. We weren't evolved for this. I'm already seeing the signs aboard. I know the symptoms. We needed the data, sure, but to put this many people at risk." She put her back against the kitchen cabinets and slid to the floor, hands covering her face. "This may be madness, not daring. We're children playing with toys we don't understand."

Dad went to her side and wrapped her in his arms, a gesture I'd never seen from him. It wasn't that they didn't share their love for one another, it just wasn't often physical. "Shh. It's okay. You aren't in this alone."

"I have to save the world," she mumbled, her words choked. "The problem is just too big. Too many factors. If I don't solve it, no one will."

"And you *will* solve it, I believe in you." He brushed back her hair and placed a kiss on her right cheek. "You'll give us a safe path out of this. We are humans, we adapt. We can thrive in the void. Just another frontier."

Part of me wanted to go hug Mom just like Dad, to tell her it would be okay, to give her an ounce of my youthful, ignorant confidence. Another part felt unwelcome in this moment, that this was between them, something a child wouldn't understand until they were grown up. Then again, there was a rock in my chest that felt it might have the same shape as Mom's, a weight resting on my shoulders heavy as the world.

Failure for her meant that others died, the same as math for me or Dad.

I came to class the following day with an unease in my heart, feet heavy as if my shoes had been filled with concrete. That all changed the moment I saw Shelly's smiling face. She gave a wave and I came running over.

The classroom was filled with a chaotic chatter, a half dozen different threads and circles of games playing out in the maze of desks. Kerrie and Harper were slapping hands, making patterns and rhythms while singing a nonsense song. Deet, Browlin, and Lance were exchanging monster growls, seeing who could sound the most like a zombie. I slid past Sander who was drawing faces on his tablet too realistic for our age and took my seat beside Shelly.

"Want to see something cool?" she asked.

I nodded, transfixed as she drew a flat, silvery object half the size of a cheese cracker from her pocket. She set it down on my desk. I leaned in to inspect its features, geometric shapes appearing on its surface, a metallic box on one end. It reminded me of a slip of aluminum foil painted with gold triangles.

"What is it?" I asked.

Shelly gave a smile. "*Wake*," she whispered.

The tiny machine made a buzz and began to form into something, its body folding along the edges of geometric lines. The resulting shape was like a crab made of angles, its body flapping as it moved across my desk.

My eyes widened. "That's so cool."

"It's a tiny robot!"

"What's it for?"

"I have no idea. But they're fun. I made them."

"Can you show me?"

She closed her eyes and nodded.

"Children!" Mrs. Lawson clapped three times, gathering the attention of the class. Shelly scooped the robot into her palm, and we turned to face her. "Take your seats. James! Hurry up, quick now, quick now. Austin, get your finger out of your nose. Right now! If you didn't bring enough for the class, you can't have any yourself!"

"Eww!" several of the other students said. "That's gross."

"Indeed."

Shelly reached out a hand and squeezed mine. She pointed to a drawing on her desk, and I leaned over to look. It was a boy and girl standing on a hill by a house, a smiling sun overhead, the boy's quiet features familiar to the person I often saw in the mirror.

Mrs. Lawson raised a hand and tapped a button on her stylus. The room went black but for a light bleeding in from the hall as the main display lit up.

"Can any of you tell me why we are aboard the *Vasco Da Gama*?" she asked.

George raised his hand. "To see the Foundry."

"That's right. And what is the Foundry?"

"We don't know?"

She clicked her stylus and the screen shifted again, showing a pattern of stars and blurry photos. "It's true, we don't really know what the Foundry is, not for sure. All we have to go on are the signals, their few words, the emotional imprint of calm the signal leaves upon us, and the data taken from the Star Reach satellite constellation. Like Star Reach's predecessor Kepler, it used dips in starlight from varied angles to measure the transit of exoplanets. And while the data is valuable, it is inconclusive.

"From what we can tell, we theorize that the Foundry is what we refer to as a mega-structure, and it's a long way away from Earth. The distance it takes for light to travel in six years. For centuries humankind has dreamed of making contact with someone other than itself. That all changed seven years ago, when Dr. Hiro Kobayashi of the Kyoto Institute of Technology, discovered a way to send and receive messages using a previously under-utilized particle known as a neutrino."

"More like pootrino," James Reed, the doctor's son, said, and the class started laughing. He was always clowning around, making trouble. If he didn't keep his mouth shut, he might just end up in time out.

"Very creative, Mr. Reed." Mrs. Lawson gave a placating smile. "Neutrinos are tiny sub-atomic particles with a mass near to zero. At this very moment, trillions of them are zipping through your body and not doing a thing. That is why they are good a communication. They rarely interact with their environment.

"When Dr. Kobayashi developed his neutrino communicator, he discovered five nearly identical signals directed at Earth from five separate, vastly distant locations. The message they sent was simple, as you know, if a bit odd. *Hello, humanity. We are the Foundry, come see us soon.*' As we might have expected, they did not say, *We come in peace,*' or *Take me to your leader.*' Just a regular hello, written in a minor variation of Morse code.

"Hundreds of scientists were enlisted to be sure this was indeed genuine, not some laboratory accident or high-tech prank. The emotional response the signal induces, the message that is conveyed through feeling, made that seem less likely. Governments worried if it was human made, that there might be a new weapon of manipulation on the world stage. A weapon which could alter emotions with sound. We focused our greatest, most powerful satellites on the source of these signals and could see nothing but the radiant light of the stars they originated from. And so here we are, headed to knock on their door and say, *Hello.*"

A kid at the front of the class raised their hand. "Is the Foundry dangerous?"

"Hard to say, which is why we must be cautious. We have enough fuel to pass it by, do an orbit, and scoop reaction mass off a neighboring gas giant to burn home. Until we arrive, however, we are mostly in the dark. We must put our faith in deduction and human intuition. As advanced as we presume they are, if they intend us harm, why would they not simply come to Earth and attack us? Would they not make an even more enticing signal? We have to learn as much as we can about—"

The classroom lights flashed red as a whooping alarm echoed. Mrs. Lawson's face went slack. I looked to Shelly, and she gave me a shrug.

"Radiation storm," a student said from a nearby desk.

"Children," Mrs. Lawson said, motioning for the exit. "Hurry to your designated shelters now. Quick and orderly. Single file."

The head of the group did as they were asked, forming a neat queue. Then a kid in the back screamed, 'Go!', and the calm everyone had adopted from their teacher shattered like brittle glass. Kids streamed into the hall, fighting one another to breach the portal. I took Shelly's hand and we dashed through the exit.

The hall was crowded. Not everyone was heading for their proper shelter. We wore numbers on our jumpsuits to make this easy. Mine was six. So was Shelly's. We made a break for the shelter, and before we'd gotten halfway there the lights turned yellow, then red.

"I think that's decompression," Shelly said.

"Bad," I replied. "This is bad."

We had to move fast, or we might not have any air to breathe. It didn't matter that the ship felt fine. The alarms told us what to do.

"Masks, we need masks," I said, and Shelly nodded. It was all part of our training in school. Not only did we need to get to the designated safety shelter on board, where extra radiation shielding would protect us from a burst of cosmic rays, we needed a way to breathe after a loss of air pressure.

We rushed to the nearest safety station and opened the storage containers. I took hold of my mask but was then hammered in the side by a flood of other kids. The rush knocked me onto the floor, the side of my hip bruised, the mask clutched against my chest despite the fall.

I turned to my right and fought to stand, catching sight of Shelly as she struggled to recover from her own tumble. The crowd was swamping the safety station, taking all the available oxygen masks without regard for anyone but themselves. We stood at the edge of the maelstrom gaping at the frenzy.

"There's no time," I said, and put my mask over Shelly's face. She moved to protest, but I pressed the self-sizing button on the side, and it formed and fixed to the shape of her face.

The alarms continued as I led her to the shelter. We jumped inside and took our seats, Shelly wearing the mask, my face naked. Mom and Dad were waiting for me, what appeared to be anger written across their hard-set faces beneath the angular masks.

Why would they be mad at me?

A deafening buzz echoed throughout the ship and the emergency lights disappeared.

"Stand down, crew," the captain's voice came over the intercom. *"Stand down. This was just a drill. I repeat, just a drill. If this had been an actual emergency, half of you would have terminal cancer. The rest of you, well, you would have been left gasping for air until your head exploded. Come on. That was a lackluster performance. We have a lot of opportunity for improvement. Please return your safety equipment and tend to your previous tasks. Thank you."*

Shelly removed her mask and gave me a blank look.

Mom snatched me up by the hand and pulled me through the door. "We have something to talk about, little mister."

"What did I do?"

The door to our quarters slid shut and I was ordered to sit on the couch, Mom and Dad standing before me with crossed arms. I was a prisoner lined up before the firing squad. At the count of three, I'd be a dead man.

"You've done these drills a hundred times now!" Mom shouted at me. I shrunk down in my seat and felt cold. She'd never raised her voice like this. Maybe if I didn't move, she wouldn't kill me. "Why didn't you follow the rules?"

"But I did follow the rules. I got into the shelter. Shelter number six. That's my shelter."

"That's not what we mean, and you know it," Dad said, his voice a low simmer. He motioned at his head like an airline attendant, an imaginary mask in one hand, its strap pulled back by the other. "In the case of a decompression event, collect an oxygen mask from the nearest safety station. Place it firmly over your mouth, secure the band, and press the self-sizing button. If you are traveling with someone who needs assistance, please *secure your mask first*, then theirs. In the event of a water landing..."

Mom gave Dad a withering stare and he trailed off.

"I just wanted to be sure she was okay first," I told them. "There were so many kids. They wouldn't get out of the way. Someone pushed her down. They pushed me down too."

"That doesn't matter," Dad replied. "Not at a time like this."

"Why not?" I protested, my blood boiling. "Haven't you told me to be kind? To help others?"

"*Estou-me nas tintas.* How can you help anyone if you asphyxiate?" Mom put in. "Tell me. How? This is the one time to be selfish."

"You never care what I think," I mumbled.

"What was that?" Mom leaned in. "Did you say something?"

I shook my head. A thought best left to myself.

Dad puffed up and took a sniff. "Have you learned your lesson?"

"Yes," I said, lowering my head.

"Right then. Two weeks?"

Mom gave a nod. "Two weeks."

My eyes snapped up and darted between them. "Two weeks of what?"

"You're grounded. Go to school, come home. No games. School only."

"That's not fair!"

"Neither is my child dying if this drill had been real."

"But that won't happen. I can't die."

Dad scratched at the top of his head. "Not how it works. We're all going to die."

"Even us. I can't lose someone else. Not my son." Mom raised a finger and pointed. "Go clean up. Go to your room. You've got snot all over your jumpsuit."

I stood and did as I was told. When I looked at myself in the mirror, I found that she was right. I'd been sniffling and blowing bubbles. I hadn't even noticed.

Strange as it may have been, I had a revelation as I washed my face. This was the longest Mom and Dad had talked to me in weeks. For good or bad, it was nice to have their attention. But was this what it took to get them out of their work? Their child's life being at risk?

Whatever. I knew I'd done the right thing. I put myself in danger for the right person. I'd put myself in danger for a friend. Lesson or not, I knew I had the courage to do it again if I had to.

CHAPTER 8

Some progressions in life happen over time, a slow gradual change, a transition from night into day, like an older person going grey or packing on a few extra pounds around the middle. Others happen like a crack of thunder and a flash of lightning, a sudden explosion that leaves you both shocked and awed. Fifth grade had many of those shock and awe moments, though most of them came in the form of unbridled verbal expression.

"The captain is such a goddamn dick," my classmate James Reed said with bravado as he sat on his desk in the center of the room, all eyes fixed on him.

The morning had already been an interesting one. They'd called us kids into one of the medical labs as we were headed for school, checked our weight, took our vitals, pinched us with some device they swore measured muscle mass, and to finish it off, collected a vial of blood. I didn't care much for needles. Soon as nurse Brennon brought it out, I turned to jelly in my chair, face pitching onto the padded arm at my right. The experience was disturbing to say the least, not to mention embarrassing. I did not expect it to be topped by words.

I was back in class, over by the sinks grabbing a glass of water to wash away the discomfort of my phlebotomistic encounter. The moment my classmate James's lips stopped moving, I felt the back of my neck and shoulders catch fire with more intensity than I had in the lab. Those words. *Goddamn dick.* That use. He was wrong, right? The captain was a good man. But what do I do? Say something to the teacher? Do I snitch?

I filled my glass and took a quiet seat at my desk. Shelly had not yet arrived, it was just a few of us. Class didn't start for another five minutes.

"James, why do you say that?" George rubbed at his round jaw. "He's an American treasure. Served on the second International Space Station for what, six missions?"

"Yeah, he seems nice to me," Austin added, reaching around with a lanky arm to scratch his hair with equally slender fingers. "Always smiling, always working to be sure everyone is taken care of. It's a big responsibility, I think. We're like, humanity's only hope or something."

"Screw that bullshit," James replied. "Responsibility? Look, all he ever does is run Mom ragged. She's the doctor on this *fucking* can, someone real important, and he keeps her working all the time. She gets up at all hours of the night and works through the next day. Never has time to do anything anymore."

Austin shrugged. "Maybe people have been sick?"

"How in Neptune's ever-loving shit cakes is that even possible?" James tossed his hands in the air. "We're out here all alone, the damn Oort is at our drive plume. My mom told me the only germs we have are the ones we brought with us." He glanced in the direction of the door just as Shelly came in. "Oh, better be quiet now. Here comes Miss Perfect."

Shelly entered the room with her backpack slung over her shoulder, her curls straightened and pulled into a pair of French braids. An uneasy look had taken residence on her usually sunny face. I gave her a smirk and she sighed before sitting down beside me.

"Alright class take your seats," Mrs. Lawson said. "Grab your tablets. Time to review your test scores from last week."

I drew mine out of my backpack and frowned at what the page showed me. Though I had gotten far better at taking tests over the past few years, it was still a weak subject for me. Math was a little better. Science was flat at best. Language arts and writing in both English, French, and Spanish, I had bombed. History? Don't even get me started.

My standardized score for this week was sixty out of a hundred, a score that had been trending down for quite some time. Mom and Dad would not be happy.

"Well fuck-a-doodle-doo," James said, and the entire class turned to look at him.

Mrs. Lawson froze in the middle of what she was doing. She slipped her tablet into her desk and made her way over to him.

"What was that, James Reed?" She leaned over his desk, arms crossed, eyes on fire.

He tossed an arm over the back of his chair and smiled. "This test is a lie. No way I scored this low."

"I checked the answers twice."

"Well, your answers are wrong, check it again."

The class let out an "ooooo." I clamped a hand over my mouth in surprise.

"Mr. Reed," she said between gritted teeth. "You are excused. You may let your mother know she will be hearing from me."

He stood and snatched up his backpack. "Good." Everyone watched as he slid between the desks, getting what seemed to be random nods of approval from other students for his daring. When he was at the doorway, he glanced back at us and dusted off the shoulders of his jumpsuit.

I could hear Shelly growl, "No respect," under her breath.

"Can I leave too?" Austin asked.

Frank chimed in. "Or me?"

"Sit down!" Mrs. Lawson said with a bit too much bite. "Today we are discussing the New England colonies and how they changed the political make-up of the colonial world. Who knows, maybe I'll put a quiz together for tomorrow."

"Aww," several of the students whined. Shelly was not among them.

"Two quizzes? That better? We can keep going."

The room went silent.

I contemplated James's actions, and was both confused and interested, compelled to seek a meaningful conclusion. He had done something that perhaps on some level all of us in the room had thought of at one time or another. School was too much at times, year-round, never ending, spinning and spinning and spinning like the habitat ring, the motion creating its own sort of gravity. Mrs. Lawson had been our teacher for years, kids to preteens. She had pushed and pushed and pushed us, as if time were against us to learn all we would need to know. It had been painful at times, and yet, she was so kind, so sweet. She wanted nothing but the best for us, and so why treat her such a way? Maybe sometimes the rules were just too much. And yet… How could someone acting in such disregard for rules and respect seem so absolutely, well… absolutely fucking cool. James was pushing back against the establishment and that felt good. The standardized test was a lie, right? There was no way I could have scored as badly as I did.

Shelly ran a stylus across her tablet as she reviewed her own test. I caught a glimpse of her score out of the corner of my eye. Ninety-five out of one hundred. I slunk down in my seat and sipped at my water.

There was a knock at the classroom door. Mrs. Lawson waved to us and made for the exit. "Review your tests and my notes. I'll be back."

A few fixed their eyes on their tablets, but most started to chat in low voices, discussing what had just transpired. This had been an exciting class.

I turned to Shelly. "Want to hang out this afternoon? I found some new VEs on the stream. One is a fourth dimensional puzzle game. It has portals and light beams. You have to solve the different levels to discover the secret of some ancient alien structure. I've been playing it like crazy."

"Sorry, Milo." She flicked a finger at her tablet and shook her head. The look she gave her work was intense. I'd never seen her so focused, a mixture of worry and determination rippling across her brows, telegraphed in the darting of her eyes. "I need to study what I missed."

"But look at your score. It's amazing. Wish my score was better. My parents are going to kill me."

"Yeah, I know mine can be better." She narrowed her eyes and circled a sentence. "I'm going to make a hundred next time."

"Is that even possible?"

"It has to be. It's the only way I can prepare myself for what we are up against."

I frowned at her. "That's a little dramatic, don't you think? It's just a test. What are your plans when you grow up anyways? Be a roboticist? A computer engineer? Neural science? Who knows, we're kids."

"No." Shelly began to chew at her bottom lip. "No, I don't think its dramatic."

"Don't be so hard on yourself. They don't expect us to know it all yet."

"Doesn't matter. The Foundry doesn't care if we're kids."

"And we have years till we get there."

"You're being naïve."

"I have no idea what that even means."

"That's exactly my point," she raised her head and stared daggers into me. "Everything is just so happy go lucky with you lately. You used to try harder. Now, it's like you don't even care about your lessons, your responsibility. You just do whatever you like."

I gave a shrug and sunk down into my chair. "Why should I? Not like hard work earns me any favors."

The night before flashed into my head. No one at home, at least not really, Shelly busy, dinner and studies left up to me. Just a night like every other.

"You just need to chill the heck out," I told her, a jagged edge in my voice.

"Shut up, Milo," she said, and turned her attention back to her tablet.

"I'm not the one making a big deal out of—" I paused and leaned in her direction to see what she had missed, "Come on. You missed a phase in cellular division. Shocking, I think that's the one thing I got right."

She slammed a fist on her desk and groaned. "Stupid. Stupid. Mistakes like this won't cut it. I'll never figure it all out. Perfect, Shelly, you got to be perfect. That starts with your lessons."

Mrs. Lawson reentered the room, and everyone snapped their attention back to her. "Alright class. Anyone who scored a sixty-five or less on their test, no need to raise your hand I know who you are, you are to spend the afternoon in Lab 6-4G for detention."

I checked my score again. It hadn't changed.

"Fuck me," I groaned. My forehead hammered my desk once, twice, three times.

"I'm sorry, what was that, Mr. Hughes?" Mrs. Lawson asked, and I felt my skin prickle with fire.

"Nothing ma'am." I coughed. "Just something caught in my throat."

"That's what I thought."

After class I went directly to detention. Mom sent my tablet a ping to ream me out by remote. Typical. The source of her message showed Med Bay. She was working with my classmate James's mom, Dr. Reed, on what they were calling the Micro-G Protein. Rumor was that if all went as she hoped this would make space travel far safer. We might even be able to start families in space, which for now posed a huge risk of birth defects and developmental issues. Humans weren't adapted for this, our bodies withered. We had been researching the effects of micro- and null-gravity for decades, only until now the sample set was small, reserved to only a chosen few living aboard the ISS2 or on short hops between the Earth and the Moon, as well as Void Striders on flyers mining for resources. The data was inconclusive with the Mars colonists as well, since the minimal natural gravity on the red world made things ever more complicated. The *Vasco Da Gama*, along with the rest of the fleet, represented the largest human population living outside a gravity well, and all that data was very useful. It might just be enough to give us a path through these dangers.

I stood before the door to Lab 6-4G, terrified to go inside. I'd never gotten in trouble before, not any real trouble. I didn't know how to act other than penitent. I prepared my best speech about how this would never happen again and how I would study harder. Maybe Shelly was right about my focus lately. I'd add a few sob lines about how no one had helped me and that the crappy food we ate on board, except what we had on communal dinner nights, was rotting my brain and this made everything harder.

"Good story," I told myself, then opened the door.

Inside the lab there were four of us, and no teacher. The room was like the majority of the ship, mostly white, floor a crosshatch of textures, the outer walls covered in an array of bulky science equipment, glove boxes and grow tanks. George Ramirez, a quiet, heavy-set brainiac from class, stood over by the microscopes, fiddling with the controls, looking through one, then the next. He gave me a silent wave and went back to his business. At the rear of the room sat Harper Franklin, a girl I'd only said hello to once or twice. She stared at a safety poster on the wall and braided her auburn hair absently. I was pretty sure she didn't like any of us with how she acted most of the time.

James was in the middle of the room in a rolling chair, spinning himself in circles. He turned to face me, coming to a stop. With a triumphant smile on his face, he said, "Welcome to Failures 101. Ready to study, asshat?"

"Hello," I said, and took a seat opposite Harper. James watched my every move, his eyes betraying an active mindscape of thought. "What do we do? We waiting on the teacher?"

"She won't come," George said, his attention absent. "Our assignment is to review our tests."

"And your assignment, George, is to help us with that," Harper said.

George lifted his eyes from a microscope and scratched at his head. "Last time I play with Mrs. Lawson's tablet."

"That was hilarious." James began spinning in his chair again. "Hilarious."

"What happened?" I ventured.

George gave a smile, then shook it off as if the expression might land him in double the trouble. "I changed her lock screen on her tablet to a picture of her in a bikini. It was photoshopped."

"Dirty minded," Harper said, giving him a lazy eyed stare.

"What? It wasn't even her body. It was someone else's. We do have access to some of Earth's internet over the stream, if maybe not all the good stuff."

I crossed my arms and considered what he said. There was no way I'd say I had no idea what a bikini was. Was it a kind of fruit? Maybe a model of car?

"Still," James said, "I bet Mrs. Lawson looks hot in a bikini. I'd fap to that."

Harper stood and laughed. "Do you even know what fapping is?"

James rolled his eyes and turned to me. "So, new kid. What you in for?"

"Grades."

"Ditto."

Harper raised her hand. "Same."

"Shouldn't we be studying then?" I asked, then reached into my backpack for my tablet.

"Hold up there, buckaroo." James extended an open palm in a pleading motion. "We're not going to study."

"Why?"

"Because bump that. That's why."

"But we'll end up in here again."

"So? This is easy time. Not like they sent us upstate or anything. We stay in here, do a little work, maybe, and spend the rest of our three hours playin' around."

"My tablet won't let me into any games. Mom's got me locked down."

"Not all games are on your tablet, bro."

"VEs? Movies?"

James shook his head. "Though that would be great. No. Can someone fetch this kid an imagination?" He gestured at the room, the storage cabinets and laboratory equipment. "I'm sure there's something we can get into."

"Look, I don't want to get into trouble," I told him. "I'm already in enough hot water."

"Don't worry about it, man, you can't get in any more than you already are. There's like a limit to this, you know? Once you reach a certain level of trouble everything else is just fun."

"Super saturation of troublesome incidents," George commented, raising a finger. "It's a scientific fact."

"What he said." James started to work his way around the room, perusing what was at our disposal for his amusement. He fiddled with several of the instruments, flicking lights on and off, revealing samples of plants in neat rows behind glass. "Here we go." He slid open a drawer and uncovered a cache of petri dishes. "Let's play lab football."

James pressed a button and a table appeared from out of the floor. He put a set of the glass dishes on one end, another set on the other. George already knew where this was going and took his place.

"Here's the game," James said. "Slide the dish as close to the edge as you can without going over. Each dish that almost goes over and doesn't is a point."

George clapped his hands and rubbed his palms together. "Better get your tears out, baby boy. I'm about to make you cry."

"You wish."

"You not afraid of breaking them?" I asked. "They're made of glass."

"Show some confidence, Milo. I never miss a catch!" George bellowed. "Bring it on, James."

"No," James said. "I think it's goody goody's turn to play."

"Who, me?" I pointed to myself.

"Yes, you." He slid one of the glass dishes across the table towards me.

I leapt forward, catching it just before it fell off the edge.

"Nice reflexes."

"I don't think we should do this. We could break it. Make a mess."

"Milo! Milo!" they began to chant.

I lifted the petri dish and stared at it, the pinkish agar substrate dominating its bottom edge. "Fine. Let's play."

We spent the next two hours making up random games with whatever we could find, killing time. Each new game I held back for a moment, seeing what they might do next. I didn't want to break anything or get into more trouble. I wasn't sure if I subscribed to this super saturation theory. When I acted too reserved, they physically pushed me into the game. One time, Harper tickled my ribs till I complied, and although it was a bit annoying, it was also pretty cool. They wanted me to be part of whatever it was they were doing. They wanted to know what I thought.

It was a relief to be distracted, to not think about what had happened, and what was happening back on Earth. *Minha avó,* my only grandmother, and many of my cousins were gone. Chances were I'd never see them again anyways, given the length of the missions, but they were family. They were part of me and that hurt. Seeing Mom check out when anything was mentioned about it hurt.

"Wasn't that fun, Milo?" Harper asked just after we finished skating around the room in our socks. She gave me a smile, her green eyes flickering, and I felt a swirl of butterflies amass in my stomach.

"Yeah. It was."

"What next, what next?" George said, making short hops across the room. "Gotta keep busy. Gotta keep busy."

We located a small cache of paper and pens—something we had in limited supply aboard the ship—and decorated the crisp sheets, then folded them into airplanes. A fierce competition ensued, seeing who could get theirs across the room the most times. Harper and I folded messy lines and lopsided wings, while James and George worked with precision, using plastic cards as tools to make the perfect plane. Our aircraft took flight time and again, cruising ahead and to one side of the room, the coriolis effect of the habitation ring's spin easy to observe by their path.

"Your plane looks like trash," James said, tossing his again. It cut a neat curve across the room to rest atop a mass spectrometer, its landing gentle as its flight.

I drew back my arm to throw my plane again, finger on the spine to stabilize it. "Well, well, your face looks like trash." After the words left my mouth, I felt terrible. Was it time to apologize?

"Ohhh! There we go." James slapped me on the shoulder and chuckled. "He isn't all goody goody."

"I think your plane is beautiful," Harper commented. "And let's be truthful, James, your face does look like trash."

"You're one to talk."

George raised a finger. "It's not his fault. Gets it honest."

"Bastard."

"Come on!" I let my plane fly. "You can make it!" It nosedived onto my shoes. I made a noise like an explosion and collapsed to the floor, the side of my head against the cold gloss of the tiles.

"Today's news report," Harper began. "Three imaginary pilots dead after the tragic crash of their paper plane. Early investigations reveal a poor design and inexperienced pilot might have been the cause."

The four of us laughed, the feeling both foreign and welcome. For an instant it felt as if the dark room I'd been living in had just been given a window, and there were stars in the distance, a promise of light, of change.

"Want to see something cool?" George asked. He went to one of the drawers and removed a blue rag. "Figured this out last time we were in here." He rolled a chair up to the far wall and locked it in place, climbed on top, and reached for a vent near the ceiling. After laying the rag flat he put it over the vent, and it stuck, negative pressure holding it in place.

"Okay." James crossed his arms and gave Harper and I a quizzical look. "That the trick?"

"Nope." He got down off the chair and directed our attention to the environmental controls on the wall. "See the humidity? The numbers are going up and up. If we leave that thing up there, this room will be sticky and damp before you know it. All the rooms have them, they're like an air return, regulating moisture. Crank up the heat a little, and you might even get a sauna."

"And how would that help us?" Harper asked. "Not like you're gonna get me in a bikini no matter what you try to do."

"Hush up." George waved a hand. "I just thought it might be funny. Can you imagine? Someone would totally freak out. They'd probably think the ship was broken or something. And in the end, all we'd have to do to fix it would be to uncover the vent. Back in engineering there's a central connection for all this. I bet you could cover it there and then no one would know who did it."

"I appreciate the dark enthusiasm," James said, a finger on his chin in thought. "But I see no practical use."

"What about for this?" Harper goosed James in the ribs.

"I hope you know this means war!" He hopped up and chased her around the room.

Before we knew it, everyone was laughing again, exchanging goosey jabs, primarily between ourselves and Harper. I wasn't sure why but tickling her was more fun than tickling the guys.

We stopped the moment George tripped and faceplanted on the floor.

"You okay?" James went to his side.

"Ouch it hurts," he replied, hands clasping his thigh. "Something in my leg. God, man, I'm exhausted."

"Me too," I said.

Harper gave me a funny look and nodded. "Weird, huh?"

"Did the nurse tell you anything this morning?" I asked.

George let out a long breath and allowed James to help him stand. "That my bone density was down. I needed to exercise more. Take my supplements. Try not to fall like this. Whatever. It's space withering or something like that."

"The atrophy crisis," I mumbled, thinking back to all the things I had overheard Mom talk about at home. According to her, time was running out. A year? Two years at most? Irreparable biological damage. That didn't seem so far away anymore. Self-care, diet and exercise helped, but it wasn't enough.

"Nurse Brennon told me the same." James scratched at his arm. "I sit around on my device too—"

"Oh crap." George's tablet pinged. He limped across the room and snatched it off the counter. "Oh crap."

"What?"

"Guys, look alive, look perfect. Time for us to study. Mrs. Lawson is on her way back."

We pretended as if we were studying until she appeared at the door. We had cleaned up our messes so there was little chance anyone could tell what we'd been up to. Mrs. Lawson said nothing when she entered, just waved us towards the door.

I left the room with the group, *my group*. Today had changed something, built a kind of bond I hadn't experienced before. We paused at one of the inward facing windows and watched as engineers performed a spacewalk along the spine of the ship, moving heavy equipment and repairing sensor spurs. One of them gave us a salute and we waved back. Harper pointed to a man in a bulky white and orange suit on the far left, identifying them as her dad.

In the halls of habitation, its bulkheads covered in soft supply packages and technical readouts, a group of a dozen adults jogged past. This had become a routine for them, taking ten or fifteen passes around the hab before heading off to Med Bay to have their vitals taken yet again. Esteban and Deidrick were at the front of the group. I found it curious that while some of the older people were thinning, their arms spindly, their muscle definition reduced, my parents included, Esteban and Deidrick seemed immune. They were just as muscular and imposing as on the day I thought they were going to space my family. Maybe they took steroids? That's a thing, right?

"*Buenas tardes, amigos,*" Esteban said, then gave us a salute.

"Esteban!" James returned the salute with an over exaggerated motion. "Keep them in line."

They maintained their pace and within a few seconds they were out of site around the upward curve of the ring.

"They sure work out a lot," George commented. "Makes me hungry just to watch."

Harper tapped him on the belly with the back of her hand. "You could do with a work-out."

"What? I'm pleasingly plump. Don't fat shame me."

As we approached the Med Bay, James tugged my jumpsuit sleeve and called our little group into a corner. We gave him a strange look but then heard the voices up ahead.

"Look, I don't care how many hours it takes, Reed. You and Hughes have got to figure this out. It's not just our asses on the line, it's all of humanity." It was the captain's voice.

"I understand," Dr. Reed replied. "But I am exhausted. If we were back home, forcing a ninety-hour work week would be considered unethical. I need rest."

"Hughes doesn't require rest."

"Well, she's a damned cyborg or something. That woman can run on caffeine and pure spite for a week on end. I am not like her. We were not created equal." She paused. "Are you okay, Captain? Your arm is red, you're scratching at it."

The captain sighed. "It's nothing. I—I was one of the last to get the bat virus, got sick in my twenties after visiting a remote location in South America with family. It just gives me a rash when things are stressful, kind of like a cold sore coming up. Nothing to worry about. Itches is all."

"I've never seen that side effect from COVID before. We can try an antihistamine. Maybe it's an allergic reaction."

"It's fine. It's fine."

"Why didn't you tell me? It's not in your charts."

"I said it's fine, Doctor."

"Okay."

"Look, I'm sorry. Tell me what we can do. How much more time will this take?"

"Projections show that for us to go gene by gene we're looking at least another six hundred hours. I can only analyze so fast."

"Then it's time we look at other options." The captain paused. "Till then, get it done. Put in the time and hopefully we'll get lucky. Go get forty winks and stay on it."

"Where are you off to?"

"To push the other ends against the middle."

"You know, for an eighteen-year voyage there sure is a lot of hurrying to be done."

"You have your assignment, Doctor. Get it done."

"Fine, fine. Yes, sir."

We heard their footsteps recede as they headed down the opposite hallway.

James gave us an angry look.

"What is it?" I asked. "You okay?"

"He's definitely not okay," Harper supplied, putting a hand on his shoulder.

"You know," James said. "I think it's time we make the captain pay. Let's give him a taste of his own medicine."

George's dark eyes gleamed. "What do you have in mind?"

"Oh, nothing big. Just a prank. Just a harmless little prank."

"Are you sure?" I asked. "Shouldn't you try to stay out of trouble?"

"Lookie here, Morality Police. I'm going to need all of your help to get this done."

"I'm in," Harper said without preamble.

George crossed his arms and nodded. "Don't worry about this guy, dawg."

Their attention fell next on me. I didn't know what to do. I know I didn't want to get in trouble, but then again, today was some of the most fun I could remember. Sure, we'd be pranking the captain and that seemed like a bad idea, but it was just a harmless little prank. We were just kids, right? I didn't want to lose my new friends just because I couldn't hang.

"Harmless little prank you say?" I asked, my voice as small as a tardigrade. "Are you sure?"

James put a hand to his chest, fingers brushing his jumpsuit's name badge. He turned his gaze to the ceiling, eyes closed in somber resignation. "On my honor as a star child."

I let out a long breath. "Okay, just so long as no one gets hurt."

There was nothing to be done.

"Bitchin'." James put his arms around the three of us. "Here's the plan."

CHAPTER 9

We spent the next few days collecting supplies and making our plans. While James's idea was similar to another, there were a few key differences. He turned out to be quite the schemer, a kid with a covert ops brain. Not only did he know how to organize this operation, but he also somehow knew where to find the things that we needed and how to get them. The *Vasco Da Gama* was punching the outer limits of the Oort Cloud, crossing into the interstellar medium. This was an event much of the crew, Mom and Dad included, approached with a sense of awe and wonder, and so while they were being inspired, we were hunting down air returns.

Using a lifted access card from his mother's work pouch, James was able to grant us access to several locations on the ship I had never seen before. One of these was the aft end of the main spine, which led into Engineering. George and I were sent in that direction to find the return leading to the bridge while James and Harper collected the rest of the goods.

"They should be up on the bridge talking about the crossing," George said as he descended a set of ladders towards the ship's fusion drive.

The passage was narrow as an arm span and terminated every fifteen feet or so with a platform, forcing you to mount a new ladder on the opposite side. Seems the engineers didn't care for the idea that someone might lose their grip and fall several hundred feet to their death. It was loud in here. The walls vibrated. Gravity was strange.

"Dad's been talking about it for weeks," I said. "It's a bunch of empty space, but there's gas and electro magnic radiation. Molecular clouds and—"

"Did you say electro magnic?"

"Yeah. That's what it's called."

"I don't think that's how it's pronounced."

"Oh."

A loud thunk came from the wall beside us, an oscillating whir following. I felt my hands go slick with nervous sweat, one foot slipping off a rung for an instant. If I just kept myself talking, the reality of where we were and what we were doing didn't seem so bad. We were in a restricted area, coming closer to dangerous equipment, and vacuum was no more than a few feet away, on the other side of space-grade aluminum and radiation shielding.

"We might just catch up to Voyager," I added.

"Voyager?" George asked.

"Dad told me all about it. It's a probe we sent into space like a hundred years ago that has pictures of naked people on it."

"What a bunch of pervs."

"Right?"

George paused at one of the landings. "Here, we need to climb into this side passage. If what the diagrams showed were correct the bridge return should be in here."

My tablet pinged. It was a text message.

James: Let us know which one. We're in position higher up.

Me: Almost there.

Harper: Hi, guys! Just wanted to say hi!

I gave my tablet a nervous smile.

"Let's see," George squeezed into a tunnel even smaller than the spinal shaft.

I followed after, careful not to touch the bundles of wires and pipes within. The temperature here was far hotter than the rest of the ship, environmental regulation somewhat lacking. Sweat began to wick from my forehead onto the diamond plated steel. I crawled forward and lost my balance for an instant, nearly putting my hand on a pipe painted in emergency orange.

"Careful not to touch anything." George pointed to a sticker. *Caution.* "Should have more like don't fucking touch written on the side, but I don't make these decisions. It's connected to the sodium-cooling system. It's molten, bro."

"Ohh." I withdrew my shaking hand.

He followed a series of pipes, consulting his tablet again and again. Several sweaty minutes later, we came to a stop. "Here it is!" he exclaimed.

"What number? I'll ping James."

"6357-L."

He returned the ping almost instantly.

James: We found it. Head back this way.

I didn't have to be told twice. George and I scurried back up the spine towards the habitat junction. Relief flooded me as we reached the top. James and Harper were waiting for us beside an open access panel. Inside I spotted the pipe's number, as well as a vent and a group of filters.

"Ready?" James asked, holding a set of wet rags that had an herbal scent.

"What's that smell?" I asked.

"Eucalyptus extract I took from the gardens. Watched a video saying they sometimes add it to bath houses. Seemed appropriate."

I leaned in and took a deeper sniff. "It's really strong."

"God this is gonna be so damn funny," James went on. "They are all on the bridge. All gonna get it. Wet, sticky, freaking out. Here, Milo. Do the honors."

"I well, no."

"Come on," Harper said, nudging me with her shoulder. "Do it for me."

My heart gave a start at her words. I took a deep breath and stepped forward, reminding myself this was just a little prank. Once this day was behind us, I'd have not only a funny story to look back on, but a set of friends forever.

"Fine." I took the rag from James and placed it over the slotted vent inside the wall. The damp rag clung to the filter just like it had in detention. We slammed the panel shut and took off running.

"Let's get to the network room!" George said as we reached the lift. "We can watch the bridge from there."

"Wicked!" James chimed in.

The habitation ring was mostly empty, so we laughed the entire way. Many of the adults had made the call to be on the bridge along with the captain. I sure hoped that they enjoyed their sauna.

We entered one of the data network rooms and James cycled through the different feeds. We could see the senior staff, my parents and James's mom included. Everyone was talking and laughing They looked happy, as if they were having a good time. I wondered what their conversations were about.

"This ought to show the captain." James took a seat on one of the chairs mounted to the wall.

I found my own and Harper sat beside me. She took my hand and began to squeeze, her fingers slick with sweat.

"You okay?" I whispered.

She shrugged. "Don't know. I've never done… well…"

George paced the room, his eyes narrowed, attention fixed on the screen. "Come on now. This shouldn't take long. There's plenty of pressure in that line."

"You haven't what?" I asked Harper.

"Nothing. Just…" She squeezed my fingers harder. "Done anything like this for fun. I'm such a goodie goodie."

I blinked. That was hard to believe given the company she kept. The company I now kept. How should I respond? It's okay, you're not so good? That sounded terrible. You're the goodiest person I've ever met? Again, not the best context for this. I think she wanted to feel like what she was doing was okay, that the swirling mealworms in her stomach, the mounting dread at her back was acceptable.

"It's just a little prank," I told her, unable to think of any other comfort.

"Guys." George pointed at the screen. "Something is happening."

One of the crew members at the main console started to wave his arms. Lights flashed on his panel. He fought to get the captain's attention, but Tobias Williams was too absorbed in conversation. The man pushed away from his console and moved to rally the help of others. Several of the adults began to yawn, appearing tired of a sudden. Many fell limp where they floated.

Something was wrong.

"What's going on?" Harper asked, her voice small. "I don't see any moisture forming."

George blinked. "I—eh…"

"Oh shit, oh shit." James started raking fingers through his hair. "Oh shit, oh shit."

"What's going on?" I stood up and went to one of the monitors. "George?"

"I don't know. It's not working. It's like… Guys, it's like they're passing out."

Alarms sounded throughout the ship. Emergency personnel appeared from hallways and rushed towards the bridge lift, first-aid and technical kits in hand.

George put his hands on his face, pressing against his temples with his forefingers. "What did we do?"

"Quick." James waved us into the hall. "If we get back to the return fast, we can undo this."

We followed him to the secondary lift, avoiding the emergency response teams like a set of spies dodging security. The alarms had ceased but the ceiling was yellow. A soft alert. The lift doors opened, and we nearly leapt inside, our group falling into a heap in the corner. George rolled out of our pile and slapped the lift button for the proper deck. We rose towards the spine of the ship.

"Come on, faster," he said. "Faster."

As soon as the lift's doors slid away, we bolted off down the hall to the access panel. James swung it open and with Harper's help, they cleared the return. Air hissed and the vent began to sound normal. James threw the balled rag at me and I tossed it on the floor, my hands stinking of eucalyptus, a new kind of shame.

"That was scary," George mumbled.

Before we could think to run and hide, one end of the hall was blocked. I turned to look the opposite direction, but there was no use. Where would we run?

"What we got, eh?" Esteban asked from the end of the hall. The two of us needed to stop meeting like this. "Dis the cause of all that?" He gestured for us to follow him. "Come on. Time you go see Captain Williams."

I swallowed. "Do we have to?"

"I'll go." James stomped a foot on the ground, his arms thrown down at his side, fists clenched. "I'm not afraid of him!"

"Tough guy?" Esteban mused. "See how you feel after a few days in solitary isolation. This serious business, ya? You almost killed crew members."

George raised his hand. "How bad is it?"

"Bad, little man." Esteban gestured ahead with a wave.

Harper and I exchanged worried looks and followed after, making no protest.

He led us to an emergency shelter near the bridge. The room was not much more than a closet stuffed with people, most of whom were breathing from oxygen masks, a few being looked over by Dr. Reed and her nursing staff.

The moment James saw his mother was there, he turned almost as white as a ghost.

At the corner of the room sat Captain Williams, coughing into his mask.

"Over here," he called to us, puffs of moisture flaring within the mask. It was hard to read his face at this time, a furious calm had come over it. The kind of calm that was far more terrifying than someone who was screaming.

James, Harper, George and I stood before the captain, coming shoulder to shoulder with those we had seen over the network monitors. Everyone in the room's attention fell onto us, three dozen eyes like tiny drills burrowing into our brains.

"Do you know what you did?" the captain asked, his voice low. "Do you even know how this ship works?"

"We made a sauna?" George ventured, his right thumb massaging the meat of his left palm.

"A wha—what?" The captain shook his head in disbelief. "Sit."

We did as we were told.

He picked up a tablet and flicked through a couple of screens, then handed it off to an emergency responder. "Do you know what the system that you played with does? And before you try and deny it, yes, we know it was you. We reviewed the video as Esteban was escorting you here. Come on. Anyone want to speak up? Tell me, master engineers, decorated astronauts, what UEI system was it that you prevented from doing what it was designed to do? Surely you learned all about it in flight school."

None of us dared respond.

"I think it's time for a little science lesson." The captain paused to take a series of labored breaths. His eyes were heavy, his body limp. Nurse Brennon reached in her bag for an injector and applied It to his arm, nodding after she was done.

"So, you see, children," the captain continued, "when living things like humans metabolize, we create a byproduct through cellular respiration. Oxygen and glucose create energy and carbon dioxide. This might all be a little over your fifth-grade heads, but I believe now is as good a time as any to learn the wonders of life.

"There are only a few living things in this terrible universe that love carbon dioxide, things like plants, but the thing is, on the bridge of an interstellar space craft we don't have lots of those. In fact, we don't have a single one. Plants are for the ship's gardens and living quarters, not here. Control panels and monitors, processors and other electronic equipment don't tend to care about CO2. So, when we're making all this dangerous gas, breathing it moment after moment, and it has nowhere to go, the air starts to get a little, how can I say, toxic?"

I swallowed. My thoughts had started to drift. I could conceive of at least fifteen different ways my life was over. Being stuffed in the airlock seemed most expeditious.

"Humans don't do well breathing a concentration of CO2. We tend to, well, pass out and die. That's why we have a special system just for this!" He paused to catch his breath, a palm against his chest. "Now do we have zeolite CO2 filters on the bridge, sure we do, but they require negative pressure to work. And what happens when you cover the air returns? Hmm? Are we understanding by now?"

I shrank down in my seat.

"I thought we were making a sauna!" George blurted. "I swear!"

"This old story again," the captain shook his head.

"I thought it was the moisture control."

The captain put a hand to his face and rubbed around the edges of the mask. "Moisture control is managed on each section independently. We recycle the water and add it to the local stores."

James gave a harrumph. "How were we supposed to know that?"

"Best to leave things you don't understand well alone."

"Hypocrite," James growled.

"What did you say?"

"James Parker!" Dr. Reed shouted across the tiny shelter. "You will show the captain the respect he is due."

"You heard me, *sir*. I said hypocrite." James sat up straight and tossed back his chin in defiance. "What are we doing on this ship? I may only be a kid, but aren't we messing with something we don't understand?"

The shelter fell silent at his comment. It was true, even I knew that. We were roaring our way towards some unknowable machine that could be the savior of humanity or… or what? Due to the captain's ban on violent entertainment, books and movies, I had little inspiration in this to draw upon. Maybe little green men would hollow out our brains? Poke us with sticks? I tried not to think about it too much. Yet on some level I knew we were all terrified. For those who joined this crew of their own free will, their curiosity was more than enough to overcome these fears. For us, though, kids stuffed into their parents' cars in the middle of the night to embark on a new life, we had no choice.

What seemed an endless moment passed, and Shelly rushed into the room and threw her arms around Captain Williams. He returned the gesture and gave a relieved sigh.

"You're okay, Daddy," she said. "I'm so glad you're okay."

He gave a nod and patted her back. She glanced over at us, and her attention settled on me, a scowl on her face. I wasn't sure why, but in that moment all it did was make me angry. Didn't she understand that I didn't mean to hurt him? What was I supposed to do, tell the others no?

"It was just a prank," I told her, more a frustrated excuse than a plea.

She said nothing in response. Neither did the captain.

My parents appeared in the doorway and by the look on their faces, I knew that my life was over.

"Milo, come here," Mom growled. "We're going home."

I made the walk of shame through the gauntlet of crew members who coughed and glared at me as I went, wondering to myself if there was a means of time travel aboard this ship. It was about the only thing that might keep me from being grounded forever. My former self, that naïve child of three hours ago, deserved a serious warning.

CHAPTER 10

Punishment over my lack of judgment was short and swift. Despite being furious at me for almost killing a third of the executive staff, Mom and Dad did not have the time or attention to enforce their rules. The official punishment was that I was grounded for a month. I was required to remain in our quarters, not just by my parents but also by the captain, unless escorted. I was restricted to the habitation ring and my access to the ship's internal network was limited to educational channels only. No crew-to-crew pings. No games of any real entertainment value.

This was fine for the first few days. Mom and Dad did their work from home, something with which they were perfectly familiar, but soon they were called into their respective labs. Again and again, they would setup their workspace at home, and a ping would force them to head out the door grumbling. I spent almost all this time alone, eating, lounging in my PJs, playing any match-up or building games I could find on the fringe of network limitations. It was fun for a time, a kind of vacation from life, an opportunity to forget where we were and what we were doing. But even that became boring. When no one was watching, I began to venture out, looking for anyone of my group to talk to. Dodging Esteban, who I had come to think of as the captain's soft enforcer, wasn't easy. He had the knack of appearing just when you didn't want him to. Still, I had to do something. Grounded or not, isolation was making me twitchy.

When the month was up, Mom and Dad hardly gave it a mention. The limitations on my tablet lifted and I went back to school. Shelly wouldn't talk to me anymore. She moved her place in class to be on the opposite end of the room, beside Austin and Deet. It was clear our friendship had become a vestigial social attachment she opted to have surgically removed, lanced away like a developmental genetic defect. I didn't know how to feel about this. I'd never lost a friend before, and over what? I made a single, poor choice. Couldn't she see I was sorry?

A couple of years passed, and by the time the *Vasco Da Gama* reached cruise velocity, one third of light speed, this particular isolation hadn't ended. Shelly didn't need me anymore.

James, George, Harper and I remained a tight group. We continued to play pranks and get into trouble, but instead of nearly killing people by fiddling with environmental controls, our activities were far more benign. We put disposable waste bags full of air in people's chairs to make them fart when they sat, made water guns out of syringes, and sent group pings during class which made music. The four of us were inseparable. We were the best of friends.

As it usually went, James would propose an idea, George would puzzle it out, I would gather what we needed, and Harper... Harper became more interesting by the day. That long red hair. Those bright green eyes, the splash of freckles around her nose, the way she laughed at awkward jokes. It was hard to say no to anything when she had said yes.

Our shift from adolescents to teenagers wasn't like it was for most human kids. I didn't go home for summer break one year, loving crayons and trading cards, only to come back and realize that every girl I saw occupied my thoughts, them having blossomed and grown a pair of melons my thirsty eyes couldn't keep away from. Our journey was less of a leap, and more of a covert operation. It was subversive, surreptitious. Everything just felt different, the brush of my clothes against my skin, the friendly hug I received from a female friend. All of it was exciting.

At the end of seventh grade, I began to notice that some of the kids from our class had started pairing off. They were pinging, bread-crumbing, hooking-up, handing, and hell if I knew what else. I pretended I understood what was going on, but I didn't. All I knew was that other people were getting into relationships, and it was the buzz of the ship. The adults did their best not to seem interested, but they had bets going. Quiet discussions heard in hallways. They were hoping, praying, coercing those who were genetic matches to spend more time with one another and form pairs.

As for me, there was no pair. I wasn't supposed to be here. I wasn't part of the system. Not part of the plan. God's reject. I was alone in this space; the unspoken sentiment undeniable.

That changed on a particular evening James and George were called home early. We'd been running around the second deck of the habitation ring shortly after school and just before dinner, occasionally stopping in the VE suite to piddle around. We took a trip to the forests of the Pacific Northwest in summer, hiking our way up Mt. Rainer. James was pinged first to come home. A moment later, George. They grumbled in unison, tossed their goggles and haptic gloves onto the floor and stormed out, waving at us from the hall. This left Harper and I alone for what might have been the first time ever.

My heart pounded in my chest.

"Wonder what we should do now?" I mused. A group of adults jogged past us, their steps without rhythm, a couple of those at the back giving us nods of hello.

Harper twisted the toe of her shoe against the floor, her left hand rubbing her right arm, and shrugged. "I don't know. Do you have to be anywhere?"

"Dad's in the lab. I think Mom's passed out. It's been a long week." I turned and gave her a crooked smile.

We stood there for a silent moment, only the white noise of the ship brushing our ears. I felt an urge to both run and stand in silence forever, unwilling to let it go. These imperatives warred against each other.

"I need to go home," I said, but my feet didn't move.

Harper grabbed me by the hand and slipped her fingers between mine. She gave me a smile, and I felt my heart melt under its intense heat.

"I don't want to go home," she pleaded. "I'm not tired or anything. Want to walk the outer loop? It's quiet this time of day."

"I—I—" my words came out in a stammer. My feet led me in the direction her hand was guiding me. "Okay."

"It's nice to be away from the other guys."

"Yeah?"

"Yeah. I feel like they can't ever be serious. Sometimes I just need someone to be serious."

"Serious how?"

"You know how James is always talking about his mom and working all the time? That's not just his story. Dad has been down in engineering tweaking the ship's main drive based on tests they did back on Earth. Should help us during slowdown, make it faster, give us options. This overworked parent business is my story, your story too. It's all they ever do. But, you know, maybe that's just how it is. Maybe that's what it means to be an adult."

"Maybe. We are heading towards something we know almost nothing about."

"Exactly!"

"Just a few words from the Foundry, a bunch of theories, and a pink light made from sound stuck in our heads."

"That feeling. It's..."

"Like everything is going to be okay, but I'm not so sure it is."

"It's not their fault really," she said after a moment. "And still, it kind of leaves me lonely. It's like, when I'm home they're not even really there."

"At least we have each other," I said, squeezing her fingers.

She paused where we were and smiled at me. "Want to go somewhere cool?"

I nodded and she led us a quarter turn down the ring to Stellar Observation, my mind swimming in possibility. I knew this was leading somewhere significant, but where that was, I couldn't say.

Stellar Observation was a circular space the size of an average living room bolted to the exterior of the habitat ring, a bump facing out of the hull, its lights dim, lambent illumination seeping out from the margins of the floor. Around the edges of the room spanned a series of white, endless couches upholstered in a kind of faux leather stuffed with memory foam. At the center of their circle was a cupola that served as an open eye, its gaze fixed on the endless void.

We were alone. Harper took a seat on the infinite couch and patted the space beside her. I did as I was instructed. I was dizzy. Had my consciousness been swapped with someone else's?

She flicked a switch, and the cupola came to life, giving us a digital overlay with the names of stars swirling in the dark. The habitat ring spun, our outward view streaking. The swirling lights became hypnotic. Harper put her head on my shoulder. I took a deep breath and slipped a nervous arm around her. She gave a contented sigh as I pulled her close.

"It's beautiful," she whispered, then turned her face to meet mine.

Color danced in her emerald eyes, a veritable aurora of lights skittering upon the atmosphere of an alien world. It was hard not to get lost in the sight. For the first time in a while someone had seen me, taken notice that I was here, that I was breathing, acting, thinking. Feeling. I wasn't just a burden, a square peg meant for a system of circles and triangles. I belonged.

She blinked and took hold of my face, then leaned in and pressed her sweet, strawberry flavored lips against mine. I closed my eyes and trembled, a shiver cascading down my spine, my head going swimmy. I felt my face flush and my chest catch.

No judgement in this moment, just… Just what?

She pulled back after an indefinite amount of time. "Wow," her word came out in a whisper.

My heart pounded against my ribcage. "Yeah. Wow."

We let another hour pass, ensuring that the pleasure of this first experience was not just a fluke. It was not. We were crew members of the *Vasco Da Gama,* born to be dedicated scientists who did our best to test a sound theory. The result? Genetic match or no, our lips worked just fine.

Harper's dad pinged her tablet.

"Want me to walk you home?"

"Sure," she said. "Just a sec, I'll be right with you."

I was the first back into the hallway, Harper fiddling with her tablet on the infinite couch. Another group of adults jogged by. It seemed this was about all they did in the evening, their ages ranging from mid-thirties to late forties. They were thin as rails, as were we, a condition not likely to change anytime soon. The super thin, sexy look might have been fashionable on the home world, but here it made Mom and her team increasingly nervous. She was obsessed with the crew's weight and muscle density, cases of low blood pressure or sudden bouts of unconsciousness. It didn't matter how much we ate, how much we exercised. Keeping meat on our bones, "countermeasures" as she called them, was an unending challenge.

The group passed and as they cleared, I could see Shelly plodding after them, her face buried in her tablet. She took an awkward step, tangled her left foot with her right, recovered her balance with a swing of a hand, and gave a laugh at herself. Despite my anger, it was good to see her face. I hadn't intended for anyone to get hurt the day of our prank, and still, she had spent the past two years ignoring me. On a ship this size, a feat like that took effort.

"You okay?" I asked, attempting to be the bigger man. "Nearly busted your butt."

She shook her head and looked up. "Oh, hi, Milo. How are you?"

I scratched at the back of my head. "Pretty good."

"Good. Good. We uh—well…" Shelly swallowed and took a step towards me. "See the update on the trip? The photos the astrological team took?"

"Yeah. Dad showed me yesterday. There's a shape to the structure."

She scratched at her arm and averted her attention. "Oh, of course, yeah. You would see that first."

I gave her a noncommittal smirk. "Still, it's pretty cool. The thing is big, we just don't know how big."

"Real, real big."

"Yeah…"

A silent moment passed between us, an expectant pause. We both had something to say, but it seemed that neither of us were fully committed to follow through.

"It's been a little, you know," Shelly ventured, her shoulders rising. "I mean things and stuff."

"Yeah. I know."

"Look, I feel terrible," Shelly stammered. "We haven't. I mean. It's like ancient history. But the accident. I just."

"Hello, Miss Williams," Harper said, appearing at the door behind me.

"Harper," Shelly responded, her voice cold and surprised.

My blood went hot. Harper slipped close beside me, reaching for my hand. Shelly took a step back and licked her dry lips.

"Oh, I'm sorry, didn't mean to interrupt." Shelly clutched her tablet against her chest. "I mean."

I froze, unsure what to do, unsure what Harper and I were, what Shelly and I were. A part of me was still angry about what Shelly had done, for not forgiving me, cutting me off by actively ignoring me. Another part knew that she was still important, and that I had made a big mistake. I had never wanted to hurt her.

Harper turned my face towards hers with a set of soft fingertips. "Give me a kiss, boo."

I hesitated for a moment, letting Harper's hand go. The shock forced her eyes wide. Shelly's gaze darted between us. Harper took a step back. There had been no other option. To save face with Harper, I had to draw her chin towards me, and press my lips to hers. She fell into me, and we breathed deep, our kiss a bit too hard and not at all pleasurable under Shelly's uncertain scrutiny.

"I can see you're busy," Shelly said. She took off running down the hall, and out of the corner of my eyes I could see a palm against her face. Was she crying? This was not how this was supposed to go.

The kiss between Harper and I broke like a snapping bone. I spun to see Shelly flee, my heart ripping down the center at the sight. Why had I done that? What had it accomplished? We were talking for the first time in forever. Why was I such an idiot?

"Later, bitch," Harper said under her breath.

I whirled on her. "What did you say?"

"Nothing. Just joking." She took me by the arm and gave an innocent smile. "Take me home."

Now that I had tasted the sweet honey of time alone with Harper, I wanted more, awkward moments or not. We made plans and schemed scenarios in which James and George would not be around. We found storage closets and maintenance access areas where prying eyes tended not to venture. We kissed and sat dreamily, talked of nothing for hours at a time. It was all I looked forward to. What I dreamed about in class.

We had plans to visit the Stellar Observatory, then go on a date in the VE suite one Saturday night. I pinged Harper and she did not respond. I waited a while, tried again, and got nothing. I told Mom and Dad I needed a walk and headed out to look for her. This was not like her. She didn't keep me waiting. I searched the ship for hours and found nothing. Harper was nowhere to be seen.

I went home defeated, shoulders heavy, and crashed onto my bed, clutching Jasper and staring at the ceiling.

Mom stuck her head into my room, a frown on her face. "You okay, *meu lindinho filho*?"

"Mom…" I shook my head and rolled over, pulling sheets over my shoulder.

She took a seat beside me on my bed. "What is it?"

"Nothing."

"Are you sure?"

"Yes." I kept my eyes fixed on the tablet propped on my bedside table. No pings. No responses.

Mom gave me a kiss on the head and rubbed my back. "Get some sleep. You'll feel better in the morning." She paused at the door and turned back around. "Girls can be fickle," she went on. "Don't take it personal. Everyone's a bit foolish at times. Especially red-headed angels."

She closed the door and left me alone with my thoughts.

I'd been stood up, and that hurt.

The following day, Harper rushed me at school and gave me a bear hug. All the anger over being stood up evaporated in an instant.

She hadn't stood me up.

Something had happened. There were rational explanations for this.

Her tablet had been acting strange, it needed an update.

Her dad asked for help around the house, and she hadn't seen him in a while.

It was just a crazy night. That's all.

"We all have crazy nights," I told her.

"Right?" she said, giving me a grin.

I went to reach for her hand, and she slapped it away.

"Not at school." She glared at me, her severe look leaving no room for discussion. "No PDA."

"What's that?"

"Do I have to spell it out for you?"

She took her seat and gave a chuckle. My empty hand went cold.

It was clear who had begun to pair off in our class. Many of our classmates gave each other eyes, suggestive smiles, pings between desks on their tablets. Why wasn't that Harper and I? It should have been us. That's where things were going. She was my girlfriend, wasn't she?

James and Harper fell into a conversation. George gave me a glance and shrugged. I stormed over to my chair and suffered in silence. Maybe we'd get lucky, and the classroom would decompress, killing us all.

Another night passed, another evening spent lying in bed alone. I had mentioned going to the null gym near the spine for a few games of NetBall with Harper. She had told me it sounded great and never got back. I pinged her once. Twice. Three times. No response. I sent George a message and he said he'd not seen her since class.

It was clear what was happening. She hated me. I wasn't cool enough for her. I wasn't good looking enough. I wasn't smart enough or funny enough. I should have made her a gift or gotten the botanist to grow her a flower. I was a loser, and she knew it. This was self-preservation on her part.

Mom stuck her head into my room, carrying a bowl. "Is it safe to come in?"

"Why wouldn't it be?" I grumbled and tossed my tablet onto my sheets. What a worthless block of blue junk.

"Want some ice cream?" she asked.

I gave a shrug and gestured towards the bedside table. "Okay."

She set the bowl down and gave me a curious look. "Want to talk about it?"

"Not really."

"Look, Milo, there's something you need to know about girls your age. A lot of times they don't really know what they want. We're all just trying to find our way, find what we care about and what really matters. Most of the time the hurt is indiscriminate. They lack the emotional awareness to make good choices."

I glowered at Mom. "I said I don't want to talk about it."

"Alright. Alright." She raised her open hands. "I'll be in the dining room working if you need me."

I flicked my tablet back on, chose something depressing to watch, and ate my ice cream in seething quiet.

A pattern emerged over the next few days. Harper and I would make plans, then they would fall through. I would try to ping her, and she would not get back. But when she was with me, she seemed interested in getting to know me more, yet when we were apart, I was an inconvenience.

At the stroke of 01:00 a week later, Harper sent me a ping.

Harper: *Meet me on deck three, section five.*

I was out of bed before I could take a breath. I slid into the living room, checked to be sure Mom and Dad were asleep, then skidded off down the hall.

Harper was waiting for me in the dim, night-time halls of deck three. She swiped a card before a door and led me into a dark room. The door shut behind us and the lights came on. We were standing in a living room much like my own, besides the fact that it was clean, didn't smell like old food, and the dining room table wasn't also an office.

With a spin, Harper gestured at the empty space, the doors leading into the two sets of bedrooms, and the oversized white couch in the center of the room.

"What is this place?" I asked.

She licked her lips in thought. "Turns out we have an extra set of quarters on board. Maybe they thought it was a good idea just in case."

"So, no one lives here?"

"Not right now." She plopped down on the couch and tossed her legs up onto the arm. "Display," she commanded. "Go to movies." The screen came alive.

I took a seat beside her, and she nuzzled closer to me. "Movie time in the middle of the night? It's like 01:30."

"So?"

"We have school in the morning?"

"You can't live without a little sleep?" She patted my arm. "Weak."

My heart pounded in my chest at the word. I wasn't weak. I was a Hughes. Everyone knew Mom hardly ever slept. If she was strong enough to stick through the days, why couldn't I?

"Fine," I said. "I'll sleep when I'm dead."

"That's the spirit!" She took my hand in hers, then leaned against my chest. "Let's see. What to watch? Ahh! Here we are. Display, third down."

The movie began and the room went dark, ambient light adjusting for the best viewing experience. The moment hit me like a ton of bricks. I was alone in an empty set of quarters with Harper. She was leaned against me, breathing heavily. I wrapped my arms around her and held on to this fragile moment like an emotional life pod, a tin can of heat and oxygen suspended in nothing.

We watched the movie for a while, but neither of us paid attention. I can't tell you any of what it was about. Wizards? A war? Was there a bookstore and a guy with a cat? It was only meant to give us an excuse while we had our mind on other things. She spun around where she sat and brought her lips to mine. We kissed for a time, the movie droning on, white noise to serenade our awkward exploration. The intensity of our endearment magnified until our bodies began to join in. She pressed her hips against me, and a sort of rhythm worked into us, lips and limbs following suit.

Several long moments passed. I was purely content at where we were. Everything was okay. She was just going through a hard time. Things had been busy. The thought that I was a toy got pushed away. I was important to her, right?

Yes.

I was important. I was important.

She put her hand down my jumpsuit and I pushed back.

"What's wrong?" Her expression twisted in surprise.

"Don't you think this is a little far? A little too fast?"

"What do you mean?" She grabbed my hand and put it on her left breast. I felt my forehead burst with sweat. "Doesn't it feel good?"

"Yeah." I paused. Something swelled beneath my waist. "It feels great. I just—"

"Fine." She slapped my hands away and let out a long sigh. "You're probably right."

I shook my hands in the air before her. "It's not that I don't want to. It's just. Maybe this is too fast. I don't know if I'm ready to get you pregnant."

Harper blinked at me for a moment, then let out a belly laugh. She went on for an uncomfortably long period of time, then dabbed the moisture collecting at the corners of her eyes with her jumpsuit sleeve. "Pregnant?"

"Yeah?"

"You have got to be fucking joking me!" She slapped her knee. "You think we were going to have sex?"

I gave a shrug. "Maybe?"

"We can play around and not have sex, silly. Besides, no one can get pregnant on this ship."

"Wait, what do you mean?"

"It's all part of one of those shots Dr. Reed gave us. Until we get the counter shot, we're all, what's the word, sterile? No, maybe that's not it. Oh! We're all on birth control, even the guys."

"Say what?"

"Yeah. It's a big thing. I thought you would know, Adriana Hughes being your mom and all."

"No, no, I didn't." I hung my head and thought about what she had said. It made sense. We didn't need anyone getting pregnant till we figured out all the effects of space travel on the human body. Babies, adults, whatever.

The lizard part of my brain pushed these rational thoughts away in lieu of another. My jumpsuit stirred once more without any command. That thing had a mind of its own.

"Look, Milo," she whispered. "If you're not like emotionally ready, whatever. But if it's just something stupid like you thought you'd knock me up..."

I reached out, grabbed her breast, and started to kiss her. She pulled me in and forced me back onto the couch, throwing herself astride my hips.

"We'll only go as far as you're comfortable," she said, then turned the display off, plunging us into dark.

Several hours passed and I snuck my way home. I slipped into our quarters and found Mom sitting up in bed talking on her tablet, bleary eyes glowing in the screen's backlight. I paused outside their room, curious what it was about so late at night.

"He broke his leg," the tablet's speaker said. I recognized the voice immediately. Dr. Reed.

"How?"

"Nothing unusual. He was climbing one of the maintenance ladders and fell. Just two feet. I've seen breaks for falls that short before, but that's not all. He has large bruises that aren't healing quickly. I've seen the same ecchymosis on others as well."

"And I am guessing he is one of the people on our risk list for side effects?"

"I'll ping you his file now."

Mom's tablet chirped.

Dr. Reed went on, "Low muscle mass. Low bone density. We're seeing it across the board. Despite the artificial spin gravity, we are suffering somehow. What's going to happen when we make planet fall somewhere that gravity isn't normal for us? People will be sick."

"I know. I know. We're at a tipping point, if we don't take action soon, we're doomed. Some of our measures have helped, but we haven't found the silver bullet yet."

"Look, there's nothing to be done about it tonight."

"Night?" Mom chuckled. "It's 04:00. People are going to start waking up soon."

"Get some rest, Adriana. I'll see you in a few hours."

Mom gave a nod and switched off her tablet. Dad rustled around in the bed, letting out a snort. I took off for my room and hopped under my sheets as quickly and quietly as I could. There was no time to take off my clothes and get comfortable. A moment later Mom came into the room, pausing at the doorway to look at me. Though my eyes were closed, I could feel her watching. She approached my bedside, leaned down, and gave me a kiss on the forehead.

"I won't let you down," she whispered, then tiptoed out of the room.

I didn't get much sleep that night. Between Harper and Mom, there was a lot to think about. On the one side, mortality, the frailty of our position screaming through the void between systems, our bodies breaking down, evolution not intending for us to be in this environment. On the other, life, an auspicious connection of the first order, beautiful and all consuming, the embrace of another, of touch and tenderness.

In the end, life won out, and I closed my eyes to get some much-needed rest.

All two hours of it.

CHAPTER 11

I never knew life could be perfect until now. It didn't take much for everything to change, just someone to notice me, really notice me. The events of the previous night had left me in a state of distracted bliss. Nothing else in the world could ever matter as much as how I felt in this moment.

As I ate my breakfast, Mom scurried around our quarters looking for something. I took a bite of a protein cake and swallowed it down, the taste salty and smoky, the texture dense like cold cream cheese.

"Need help?" I asked.

"Where are they?" She flipped through a stack of papers and groaned. "Where are they? *Você está de brincadeira comigo?* I can't believe I lost them. *Idiota. Idiota.*"

"Where are what?" Dad asked, stepping into the living room naked but for a towel tied around his belly, his hair dripping wet. "We lose a gremlin?"

"No. My notes. My notes."

"That's what we have tablets for, Adriana."

"Not now!"

Dad gave me a look and shrugged, then vanished back into their room to get dressed.

"Here!" Mom said after another moment, a stack of papers held triumphantly in her right hand. "Finally." She bolted for the door.

"Bye, Mom," I said.

She waved a hand. "Sorry I don't have time right now, maybe later," she said before vanishing into the hall.

I shook my head and put my attention back on my breakfast. This block of lard wasn't going to eat itself.

Despite the changes within myself, school was pretty much the same. A level of unadulterated bliss had overridden my usual thoughts, but no one else seemed to notice. I took my seat in class, talked to James, George, and a couple of others, before Harper and I exchanged knowing looks. Far as I could tell last night had been fun for her as well. Mrs. Lawson went on about gravity and the theory of relativity, time dilation and our current predicament aboard the *Vasco Da Gama*, as several paired-off students exchanged pings on their devices.

We moved from astronomy to biology, how the human body changed and developed. It was far too convenient a topic, given the season many of us were transitioning into. Girls were becoming ever more interesting. Guys more aggressive, driven by primal instinct to find a partner and hold on tight. As Mrs. Lawson discussed testosterone and how the male body produced millions of sperm a day, classmates laughing and making jokes about gonadotropins, my forehead and palms began to sweat.

I felt hot. Nervous. An intense desire to take Harper away from this room to be alone. My body vibrated. I wanted, no I needed, more of what Harper and I had done. And more…

Shelly turned her head and glanced at me from time to time, acting as if she was avoiding the nude figures on Mrs. Lawson's screen. I felt a pang of shame for my decision to kiss Harper in front of her. I had hurt her feelings, and over what? It was stupid. But you stand up for your girlfriend, yes? Had I made the right choice? Didn't feel right.

Desperate to make sense of all the thoughts in my head, I did everything in my power to pull Harper aside during open discussion breaks, but somehow, she always managed to end up talking to James. We were coming up on lunch and I thought I had a perfect opportunity. Before I could tug on her sleeve or toss her a note, she and James stepped out into the hall. Their voices low, postures secretive. George, Austin, and I watched them go.

This was fine, right? I was just being paranoid. If you care about someone, you have to give them space. Don't smother them. Girlfriends can have male friends, right?

"Well, that was weird as hell," George said, taking a seat on top of his desk.

"Why weird?" Austin asked. "They do it all the time."

"Do what all the time?"

"Walk off together."

"They do?" I asked, suddenly uneasy.

"Totally, man. I see them chillin' out up in the NullGym two or three times a week. She's pretty good at NetBall. If I was coaching her, I'd say she needs to improve her serve but she can throw a mean spike."

My hands shook.

"Whatever, dude," George said and gave a sigh. "Let's go get some lunch. I'm starving."

"Me too," Austin echoed. "You coming, Milo?"

I nodded. "I'm coming."

"Heard we were having pizza," George went on, patting his belly.

Austin rolled his eyes. "Pizza? What is pizza anyways? Can any of you remember?"

"Cheese on bread?"

"Doesn't look anything like the pictures. None of our food does. They form the protein up into shapes, but it never quite matches up with the real thing."

"Not pizza, anyway," I said, stepping into the line and taking a tray from the stack at the end.

I placed the aluminum sheet on a set of rails and slid to the side, inching my way up the line, inspecting what was on offer behind the sneeze guard. Drago Babić, one of the ship's cooks, stirred vats of steaming beans, rice, and cheese sauce. These were standard items at lunch, foods easy to produce on board, but to my surprise, there was something new that truly looked like pizza on a baking sheet at the end, round discs likely made of a protein substrate with a layer of red sauce and melted mozzarella on top.

"Is it any good?" I pointed.

"Maybe," Drago replied. "It is better than same old thing. It is not my recipe, mind, I found it on the stream. Thought we might give it a try, no? Looking tasty."

"What the heck. I'm adventurous."

"Aren't we all?" He scooped one up and placed it on a plate, handing it to me over the top. "This is *Vasco Da Gama*, after all."

About the time I grabbed the edge of my plate I heard a shout behind me. I pivoted to see James stomping his way through the lunchroom, a look of fury on his face. Conversations, such as they were, went on without little notice, the room a jumble of a thousand crossed words.

"What's up, man?" I asked.

James puffed out his chest and invaded my personal space. "I heard what's been going on."

"What?" I scowled at him. "What do you mean?"

"Don't play coy with me." He poked a finger at my chest. "I heard about you and Harper."

I slapped away his hand and took a step back, feeling uncomfortable as close as he was. "Heard what?"

James growled, "That you are sneaking around making out with her!"

What few conversations were happening around the room died as we became the center of attention.

"Who knows what else," he went on.

"Why should that matter?"

"Because she's my girlfriend!" He gave me a shove with his open palms.

I stumbled back several steps, Austin catching my balance. "Your what? What are you going on about, James? The hell is your problem."

"My girlfriend, asshole!" James took a swing at me but missed. "I trusted you."

One of the kids at the back of the room began to chant, "Fight, Fight, Fight." The room picked up the call. James came at me again, fists whirling.

"Kick him in the nads!" a single, shrill voice shot through the chaos.

I threw up my arms to block a set of knuckles and they connected with my elbow. A throbbing sensation resonated up my arm and into my fingertips. James cursed and shook his hand. Drago shouted something in Croatian, likely telling us to stop, but it faded into the background.

Harper chose this moment to appear in the room. She stood in the far corner, arms crossed, a smug grin on her freckle speckled face. I slowly realized this was actually fun for her, a payoff for her best laid plans. The pieces were fitting together, falling into place before my eyes. All the nights she didn't have time for me she was with James. I wasn't sure who to be angry with, but at this moment, James was a convenient target.

"You had no right," James growled and shoved me onto the floor. I skidded back and rolled over; my ass screamed. I struggled to my feet and barreled into him, shoulder first.

"Fuck you!" I screamed, then hit him in the stomach. James folded in half as his breath was squeezed out of him. "You kept it a secret from all of us. Want to talk about trust? We've all had eyes for Harper."

James shoved back at me and the both of us fell on the floor. We were in a position to wrestle this out if we needed to. I was furious. It was his fault, right? He ruined my perfect relationship. He had taken her from me, split her interests. I would pin his ass to the floor and make him beg to be let back up.

"This is great!" Harper whooped, a fist in the air. "How lucky can a girl be that two men would fight over her?"

One second my focus was intent on how I'd get the best grip on James, the next, I was watching beans and rice scatter across the room. Harper was on the floor, a palm to her face, blood spewing between her fingers, the sound of ringing metal ringing in my ears. She let out a series of gasps and screamed. What in the hell had just happened?

I blinked, shook my head and tried to resolve what I saw, make sense of it somehow.

Shelly was standing over Harper, bean-smeared aluminum lunch tray in hand. The moment had happened so fast I hardly caught sight of anything as Shelly had darted across the room, curls flying in a train, her lunch tray drawn back like a swinging baseball bat. She struck, and thunder cracked along with the cartilage in Harper's nose. Shelly might have missed her calling in life. That swing could have put a baseball clear into orbit.

"Bitch," Harper growled and leapt onto her feet, coming after Shelly, her face smeared with blood.

To Shelly's testament, she did not back away. She threw herself at Harper, claws out, and the two began shoving, pushing, pulling each other's hair. I glanced at James and he gave a shrug. Whatever anger we had for one another vanished the moment the scene had pivoted. Neither of us knew what to do other than shake hands and apologize.

"Sorry, man," he said.

I breathed the word, "Bro."

Harper broke free of Shelly's grasp and tried to get around her back, but Shelly was too fast. She swung at her and landed a punch on one of Harper's breasts. Harper screamed and began to cry. Pain or no, the fight wasn't over.

"It's okay," I replied, shaking James's hand. "She was playing us, wasn't she?"

"Looks like it."

"Do we like… Stop them?"

"I don't know."

"Me either."

The two of us began to laugh. Because why not? The scene was absurd. We were in such a small community and yet we had let our puppy dog infatuations blind us from the fact that the girl in our group just liked attention. It hurt, sure, but it wasn't all bad. It had been a fun ride, short but fun.

The scuffle between Harper and Shelly rapidly cooled when Mrs. Lawson burst into the room, hands waving.

"You know what?" James asked.

"What?"

"I think I was tired of being jerked around anyways."

"She do that to you as well?"

He hung his head. "Yeah. Never there when I wanted her to be. I don't think that's how it's supposed to be."

"I don't either."

"You're lucky, man."

My brows crowded the middle of my face. "Why?"

He gestured in the direction of the girls. Shelly was standing back up, her jumpsuit covered in protein paste and cheese sauce.

"I think she really cares about you," he said.

"Maybe."

"Why else would she fight?" James gave a chuckle. "She was defending your honor, or something."

"My honor?"

"Yeah. I think there's still a soft spot in there for you."

"Even after…" I let the words hang.

"Yeah. Even after." James reached out a hand. "Help me up?"

I gave a nod. "Sure."

We crossed arms and pulled, groaning together, our bodies sore from our pathetic melee.

Their fight had burned itself out, the two girls staring at one another with smoldering eyes, their chests heaving as they fought to catch their breath. Mrs. Lawson rested a hand on one hip, a finger extended, scolding the girls for what they had done.

I hobbled my way over to Harper, and our teacher quieted. Before James could speak, I told this fickle girl we had been fighting over, "I don't think this is working out."

"What?" Harper's eyes widened. "What are you even talking about?"

"I'm done."

"Fine," she replied, a hand to her face. Her nose hadn't stopped bleeding, a line of red drops running down her palm to the front of her jumpsuit.

"Same here," James said. "We're done."

"I don't need you anyways. Either of you. Good-bye." Harper stormed past Mrs. Lawson out of the room.

"What a mess," Drago commented.

"I'm sorry," Shelly apologized, and began to clean up.

Mrs. Lawson clapped. "Students, back to class."

"May I stay and help Shelly clean?" I asked.

"Seems only fair. But I want to see you this afternoon. Both you and Mr. Reed."

"Yes, ma'am," we replied.

James followed the rest of the class back, giving me a wave as he went. It was weird, but I had a feeling this fight had only deepened our friendship.

I remained behind with Shelly, helping her clean up. Not only were we tasked with taking care of the mess we had created, but we were also instructed to scrub the rest of the lunchroom while we were at it. Drago was more than happy to supply the proper equipment.

"You okay?" Shelly asked as she swept wet rice into a dustpan.

I gave a shrug. "I'll be fine. Just took a couple licks. Some pretty hard ones in there. James can throw a punch."

"No, that's not what I meant."

"Oh." I swallowed. "Well, yeah… I guess. Sucks being lied to. Why did you do it?"

Shelly let her mess of curls down, gathered it up and tied it back into a ponytail. "I don't know. She just made me so mad the way she was acting, that self-righteous look on her face… Made me want to slap it the hell off. Besides," she paused, considering her words, "it hurt my feelings to see you treated like that."

"So, you were defending my honor?" I chuckled.

"I was what?"

"Never mind." I brought her a trash bag to dump the contents of her dustpan into. "Thanks."

"Why thank me?" She gave me a smile, and I felt something shift in my chest. "You're the one helping me clean up."

CHAPTER 12

Though the fight had ended quickly, James and I were not let off the hook. There was an investigation into the matter as to where we had gotten our violent impulses. Psychologists were called and professional opinions gathered. This was the first physical confrontation involving any crew members since we had embarked. Like the rest, neither of us had been exposed to anything you would consider explicitly violent. And so, after weeks of analysis, the two of us grounded, no direct contributor discovered, the final result was that teenage passions didn't require a blueprint. Violence was natural.

With Harper and the fight behind us, James and I became even better friends. The old squad collapsed and the two of us became a duo. Harper and George started dating, and from the looks of it she was being kind to him. Nevertheless, this threw the dynamic of our little group out of balance, and we moved on to new things.

James and I spent our afternoons playing NetBall or talking about girls, checking out VEs and keeping ourselves occupied. Soon even this had begun to feel boring. There was something our hearts were searching for, but we had yet to find it. We weren't alone in this. Austin and Deet had been feeling it as well. While the general meeting place up till now had been the lunchroom, we felt we needed something more appropriate for our age. Upon hearing that there was an empty set of quarters, several of us went to the captain to see if it was possible to make use of them. With a little give and take, a few negotiations, the *Vasco Da Gama* gained its first dance club, Plasma.

Plasma became the only place to be after school, a crowded set of rooms with loud music and walls of shifting LED lights. While some kids would sit in what was the second bedroom studying, or let's be honest, canoodling, the majority of us lounged around throwing back juice bulbs, talking shit, and complaining over the songs Austin had picked for Plasma's playlist. He was the de facto DJ, and it was hotly debated if we should plan a coup and overthrow him. I preferred mostly instrumental electronic music, whereas the opposing factions wanted more pop-hop or tech grunge. There was no pleasing everyone.

And so, all of us talked, danced a little, and mostly just tried to be normal kids in a place where nothing was really normal. However, within a few weeks, single guys like James and I started to have less of a place. Competition for lady folk was fierce in such a small community. Decisions on lock down. There were not that many more fish in the pond.

One afternoon leaving Plasma, a bit frustrated over this irrefutable fact, James and I made an unrelated discovery. Neither of us had spent a great deal of time on this deck, and yet when you live somewhere your entire life, you start to believe you know everything. Down the hall and around the corner was a nondescript door with hardly a seam set into the wall, beside it a keypad that blended in with the bulkhead.

We looked to each other and smiled. Something new.

"Has it always been here?" James asked, then flipped through his tablet. "Weird."

I leaned over his shoulder to peek at what he had found. "What's weird?"

"This door is not on the *Vasco's* plans."

"How's that possible?"

"See for yourself. There ain't shit here."

Voices echoed down the hall towards us. We gave each other a glance and a primal instinct told us to run. We bolted off into a nook and held our breath. From the cubby we slid into, we could see nothing but the hall directly in front of us.

"We got to be ready, ya?" It was Esteban's voice. "They getting' ready for the big day, so should we."

"I get it," Deidrick replied. "It's just the longer we're on this ship the more exhausted I am. It's like I never get enough sleep."

"Old man." There was a sound like a slap on the shoulder. "Got to stay strong like Este, here."

"You're a freak of nature, bruh."

"You callin' a freak? One to talk, ya?"

A door whooshed open, then closed. Esteban and Deidrick's voices quieted.

"They went through the door," I said, poking my head out into the hall.

James scratched at the back of his neck. "I wonder what they're doing?"

"Let's find out."

We camped our butts in the hallway's nook, passing the time by playing games on our tablets. At around 17:00 they reappeared. I slid my tablet around the corner, using the camera to catch a video of them leaving.

"They're all sweaty," I said, playing back the video.

"You know, come to think of it," James ventured, "I've never seen either of them talking to any of the single ladies on board."

"You think they're gay like Mr. Terrence?"

James shrugged. "I don't know."

"They don't strike me as gay."

"And how would you know?"

"Don't gay guys have like a thing for fashion and interior decorating?"

"I think that's just on the vids." James gestured for me to ping him the video I just took. I obliged. "Besides, didn't you know? Deet's gay."

"What?"

"Yeah. Austin and he went out for a while."

"Austin's gay?"

"No." He scrubbed back and forth through the file. "He's bisexual. Curious they call it."

"So, he likes kissing boys."

"Guess so."

"I can't imagine kissing another boy."

"Well, you know what that means?" he asked, a wry tone to his voice.

"What?"

"You're probably not gay." James paused for a moment, then laughed. "Oh look, Deidrick is married. I didn't know Yvonne was his wife. Damn, they sure don't act cozy with one another."

"Married still doesn't mean he's not into Esteban's meat, does it?"

"No, it does not, but I don't think that's right. I believe we have us a mystery to solve."

"More data to gather?"

"Yup."

We started to walk away, and as we approached the hallway's junction, Shelly rounded the corner. I felt my heart skip at the sight of her. I rifled through my dizzy mind to find the words to say hello. To ask her how she'd been, and what she'd been up to. I would never forget how she'd taken my side with Harper. It had taken that crazy moment to realize just how much I missed her being in my life. But before I could vocalize these thoughts, before I could put myself on the path to repairing what we once had, Lance Brittan appeared at her side.

This guy was smart, good looking, with shampoo commercial perfect long hair and lean muscles. In that moment my self-perception shifted so that I was small, ugly, dirty skinned and awkward.

What a bastard.

"Afternoon, guys," he said to James and I.

Shelly reached over and took his hand, an uncertain expression twisting her lips.

"Hi," I choked, then paused to watch them head off towards Plasma.

"Oh yeah," James said. "I forgot to tell you. She's seeing Lance. He's, well, whose kid again?"

"One of the shuttle pilots."

"Oh yeah. That's right." James put a hand on my shoulder. "You okay?"

"I just want to go home."

"See you back here at the same time tomorrow?"

I gave a nod and headed off, trying not to dwell on what I'd just seen. Shelly had moved on. She didn't have time for a stupid distraction like me. Lance's father was a pilot, the very one who had brought my family aboard the *Vasco*, an important person. When we reached the Foundry, his father would be the one to ferry us down onto the station and bring us back safe. Not to mention, Lance was part of the approved genetic pool.

A group of medical personnel came dashing down the hall with a gurney, shouting for us to get out of the way. I plastered myself against the padded walls. Mom and Dad chased after them.

I ran to catch up. "What's wrong?"

Mom responded before Dad had the chance, her words breathy, "Samuel Franklin fell while working in engineering. He has several fractures and internal bleeding."

"Samuel? Wait, is that Harper's dad?"

"Yes," Dad replied. "They were working on the drive overhaul. It shouldn't have happened. He was lifting equipment well within his weight tolerances."

"It's the trip, the atrophy," Mom put in. "He was too weak. Dr. Reed told him to take a few days off. She had a special diet ready to go, a whole physical therapy routine. He would have been fine, right?"

Dad gave her a grimace and did not respond. I hadn't seen either of them in a few days. Their faces were drawn.

"He's going to die," Mom said. "It's all my fault."

"Don't put that guilt on yourself."

"What can I do to help?" I asked.

"Go home, Milo," Dad said. "Please. Go home."

"But I want to help."

"I know, son. There's nothing you can do. Go home. Be safe."

They slipped into the Med Bay and the door shut behind them. I did as I was asked and went back to our quarters. I spent the rest of the evening trying to keep myself busy. Even though I didn't enjoy cleaning, I tidied up our quarters and scrubbed them from top to bottom. It was something to do, and I had to do something.

Word came a few hours later over the intercom.

"Attention crew," the captain's voice. *"I regret to inform you that our dear friend, Samuel Franklin, passed tonight at 22:00. He was involved in an accident in engineering*

which resulted in internal injuries. Dr. Reed and her staff fought valiantly to keep him alive, but it was too much. Please, if you are feeling weak or have injuries that are not properly healing, see Dr. Reed immediately. This is not a request. This is an order. Services will be arranged over the next few days. Please support one another during this challenging time. That is all."

Angry or not, my thoughts reached out for Harper. She had lost her only parent to the very trip itself, a shift in environment that humans were not made for. No one deserved this. What if my parents were next? Dad lifting a box too heavy, a trip, and a broken rib pierces his heart. What if Mom took a nap one day and did not wake up again? They were looking sick, frail, weary. Their skin was pale, colorless, pasty. I paused in front of the bathroom mirror and saw myself looking much the same.

"I need rest," I said, and reached for a dose of sleeping pills.

Oblivion was the only answer.

I swallowed them down and crashed onto my bed, closing my eyes, letting darkness take me. My body became increasingly heavy, my soul tumbling over the edge of a black hole's event horizon, pressing down and down, gravity increasing, redoubling, until...

CHAPTER 13

James and I stuck with our plan to gather more information about the secret room. Like clockwork, Esteban and Deidrick appeared every day at 15:00, entered the room for two hours, then emerged covered in sweat. We made notes, took short videos, and did our best to glean what the lock code might be.

"Okay," James said. "Maybe you're right. That's the look of a hook-up."

A raised an eyebrow at him. "Right? I mean whatever, no judgment, just seems like a lot of sex. How much sex do people need?"

"Like seven?"

"Seven? What does that even mean?"

"Look, let's explore other options." James tapped his chin with a finger. "Maybe there's a laboratory of horrors in there?"

"Like the mess you leave in your quarters? I think mushrooms were growing on your pile of dirty clothes last time I was over."

"Shut up."

"I'm sorry, dude, but my mommy doesn't clean up after me. I have to make an effort."

"Whatever. Here, I think I've got the code figured out. Soon as they're gone, we'll give it a go."

"Alright."

The coast cleared, and we made for the door. James inspected the keypad, his eyes two inches from its buttons.

"Greasy fingers," he mumbled, then removed a slip of paper from his pocket. "Pretty sure I know the code. I've seen them press it so many times. The buttons that are dirty are the only ones used for the code I have."

"Give it a shot."

"Alright…"

The door whooshed open on his first try. He'd gotten it right.

Inside, the hidden room was not much bigger than one of the emergency shelters. It smelled of fresh sweat and anger. At the center of the cramped space, a pair of circular platforms sat beside one another, a tiny, handrail-like apparatus rising from their circumference. From the ceiling hung a pair of VE goggles, and to their sides, each had a fake rifle with a plastic trigger.

All became clear. The regular occurrences, the sweaty men. They weren't hooking up in here, they were training, but for what? They were using these VE rigs to keep their skills sharp. The guns, the goggles, the haptic gloves and feedback vests.

James and I glared at the equipment in shock. There was no way this did not violate at least a dozen of the captain's rules.

"What's it for?" I asked, not expecting an answer.

A meaty hand rested on my shoulder and squeezed. "Combat simulations," a torrid voice hissed into my ear.

If it were possible for my heart and all the nerves attached to it to flip inside out and appear on the outside of my skin, I still don't believe it would match the shock I experienced in that single moment. I threw my arms into the air, let out a shriek like a banshee, and stumbled backwards, tumbling onto the floor.

Esteban was standing over me, laughter roaring from his belly. James had done little better, his body plastered to the opposite wall with eyes wide as dinner plates. His mouth was open and silent.

"Got caught, ya?" Esteban said. "Why you be putting your hand in the cookie jar? Might be sweet but you gotta be careful *tu abuela* don't catch."

Deidrick appeared at the doorway. "I guess you were right, bruh. The kids were watching us."

"Kids?" I bristled at the comment and recovered my composure. "I'll have you know!"

"Yeah, yeah, yeah." Deidrick waved it off. "Tough guys and all that. I seen you around, starting fights, getting in trouble."

I scrambled back onto my feet and put my face in my palms. It was going to take a moment for my heart rate to return to anything close to normal. The readings on my smartwatch were red, an alert informing me my pulse was at a dangerous level.

"What are you doing in here?" James recovered his words. "The captain would be furious."

Deidrick turned to face Esteban. "Can we tell them?"

"No," Esteban replied. "I don't think we can."

"Still, we gotta keep them quiet somehow."

"This is for true." He crossed his arms and tapped his elbow with two fingers in rapid succession.

"Airlock?"

"Too brash."

"Toss 'em in a pod?"

"People will come looking for them. Besides, the rot will make them stink."

James and I exchanged a look, my terror from an instant earlier returning. Were they serious about going through with this? Had we stumbled into something that would see us killed?

"Two can keep a secret, if one of you is dead," Esteban said.

"Dead?" James croaked. "Now wait a minute."

My mouth had gone dry. I was unable to speak.

Deidrick frowned. "I don't think that works here, Esteban."

"*Por que no?*"

"Bribe, then?"

Esteban raised a finger and nodded. "Ahh. Bribe just might motivate two troubled youths."

"A bribe?" I swallowed. "What's a bribe?"

Now that the cat was out of the bag, or at least its head and forepaws, James and I were given the right to make regular use of the combat simulation VEs hidden here in exchange for our silence. Far as UEI regulations, and Captain Williams' explicit rules, this sort of entertainment, training, whatever it turned out to be, was illegal. Why were Esteban and Deidrick using it? What were they training for? They would not say. It wasn't on the official schematics of the ship, and yet, how had so much time gone by, and no one had noticed it? We had a boatload of questions, and they weren't answering them. We were to keep our damn mouths shut, and so we did.

James and I spent hours inside the simulations, playing both co-operative and vs scenarios, our battlegrounds a variety of locations from ruined cities to zombie infested jungles. Though I might have been the better shot, James was far more aggressive, willing to take risk when the moment warranted. It all felt so real, VE goggles or not, the weight of the weapon, the rig allowing us to run in any direction as if we were there. A few months of this, and I was confident if I ever had to fight in a live-fire situation that I'd do just fine.

Bring on the little green men. I got this shit.

"I need to swing by and get something from Mom, want to come along?"

"Sure, man."

"Good game?"

"Hell yeah." He shook a fist in the air. "Did you see the dude I sniped up in the tower? Got him right between the eyes then one of his buddies popped up in the hut. Dropped my rifle and pulled out the twelve gauge. Blap to the chest. Two-point spread."

"Nice."

We made our way around the habitat ring, not a care in the world this quiet afternoon. School was done. Homework was finished. Tomorrow was a day off, a perfect time to stay up late and get into trouble.

We entered fluid recycling to find Dr. Reed standing beside a section of pipes, the balance balls in her right hand rotating slowly. James was about to ask her a question, but when we rounded the corner of a pump assembly, we could see she was not alone. Mom and Dad were here, as well as the captain. From the look on their collective faces, the discussion had been heated. The captain was bowed up, stretched to his full posture, his eyes narrowed, jaw hard set.

"Mom?" James mouthed to Dr. Reed. She shook her head and frowned.

"Can't you just listen?" Dad pleaded. "We're going to have to face some tough decisions ahead. This is likely the first. Someone has to give it a shot."

"You can't do this," Captain Williams growled, his finger pointed at Mom, not Dad, the source of a dangerous question *in flagrante delicto*. "This is an unnecessary risk."

"Is it, Tobias? Is it really?" Mom whirled on him and stepped into his personal space, a hair from chest to chest. Dad went to the corner, his eyes averted. "We've already had one death. More are just months away. What is unnecessary is to have any more. We have a potential treatment for the atrophy crisis. We're up against the proverbial wall. If we don't take action now, more will die."

"Look, Sam was an old friend of mine and it hurts. Putting another of our chief engineers in danger isn't going to bring him back. I don't care if Perry gave you consent for this test or not, this isn't happening."

Mom spun on her heels and walked off.

"A word of advice," Dad told the captain. "Don't get between Adriana and a cause."

"I am responsible for the health and safety of this crew. It is my job to make the executive call."

Dad put a hand on our steaming leader's shoulder. "Not in this."

Captain Williams closed his eyes and shook his head. "Be careful then," he whispered. "Please, just be careful."

Dr. Reed gave James a hug and patted him on the back. They smiled at one another, and she shook her head, signaling for him to stay quiet.

We followed them to the Med Bay, hurrying to catch up, the captain left to ruminate on his thoughts. Our parents moved with a uniformed purpose, each step like that of a swiftly moving attack force determined to rid the world of a great evil. Doors swooshed open and Perry was waiting on them. He gave them a smile and nodded. Dr. Reed called for Nurse Brennon, and they went into immediate action, checking Perry's vitals while collecting several kits filled with vials and fine, handheld instruments.

"Are you sure you're ready?" Mom asked him, her breath held.

"I am," he replied. "For the good of us all."

Dad turned and waved James and I off. "Sorry, guys. Not now."

The door sealed shut without another word.

We weren't sure what to say, and so we stared at one another, our mouths slack. Dangerous human experimentation, voluntary or not, had found the *Vasco Da Gama* and both our mothers were involved.

It suddenly didn't seem right to spend the rest of the afternoon palling about. We went to Stellar Observatory and sat in silence, lost in thought while waiting for news over whatever had happened. After several hours without a word, we returned to our respective homes.

At about 03:00 I woke to the sound of Mom and Dad shuffling back into our quarters. Mom was disconsolate, sobbing her eyes out. Dad held her in his arms and led her to the couch. I roused myself from bed and grabbed her a glass of water. Dad gave me a smirk and took the glass.

"It's okay, Adriana," he told her.

"No, it's not. It's all my fault." She paused, sniffling, breaths coming in short, rasping waves. "I pushed for this. I did it."

"We were in agreement. We entered into this conspiracy and wanted the same result. The blame goes three ways."

"We were to do no harm."

"And you are here to protect."

"What happened?" I took a seat at the end of the couch. "Is Perry dead?"

Mom took a deep breath, then wiped her wet nose off on the sleeve of her jumpsuit. "No. The protein injections, they—it's all my fault."

"What's your fault?"

"Perry's blind. He trusted me, and now? He'll never see again. My arrogance stole that from him."

The admission of this guilt did not absolve her from it, it only renewed her lamenting fervor. Mom put her face in her hands and began to sob, her back jerking with each surge of sorrow. I wanted to do something to ease her pain but couldn't. What power did I have? And Perry, blind Perry, would he be okay?

"It's not your fault," I whispered, and lowered myself into a crouch before her on the floor. "You did what you thought was best."

"Maybe so, maybe not," she said between shudders. "But that doesn't matter. Even when we do what we think best, we can still fail. You don't always get to choose the failures you live with. Perry is blind because of me. He's blind because I wasn't smart enough."

CHAPTER 14

Life on Earth went on with or without the crew of the *Vasco Da Gama*. Wars continued to rage across the continents, petty disputes over economic gains and perceived scarcity, totalitarian regimes grasping for power and propogandist dogma spreading misinformation. From my perspective, almost all of these conflicts could be resolved if compromise could be found, egos removed from negotiations. With a population of now over ten billion humans, resources were getting scarce. Where once everyone fought over the oil fields, fossil fuel energy, now we fought over dry land to sow crops, water to drink. All these years after *minha avó's* death, and Boulder, Colorado was still recovering.

News reports declared that a recent engagement between super-powers had reached a cease fire only after the use of a tactical nuclear weapon. Close to a million people were turned to dust in an instant, all over inflammatory messages exchanged online. It was too much to take in. All the destruction, and yet from this distance it felt like a footnote in an old book, the reality of those who had lost their lives several steps removed from my own.

I told myself again and again that the Foundry would save us, one way or another. The signal made it all true. The signal gave us peace in this place. That pink light. That sense of understanding.

These regular data uplinks gave us the news we needed on world events, as well as a wealth of scientific breakthroughs. Where corporate trade secrets and patents might be kept under lock and key back home, these same companies felt a great deal of freedom in sharing the information with us and the FICSE fleet at large. We were given new ways to synthesize medicine, better systems for resource allocation and recycling, and latest of all, a most curious advancement which until now had only been a thing of science fiction.

"Here are the neural implants," Dr. Reed said, turning a slim display mounted on a swivel around so that Mom, Dad and I could see.

The three of us were seated in her office across from her work desk, relaxing in soft orange and white armchairs. This space was just off the Medical Bay, a private room with two desks, one for her computer, the other for a microscope and limited chemical testing, as well as a collection of house plants in hanging pots, peace lilies, dracaena, and a half-dozen varieties of ferns. Their leaves and fronds waved as the air circulated, their motion hypnotic.

"The captain has approved the use of flexible meshes and I have done several operations already," Dr. Reed went on, then advanced the slide on the display, showing images of the brain with what looked to be a fine, sheer net covering most of it. "More than a billion people on Earth already enjoy the benefits. Instant interfacing with computer networks, onboard functions far surpassing many mobiles, hand terminals, and tablet devices. Communication and data on demand, why not you?"

Mom crossed her arms and glared at Dr Reed.

"Adriana, come on."

"You know why I'm against this," Mom replied, her nose twitching. "*Bicho de sete cabeças.*" The seven headed beast. The very devil.

"Perry was test subject number one. It was a mistake."

"And yet he's still blind."

Dr. Reed let out a slow breath. "Fine. I get it, I understand. But we are talking ten percent of the human race have gotten them with little or no side effects. That's quite a test group."

"It seems an unnecessary risk."

"Way to use the captain's words against me."

"Maybe he was right."

"And maybe now he's changed his mind."

"Only because of the pressure we put him under." Mom unfolded her arms and readjusted in her seat. "He realized we were running out of time."

"And he's right. Jackson, Adriana, you could work twice or three times as fast with implants." She drew up a series of charts outlining beneficial statistics, increased neural processing, intelligence augmentation, computational overclocking. "Cheating death may still allude the human race, but time is relative. If we make better use of it, we might as well have lived a longer lives."

"But the dangers," Dad interjected. "It's in my brain. My brain. That's where I live, ya know? The me who makes me me. What if it itches, how do I get it out? What if it erases my personality? Will food taste different?"

Mom pointed at the display, a slide showing a model of the data flow from digital networks to the various lobes of the brain and back. "What if we get hacked?"

"You have full control over its access." Dr. Reed drew our attention to a series of boxes on the screen. "If the device is compromised you have a deadlock switch that works like a circuit breaker. It closes off the flow of all information. To put it in computer terms, your brain has read/write capability, the mesh does not. The mesh may only display information for your brain to read. You have to choose what information to receive or reject. It cannot under any circumstance take control of your functions. It has no access to the autonomic systems of your body. You'll be able to think faster, work faster. Hell, you'll even be able to fully immerse yourself into VEs with this. No more clunky peripherals. Direct connection from brain to environment."

My eyes widened at the mention of this. No way Mom would not allow any of us to make use of this, and for obvious reasons. Then again… I sat up straight in my chair. "Did you say VEs?"

Dr. Reed nodded. "And so much more."

What worlds could I explore if I could go outside my body into a virtual space? James and I could become even better with the combat VEs, maybe travel back home and see what we were truly fighting for. Earth was a distant memory I did not wish to forget. The decision was easy. And besides all that, I was expendable. If these implants lobotomized me, the mission would carry on. Maybe this was an opportunity for me to be useful. My way to contribute.

"I'll do it," I told the doctor.

"Milo!" Mom whirled on me. "*O que foi que você falou?* It's too dangerous."

"Come on, Mom, how dangerous could it be?" I stood and found a wall to lean against, my arms crossed, eyes fixed on the ceiling. "We're literally screaming through a gulf between star systems with nothing but a tin can keeping us alive. If anything goes wrong, we're all dead. I may not be old enough, or mature enough to understand everything, but I feel like this could be useful. Dr. Reed makes some really good points. You know, it might even keep us out of danger. Help us to make quicker actions."

"He's not entirely wrong." Dad tapped his lips with a forefinger. I brought my eyes back from the overhead lights to regard him. "Would make us superhuman in a way. Ooo, I like that idea. This will give my brain preternatural speed. I could do anything. Do I get mental powers with it? Telekinesis? Cause you know, that would be badass."

Mom began to scratch at the back of her head, fingers pulling at her hair. "Jackson R Hughes…"

"What, Adriana? If it doesn't itch, I'm okay with it. To be honest, that was one of my biggest concerns. Maybe I could work from within a VE? Sure would give me a lot of options. An infinite virtual desktop."

"So, can I get mine?" I asked, thrilled at the prospects this device would open up.

"Sure, buddy," Dad said, offering me a thumbs up.

Mom's face went hard. "No. Absolutely not."

"Yes."

"No!"

Dr. Reed gave me a conciliatory look and stood. "Milo, would you like to go grab something to eat? James is meeting me for lunch. I'm sure your mom and dad could use some time to talk this over."

"Sure." I followed her out of the room, allowing my parents to continue their argument.

We took our time eating lunch, a meal of steamed hydroponic vegetable medley and Thai spice protein cakes. While we were out, we ran into Perry, his now turquoise-headed sister helping direct him down the hall, a long stick in his right hand used to feel what was before him. They were training Perry to memorize the ship so he could get around on his own. James gave his mom a hug, holding her for a while as she fought back tears. Mistakes had been made, but it wasn't their fault.

Once we returned to Dr. Reed's office, a decision had been made. Mom had given in. I'm not sure how Dad convinced her, but the decision was made. He and I were getting implants. Mom would abstain.

The following day Dad and I went to the Medical Bay, laughing and cutting up all the way. It was great and yet troubling. Was this what it was like to spend time with Dad? How long would it last? We'd never been that close, never spent any real time together. I didn't know how to act around him, and from what I could tell, neither did he.

"Did I eh… I ever tell you I used to ride motorcycles?" he asked as we were getting settled in the operating room.

I shook my head. "Never came up."

"Before you were born, I had a Ducati. A crotch rocket, they called it." His eyes gave off a glitter of nostalgia. "Used to take it up and down the highways in Montana. To feel the wind against my skin, the thrill of the ride, see the endless expanse of mountains."

"Why not go again?"

"What's that?"

"You know, for a ride on your bike. Surely with this neural integration you could do that easily."

"You know what…"

For the first time in my life, Dad and I had something we could do together. Over a blissful series of weeks, as soon as I got out of school, we met back in our quarters and connect to the ship's network via implants. An instant later, the physical world we occupied would vanish, and the two of us would appear at the end of a set of rolling grey mountains, slopes studded with evergreens and brushstrokes of scree. The sheer magnitude was dizzying, my mind grasping to comprehend its expansive scale. Being within the *Vasco Da Gama*, I had gotten used to seeing objects no more than a hundred feet away, the longest continuous distance either looking down the curve of the habitat ring or up the main spine. Here, in the foothills of the Rockies, there was almost too much world for my brain to process.

Not only did the implants do well emulating the visual responses of the brain, it translated touch, temperature, and smell at a high level.

I was sitting on a motorcycle at the end of Beartooth Pass in Montana.

I was giving Dad a nod and a smile before slipping on my helmet.

I was revving the Ducati's motor and shooting off down the narrow highway, negotiating its dozens of switchbacks and curves, cool wind rushing over my leather jacket. We were a pair of candy-red blurs cutting twisted hairpin lines under endless blue skies. Crotch rocket had been an accurate description.

This felt right.

We raced each other up and down the pass, as well as pulled over often and enjoyed the sights. We cut up and made jokes, looked for secret hiding places, and even ate dinner in a small mountain town along the way. It didn't matter that none of it was real. What was real anyways? Connection. Connection was real.

I pulled my bike off into the gravel at the edge of town, watching as a computer-generated person stood on the back of a rusty pickup truck, a bulky black controller with two joysticks in his hands. He was a guy in his twenties with long hair, a set of goggles covering his eyes, the name of a company, *Top-Shot Photography*, written in bold letters on his t-shirt. Above us came the whirr of a quad copter drone, its blades slicing through the air at thousands of RPM, producing a noise that reminded me of a hive of angry honeybees.

Dad rolled up on me a moment later, a curious look on his face. "What is it, buddy?"

"I have an idea." The drone panned overhead, its movements smooth as if were mounted on rails, its camera lens shimmering in the sunlight.

"What idea?"

"What if Perry wasn't blind?"

"What do you mean?"

"I mean, what if he wasn't blind? What if there was another option?"

"Where are you going with this?" Dad turned his attention up to where mine was fixed. He watched the drone buzz around, attempting to puzzle out my conclusion. After a moment, his lips split and twisted into a grin. "Why didn't we think of this before?"

"I don't know."

"We have to tell your mother."

We unjacked from our virtual environment and went straight to Mom. Within the hour we had gathered up the optics and fabrication teams, gotten their feedback on our rough concept, then called Perry into Medical. His sister Mary helped the optics members take measurements of her brother's head, her hands shaking as excited as she was.

Mom, Dad and I held our breath with anticipation.

After measurements were taken, one of the mobile 3D printers began to churn out the headpiece. Mary took the final product, sanded the edges, then slid it over her brother's head, tightening the band that held it into place. Optics were then slid into two round holes at the front of the rig.

"It's not a perfect fit, but it should work," Mary pronounced, her expression hopeful, turquoise curls pulled back into ponytail as if ready for action. "Is it comfortable, little brother?"

"Not bad," Perry replied scratching at the back of his neck. "A bit awkward, but not bad."

"Link it up, Dr. Reed."

"Here goes nothing." The doctor made a series of keystrokes in the air, connecting to her systems through the very type of implants she was setting up for Perry.

"Holy shit!" Perry shouted, palms gesturing to empty space. "Too bright. Too bright."

Mary grabbed her brother's shoulders. "You can see?"

"Yes yes." Perry waved in the direction of the doctor. "Lower the gain by like fifty percent."

"On it," she replied.

"Stop!" Perry reached out. He took a deep breath, then moved to try and stand. "Mary, you can put your hands down. Wipe that stupid look off your face. I'm okay. Let me do this on my own."

"You're okay," she said, and the joy on her face only blossomed.

Perry took a step. Then another. He shuffled around the room and looked at each one of us in turn, his optics reflecting light back at us. It was a touch unnerving to look at, a bulky machine strapped to his face, but from his expression he could see. He could see.

"Wicked cool," he said. "I'm like Geordi freakin' La Forge."

"Who?" I asked, offering a curious smile.

"Before your time kid, way before your time."

Mom rushed over and gave Perry a hug. She then turned to me and did the same. Dad nodded at me and shook my hand.

"Your idea, huh?" Perry asked me.

"Someone would have thought of it eventually."

"Maybe," he said. "You got there first. Thanks, man. I owe you my sight."

I felt my face flush. "Just an idea. I didn't do the hard work."

My time with Dad had not only been an opportunity to connect, but to do some good for someone else. Perry could see again, if not exactly how he did before, but moreover, this gave Mom a renewed inspiration in her just cause. She picked her project back up with vigor. She could see the light at the end of the tunnel.

There were more days riding bikes with Dad, and during that time a new interest arose. If an idea could help Perry, what else could I learn? What else could I use this technology for? I found myself studying how VEs could be manipulated by my thoughts. How I could reach outside my body into a space between worlds, between the physical and digital. Computer architecture was fully explorable with the aid of my implants. Dad encouraged this exploration. I learned to navigate networks and move around the ship, dig meaningful data from deep stacks of binary sectors gathered by a hundred sources and deliver them back to Dad for help in his research. The world the implants connected me to became an extension of baseline reality, not separate. A place I could teach tiny machines to work out complex problems and release them into the world, or at least try to. Everyone was always trying to get me to look at how big the universe was, and I always found myself seeing how small it could be.

For the first time in years, I was happy.

But as life seems to turn out, I learned a hard lesson that season. All good things come to an end. Even though for years Dr. Reed had been able to synthesize a workable version of Dad's bipolar medication, his current prescription no longer did the job. Even with therapy, Dad began to withdraw and soon fell into a depressive state, cutting himself off from both Mom and I, spending most days sleeping and sitting alone in the dark. We tried to snap him out of it, give him something fun to do, cook his favorite foods, take him out on activities and outings. None of it worked. Weeks went by, and Mom dealt with this stress and rejection by working ever harder, putting in more hours, giving more focus to whatever project she was on now. As for me, I dealt with it by not dealing with it. When my concerned friends caught word of what was going on, asking if Dad was okay, I ignored them. I pushed his depression deep into the back closet of my mind where I did my damndest to ignore it. It felt like a death. We'd come so far, and I'd lost it all. I missed him.

For good or bad, I tended to follow my parents' example. Dad was ever determined to understand our place in the greater universe, how us tiny, insignificant things brought value to the endless. And Mom, she felt that space exploration was humanity's best hope to escape the damage we'd done to our world.

It was no wonder I was their product.

***

Time carried on within our subjective frame. Soon, we would arrive at the Foundry. Just a few more years, just a few more awkward moments, murmured conversations on how Milo wasn't a genetic match to any girl on board. I would be a mature adult by the time we made contact, and so I had best start acting like one. I had to accept that I was not part of the plan. These engineered lives the UEI scientists had designed for us did not fit my own. I was a stowaway, my Dad was a basket case, and my Mom took the weight of the world on her shoulders. I needed to find a way to make myself valuable. I needed a passion to throw myself into, a grand work to devote myself to like both of them. It was time to choose what I did with my life, and I didn't have a clue. I had interests, but not a calling.

Mom's renewed vigor for her project, along with avoiding Dad's depressive stage, led her to a breakthrough. She had been off the tiniest degree with the protein treatment, and Perry had been the unfortunate result. It turned out that the original protein caused a chain reaction in Perry's body, which triggered an auto-immune response in his central nervous system. The result was a severe, acute case of neuromyelitis optica, a hormone imbalance which caused his body to target the aquaporin-4 proteins in his nervous system. It placed increased pressure on his optic nerves to the point of failure. As bad as the result, it was fortunate his neuromyelitis optica did not extend beyond his eyes into his brain stem or spinal cord. This could have left him paralyzed, or worse. Mom had been between a rock and a hard place, there was no doubt the crew was being slowly killed by a lack of true gravity, our muscle and bone density withering away by the day. Risks had to be taken or we would do more than fail, we would wither and die.

Now that the problem with her treatment had been found, several others were brought in for testing and passed with flying colors. Within several weeks each of those treated began to grow more muscle and bone density. Their red blood cell counts increased, along with their energy and focus. She had found the silver bullet. The way was paved not only for the crew of the *Vasco Da Gama*, but for all exo-colonists.

Mom's paper, *Promoting Cell Regeneration Under Asymmetric Gravitational Stimuli*, was soon published in the Journal of Medicine. It fast became one of the most cited works in medical history. Within a few weeks of this crowning achievement, Dad won a Nobel prize for his discovery of a new class of star, and was awarded the coveted Silver Snoopy by NASA, both of which would be crowning achievements for his career, yet even these did not draw him from his depression.

The crew of the *Vasco Da Gama* was tasked to make contact with the Foundry, as well as to study it as we neared its location. This was the primary mission of all exploration ships en route, of which at this time we were still in contact with all four. As we closed the last half of a light year, we extended an array of telescopes allowing us to scan Barnard's Star system with unprecedented resolution through all spectrums of visual and ultraviolet light. The challenge, a Dad cried into his armchair on the evenings he was able to rouse himself and work, was that since we were traveling at such a great velocity the deviation in light frequencies made observations skewed.

Doppler shift was compressing and stretching light waves. Dad was unable to get the pictures he was hoping to have. The pictures the captain was demanding.

I came home one evening to an empty bottle of whiskey on the kitchen table, Dad curled up on the floor with a pool of vomit beside his mouth. Mom was in the other room, her goggles on, lost in a VE analyzing climate data recently uploaded from Earth. It took both of us, but we carried him to the shower and cleaned him off before putting him to bed.

"Something's wrong with the stars," Dad mumbled again and again.

Mom glared at me and swallowed. The tired lines at the corners of her eyes had grown deep as valleys, drawn out by a life committed to saving the world and not her family. She might have had a great victory, but she knew her journey wasn't over.

"What's wrong with them, dear?" She asked, crouching down beside him.

"They aren't right."

"What do you mean?"

"It's like they're on acid. The colors are all wrong. Why are the colors wrong?"

"I don't understand."

"The colors, Adriana. The goddamned colors!" He let out a sob, his lip quivering. "They've gone crossed. They're too close, too far. We're too fast. Too slow. We're adrift in a sea of uncertainty. Where are we? Can we navigate by the stars when the stars are wrong?"

I let out a slow breath, taking a seat beside him. Never in my life had I feared being lost. Could something have gone wrong with the navigation star fixes? That was how we stayed on track, much like the ancient Vikings. Was the *Vasco Da Gama* even headed towards the Foundry? "How can colors go crossed?"

"They flee from me. Squeezing, twisting. No no. This is not it. Not what we need."

"Jackson," Mom whispered. "Get some sleep. Shh. Shh. Get some sleep." She brushed his forehead with the backs of her fingers and drew up his sheets, tucking him in.

I took this as a cue to leave them alone.

Dad's words rang out in my head again and again, leaving me with a chill as if the environmental controls had broken.

Why were the colors wrong, Dad? What did this mean?

CHAPTER 15

Finished with my grade school- equivalent education on board the *Vasco Da Gama*, I graduated along with my class and put high school behind me. As we were all required, my studies now shifted from general to applied sciences, my final choice of subject, nano construction. What can I say? I enjoyed things that were small. Can't get much smaller.

With the advent of our implants and their ubiquity, many people in the scientific community saw our future in not how big we could make things, but how tiny. Nano machines had ever been a curiosity of man, a theoretical arena where debates had been lost and won in the academic stages, but they were now a reality. Feeling dangerous and powerful, I assisted Perry and Mary to synthesize the first batch of nano-fluid on board using detailed instructions that were part of my self-directed pre-grad curriculum. Being our engineers, they were just as interested as I was. The possibilities of the material were endless. We could repair tiny sections of the ship under pressure, or in vacuum, knit together failures in chemical tanks, stitch flesh, form simple shapes or tools at a single command, even fight foreign bacteria and viruses living in our bodies.

Our first batch of nano-fluid was a total bust, weeks of hard work creating nothing more than a mass of quicksilver, inert machines filling a basin no larger than a cereal bowel. We flashed the batch with high voltage and heat, ensuring the fluid was deader than dead, and tried again. It took three additional attempts before the silver fluid responded to our call.

As a test, I was tasked by Perry to repair one of the waste recyclers. For the past few months, sewage had been piling up, the tried-and-true processors of the ship unable to do its job. Within another six months, this issue would become critical and put the crew in danger. Everything was recycled on board, an environment in near perfect equilibrium. The captain thought it time to let a bright student make use of his newfound skills and hopefully not screw it all up.

I studied the waste recycler, determining the exact process by which it worked. Unlike other treatment systems in short-jaunt spacecraft, ours had to make best use of every atom on board. Not only did we need to break down our waste, we needed to use it for things like farming, a process commonly frowned upon for the diseases it could spread, but which was safe aboard the ship. We needed to reduce its mass without destroying its biologically active qualities.

Observing the bacteria of the waste tanks, I was able to model some of the behaviors using the ship's primary computer. The nano-fluid was then given a set of instructions, tested on a small batch, then released to the larger volume. The tiny machines moved together, breaking up the berms and allowing bacteria to flourish. Within a week the filters were clean, and the recycler's balance restored.

For this victory, I was brought to the command section and given a special commendation from Captain Williams. There were others present, Mary and Perry, Dr. Reed, and a few of my friends from class. We had a reception of a sort, where excremental jokes were made, and bulbs of adult beverages enjoyed. It was awkward having a party in null-gravity, pushing off to join a different conversation, fancy clothes merely a jumpsuit with different stripes. Still, the experience was unique. A party just for me. It was the first time in my life.

"Always good to find something to celebrate," the captain said, giving me a firm handshake. "Good job, son. We'd be knee deep in shit if not for you. You're a smart kid. I see a bright future ahead. Work hard, stick to it. You'll always have a place."

I gave a smile and nodded. "Thank you, sir."

Across the room, I spotted Shelly among the crowd. Her boyfriend, Lance, was absent from her side. We made eye contact and froze, my stomach twisting into knots at the thought of her. She was beautiful, her dark, curly hair floating as we cruised in freefall. Her eyes smoky and yet somehow auroral, alive with both mystery and promise.

I wanted to say something to her but couldn't.

She pushed off from the bulkhead, her trajectory set to intercept me. I sucked in a breath and chose to float in a different direction. Perry gave me a smile and waved me in on an ongoing conversation, an easy escape, his optics glowing like alien eyes.

"Can you believe we're nearing the site?" Mary said, a bulb of wine in her hand. "We've extended the optical telescopes to start taking pictures. A bit blurry for now, the color shift is all wrong, but it's there for sure. The structure's massive. I'd estimate at least a few hundred kilometers in length."

"A few hundred kilometers?" Janice Parks, the woman from xenobiology she was chatting with, replied. "What kind of species do you have to be for this to be possible? Have you put much thought into it? Are they bipeds? Do they look like humans? Popular culture wants to make out like they will appear humanoid, but there's nothing saying this for sure. They could be akin to platypuses."

"No opposable thumbs."

"Maybe they have another adaptation for holding and using tools. A collection of claws or tentacles? Then again, maybe they are like koalas?"

"Or land squid," Perry added, then began to laugh, a hand on his belly.

Dr. Reed leaned in, taking a sip of her drink before contributing. "Given what we know about the planet the Foundry is orbiting, there's a good chance that life requiring a high concentration of oxygen should thrive. If this is the case, insect life could have evolved into great size. For all we know these people could be giant wasps or spiders."

"Stop." A shiver ran down Perry's spine. "Now you're giving me the creeps."

"As for meself," Gareth Baker, a balding astronomer in his fifties with a five-o'clock shadow started, "I think they are simians of a sort. Come on, all the God-given advantages in all."

"Careful now, don't break the rules," Captain Williams said, butting in on the conversation.

Gareth gave him a withering look. "Pretty sure God can be used as an adjective."

"What a narrow-minded view, Gareth," Dr. Reed went on. "For all you know they could be sea sponges."

"Bah. Now you're just being daft. How does a sea sponge grow a complex enough neural network to even have the intelligence to think about spacefaring? Not enough opportunity for neurons. Look at that structure! I'd love to see a kitchen sponge hold a hammer. Like to see 'em bodge something with that setup."

"I suspect it would work about as well as your last marriage."

"Now see here!" He raised a finger and tapped her on the chest. "I'm not sure how that should offend me."

They began to laugh. I stared at my sour drink and questioned their sense of humor.

"We'll start the slowdown burn soon," Captain Williams said, simmering down the gathering, "shaving off speed so we may slip into a gentle orbit around Barnard's Star-3. Rest assured, you'll get your answers in due time."

The great discussions of the Foundry went on. I contributed little on my part and extricated myself once enough drinks had been downed. I was honestly too young to have alcohol, and the single glass of wine I drank was more than enough to make me sleepy. I was *knackered,* Gareth said when it made me yawn.

I wandered the habitation ring for a while, not sure if I wanted to go home. The captain had given me praise for contributing to the good of the ship, and my parents had been too otherwise engaged for it to matter. It felt good to be given praise, sure, I just wish the source was different.

"Walking off your thoughts?" Shelly asked from a side hall, her arms crossed. I hadn't expected to see her here. I'd done my best to avoid it. "I've been counting your laps. Ten more. Maybe then you'll be able to sleep?"

My attention crashed onto my feet. "I don't know."

"It takes me a good fifteen laps sometimes. The monotony helps my mind drift." She took a step towards me and I felt my heart skip. "Sometimes, it's like I have a rock in my chest and all I can do is walk until all the edges become smooth, blood flow rushing over it like a river. It doesn't go away, not really, but it hurts less."

"What kind of rocks do you have in your chest?" I asked, raising my eyes, a touch of spite in my tone. "You're the captain's daughter. You have the perfect life."

"We all have rocks." She paused for a moment. "We're all just doing the best we can."

"Some peoples' best isn't all that good."

"You, uh, got that right."

I wasn't sure where she was going with this, or even why she was talking to me. Our previous friendship or not, I was still a stowaway, a misfit, not a genetic match for any woman on board. My feelings were something I kept bottled up, not sharing with anyone, even James, and yet she was prying. Best to keep my emotions buried deep so my eyes stayed dry and arguments were avoided. Yes. This was for the best.

I turned to leave, and she took hold of my hand.

"We haven't talked in forever." She raised my lowered chin and looked at me dead in the eyes. My face tingled where her fingers met flesh. "Why?"

"I, eh…" I took a step back, feeling sick all of a sudden. My feet tangled and I lost my balance for an instant. Shelly caught my arm before I could bust my ass. "I'm sorry. I didn't mean to…"

She smiled, her expression soft and genuine. Her eyes… "It's okay."

"Look, you're spoken for. I wouldn't want to get in the middle of…"

"Lance? Oh, geez, that's been over for a while. He's too full of himself. Spends more time working on his hair than I do."

"Oh."

"Talk to me." She took my hand in hers and held tight. "Please?"

I reached for an excuse, unsure why. "I wish I could, but I can't. You see it's just. I can't."

"Can't what?"

"I—all the—well."

She folded her arms around me, squeezing tight. I can't say what happened next, the world became hazy fast. I'm pretty sure I left her shoulder wet and made a fool of myself. I'm pretty sure she didn't judge me for my uncontrolled actions.

What I can recall was her saying, "Never forget, you are important. You have value."

An hour went by in a blur, the habitat's hallways empty but for us. At the ten o'clock chime we parted ways. I watched her go and felt a combination of relief and longing as she went. Years might have separated the active pieces of our friendship, but something deeper still lived. The girl who wanted to color with me, and the boy who sat by her side in rapt attention, still recognized one another.

Back in my quarters, I found Mom sitting at the dining-room table working. She was just where I'd left her, no surprise at that.

"Hey," I said, and headed off to my room.

She raised a hand and nodded.

At that moment a gasp came from their bedroom. Out of the corner of my eye I saw Dad shoot up in bed, his body rigid.

"Dad?" I shouted and ran to his side, Mom fast on my heels.

He ran fingers through his hair. His eyes were wild with recognition.

"I finally know what's wrong," he hissed. "Finally."

"What do you mean?" Mom asked.

He regarded us one at a time and swallowed. I'd never seen Dad so afraid. "The stars. The stars are wrong."

"I don't understand."

"We should be slowing down, but we're speeding up. The Foundry is pulling us towards it."

I blinked at him, unsure of his meaning. Dad might have his episodes, but he was not one to make false claims in moments so lucid. Though he might seem mental at times, more often than not, he was able to see over horizons others lacked the ability to. Something in the data had him spooked. I could see that this wasn't his bipolar disorder. We were in danger. Real danger.

"Show me," Mom said, and we helped him out of bed.

CHAPTER 16

"What do you mean we're speeding up?" Captain Williams asked.

Mom, Dad, and I were now on the bridge, bleary eyed and fatigued after a night-long debate. Mary and Perry were there as well, ready to verify Dad's claim.

"I can't believe it," Mary said, her attention fixed on the main display. She pressed several keys and drew up a model, waving a hand as her curls, which were now bright purple, fell into her face. How damn often did she dye her hair? What was it last time? Pink? Blue? "The data tracks. How did we miss this?"

"Because it made no sense to look," Perry said. "Made no sense at all."

The captain rubbed his face and let out a long sigh. "Why is it whenever we have a little chat on the bridge it turns out to be something Earth shattering. Can we not just meet for coffee? Janice raises beans that taste just like Ethiopian Yirgacheffe, I swear. Medium, not too much bite."

"Oh, coffee!" Perry pushed off from his console. "Back in a tick, who wants cream?"

Mom waved him off. I raised a hand. It had been a long time. Coffee sounded perfect.

"Take me through it again," Captain Williams said. "How did you discover it?"

"Okay," Dad started. "I was taking multi-spectrum pictures of the Foundry and its surrounding system. I came to discover that, well, none of the colors were right. We've all had a bit of studies as far as astronomy so I will not insult your intelligence. We all know about the redshift and blue shift of light. Traveling at the relative speeds we are, the shift is quite drastic. If you were to go out in a space suit, not only might you be cut to bits by x-rays, you would see that the stars before us have a different look than those behind us. Look back, and everything is red. Look ahead, and everything is blue."

Perry returned with bulbs of coffee. He handed me one, then the captain and Mary. I clutched it in my hand and sipped slow. The contents were warm and sweet, settling into my belly and radiating a sense of borrowed comfort.

"Thanks, man," I told Perry.

He gave me a two-finger salute.

Dad continued, "The waves of light are compressing as we travel towards the stars ahead of us and lengthening at our stern. We knew to expect this from the start, which is why the telescopes were given an algorithm to compensate for this. It has worked like a charm until the past few weeks. Something about the pictures weren't coming out clear. And since I am no idiot, far from it, I dug deeper."

"You discovered an error in the image correction algorithm?" the captain supplied. "Improperly calibrated factors."

"Once I let myself drift, entering a state of not quite sleeping or being awake I use when I really have to think, it was plain as day. There can be no doubt now. The level of shift we are experiencing is that of an increase in velocity, the bands are widening, shortening. Best I can tell, the *Vasco Da Gama* is close to approaching three quarters of light speed."

Perry nearly spat out his coffee. "I'm sorry, what was that? Three quar…"

"And he's not wrong," Mary added. "I can't explain how, but the data supports it now that we're looking for it."

"How's this even possible?" The captain started ticking keys on his console. Implants or not, we all have habits. "Let's see. The amount of energy it would take to bring us up to that velocity is unheard of. The nearer we approach the speed of light the energy requirements increase exponentially. We don't have enough fuel. Besides, we've already started slow-down. The Foundry is not only drawing us in, it is drawing us in against nearly fifty meganewtons of fusion thrust."

"What is it even tractoring us with?" Mary asked. "There's no electro-magnetic interference. I see no physical tether of any kind. Pretty sure there's not a lasso wrapped around the spoke. What could it be?"

"What about a manipulation of space-time?" Perry responded. "A focused gravity well? I mean, not trying to get all sci-fi but we have literally no idea what these guys can do."

"Now that's a scary thought." Mom narrowed her eyes. "What happens when we reach the end of this trip? I can't imagine whoever is behind the Foundry wishes to make us into a projectile. Is it impatient to meet us? Are we taking too long to get there?"

"Perry," Captain Williams said.

"Yes, sir?"

"Any word from the other ships? Have they experienced similar phenomena?"

He shook his head. "We are going to be the first to make contact, no way around it. The others have many years before they reach their target stars. Since the *Brilliance*, *Galileo*, *Star Stream*, and *Revelation's* signals are being routed back through the deep space network in Sol, then out to us, we have no way of knowing till it's too late. We can't signal one another peer to peer, too complicated to calibrate such a thing. We're on our own."

Mom let out a huff. "What do we do, Tobias?"

"I don't know." The captain put his forehead against the main console and closed his eyes. His tired expression was framed in the glow of the panel's lights. "I want to believe this isn't an act of aggression. They have the means to construct a machine several hundred kilometers in length, the purpose of which we don't yet understand. And not only have they made one, we know of at least five more, each similar in design. They are a powerful and advanced species. Let us hope we have not incurred their ire."

My imagination ran away from me.

Images of brutalist starships large as cities, made of bizarre angles and lines appeared in my mind, brilliant flames as bright as stars trailing behind them. As they entered Sol, humanity's home system, swarms of smaller craft broke away from the craggy flesh of their motherships like a molting exoskeleton. They descended upon the dozens of human colonies first, ripping apart each habitat, each human being, using the information we gave them to work with frightening efficiency. Earth is all that lay before them, a green world rich with rare biodiversity even if it is in decline. They need it for themselves, for their purposes. They need it to grow, to survive. They need our fertile, terrestrial soil to plant their alien seed.

"If we cut thrust, this tractor force should increase," Perry said, his words breaking me from my nightmarish vision.

I blinked and shook my head. Cold sweat was collecting in my hair. My hands were balled into fists.

He went on, "Then again, we don't have the thrust to fight it, that much is clear. Looks like we're resigned to this fate. Might be a good idea to save reaction mass. Anyone want more coffee? I could use more coffee."

Mary passed her brother an empty bulb.

"It would shorten our downtime for the return trip," Mom suggested. "The fuel collectors would have to scoop half as long. Might get us out of trouble if things have gone bad."

"But what kind of trouble?" The captain raised his head and spun around. "We all knew this could happen. Now that it's here, something feels different. It's toying with us."

"What if the Foundry is a trap?" I mused. "Like honey to a fly?"

The spell of adult-to-adult attention snapped. They turned to regard me as if I had magically teleported into the middle of the room, bursting in on their private conversation.

"Truth is, it might be," Dad replied. "I sure hope it's not."

Mom began chewing on her fingernails. "I pray they help us, not kill us. Don't give me that look, Tobias. I can say pray if I damn well please. A time like this warrants it."

"I said nothing." He raised his hands.

"Do we have any way to fight back?" I asked.

The captain smirked at me. "A great idea, and terrible at the same time. First of all, no, we do not have weapons. Second, even if we did, there's no way they would be enough to combat what we are heading into. Then there's the fact that it might be seen as a provocation. If we want them to follow us home and burn it to the ground, I'd say that would be a good way to see it done."

"Would this event not be considered first contact?" I asked. "The tractor."

"He has a point," Perry replied. "Might be a good time to send some of those pre-recorded UEA approved messages."

"Good thought, Milo. Perry, get the packets ready. They have made contact with us, and in a physical way, even if it's across a great distance of space. Might as well return the favor and say hello. Maybe even more."

"Plan then?" Dad asked, eagerness in his voice. This is the sort of thing he lived for. Adventure in the real world, or only in his head, it did not matter.

"Perry," the captain started, "cut thrust. Let's allow the Foundry to bring us in. No more fighting it. Jackson, make the necessary changes to the algorithms and get us the best pictures you can. You've got the whole research staff with you on this. Take what resources you need. I want to know everything about it. This was always the plan, but we're going to get started ahead of schedule."

Dad gave a salute. "Aye, Captain."

The captain crossed his arms and took on a stern look. "And Adriana."

"Yes, Tobias?"

"You're not alone in this. You have an army at your back."

Mom let her attention drift to her feet. It was a look unbefitting her confidence, a vulnerable side I had never seen. The captain had touched a nerve and Mom somehow seemed smaller, younger.

"*Sim claro*, I know," she whispered.

"Then start acting like it." He gestured to the rest of us with an open hand. "It's okay to ask for help."

She curled up into a ball and rested a cheek on one of her knees. "What if they let me down?"

"Then you'll finally learn they're human. Just like you." He let that hang for a moment before moving on. "Alright. You've got your orders. We'll see this through together. Ten billion people are counting on us. Let's not let them down."

CHAPTER 17

The *Vasco Da Gama* slowed as we approached the Foundry without any action on our part. Whatever force had been drawing us in also ensured a proper approach. I wondered if the aim was to protect the structure itself. We were an unknown, something that had yet to be studied or understood. We were an invader into its space, so in a sense it was fair for them to be the cautious ones.

It was a moment of awe, the tiny human craft reaching its hand out to say, "Hello."

It's one thing to be told we aren't alone in the universe, and yet, it's another thing to look out the proverbial window and see it for yourself. Academic discussion vs experience. Logic vs emotion. Scale is difficult to comprehend or put in context with such great distances in evidence. Nevertheless, with about a million telescopic pictures, multi-spectral scans from detachable probes, and the use of artificial intelligence that could stitch it all together, it was possible to get a small glimpse of the truth.

Dad and his team had spent seven weeks taking pictures of the Foundry from every angle they could manage, scanning inch by inch down its hundred and fifty-three-kilometer reach. This great cache of data allowed them to render the most incredible virtual environment humankind had ever seen. The Foundry in three dimensions.

On my part there was nothing to do but wait for our arrival. The days leading up to first contact were frantic. We had eighteen years to prepare for this moment, and yet it felt as if that was not enough. Linguists were on standby. Astronomers ready to collect data and plot us a path home when this was over. Photographers set to capture a brilliant moment in human history. And for my contribution? Well, I had made tiny machines set to repair key systems if all went wrong, power relays, environmental sensors, and oxygen condensers. So fancy.

I received a ping from Dad when the VE was finished, and I was eager to explore. There was time. At our current rate of deceleration, it would be about forty hours till we reached whatever position it was we were being drawn into.

I took a comfortable seat in my room and leaned back, taking a deep breath. Our fate was in the Foundry's hands.

"Lets see what all the fuss is about," I whispered.

With a flicker of my eyes and a mental command, my physical body dissolved, and my digital form was transported to a place just a few hundred kilometers before the Foundry structure.

My chest caught for a moment, my breath frozen by feelings of both awe and terror. The Foundry, great and powerful, shone before me, scintillating like a harvest moon, a torus of gold and silver flickering beneath the crimson rays of Barnard's Star, its hull studded with geodesic domes of ivory and obsidian. As the structure orbited the bluish green world beneath, I could see what appeared to be fine hairs sticking from the surface. I closed the distance in this virtual space to discover its endless arrays of spines and towers. The Foundry let off a soft flash, and the spines lit one after the next, transmissions of blue energy traveling across the matrix like an aurora. Curiosity drew me in.

Between the spines were great connections miles long, and along their many nodes, shapes began to coalesce into form.

"Ships," I mumbled under my breath, and then felt a hand on my shoulder.

I turned to see Shelly floating beside me and felt my heart swell.

How had she known I'd be in here and in this instance of the simulation? Not that it mattered. The couple of years since Dad's discovery over us being tractored, she and I had come to a new place. Hitting age twenty-three made me, and her, look at the world in a different way, see what had happened through a longer lens, and so we had become friends again, yet I felt we were something far more. So many quiet moments there was a sense of becoming whatever came next, and yet the both of us only retreated and hid, our defenses raised like deflection fields on science fiction battlecruisers.

"Those look like ships," I said after some time. "How many are there?"

She let out a long breath, finger extended as she briefly attempted to count. "It has to be thousands. That cluster there is ten by fifteen. And there's rows and rows of clusters."

"Is it okay to be afraid?" I asked, my voice fragile in the void. I had always known we were but a grain of sand on the beach of infinity, but beneath the structure's control, that feeling was oppressive. I was nothing and no one.

"Yes," she said, and took hold of my hand. I did not resist. I did not run.

We skimmed across the surface of the Foundry together, exploring every nook and cranny the scans had allowed us to access. Tiny craft moved about its surface like ants, ferrying materials from barges in orbit to its molten forges, fully formed superstructures sliding free through membrane-like space docks, those pieces then attached to others, great latices of interstellar intent. The Foundry was just as it had called itself. A crucible of construction, a builder of ships.

"Many of these craft didn't show up on any of our scans," Shelly said, pausing us for a moment. "I wonder why that is? What are they made of?"

We floated in the shadow of a cigar-shaped vessel covered in segmented plates of armor, our legs weightless and bending back behind us. One end was mounted with a cluster of massive tubes, a soft blue emanating from them. The drive. The other end, a collection of mechanical cylinders of varying lengths with orbs mounted at their tips. The VE returned measurements back to us, declaring that this craft was five kilometers in length. Five kilometers…

"I wonder," she went on, "are these for organics or is the Foundry autonomous?"

"That's a good question." I pointed to the ship. "Pay attention in biology?"

"You know I did."

I rolled my eyes. "Those panels. Are they protection from cosmic radiation? Military grade armor? Who can tell? But notice, they look like the thoraxes of small insects, maybe ants. Note the coloration, it transitions from one end to the other."

"And yet, not all of them are like it."

She was right, this particular design was among a minority. There were a half-dozen different hull textures, shapes, and sizes, implying either a great degree of creativity or varied requirements. Some were elongated and smooth, others were curved like crescent moons, their drives centered at the inside of the shape. And yet others had complicated, fractal structures, buttresses and gothic arches connecting a network of fine modules mostly hollow at their center, friezes and bas-reliefs showing complicated markings and symbols.

The work was beautiful, directed by a mind more advanced than humans could comprehend.

"I half expect a hunchback to be swinging from the tops of that one," I said, and gave a laugh. "The design is baroque in nature."

Shelly shook her head and rolled her eyes. "I don't believe that's Notre Dame. The French had nothing to do with it."

"I wonder if this thing works on order? What kind of currency does a hyper-advanced species like this take?"

She took a deep breath and crossed her arms. "I'm not sure, but if they have a restaurant on board, I sure hope it's not called Neutrinos."

"Why is that?"

"Because that stuff just goes right through me."

I paused for a moment, then let out a ridiculous belly laugh, my body flipping end over end through the digital void. Shelly reached out, taking hold of my shoe to stabilize me and pulled me back.

"Did you just make a pun?" I asked, finally back under control of myself. "Because neutrinos go through anything?"

"A pun? Maybe. Maybe not."

"There's hope for you yet, Miss Perfect."

She gave me a gentle punch on the shoulder. "Keep calling me that, and I might just take it as a compliment, not an insult. No hope for you at that point. I do like being perfect."

"Whatever," I said, grinning.

We watched The Foundry do its work, the great task tireless and mechanized. Flashes of light. The birth of new structures. Sparks and bonding metal. Metallic beams as large as skyscrapers twisted into shapes. Glimmering filaments of metal spun around house-size dynamos.

There was no sound. We kept our mouths closed for a moment. The activity was hypnotic, like the plants that waved in the breeze of Dr. Reed's office, or the swirl of stars in observation. My mind began to drift into possibilities.

What happens now? Sure, we'll make contact, explore. Hopefully, we will find the help that we need. But then what? This moment changes humanity forever. Even if we learn nothing more than we already have, the VE alone was worth the trip.

Lost in thought, I had not realized I put my arm around Shelly and had drawn her in. She placed her head on my shoulder, snuggling close against my neck. We were free falling, the Foundry and its machines a dazzling, pulsing agglomeration beneath us. She was warm against me, so warm it made my heart ache. Did I deserve to feel so good?

"What are you thinking?" I asked her after a moment.

She began to speak, then paused as if she wasn't ready to let go of the words tickling her lips. After a moment she said, "What now?"

I closed my eyes and put my nose against her curls, breathing softly enough she might not notice. The aroma was heady and sweet, smelling of cleanliness and tropical fruit. Was this how her hair always smelled? Or was this a projection of the simulation?

"I—eh—I don't know." My heart quickened. "We figure this out or I guess we don't. We go home?"

She shook her head. "I think we are home."

"On the Foundry?"

"No, silly, *the Vasco Da Gama*. We've lived here our whole lives. Eighteen years is a long time. But I didn't just mean..."

I turned to face her, clasping her hands in mine. The Foundry flashed as its forges were refilled with raw materials by swarms of drones, her eyes glittering in their light like black diamonds.

"Look, I know we haven't always had the easiest relationship," she started. "But I can say that we have had the most honest relationship of anyone I've been with, even my family. We might be on the edge of something remarkable as humans, and yet, it all feels meaningless to do alone."

My mouth went dry. "What are you trying to say?"

She lifted her hands, taking hold of mine, then pushed our palms together, allowing our fingers to intertwine. We stared at one another for a moment, then a kind of gravity took over. Our hands began to drift away, and our faces, our lips, began to fall towards one another.

I closed my eyes and let it all go. All the worry. All the hurt. All the fear. I wouldn't be alone. Shelly wanted to be with me, and in my heart, I knew that I had always wanted to be with her. There was no one else who got me, really got me.

A voice cut in on our environment and we paused. I opened my eyes to see our lips were an inch apart, unable to advance past the interruption.

"This is Captain Tobias Williams..." the voice said, and Shelly's back went straight, but she did not let go of my hands. *"We have sent communications and heard nothing in return from the Foundry. The tractor force, whatever it is, seems to be drawing us to a dock on what we will refer to as the north end of the torus. Everyone stand by, you know your places. Let's do this by the book. First contact in less than two days. May this go down in the—"*

The virtual environment collapsed, the image of the Foundry and Shelly reeling away as if someone pulled a drain plug on reality. I found myself back in my quarters, lights off. Shocked by this sudden shift in perspective, it took a moment for me to regain my bearings. My body was cold, my head dizzy, fingertips tingling, eyes dry.

Once I had my balance I blinked and evaluated the situation.

The ship was quiet, too quiet, the familiar vibration of reactors and fans and machines throughout the hull, absent. The lights were out, near total darkness encompassing my room.

I reached into my jumpsuit for a flashlight and stumbled into the hall, attempting to use my implants, tablet, hand terminal, watch, anything I had to ping anyone. No response. No network.

Screams echoed from up the habitat ring. I shone my flashlight one way, then the next, then began heading towards the source of the noise.

Details began to fall in line.

The moment we approached the Foundry, reached some sort of threshold, the *Vasco Da Gama* had lost all power. We had been drawn into the great structure against our will. Were my worst fears coming true? Was the thought I had worked so hard to push to the very back of my mind becoming a reality?

This was no coincidence.

"Shelly," I mumbled under my breath and scurried off into the dark, nothing but a flashlight to guide me down the *Vasco's* black halls.

Fear gripped my heart. The words, a trap, a trap, a trap, a trap, a trap, repeated in my head. A trap. A trap. A trap.

I had to gather everyone up if we had any hope of seeing another day. Help them get the power back on. Lights, environmental control, networks, the main drive. That objective started first with her.

PART II

CHAPTER 18

Despite wanting to be good at everything, the older I got, the more I came to realize this was impossible. History was not my favorite subject, yet it was a big part of our education on board. It is difficult to understand the future, without first understanding the past. And while I might not have cared less about the subject as a whole, it was interesting enough that I had uncovered recurring patterns throughout the ages.

Exploration has always been fraught with danger. From the days of early man, it meant venturing out of our caves to war with neighboring tribes while wrestling with beasts, all so that we could acquire scraps of meat and verdant lands in which to forage. Yet all the while, we were looking over the next hill, wondering what was there, taking inventory of what we had, the food that smoked in our domicile, the skins that dried beneath the sun. Anticipation and vision drew us forward, compelled us to act.

We thrived in this spirit, built great cities, and expansion began. Sprawling empires like Rome set out to civilize our wild, untamed world, imposing a single culture and will. What arose as the result was a man at the top, an emperor, a figure who reaped the vast majority of these benefits in power, influence, and luxury.

By this model, many nations rose and fell, and despite what most might desire, the cause was typically economic rather than ideological. Sentiment and morality are often malleable, ever shifting from parent to child, whereas the need for food, water, and shelter are not. Practices and traditions acceptable today may not be the same in the next generation.

Thus, we found ourselves in the Age of Exploration, in which an inexorable desire for riches and fame drove trade. Prince Henry of Portugal, even *Vasco Da Gama*, our ship's namesake, set off against the dangers of starvation and storms with fleets of ships driven by the wind. Routes were made from Europe and around the tip of Africa, connecting markets once thought unreachable. Hard goods were traded to drive wealth back to the homelands. Even people were traded, a concept abominable to us in our modern age.

Christopher Columbus sailed into the new world under the rallying cry of *God, Gold, and Glory*, landing on the shores of a foreign land to subjugate and control as all explorers of the age were like to do.

For all its daring, the true motivator, the prime mover of this grand expedition, was a dream to obtain riches at the expense of others.

Humanity has ever suffered for want, not need. That which we have needed has always been in abundance, our very biology evolved to make use of the Earth's seemingly endless bounty. But want. Want is lack. Want is the result of greed, a force compelled by our deepest fear. A fear that one day we would lose everything, and that by hoarding our riches we could escape that inevitability. This primal form of want is so fearful of scarcity that every action becomes self-serving.

And yet, there is a flip side. Mere want is also a choice, whereas need is a requirement. Can the want for knowledge, the choice to pursue it at any cost, become intellectual avarice? Were we at this place in history out of want, or need?

We lived in unprecedented times if humanity could stand for a just cause beside its own greed. Setting the five of our ships on course to reach the Foundry took trust. It took an intense need for survival to overcome the short-term losses of an international undertaking. Humanity, not just America, had reached a fork in the road. Our infinitely rising economy had led to lack, bringing us to a point of crisis. A point where making a choice was really no choice at all.

The Foundry had known this. It had positioned itself in such a way as to use this fragile moment for our species as leverage. It had called and we had come, our motivation part curiosity, though mostly fear.

Fear was an emotion I was just coming to be familiar with. Until this point, everything in life had been perfect, or at least safe, everything was controlled and rationed out in neat little portions. And now…

"I don't want to die," I mumbled as I scurried along the dark halls of our ship, flashlight gripped in hand. "I don't want to die."

Lights appeared up ahead, voices trailing after them. The crew was mobilizing, assessing the situation. There was no clear leadership in the moment, just collections of people doing the best they could. We had procedures for this, but the shock of our predicament seemed to have plucked this knowledge from their heads.

A hand reached out for me in the dark, taking hold of my arm. I gave a start and whirled.

"James?"

"Milo, you're okay," he replied, gasping for breath. "Wait, *are* you okay?" The front of his jumpsuit was smeared with black and brown, mashed beans having fallen from a shaking fork when the lights winked out.

"I'm fine."

"What's going on? Why is the power dead? People are freaking the hell out."

"Are you freaking out?"

"No," he replied, a bit too quick, the fingers of his right hand rubbing his jumpsuit's chest in a pacifying gesture.

"I don't know why." I waved for him to follow. "This way, let's find Shelly and head for the bridge."

"Good idea."

We hurried down the hall to her quarters, passing other crew members along the way. No one was hurt so far, other than minor injuries that occurred any time humans stumble around in the dark. No one had an answer for what was going on. Internal communication channels were dead, our implant connections to the network timing out.

"Do you think we're okay?" James asked.

I gave a shrug and rounded a corner, jumping back as a series of emergency responders rushed past with tools in hand, the three of them arguing over what systems had gone down.

"We're okay right now," I replied. "There's her quarters."

He popped open the manual release panel. I reached inside the access point and began to twist a tiny wheel, a ratcheting click-click-click issuing with each quarter turn. The panels of the door split down the center and began to retract into the wall, an open slit appearing.

A hand shot through the opening like a zombie seeking fresh victims. James and I sucked in a breath at its sudden appearance.

"Milo!" Shelly exclaimed. "Get me out of here, please. The release isn't working."

I collected myself from the scare and gave a nod, turning the wheel until the door opened wide enough that she could slip through. She was okay, a bit shaken up like the rest of us, but okay. What a moment for all this to go down. She gave me a smile and squeezed my fingers, a gentle promise our business wasn't over.

"Do you guys feel that?" she asked.

"Feel what?" I glanced up and down the dark halls, no activity but for the distant voices of unsettled crew.

"I don't feel anything at all," James answered.

"Exactly. The air isn't recycling either."

My eyes widened at the prospect. If the air wasn't circulating, we needed to either keep moving or procure breathing masks. If we remained in one place for too long, we might find ourselves caught in a carbon dioxide bubble.

Of all the things in the universe to die from, I did not want loitering to be what took me out.

We decided to work our way to the bridge, grabbing masks along the way. The rush was not like it had been that fateful drill when we were young. In fact, the response crew were informing non-emergency personnel to remain in their quarters till we had it all sorted out. This was procedure, but I didn't care. I had to find my parents and speak with the captain, and from here there was no way to figure out how much shit we had found ourselves in. I was done being stuck in a position of no control.

The maintenance hatch accessing the primary lift was jammed. For all our best work, it had not needed to be used but only a handful of times over the years. This had resulted in stiff hinges and sticky bolts.

"One, two, three," James said, and we pulled and twisted. The hatch gave for an instant. Shelly slid a metal rod she found in a maintenance toolbox through the gap, hoping for leverage.

"Someone needs to spray some WD-40 on this bitch," I said through gritted teeth.

Shelly leaned against the rod with all her body weight. It was clear this wouldn't be enough, and she knew it, yet in spite of it she gave it her all.

The hatch widened an inch, then fought to shut again, emergency pressurization systems operating at full strength.

"Come on, come on!" James struggled with the release.

I let go, my palms sore from gripping the tiny handle along with him.

"I don't think it's coming open," Shelly said.

And at that moment lights began to flicker up and down the halls of the ship, coming back online. The hairs on my arm rustled for an instant as the recyclers were restored. A light on the lift door turned yellow.

"Emergency power's up." Shelly reached out and called the lift. "I wonder if the fusion reactor is down."

"That would make sense," James replied.

"Why would the reactor be down?" I asked, though I already had a good idea why. It felt good to talk it out, to keep my mouth moving.

"Don't be stupid, Milo." James wrung his hands. "How else were they planning on disabling us without firing any shots?"

Shelly leaned her head against the bulkhead and frowned. "We are toys to them."

The lift arrived and the doors opened, though slower than usual. The low power situation meant that it was running on conservation mode and not optimal speed. We rode the lift to the spine of the *Vasco*, my stomach dropping as spin gravity diminished and soon vanished.

On the other side of the lift, people rushed to the bridge, taking handholds in null gravity to move as quickly as possible, before firing down the hall like human bullets. Perry joined our party, his latest set of implant driven optics in evidence, their design far less bulky than the others, more like a pilot's set of black goggles than an early VR headset. They were comfortable looking, unlike their predecessors.

"Are you guys okay?" he asked, surveying our condition, optics scanning us top to bottom. "When the lights went down, I thought my headset had gone dead. Wasn't till I cycled through the various modes and found an infrared setting that I realized we were in real trouble. Network is down for the moment, so I'm headed for the bridge. Mary's looking at the reactor. We're running on batteries. Won't last forever, though."

I curled into a ball for a moment, free floating, my right hand caressing my knee. "How long?"

"A few—well—days at most," his words were broken, a pervasive nervousness in his tone. "Takes uh—it's lots of energy to keep us running."

Shelly reached for Perry's jittery hand and gave it a friendly squeeze. "And if this thing keeps up this remote manipulation that might not be the worst of our troubles."

"Might not. Doesn't take a PHD to figure that out."

As we approached the bridge several arguments grew louder. The main doors were open and most of the lights were still off. The displays were dead, lights flickering on and off as if the bulbs had reached the end of their life.

"What do you expect me to do?" the captain shouted; his attention focused on one of our astronomers, Gareth Baker.

"We need to turn this torch about and burn out. Nuffing good is going to come of this. We're standing on the edge of the rabbit hole and I ain't got a mind on stumbling through the looking glass."

"Gareth, calm down." Dad said, a hand on the Brit's shoulder in an awkward, calming gesture. Mom was at his side, a determined, hawkish look on her face. She gave me a nod, acknowledging my arrival.

Others were gathered, a few scientists, Nurse Brennon, but mostly senior staff. Esteban and Deidrick lingered to the side, arms crossed, coiled and ready as if they were waiting on orders. Gareth was by far the most upset of the lot.

Shelly, James, and I were not supposed to be here. I only had half the needed clearance myself, with my nano-repair machine duties. Shelly had become a neural connectivity researcher, and James, a chemical engineer. Their parents' positions or not, they should have stayed secured on the outer decks.

"We're all scared," Dad went on, "but insofar as we know right now, nothing has violently attacked us."

"Not violent?" Gareth turned his face to show the bloody gash tracing the side of his cheek. "What do ya' see in this?"

"I think you tripped and hit your head on the bathroom sink when the lights went out," Mom replied.

"Remain calm." The captain raised his open hands. "Perry! Thank Go—" he paused to reconsider his words, "thank goodness you're here. What's the situation?"

"Mary says that whatever hit us has killed the fusion reaction. The tokamak is cold. She's working to see if it can be restarted. Tritium is nothing to toy with, we didn't expect a total shut down out here."

"So not the end of the world." The captain gave Gareth a look meant to say, *I told you so.* "What's our next step?"

"Get the reaction started back up and go ahead. Beyond that, it's your mission, sir."

The captain took a moment to consider his words. Shelly and I gave each other a look. I wanted to know what she was thinking but could not ask in front of the captain, let alone her father. Part of me, the hind brain primal man, felt running would be the best option. We'd turn tail and burn hard as we could until this discovery was nothing but a fever dream brought about by weary explorers. Shelly and I would be safe, we could live our lives out on the *Vasco Da Gama,* and when we reached home find a place on Luna. We could have a child, give it the same kind of life we had, a safe environment and a good education. A better life than ours, the end of our child's journey a warm bed and plenty of human company.

"We can't tuck our tails," the captain finally said, "we didn't burn for eighteen years only to run. Unless they open fire on us, we *are* going down there to find out what we have gotten ourselves into. We will dock or take an orbit or whatever this structure will allow us to do, and the field team will head over and start untangling this mess. We are here to make first contact, to figure out what the impressions, the promises in that signal, are telling us. Things are bad back home, and we're not turning our back on that. We can't. Any response to the communication signals?"

Kathy Vespier, one of our head linguistics experts and anthropologists, shook her head as she pressed several keys on a glowing panel. "Nothing, sir. All bands, all messages. They aren't responding."

"You're putting us at risk, Tobias," Gareth went on, crossing his arms. "You're a short-sighted prig. We're dead men."

I pushed off from the doorframe and made my way over to Mom and Dad, not sure what I was planning on saying. This was not the first time I felt part of historic events that were out of my control.

"Why aren't you down in the habitat," Mom stated, not asked, her voice cold.

"I had to see what was going on."

Dad gave a humph. "That kind of curiosity will get you killed."

"I'm tired of being at everyone else's mercy." I took in a deep breath, my chest swelling, nostrils flaring. Here it was again. They were treating me like a kid. I was twenty-three. If we were back on Earth, I'd already be on my own, maybe even have kids. "I'm not a child."

"Spoken like the truly immature," Dad mumbled under his breath, attention still focused on Gareth and the captain's heated debate.

I raised my hands. "What's your problem, Dad?"

He whirled on me. "My problem? My problem is that we are eyeballs deep in something that could be shit or could be the magical healing waters from Ponce de Leon's fountain of youth. Trouble is, we can't tell the damned difference at the moment. I need *things* to be where they need to be till I can sort this out. Safe. Tucked away."

"Things?" I leaned back where I floated. "Things?"

Mom let out a sigh and punched Dad on the shoulder, pushing him away from us, forcing him to reach for a handhold on a bulkhead. "What he means to say is that we want you to be safe."

"No," I replied, not letting his word go. *Thing.* There was a truth to it, something so deep it was wrapped around the roots of our relationship like an invasive species of creeper. "I see how you feel."

"Milo," Dad said, backpedaling. "I love you with all my heart, it's just that there is a place for everything, and your place right now isn't here."

"Jackson, *cala a boca!*" Mom growled and drew the attention of a few of the gathered crew. Perry closed his mouth, words cutting off. "You need to apologize to Milo."

"*Chega!*" I spat in Portuguese. *Enough.* "Don't bother. I've always been an object to the both of you, a *thing* to manage. How many nights did I come home to an empty house? When I drew pictures and just wanted you to look, where were you? When I had my break-up, were you there? I found all the friends I needed, but you know, what I really wanted were parents. My friends had parents."

Mom pointed a finger at me. "That's not fair. We are working to save humanity."

"It isn't fair?" I met her gaze and narrowed my eyes, my body filled with a sudden furious confidence. "You know what's not fair? Being left alone to figure life out on your own. No kid should ever have to do that."

"Would have been okay if you just listened to us," Dad interjected, his face darkening.

"I can't say your father is wrong," Mom added, her face transitioning a new shade of red. That was something given how dark her skin was. We were on the brink of disaster, yet it was me that pushed their buttons, not the prospect of death far from humanity's cradle, but old, petty arguments from our home life boiling to the surface.

My hands began to shake, heart thundering against my ribcage. The bridge was stuffy and warm, my vision shaky.

"I hate you both," I growled, the words burning like acid on my tongue. The words had been said and I couldn't take it back, and you know, I wasn't sure I wanted to.

Mom and Dad's eyes widened, the pair of them looking as if I had just punched them in the chest. Everyone in the room was silent. After a pregnant moment, Mom's lips moved. I wondered what she wanted to say, anticipated and prepared myself for the verbal blows, but nothing came forth.

"Oh, shit," Perry squawked, his eyes staring off into space, his mind once again connected to a virtual space as the ship's network was restored. "Guys, the uh, aft security cameras on the hull are showing movement. Something is attaching itself to us."

The captain's eyes went wide. He pushed himself off and floated over to Perry. "What something?"

With a flick of his hand, Perry put it up on the main display. From what we could see in the black of space, an object resembling a white and gold beetle had latched itself to the aft end of the ship just north of the fusion drive. Its hull reminded me of the cigar shaped vessel Shelly and I had seen within the virtual environment. Appendages extended from its flanks and dug into the hull. The mechanical creature lowered itself till its bone-white belly came in contact with our carbon fiber skin. Our vessel rocked and began to vibrate.

Perry switched our view, splitting it into several angles. One took us inside the maintenance shaft leading to the drive. Sparks were cast into the cramped space, a stream of lights as intense as the sun tracing a geometrically perfect circle through the exterior hull.

"We've got visitors," Esteban declared. "And I don't think is a friendly knock, ya?"

The captain motioned a hand towards the elevator. "Esteban. Deidrick. You know what to do."

They nodded to the captain. "Yes, sir. Make contact, wait to fire. Assess their weapons, see if they are hostile. If they are, keep us safe. Fight them back."

"All we need is time."

"Call up the others, ya?" Esteban confirmed.

Captain Williams frowned. "There's only ten of you in all, but it will have to do. All we have."

"What's going on?" Dad asked, his words frantic. Esteban answered him by removing a series of MJ-6 submachine guns, familiar short-range weapons from the combat VE, from a hidden compartment on the bridge. "Oh, for the love of…"

Mom pushed off to meet them. "We have guns? We came here with guns? What's wrong with you?"

Murmurs burst out across the bridge. Gareth's eyes bulged out of his head. The rest of those gathered were just as shocked as Mom and Dad.

"And it's a good thing, ya?" Esteban readied his weapon and collected several spare clips of ammunition, stuffing them into his jumpsuit. "Could use a little backup. The rest won't be able to connect with us for several minutes. We need quick."

"I'm in," James said, and extended a hand. Esteban tossed him one of the submachine guns.

"You sure about this?" Deidrick asked James. "You haven't had any real combat training, just the games. You're about as likely to hit the enemy as you are me. What if you break under pressure?"

Esteban gave me a glance and I nodded, making my decision. He tossed me a weapon, magazine already in place. "James has had as much training as I have." I pulled the slide back on my MJ-6 and ensured the safety was on. "High scores and everything. Achievement unlocked."

"Which again, is only a game. A game, bruh."

"We got this."

"Suit yourself. If these things are hostile, we're probably dead anyways."

"This is madness," Mom said, her mouth wide. "First contact is to be peaceful."

Dad shook his head, palms against his cheeks. "I'm with Adrianna, how is this a plan? We go shoot the aliens in the face and hope for the best?"

The captain turned towards the main display. "We need to get our feet on the Foundry. If we can save the ship, put it in a stable orbit or dock up as planned, let's do so. But if they are hostile, and they take the *Vasco Da Gama*, with us on it, whoever they are, all is lost. Something in my heart tells me that everyone needs to get to the capsules and find a way down to that structure, that we'll be safe there. We came to see the Foundry, and by damn it, we are going to. We have a mission. I will not see FICSE fail."

"But what about the invaders, Tobias?" Mom asked. "Won't there be more on board the station? Chances are that they are The Foundry."

"I don't have all the answers, but there's one way to find out."

The four of us now armed, we made for the spine of the ship. I glanced back over my shoulder to see Shelly glaring at me. I gave her a smirk and followed Esteban towards the aft end of the spine. She'd be okay, right? That was our mission. We'd make sure of that.

"Time to fuck them up," James said, and pushed off the bulkhead with both feet, rocketing ahead of us down the seemingly endless hall along the ship's spine.

Esteban fought to keep up with him. "Don't be so eager to die, *amigo*. Hold your safety. Wait on my command. We the first to say hello to aliens, let's no put our foot in it."

CHAPTER 19

We were idiots, rushing into what was almost certain to be a fight with an unknown threat, using weapons we weren't even sure would be effective. We'd traveled six light years in a pitifully primitive craft, a bunch of sun worshiping rock-splitters come to touch the wrathful face of gods. And despite all that, the fear swirling in my stomach, all the danger processing at the front and back of my mind, I was experiencing a momentary thrill at the prospect of change. Good or bad, life or death, this was different, and different was welcome.

"They're working towards the forward end," Perry cut in over an implant-driven communication channel. *"You'll likely hit them on the ladders. Still can't get a good look at them."*

"What's the plan?" Esteban pushed himself towards a hatch leading to the *Vasco Da Gama's* drive and scanned the space ahead over the barrel of his submachine gun. "Clear."

Deidrick floated through the opening and up to the next. Without thrust or spin gravity, our progress was swift, far more so than when George and I had climbed down these stuffy tunnels as kids.

"The captain has emergency evac preparations underway," Perry cut back in. *"We're working to get everyone ready to get into capsules and ascent vehicles if needed. It's the only real play we have."*

"So it all hinges on us?"

"Pretty much. If this goes bad, we'll be ready to tuck tail and run."

"Clear."

We moved to the next opening and Esteban peered through the hatch. He put his palm to his ear then nodded. "The other two teams are getting into place. One will back us up. Another stand guard at the lifts."

"Good," Deidrick whispered. "See anything?"

James and I were positioned against the bulkhead, hidden from the hatch's line of sight, weapons ready. I narrowed my eyes and wrinkled my forehead, attention focused, forefinger ready to flick the MJ-6's safety.

When, not if, something dangerous came through, we were ready to unleash hell on it. Whoever they were, they had forced us into action, popped open our ship like a can of beans without a word of greeting. Under normal circumstances, I would have been concerned there might be a diplomatic issue, raising arms against an alien species we had barely met for the first time, but they were the ones taking hostile actions. We were disabled, without communication, and were being boarded. I hoped for the best but feared the worst.

"I'm not. Wait. Okay. I see something. Oh, shit." Esteban flung himself away from the opening just as a series of white-hot projectiles sang past his face back up the way we had come, striking the deck at our backs. The shots made no holes, but left hotspots where they landed, sizzling quarter-sized circles of impact.

Whatever reservations I might have still had vanished as I watched the damage smoke.

"First contact, *no bueno*," Esteban said. "We have a choke point here, ya? No way to say what bombs they got maybe. I hate to move, but I think we gotta press down on them."

"Okay," I said and gave a nod.

Deidrick craned his neck around the opening, searching for an angle. "How are we going to all fit through the hatch at once? Too tight."

Esteban took in a sharp breath as if to reply, and then our answer was given to us in a flash. What had once been the floor when we were under thrust, now acting as a wall, folded up like a spent aluminum can in a sudden shriek of twisting steel. It fell away towards the enemy, shrinking ever smaller by the millisecond. Nothing stood between us and our quarry.

The four of us threw ourselves flat against the outer bulkhead, seeking cover that was in short supply. We pointed our guns ahead, watching as the twisted ball of metal was squeezed down to the size of a backpack, a ball of crumpled foil. That was one hell of a room-breaching device.

We might not have liked being in the open, but it had given us something we required, a clean line of site to the enemy. A long moment passed, and no shots were fired, the enemy regarding us, us them, both dumbstruck.

For the first time in human history, we were making face to face contact with extraterrestrial life. It was a moment that should have come with awe and peace, but instead I was given both panic and dread. First contact gone to shit. By the next hatch were a trio of insectile creatures six feet in height, their bodies brown carapaces striped in tan, gleaming belts of silver and black equipment strapped to their thoraxes. They steadied themselves on six pairs of spindly, multi-jointed legs covered in fine hairs, their clawed hands clutching tube-like weapons. The short wings that extended from their backs flittered, antennae jerking with all the adrenaline-fueled anticipation of a fight. They glared at us with their bulbous faces and black eyes, pincers working at the air as if chewing on a deep thought. I couldn't recall what insects looked like, not really, those days playing in the dirt belonging to another kid. Still, the very sight made my skin crawl. Were there any varieties on Earth that grew to this size? I didn't think so.

We raised our barrels.

James shot first, and the space was filled with the roar of gunfire, the smell of spent chemicals, a barrage of hollow pointed slugs unleashed at the insect creatures. They didn't expect this response, and two of them were shredded apart, ichor and bits of their hardened carapaces littering the passage. The recoil pressed him into a nook on the wall and he groaned, his last few shots going wild, piercing the bulkhead of the maintenance space before the outer hull. No decompression.

The last of the insects lifted its weapon and aimed at me, but before I could blink, Deidrick put it down, three short bursts to the face and upper thorax. It slumped back and ceased moving.

Esteban pushed off and made for the bodies, sticking his head through the following hatch to be sure there were no others.

"The fuck are these things?" Deidrick checked over the fallen enemies. "I knew they'd be different, but—but those give me the willies."

"Be careful." I sidestepped a cloud of ichor and guts. "You don't want to breathe this stuff in. No telling what it will do."

His eyes widened and he leaned back. "Good point."

"Aft clear," Esteban reported. "Ingress here."

James shook his head. "Just three of them? Not much of a boarding party if you ask me."

"Depends on how much resistance they expect."

"Scouts?"

Esteban grunted.

I slung the submachine gun over my shoulder and picked over the alien equipment, attempting to divine their uses. There were belts of tubes made of similar materials to the rifle-like weapon they carried worn across the body like a bandolier. A series of squares the size of my fist were clipped at their middle. I plucked one of the cubes from the dead and felt around its outside. It was made of a smooth, black metal, its corners hard and sharp as a razor.

"No breathing masks?" James poked at one of their lifeless faces with the barrel of his weapon. "They breathe oxygen like us?"

Deidrick snorted. "Looks like it. I wonder for how long. The air mix has to be different than on their ship. How would they know?"

"But how do they breathe?" I raised the cube to catch it in the light. The object captivated my attention, its black surfaces so dark it absorbed almost all visible light. Looking at it was disconcerting, as if where it existed, reality were being edited out.

After a moment I felt a small button along one face and depressed it slowly. Barbed spikes extended from the opposite end towards the others.

"What are you doing, bruh?" Deidrick slapped my hand and I let go of the cube. The spikes retracted into its void-like form with a snap. "Pretty sure that's the thing that tore up the floor."

"Oh."

"Yeah, oh."

"Situation?" the captain called into the comm channel on our implants.

Esteban put a hand to his ear and spoke, "Three down. I can't say what they are. Big bad insects."

"Termites," Perry chimed in.

"Termites?" James gave me a confused look. "The hell are termites?"

I smiled at him, knowing the answer for once. "They live in houses and trees, eat wood."

"Oh."

"Let's call them something," the captain suggested. *"Might be easier in dealing with them."*

"Isoptera," Perry suggested, and the line went silent. He went on to explain himself. *"It's, well, that's their infraorder. Taxonomy is a hobby of mine."*

"Isoptera?" Deidrick mumbled. "How about Creepy Fucks? Try and get a termite bond that stops those shits."

The captain gave a grunt. *"Good as any. Isoptera it is."*

Esteban shook his head and climbed through the hatch, moving to inspect their craft.

"It's too bad," James said, his head hung low.

"What is?" I asked.

"That this was all the Foundry sent for us to chew on. I was looking for some real action. A chance to really show what I could do."

Esteban climbed back out. "I don't think the Foundry be sending this, ya? Instincts giving me the wrong advice. That signal an' all."

"Same here," Deidrick echoed. "This is different."

The *Vasco Da Gama* chose that moment to give a violent shake. I was grateful for the fact that I was floating freely, instead of pressed against the bulkhead. Esteban banged his head against a pipe and James took a blow to his shoulder. The hull of the ship vibrated, then stopped, vibrated, then stopped, a square wave of frequency resonating through its structure.

"We've got more incoming," the captain called, his voice panicked. *"For a moment I thought we might could keep this together, but it looks like everyone needs to get off the ship now. Right now."*

"Where are they?" Esteban replied, then pushed off in the direction we had come. The three of us followed after without a question.

Perry pinged in, *"Second and third boarding craft have attached to opposite ends of the habitation ring."*

"Oh, shit," I mumbled.

"On our way," Esteban called, then swapped frequencies. "Team two. Redirect. Take up positions at crossing 35-C."

"We don't have the numbers," I went on.

"No. No we don't."

"Anyone else on the ship armed you can call? What did I hear the captain say? Ten of us? That's it?"

"A handful of cowboys." He pressed off the bulkhead and led us back to the lifts.

"Great idea," James started, "let's put eight guys with guns on an exploration ship, then find a couple kids and teach them how to fight using a video game. If we go to war, sure, this will be enough. Well, at least we'll get some more action."

"The guns weren't for the aliens." Deidrick gave him a glare. "Never know when someone's gonna lose their shit on a historically long voyage."

"Oh."

I scanned the various onboard communications channels with my implants. The network was abuzz with terrified people. The Isoptera were coming from everywhere at once, and we had little to nothing we could use to fight them off. I wasn't ready for this. Every scream I heard through the ship's network heightened my sense of dread and inadequacy.

"I was right. We're going to die," I mumbled, not thinking I had said it out loud.

Deidrick glared at me and shook his head. "Not dead yet."

"Not dead yet," Esteban echoed.

We hit the lift and I pinged Mom and Dad. They didn't respond. The Isoptera had boarded the habitat ring and everything was chaos. For us to evacuate the ship, everyone needed access to the lifts. We had to neutralize the threat to make that possible. The capsules and ascent vehicles were docked to the spine, not the ring. This created a bottleneck.

Spin gravity reasserted itself and the four of us hit the deck. I followed Esteban's example and put the submachine gun's butt against my shoulder with my view lined down the weapon's sights. The door to the lift opened and we stepped out into the hall.

"Oh, thank God," someone said, and rushed into the lift with a dozen others. Harper and George were among the mix.

"Get to the capsules," Deidrick instructed them. "Captain's orders."

A man at the front of the lift nodded and closed the doors. I felt a sudden wave of panic now that the exit was closed and forced myself to take a series of slow breaths.

Esteban waved ahead and led us down the hall in formation. We could hear our fellow crew members in distress, and so we headed for the noise. We reached a junction in the hall by the Med Bay and found a squad of Isopteran soldiers standing over a collection of several human bodies, guns laying on the ground beside them. Team two was down, but in that moment, the enemy appeared more curious than hostile over the outcome, staring lost as if in deep thought at the bodies they had slaughtered. I did not share their dispassion. Bile rose from my stomach and I doubled over. There was no time for this, I had to tamp it down.

"Get them," Esteban growled, and we opened fire, ripping apart the unaware Isopteran squad.

Of the five of them, three didn't have a chance. The wall behind where they stood was soon an atramentous impasto of minced organs and viscous fluid. The remaining two scuttled into cover around the corner of a junction, a ring of chittering exchanged between them.

Esteban and Deidrick split up as if on cue, Esteban putting himself against the left wall, Deidrick taking the right. James shouted at my back and I spun around. From our rear came a flurry of white-hot projectiles. I threw myself onto the ground and rolled towards the wall, attempting to make my way to a door. James stood tall, taking slow steps towards the oncoming enemy, their weapons' fire zipping past him without hitting. The Isoptera were a long way down the habitat ring, and they didn't have the best aim.

"Get down!" I said, but he didn't listen.

A moment later, something rolled its way into our group, made of the same light absorbing material as the cube had been. I tossed my MJ-6 on the ground and scurried over to it, all too aware I was in the open. I took hold of the ball and found it weighed about as much as a portable instrument kit, twenty kilos at least, yet it was no bigger than my fist. The surface sizzled and I felt a shock go through my palm, forcing me to drop it back on the deck.

"Bruh, get rid of it," Deidrick called, then laid down a line of suppressive fire, attempting to keep the enemies before us from advancing.

I reached into a pocket and removed a cloth I had used to clean a filter earlier that day, then wrapped the weapon with it. The light of gunfire, human and alien, flashed all around me. I gripped the ball and groaned, feeling the dampened electrical charge dance through my skin. As heavy as the object was, all I could think to do was spin around in circles and then let go like someone competing at hammer throw. The ball went soaring up the hall to land in the junction Esteban and Deidrick were covering. They exchanged a look and took off running towards James and I.

"In here," Deidrick said as he yanked us into a set of quarters by the fronts of our jumpsuits.

I tripped over my feet and fell face first onto a living room couch. An instant later, there was a flash of light and heat from the hall.

We stood and looked at where it had fallen. There were no holes in the bulkhead or deck, but everything was singed black in a starburst pattern originating where the object had landed. The remains of our fallen crew members and the Isoptera were gone, all organic matter vaporized in a flash. I finally understood their weapons. These were specifically designed for boarding ships and taking control, not destroying them. They were energy weapons that would not pierce the bulkhead but destroy organic matter. Weapons that would kill without endangering those who boarded with the risk of decompression.

A ping came through on my implants and I connected. James glanced to me as if he had received one as well.

"Milo?" Dad asked, his transmission glitchy as his signal experienced severe packet loss. *"Where are you?"*

"In the habitat ring. Are you okay?"

"Your mom and I are pinned down in our quarters. Went back to get a few items before getting off the ship and they caught us."

My heart gave a start. For an instant it was hard to breathe. Was it the alien weapon or something else?

"Okay," I replied. "I'm on my way."

"Please hurry, Son. They're breaking in."

"We got to move," Esteban said, and leaned out into the hall, barrel first. He squeezed off a series of rounds and drew himself back in, panting. "That other group's on us. Team three isn't responding neither. No backup."

"They don't matter, no one does," James blurted out of nowhere. "I've got to go save Mom… Dr. Reed. She's hiding in the network room."

"We'll get to her when we can, bruh," Deidrick said. "But we got to eliminate the threat first. Tell her to keep the door locked."

He shook his head. "I can get to her, I just need help. Milo. Come with me. Please. Come with me."

"I can't." My body slumped and I swallowed hard. "Mom and Dad are in trouble. I have to help them."

Esteban raised his hands in a gesture of exasperation. "Damn it, you two. This isn't time to be chasin' down your parents. They're all grown up, and we got people to protect not fifteen feet away, not just them. We don't get to pick cherries and all that."

"But they're my family," I said.

"Don't you see by now," Deidrick whirled on me. "We're all your family, bruh."

The sound of gunfire and screams returned. We had to get a move on.

"Milo," James looked me in the eyes, and I could see the tiny muscles just above his cheekbone quiver, "you coming with me or not? I need help saving Mom. I can't do this alone. How long have we been friends? I need your help. I can't do this alone."

"I—I'm sorry," I said, then turned and took off running.

"Milo!" Esteban roared, and reached out with one hand, but too slow to stop me.

Gunfire rained down on me from up the hall. My parents may not have been all they could have been, but they were still my blood. I wasn't leaving them to die, not if I had a chance to save them.

Halls and doors and emergency lights blurred past, the once-familiar habitation ring now a war zone. There were bodies and people fleeing, scorch marks along the bulkhead and trails of blood on the ground. It was more than I could process at the time, so I didn't. A piece of me dissociated. I skidded around a corner and came face to face with an Isopteran soldier, the creature too close for me to fire my weapon. Before I could step back, or get myself in a better position, he swung the tube held in his claws and clipped me on the chin. I went sprawling back, my weapon clattering to the floor. Blood poured down from where my skin had split open.

It placed the weapon it carried into a holster and approached me slowly, its claws and pincers working. I scrambled to get onto my feet, and it took hold of my leg, dragging me in. Its claws began to dig through my jumpsuit into my calves. I gave a wordless shout and tried to flee, but its grip was too much. This creature was too strong.

"Get off me," I shouted, and began beating at its arms. It was unfazed by my effort.

Once I was close enough, it leaned in, putting its facial pincers against my cheek. The chitinous flesh was cold and hard and smelled of copper. Blood was on its face and mouth. It had been feeding, feeding on humans, feeding on my extended family.

It drove its claws into my shoulders and legs, and I screamed for help that did not come, the pain washing all other senses away. I blinked and found my vision blurring with moisture. What can I do? What can I…

I reached out and felt something cold and black and square hanging from its belt. I felt around the object until something began to give. A button. I pressed hard as I could, and in an instant, the Isopteran soldier was no more, a set of hyperspatial claws having extended and taken hold of its form to compress it into a space no larger than a basketball.

The cube clattered to the deck and I let out a breath. I sat there for a moment collecting myself. I sent a ping for anyone to help and got no response. It was stupid to go out and try and help them on my own. Stupid.

The barrel of my rifle acted as a crutch to help me stand, and I hobbled down the hall towards my parents' last location. All I could do was try and save them, but at this point I wasn't sure I could even save myself. Blood covered my jumpsuit where the creature had cut into my soft flesh. My body throbbed with waves of sharp, burning pain.

I could see a group of half a dozen familiar faces up ahead. I hobbled towards them and gave a shout of hello.

Someone waved back, and there was a flash of light.

The ceiling fell away, floor rushing up to meet the back of my skull. The world went hazy. Were they still there? I couldn't hear anything. I couldn't feel anything. My body was numb, darkness creeping in at the edges of reality.

I found myself drifting in a space between dimensions, third and fourth walls as thin as water vapor. Images of myself persisted, yet I knew it was a mirage, a vision. I could do things, see places, but I could not get my body to respond. We, the *Vasco* and crew, were suspended in nothingness, a void thick as cooling gel, a viscous medium of black.

Where were Mom and Dad?

Where were the rest of the crew?

Where was Shelly?

It was hard to say how much time passed, but at some point, I became aware I was moving. There was little pain to inform me if this was good or bad. Perhaps I was next on the menu. Perhaps my entire life had been a dream.

My eyes creaked opened for an instant, saw flashes of light, then closed. Sleep was good. Maybe it was time to sleep forever.

I felt a prick on my arm and awareness flooded back into me along with a deluge of pain. It took me a moment to realize I was no longer aboard the *Vasco Da Gama*. I was in a closed space filled with acceleration chairs and controls. In those broken moments, I had been transported onto one of the capsules.

Anger rose in my chest, restrained by the five-point harness of an acceleration chair. Esteban sat across from me. A pilot was at the main controls.

"What are you doing!" I shouted at them. "We left them."

"There was no other option," Esteban replied while checking his harness. "We aren't the only capsule, no?"

I glanced down to find I'd been buckled in. I fumbled to unclip my belt and get out, but Esteban reached back and put a hand over mine.

"Can't do it, *amigo*," he said. "It's bad, we got to get out."

Our pilot, Henry Brittan, the father of Shelly's one-time boyfriend Lance, coughed into his hand, the sound wet and labored. "He's right. This went shit sideways fast. We can only save as many as we can."

"Why only three of us?" I pressed. "Where's Deidrick? James? Where are my parents?"

Where's Shelly?

"All we could get before we were cut off," Henry said. "After you went down for a nap, they dropped three more of those beetle breaching pods on us. The *Vasco Da Gama* is crawling with them." He gave another cough, flicked a series of switches, and the capsule sputtered.

"But… my family."

Esteban gave me a consoling look. "Ain't over yet, *amigo*. We're all headed to the same where."

Henry worked his way down a checklist and put his hands on a set of control sticks. "Here we go."

My stomach dropped as the capsule fell away from the *Vasco Da Gama*. Through a tiny window on my right I watched our home grow smaller, the white spoke and spear which had been my entire world now cast in the blossoming crimson light of orbital dawn. She was helpless, her skin crawling with golden beetles, plumes of gas bleeding from all along her hull. I scrubbed the moisture from my eyes.

"*Ay dios mio*," Esteban exhaled. "Bastards drew us in to have for dinner."

Henry coughed again, then tapped the control sticks. The capsule pitched and spun. I became nauseous, stomach twisting at the shift in inertia.

"It doesn't feel right," Henry wheezed.

"No, it doesn't. *Muy malo.*"

"None of this makes—sense. We might… We, em…" his words trailed off as he slumped over in his acceleration chair.

"Oh, shit," Esteban growled, then started to unbuckle himself. "Henry, get up. Get up."

An alarm wailed, and red lights blinked across the main controls. Proximity alarm.

"We're going to hit it. Esteban, do something."

"I don't know what." He gave Henry a shake. "Wake up, my friend. *Amigo*, we can't pilot for shit."

Through the window came a flash of white light. The *Vasco Da Gama* began to break apart, its spine snapping in two, habitat ring twisting and cracking. The base materials of the ship bisected and grew smaller, more numerous, a scattering mass of metal and ceramic. It was impossible to tell among the madness what was debris and what might be additional capsules.

"Wake up!" Esteban shouted.

Henry lolled in his chair, his eyes blinking as if he wanted to wake, but did not have the energy. The alarm screamed on, the display beside it showing our relative velocity to the Foundry of twenty thousand kilometers per hour. At that speed, we would be rendered into dust upon its surface.

"Ten seconds to impact," I said.

"Wake up Henry!"

"Six."

Henry mumbled and reached for empty air, trails of blood gleaming at the edge of his lips.

"Four."

"*Ay Dios mio.*"

"Two."

I squeezed my eyes shut, tensing as if this instinct would help me survive the impact. A fresh alarm went off and I opened my eyes again. The screen displaying our velocity jumped from twenty thousand to ten thousand to five, four, three. One moment we were traveling at orbital velocity, the next, a gentle drive through town on a Sunday. Whether it was for self-defense, or to protect the passengers, the Foundry had reached out and taken hold of our fragile craft with invisible fingers.

"It's pulling us in," I said, as the light beaming through our window vanished, the structure having swallowed our tiny capsule whole.

We had made it out of the chaos alive.

We were inside the Foundry.

CHAPTER 20

"He's dead," Esteban said, sitting the portable defibrillator to the side. He had given it his all, bandaged the pilot's wounds, performed CPR, attempted to restart his failing heart. It hadn't been enough. "He lost too much blood and his body just gave out. I doubt Dr. Reed could have done much more. Sorry, *amigo*."

"He was a hero, and he got us here," I said, and for some reason I put a hand on Henry's shoulder. I didn't really know the man, but it pained me to see him pass. It pained me to see anyone pass. Death was not something I considered often. Henry was a part of the crew, a fixture in our shifting world-scape. Now he was gone, and I could only hope he was the last. "What now?"

Esteban took the copilot's seat and began to try and reactivate comms. For all the extraordinary events we'd been thrust into, neither of us had mentioned that now that the capsule was inside the Foundry, there was gravity.

The *right* level of gravity.

"We've got to try and get in touch with the rest, ya? Your implants connecting to anythin'?"

"Just the capsule."

"Damn. Same."

"I hope everyone else is okay."

"Me too, ya?"

I reached out again with my implants, hoping beyond hope I might find a fresh signal, then felt something brush against my perception. It wasn't a network connection as I would normally have described it, but it was a something. Something blue and pink and organized. It was familiar, like that feeling we got when listening to the signal which brought us here. I focused on this impression, feeling around its edges for a virtual shape.

We looked to one another and blinked.

"What the hell was that?" Esteban gave a shiver. "You feel it?"

"Yeah."

The escape hatch at the back of the capsule started calling to me. It was okay to open it. How did I know it was okay to open it? I had no concerns with breathable air on the other side. We could forgo environment suits, take a stroll without a care.

Where did this information come from? Why did it give me such peace?

Before I knew what I was doing, my hand was on the controls opening the hatch. Esteban watched in surprise but did not stop me. The exit hatch gave a hiss and the door swung open, revealing a spacious hallway with smooth golden walls and white decking. I stepped over the lip of the opening and drew a breath of clean, alien air.

"Hello?" I called, my voice echoing. "Hello? Anyone here?"

Esteban appeared beside me, offering me my weapon. I took it back but left it hanging over my shoulder.

The strange color and shape appeared in my mind again, and then the floor began to glow in sequence, cutting a path ahead like the locator lights had on the *Vasco Da Gama.*

"Come on." Esteban took the lead.

The inside of the Foundry was cool yet comfortable, no wind or apparent air circulation other than what we felt while moving. With all the machinery seen from the outside, the great forges and assemblers, I expected the interior to be loud, the entirety of this structure vibrating as it churned out starships by the hundreds. Yet it was quiet, like the lobby of an abandoned hospital, clean with smooth angles and endless views, no visible doorways down the gold and white passages.

Trails of light dashed ahead, taking us down series after series of passages seemingly miles long. Did we take a left, and then a right? Or two rights, then a left? Anxiety seeped into my chest and shoulders, tightening the muscles. We had no idea how to get back to the capsule, no trail of breadcrumbs left at our heels. If we felt the need to escape, there was no clear path. Then again, what good would a capsule do? Controlled falling, which is what they did best, would not help us now. Our home was destroyed, our ship disassembled. We were committed.

A half dozen paces ahead, a featureless wall resolved itself into a doorway. We paused in our steps, watching as a small room appeared on the other side of the opening. I gave Esteban a worried look and he shook his head. What else were we to do? We had been at the mercy of the Foundry's tractor force for more than a year. Perhaps now it would give us some answers. Answers like, where was my family and the rest of the crew? Like, what were its true intentions?

We crossed over the threshold and entered the room, breath held. It was like stepping into a photo studio, light coming from everywhere and nowhere, shadows on our face and clothes perfectly brushed into non-existence by diffused, white light. This made discerning the edges of the room nearly impossible. We could see little more than a faint grey line at its corners, tracing its vertices with creation's finest pencil.

Up from the floor oozed a set of short, simple chairs, each one a single piece of white polymer. From the color and the shape of the impression left inside my head, I knew that they were safe to sit on.

"You first." Esteban gestured at the chair on the right.

I obliged. The seat was soft, comfortable. I hadn't realized how far we had walked until that instant. It was good to rest.

"Please," a word came through our implants. For an instant I thought it might be someone from the *Vasco's* crew calling out, but then it came again. *"Please."* The voice was not human.

"Hello?" I asked.

A digital speaker in the room declared, *"Please stand by."*

The shapes in my mind blossomed into a flurry of colors and sound. There was no pain at this explosion, nor was it comfortable. It was as if my neurons were working overtime, data being ripped from them by a thirsty network connection. I gave a shocked groan and held tight to the chair, unable to move. Esteban glanced over at me, his eyes wide, muscles frozen.

From out of the chair a silver fluid appeared, rushing over and into the rips of my jumpsuit to make contact with my injured flesh. The pain in my body began to recede, and the sting of my cuts vanished. Once it was done, the liquid flowed out the bottom of my jumpsuit pants into the floor and I felt control return to my body.

"You okay?" Esteban asked, his attention focused on his hands.

"I—"

"Hello!" the room said, a little too excited given the circumstance. *"Welcome to the Foundry."*

"Hello?"

"Hello!" it replied, emulating my tone if not my inflection.

Esteban scratched the back of his head. "I think it's stuck, ya?"

"Stuck?" it asked. *"Yes, the Foundry is stuck in position over what you refer to as Barnard's Star 3. The Foundry is in stationary freefall."*

I leaned forward in my chair. "What are you? Where are our friends? My family?"

"Due to the low bandwidth of voice communication, please limit queries to one at a time."

"Where are the other humans?" Esteban blurted. "Are they safe?"

"No response can be given at this time. Hostile situation unresolved. Scavenger species designated by humans as Isoptera are still a threat. Please try your inquiry again later."

"So those things are still out there." I ground my teeth. "Did you send them?"

"Hostile situation not the result of the Foundry's actions. The Foundry apologizes for any inconvenience. Intervention by the Foundry is not permitted except only within designated protection zones."

"Like close to the Foundry itself?"

"Correct."

"I sure hope everyone is okay," I said under my breath, and thought about the last real conversation I had with my parents. If I could take what I said back, I would.

"No information available at this time. Please try again later."

"Come on, asshole." Esteban stood up and began to pace the room in thought. "Tell us. How many other humans can there be on this thing?"

"No information available at this time. Please try again later."

The doorway we had entered through began to close, dissolving into the featureless walls like melting plastic. Esteban rushed over, palms slapping against the surface where it had been.

"Do not be alarmed," the Foundry said. *"The door may be opened at a verbal command. It is closed as of now for security reasons."*

"Dios mio, mas Isoptera?"

"Yes. More Isoptera." A silent moment passed, and the Foundry spoke again. *"Would you like refreshments as you wait?"*

I gave Esteban a uncertain look. "Refreshments?"

A table appeared between our chairs with a set of slender glasses filled three quarters of the way with water. Beside them sat a collection of tea cakes covered in frosting, each carefully arrayed along the edge of a porcelain plate.

Esteban strolled over and snatched up one of the cakes. "Now that's weird." He put it to his nose and then held it up to the light.

"And the rest of this isn't?" I sniffed the water.

"It is all safe, designed to meet your dietary and metabolic requirements," the Foundry said. *"No toxic chemicals or harmful biproducts."*

"What in the hell are you?" I mused, not expecting an answer.

"I the hell am the Foundry. I protect life."

Esteban dropped the tea cake back onto the plate and let out a belly laugh. I'd never heard him laugh like that. Amused. Manic. Unstable.

I rubbed my face with my palms, attempting to clear my mind. The table beside me shifted for an instant, and then a cup of steaming, black liquid appeared. "Wait, what? Is that coffee?"

"It is a synthetic analog to the substance you refer to as coffee, its taste, texture, and makeup copied from your memories."

"The implants," Esteban hissed after he had collected his breath once again. "That's what was happening. It was linking up to us."

I took a sip of the coffee and marveled at the taste. It was good. So good. "So that's why it couldn't communicate with us until now? It needed more information."

"Correct," the Foundry replied, its tone regretful. *"While the Foundry desired to make contact before this cycle, a lack of data made this impossible. Please excuse our ambiguity."*

Esteban snatched up one of the tea cakes and took a bite. He gave a satisfied grin at the taste. "You sure do give lots of apologies. You guilty?"

"The Foundry does not feel guilt."

"So, who's in charge?"

"The Foundry is here to protect life."

"Yeah, yous said that before. I just saw friends of mine die, ya? Havin' a bit of an out of body experience. People I've known most of my adult life. How's that for protect?"

"The Foundry did not order their deaths. The Foundry protected Milo and Esteban. The Foundry works at this moment to protect others."

"Then where are they!" I slammed my coffee mug down on the table, splashing the contents and making a mess. What had spilled instantly began to absorb into the table, leaving it clean. My hands shook. "Here we are having cakes and coffee and my friends and family are in mortal danger. This is wrong. It's all wrong."

"No response can be given at this time. Please try again later."

"Maybe we should just go walkabout the station and have look for them," Esteban suggested, putting a hand on my shoulder. "How big is the interior? Nothin's infinite."

"The Foundry's internal surface area is equal to ninety-three thousand, seven hundred and fifty cubic kilometers. At an average pace of five kilometers an hour it would take the two of you approximately thirteen uninterrupted days to complete this search. Taking rest and refreshment into account, however, it would require—"

"Fine, fine," he cut in before it went on. "So that might not work best."

All we had gone through, traveling the great distances between Sol and Barnard's Star, the attack, and here we were, being stonewalled by a simple policy we could not override. I scratched at the back of my neck and attempted to find a solution. I didn't realize I'd been flashing my teeth at the floor until my mouth felt dry.

"How is it you want to protect life, yet you deny us information?"

"Our imperative is to replace. Create an even playing field. This makes it safer for all species involved."

Esteban and I shared an enlightened look.

"You what?" I pressed. "What do you replace?"

"Each starfaring species who reaches the Foundry is given new, most often better ships to replace their individual creations. We cannot guarantee the safety of all sentient life in the galaxy unless each species is given no advantage."

"So, a species shows up in their old, busted tin hooptie," Esteban mused, "and you give 'em a Porsche?"

"Colloquialism not found."

I shook my head. "You take their old ships and make them new. Give them the same level of technology."

"Correct."

"Who's in charge of this process?"

"Information not found."

"What? You don't know who's in charge of you?"

"Information not found."

"Is this what happened to the *Vasco Da Gama*? Were people still on board?"

"No active human life was aboard the Vasco Da Gama *when disassembly began."*

Esteban growled, his words meant only to process his thoughts, "That's either good or *muy, muy malo.*"

I stared off into space, thinking. "How do we go about getting a ship to replace ours?"

"Due to the current hostile situation, and production queue, a new craft would not be available for two cycles. One Earth year."

Without shame, Esteban bit into another tea cake and took a sip of water. "Well shit, that is long wait."

"Is it free?" I asked.

"Nothing is free. There is a cost to all things. We ask for a donation."

"We? I thought you referred to yourself as the Foundry."

"We ask for a donation."

"Okay…" I let the word drag out. "I'll bite. What is the donation? How do we get a ship?"

A flash of light appeared along the wall ahead of me. I was compelled to stand and allow a series of blue lasers to scan my body. For the first time since having my implants installed, I had mixed feelings over their presence in my head. Maybe Mom was right. I was pretty sure the facility was hacking me on a cerebral level.

"Analysis complete," the Foundry replied. *"To replace your exploration ship, the cost would be the shortest appendage on the right side of your body, as well as the long one on your left. A small portion of matter from your cognitive center and several pints of blood will also be required."*

My eyes widened. "I'm sorry, what? What did you ask for?"

Esteban rubbed at his stubbly chin with the back of his hand. "I think it just asked yous for an arm and leg and then some."

"References match," the Foundry replied.

"But I need those things," I said. "To, you know, function."

"Each piece of donated biomass will be replaced by comparable mechanical prosthetics or possible bio replacements grown from stem cell cultures."

"That's asking a lot."

"Building a ship to support over four hundred human lives is a lot."

I turned to look at Esteban, shaking my head. He held up his hands to accept my answer. There was no way to do what it wanted at this time. My body was my body. Things were weird enough as it was. I wasn't planning on going post-human anytime soon.

I adjusted my approach.

"Look, you've been a good host," I told the Foundry, tamping down my mounting anxiety. "I just want to find my friends and family. At this time, I cannot pay your price for a ship, and I don't know what good it would do if we can't find them anyways. Are they safe?"

The Foundry paused for a moment as if thinking this over.

"Your genetic data does not closely match the leader of the remaining group."

"What do you mean?"

Esteban mouthed, *'The captain'.*

"Okay," I said. "So, if I was a match you would give more information."

"Likelihood high."

"The leader of the other group of humans is alive. Are there many others with him?"

"Yes."

"Good. Can you tell me where they are?"

"Your genetic data does not closely match the leader of remaining group."

"Then can you point us in their direction? As we have already discussed, this is a big station."

"Your genetic data does not closely match the leader of remaining group."

"Fuck, dude."

"Inquiry unclear. Do you wish for the Foundry to provide a female analog to your Shelly so that you may enjoy a satisfying f—"

"No!" I raised my hands in protest. "No! No! No!" This was a prospect both terrifying and embarrassing. What couldn't this facility create out of almost nothing?

"As you wish," the Foundry conceded.

We were getting nowhere. I was trapped in a room with one other, who for all I knew, was the only other living human within six light years. Our home had been attacked and disassembled. Now this thing was trying to placate my needs. My hands shook. Keeping my composure was...

I shot up and ran over to the wall, shouting, "Why can't you just help us? You're like a goddamned, well, god! Do you like being divine? Have mercy on us then, if you like to hear it that way. Tell me what I need to know! Where are my friends and family? Where are the rest of the humans who came with me aboard the *Vasco Da Gama!* Tell me, damn you, tell me!"

The Foundry did not respond.

"Tell me!" I hammered my fists against the wall, hoping to shake something loose. It felt like banging cold marble with the meat of my hands.

Esteban came over, whispering, "I don't see this thin' helping us straight." He put an arm around my shoulder and gave a gentle squeeze. "Keep your wits, *amigo.*"

I gave a nod and took several slow breaths. It took some time to put my rational mind back in the driver's seat. My adrenaline was running high, emotion all I felt, logic having fled to a cold, dark corner. My life had been too easy. Is that why all the scary shit had come at once?

For whatever reason, it still saw us as a potential threat to the others, or vice versa. It had a privacy protocol that kept the information under lock and key. There was no way I was giving up, but this was not going to give us what we wanted. I only hoped that by the time we found the rest that they would still be alive. Whatever the Isoptera were, I had a feeling they now had the taste for human flesh.

"Okay. What are our options?" I let out a long breath and wiped the moisture from my eyes. "I'm not willing to give up my body at this point just to have a ship. Is there a way to get a ship without giving a donation?"

"To avoid donation, you may remain on the Foundry and wait for the production queue to reach below twenty five percent."

"Which will take?"

"Estimated time, six hundred cycles."

"How long is cycle?" Esteban asked.

"Banard's Star 3 requires the equivalent of approximately half of an Earth year to complete an orbit."

"Okay," I breathed out, "so, not an option. Anything else? Searching the ship will take too long. Getting a new ship, again too long, and we won't have our friends."

"You may take the suspension transportation to the nearest xenohub, Cynosure."

"We can go somewhere else?" Esteban asked, leaning over the back of his chair. "Cynosure?" He rolled the word around on his lips. "Center."

"How far away is that?" I asked.

"Distance is not important under hyper suspension."

"As in stasis? Suspended animation?"

"Correct."

"Is it harmful?"

"Of the more than six thousand species who have undergone hyper suspension, only three have suffered negative consequences, and those in limited cases."

My mouth fell open. "That's a lot of species."

"Safer than taking a ferry," Esteban put in. "Those thin's flip."

I gave a nod. "Will the others be traveling there too? Can you tell us that much?"

"This is the only option given to the remainder of humans onboard the Foundry."

"So then, yes?"

The Foundry did not respond.

Esteban dug his fingers into the chair and narrowed his eyes in thought. "So, we take this suspension transport, ya? Meet our people there."

"And then what?"

"Fulfill the mission. We came here to find help for Earth. Save the planet from us an all. Find a way home after. Might be another way to get a ship and that."

A dark thought rose to the surface of my stormy mind. "What if the Isoptera follow us home?"

"Oh, shit."

"A likely outcome," the Foundry chimed in.

"Can you keep them from doing that?" I asked. "Can you help us save our world?"

"Not enough information available at this time."

"Fantastic."

"So, we figure that part out later," Esteban said. "Find loved ones first, ya?"

"Okay." I stood and faced the wall at the end of the room. For some reason it felt as if whatever artificial intelligence we were speaking with was standing behind it. "We've made our choice, take us to Cynosure."

"As you wish. Standby."

Without preamble, the lights of the room flickered out. I felt myself falling, falling into the dark with nothing to hold on to, stumbling into another moment where the Foundry's mercy was all that we had.

I was caught by something and felt myself shoot forward, a gentle breeze rushing over my face in a near-silent blackness.

"Please relax," the Foundry said, its voice calm.

"Esteban?" I called into the dark.

"I'm here, *amigo*," he replied, his voice nearby. "Just hold on."

"Okay." My finger dug into whatever was holding me in place, my thoughts fixed on those we were determined to find. Afraid or not, this wasn't over.

I had to believe they were alive and safe.

Alive and safe.

CHAPTER 21

For the first time in my adult life, I felt as if I'd been given a choice that was acted on, not just discussed. I had chosen not to give up parts of my body, and in exchange, the Foundry had whisked Esteban and I off into the dark that we might travel to a central meeting hub for extraterrestrials. Good or bad, it was my choice, and it was done.

After several minutes hurtling through the dark, barely able to sustain light conversation, we had found ourselves standing in a cramped space with six large tubes the length of compact cars along one wall, four of which were covered in domed pieces of frosted glass.

I approached the first of the tubes and rubbed at it with the back of my jumpsuit sleeve, clearing away the condensation. The form within was not human, or Isoptera. It was like a tree, slender branches and a thick, knotty trunk, but instead of roots at its base it had a bundle of multi-jointed legs covered in brown bark. At the top of its body where its branches extended was a bundle of eye stalks and a crooked mouth.

There was nothing I could do but shake my head. Two alien species seen within just a few hours of one another. Another six thousand, maybe more, ahead of us. What did this tree creature think? What was important to it? What sort of values did it fight for?

How did it communicate?

"See this?" Esteban said, gazing into another of the tubes, nose against the glass. "Ever read *Lord of the Rings*?"

I shook my head.

"Missed out. This like Treebeard here, sans the beard."

A porthole window caught my attention. I took two steps and looked to the planet below, Barnard's Star 3, a verdant wash of blue and green stretched out over thousands of archipelagos.

"Foundry?" I asked.

"Yes."

"Is this planet the Isoptera's home?"

"No."

"Do any intelligent species live here?"

"Yes."

"Who?"

"The Draegenintevargoque."

"The who?"

"The ones you will share a suspension bay with."

"Ahh yeah, the Ents," Esteban commented.

"Analogy sufficient."

I stood and watched the clouds drift below, a weather system moving from south to north. A collection of islands that within the next couple of hours, was in for heavy rain and winds. It was a world I had traveled so far to see but would almost certainly never step foot upon. A pity.

"It is time," the Foundry told us, and the two open tubes glowed at their edges. Drawers extended from their sides. *"Please leave your weapons in the approved containment area."*

Esteban gave me an uneasy look. I shrugged. What else could we do?

We placed our submachine guns in the drawers and climbed into the stasis tubes. I did my best not to think of them as caskets. Caskets didn't have glass windows or a cushy mattress, let alone a set of comfortable sheets.

"Make yourself at home as if you were taking a nap," the Foundry said. *"No matter what position you find yourself in when you fall into stasis, you will be comfortable and safe."*

"How far are we traveling?" I asked.

"Not far."

The tubes began to close, and Esteban vanished from view, my vision filled with nothing but rapidly cooling glass. I drew the provided blanket over my shoulder and laid on my side, head on a soft, grey pillow. Within moments, my anxiety began to recede. I relaxed, drifting off into slumber.

Time ceased to exist. Breaths. Ticks on a clock. The spin of a world, the orbit of its star, all was a singular, infinite moment. I dreamed a great and beautiful dream, its meaning and content as difficult to take hold of as grasping for water vapor with your hands. The Universe lay before me, vast and alive, each world pulsing like the light of neurons in an unthinkably powerful organism. Some of its mind was healthy and bright, other parts dark and diseased. It cried to live. To exist as all life had, for as long as it was able. It slipped away quick as it had come. Vapor in my fingers.

The only thought that escaped this endless vacuum was that of my mission. Find my parents. Find Shelly. Find my friends. Find the help we needed to save Earth.

It was good to sleep. To truly sleep.

I later found myself wishing I could have recalled the experience of interstellar travel within the Foundry's transport, but there was no true stimulus to draw upon. When it placed us in stasis, my brain fell to the very lowest levels of cognitive function. There were thoughts, sure, yet was that just my imagination? Did the fantastical part of my brain take control upon awakening and chain together a narrative to make sense of everything?

My head twitched; colors danced over neurons.

I was outside the craft. Esteban and I undocked from the great torus of the alien facility in a golden vessel shaped like a spur covered cigar, no sound accompanying our egress, no fanfare, just a sanguine twinkle of reddish light tracing its impenetrable hull.

A great flash came from the rear of the silent craft and then…

And then…

I have no idea.

What level of technology had these beings reached, other than simply hyper-advanced? Did they travel between stars by conventional means, or did they bend space-time? All was plausible.

At some point, disconnected from time, my heart rate began to increase, I felt my vision clear. I opened my eyes to see the glass covering the tube recede with hardly a noise, the dim stasis room resolving back into reality. Esteban sat up in his tube and gave me a half-hearted wave before letting out a long yawn. I stretched and popped my fingers then stepped out of the machine and went to the window. The view had changed. From the portal there was now nothing but the black of space with fresh sets of constellations in evidence.

How fast had we traveled? Had we broken the speed of light by some creative exploitation of physics? What sort of power source did the Foundry use?

Perhaps most importantly of all, I wondered how long had this taken. How much time had passed? Was it days or decades? Did a simple response seal away all opportunity for us to ever see a world we might call familiar?

What was done was done.

The other tubes began to open, clicks and hisses issuing from their seals. Esteban scrambled over to where he had stowed his weapon, but the drawer wouldn't open. He worked at the corners with his fingertips but could not pry it loose.

"I don't think we're supposed to have weapons here," I said.

Esteban let out a sigh. "How do we protect ourselves?"

From behind us, the tree-like creatures began to emerge from their tubes, sliding their bundles of legs over the sides and onto the ground. As they stood upright, they shook, and a kind of dust fell onto the floor. They faced one another for an instant, then turned to us and paused, before squeezing past towards the exit. The whole exchange felt a bit, well, awkward, as if we were the uncool kids they were trying not to acknowledge.

"That was weird," Esteban commented. "Like we were rats loitering at the mall."

"The mall?" I asked, feeling as if I had heard the word somewhere before. "Rats?"

"You really did grow up in space, ya?"

I gave a shrug. Was that such a bad thing?

"All passengers," the Foundry declared, *"please exit the transport ship."*

"I suppose this is our stop."

We followed the aliens down a long hall to an airlock. It was hard to tell where the ship was located, if we were set to board a landing craft or if we were docked to something larger. They went through first, the hatch closing before us. We waited. I found my stomach rumbling. When was the last time I had eaten?

"So, the plan," Esteban turned to face me, "we don't have any weapons, ya? We has to be careful. Get a read on this place and find where our people went."

"Did you feel us travel at all?" I asked.

"No. I took me a nap and woke here."

"Same," I replied. The airlock made a series of noises then quieted down. I watched Esteban put his ear against the white and gold hatch. "I get the feeling you're not an astronaut. Not originally at least."

"You got me." He flashed a toothy grin. "Served in the Spanish army back home."

"The Spanish have an army? You mean the Mexican army?"

He gave me a withering glance. "The Spanish have an army, in *España.* Who doesn't these days, what with the crisis? I was part of *El Unidad de Operaciones Especiales,* the eh, Naval Special Warfare force. Served for ten years before signing up to be on the expedition."

"You ever see combat?" My words came out perhaps a bit too excited.

"Milo, there is always a fight to be found. You may no can remember, being a kid, but it was bad when we left. Not enough to feed families, melting caps, high seas. It was getting where we all had beachfront property. Peoples were getting desperate."

"Feels like a lifetime away."

The airlock hatch made a click and lifted out of the way, a series of lights set into the floor inviting us inside.

I regarded the space before taking a step. "I don't see signs the Draeg were killed in here."

"Already throwing out nick names?"

"Easier than, what was it? Draegeninwhatever?"

"Good point."

"Ready?"

"Only one way forward."

We stepped into the airlock, unarmed and unprepared. The hatch closed and the air cycled. A moment passed, and then a pair of silver tentacles extended from the wall with needles at their tips. I took a leap back and fled the approaching object.

"Do not be alarmed," the Foundry boomed, and the needle paused. *"All visitors of Cynosure and other Foundry facilities must be given their universal inoculation."*

"Inoculation?" Esteban had the tentacle pursuing him gripped in his left hand, its needle pointed at the ceiling. "What's in it?"

"Custom designed nano-machines powered by the movement of your blood. During your suspension we scanned all micro-biological matter in your body to determine which were required, and which were not. The universal inoculant will seek out foreign bacteria, micro-organisms and viruses, neutralizing them before they can cause harm."

"So, I won't get sick, ya?" Esteban poked out his lip as he considered this idea. "I hope they done itch."

"Are they harmful?" I asked. "Will there be side effects?"

"Other human groups have shown no signs of ill effects."

"Others? They're here?"

"Additional groups of humans arrived before this transport."

I raised my hands in surrender. "Inoculate me."

The tentacle lashed out and pierced the skin of my right shoulder. There was hardly a prick and it was over.

"That's all?" I asked, and the Foundry did not reply.

The airlock hatch irised open and white light poured into the golden ship. The exterior world flashed against my vision, a flurry of color and activity, distance and movement. My legs went weak, my brain struggling to resolve all that was in view. It was too much to process all at once.

"We're not in Kansas anymore," Esteban mumbled and gave me a slap on the back. "Come on. Stick with me, *amigo*."

We took a step out of the ship and onto the street, boots scuffing a mix of hard-packed dirt and half-gold tiles, the space crowded with every kind of life, so many genotypes in evidence it would boggle even the greatest imagination. There were bipeds, insect people, gliding tanks filled with water with nothing but tentacles and eyes within, species that looked both organic and inorganic, marriages of flesh and machine. All melded together in a boiling mass of movement. On the left and right of the street, brutalist structures towered in neat rows, stretching fifty and sixty stories high with gilded windows and brilliant white light outlining their features. They were golden towers etched with lines and symbols and alien sigils, the languages of thousands of species and a reflection of billions of years of culture.

I wobbled for an instant and looked up, swallowing down my discomfort. We were not on a planet but orbiting one. Cynosure was a dome strapped to a rock, and above the city's chaos hung a swirling, green and red gas giant, so close it felt as if it could be touched. My head flipped end over end at the scale, just like those first days riding motorcycles with Dad in the Montana environment. My brain was not adjusted to such expansive, open spaces. Instinct called me back to the safety of the airlock, the safety of a closed ship, a cave.

"Whoa, whoa," Esteban said, and steadied my shoulder with a hand. "Keep it together, *amigo*."

I doubled over, palms pressing on my stomach. "I think I'm going to puke."

"Might want to find a waste bin first."

My eyes shut and I took a set of deep breaths. Once the wave of nausea had passed, I opened them once more and allowed myself to process what I could, attempting smaller pieces of the scene at a time.

"You alright?" Esteban asked.

"*Eu estou bem*," I said under my breath. "*Só preciso de um momento.*"

"*Que? No sey.*"

"Sorry. I said I'm good."

"You, eh, speak something not English? Like I almost recognize."

"Portuguese. Mom's family is from Brazil. Comes out at weird times."

"Ah. I see. It's like the almost-Spanish, ya?"

"You're the almost-Spanish."

"Hey now, *el Spanglish es real, amigo.*"

I swallowed down my sick and took a clarifying breath of cool, clean air. After years of breathing the same oxygen, recycled molecules sent through processing a thousand times, I realized that this air was different. It had a flavor to it, a taste which rested at the back of my throat, lacking the institutional tang of spaceflight.

"I'm fine." I straightened my back. "I'm fine."

"I don't see no humans around here."

"Me either."

"Time we go ask around. You sure you good?"

I raised an open palm.

We left the false safety of the docking zone around the Foundry's ship, venturing into the boiling mass of alien biodiversity. A wall of fresh scents hit me; nothing unpleasant, but none familiar, either. They were sweet and spicy, damp and floral. In the streets, no one stopped to give us more than a glance, or even a bump against our shoulders. They were all headed somewhere and in quite a hurry.

"Maybe there's a market or something," Esteban suggested, then gestured towards a side-street. "People are always more friendly in markets."

"What do we have to trade?" I went through the pockets of my jumpsuit and found nothing but a hand terminal, a spare protein bar, and a tube of canofluid. I broke the protein bar in half, handing a piece of it to Esteban.

He gave a nod. "Depends on what they want."

We chose a direction at random and joined the flow of traffic, the airlock of the Foundry's suspension transport soon lost to view. There was no going back, we were here in Cynosure. I only hoped this was not a death sentence. My gaze fell as a series of creatures scurried around my feet through the chaos of mulling legs. They were as varied in number as were arthropods back on Earth, sticks and talons, hairy forelegs and cloth-wrapped stumps. Some propelled themselves on bundles of roots or frond-like macro cilia. I wondered what kind of evolutionary events had to occur for life to take these forms. How did these adaptations allow them to thrive on their homeworld?

A rumble came up beside me and broke my attention from the madness. A glass tank filled with murky water, more than twice my height, hovered beside my right flank, its destination along our same general path. Within the dark liquid a dozen white and black eyes appeared, each as large as my palm, their attention fixed on me.

"I think it likes you," Esteban said. "Say hello, ya?"

I paused in my progress and so did the massive tank. Furry mammals similar to lemurs threw up their hands and scurried around it, bothered that the thing had stopped in the middle of the road.

"Hello?" I called to the tank creature.

The eyes within stared at me, unblinking, tentacles writhing at the edges of the glass. Esteban leaned in front of some of the other passersby, attempting to make contact with no success.

"Umm, hi?" I tried waving a hand and felt like an imaginative child attempting to greet a bus-size aquarium. "My name is Milo Hughes."

The cluster of eyes receded into the dark waters and the tank turned to leave.

Esteban slapped me on the shoulder. "Didn't have to be a dick, Milo."

"What the hell did I do?"

"Wouldn't you like to know?"

"Yes! Yes, I would! I really would."

We pressed through the crowd, not interacting with the aliens but observing them, attempting to understand what they were doing and why. After walking a mile or so, it became clear that groups tended to stick together, interspecies communication a rarity. It was no wonder this would be the case, how many different cultures could even one world represent, let alone thousands? Would I find it easier to communicate with people in Spain, or Germany, or even with natives in Australia, even if I didn't speak the native language? I think so. Shared humanity went a long way.

"There we go." Esteban pointed to what appeared to be a sign hanging from one of the street corners. At first the lines written upon it were just that, lines, and then they reconfigured themselves and understanding came to me. "'Exchange'? That what it says?"

"Exchange."

"Sounds like a market to me."

As promised, we entered an ever-more crowded street of Cynosure lined with colorful shops and stalls. Goods were on display, crystals and cylinders of iridescent cloth, writhing piles of grubs and peculiar plants both fresh and dried. There were as many species in evidence as there were items for exchange, each engaged in active conversation of one kind or another with whoever stood before their place of business.

I sidled up to a stall where a series of wooden boxes were filled to the brim with shimmering blue stones, acting as if I were shopping, inspecting the wares with no idea what they were. Esteban perused the shop to my left.

From a canopy above the stall, a spherical, black mass lowered itself with the use of eight spider-like legs, each one as long as I was tall. Once it settled on the ground, it spun its body to reveal a collection of two-dozen glossy, black eyes, blinking them one at a time in a rippling left to right sequence. I took a step back and dropped one of the stones on the street, my breath catching.

"I—eh"

"Of no concern," I heard spoken in my head, and the creature scooped the stone off the ground with two of its slender legs, returning them to the box with an alacrity I would not have expected its appendages to possess. "New to Cynosure?"

I shook my head and reached for Esteban. The Foundry was somehow using our implants to act as a universal translator. Would have been nice to have been given a heads up.

"Eh?" he said and spun around. "Aye, aye."

"Exchange?" the creature asked, this time of both of us.

"What you exchange?" Esteban asked. "We need information, for now."

It lowered on its legs, the eyes of its mass regarding the street in a gesture that seemed to be intended as a bow. "Information is free, for now."

"Have you seen others like us?" I asked, holding my breath in hope.

"Like you? Two arms, two legs?"

"Human."

"An unfamiliar word."

"Meaty?" Esteban offered. "Soft skin? Hair on top like mines? Clothes made of synthetic fibers?"

The creature shook for an instant and extended one of its legs. "See the Exchange? Many species, few we all know."

I let out a sigh. It was true. We were expecting this, whatever this thing was, to identify a species it had never seen in a sea of species it had likely also never seen. We were in an airport concourse where each new flight brought peoples from entirely different worlds, not just countries, and not even the same ones from day to day at that. It was too much.

"I wish the Foundry had given us more direction," I mumbled, thinking I had kept the words out of my head, if that was even possible.

"Many wish this," it replied. "The Foundry protects life yet gives little direction. You must find your own way."

That phrase again. The Foundry protects life.

"Is it dangerous?" Esteban asked.

"Anything disruptive can be dangerous." The creature gestured one of its legs over the displayed goods. "Will you exchange?"

"Not today. I don't have anything to trade. What is it you offer?"

"An oddity from asteroids in my home system. Cericite."

"Is it just pretty, or does it have special qualities?"

"Pretty?" It blinked at us. "Cericite is piezoelectric."

"Ah. I see. I have nothing to offer." I tipped my head. "Thank you anyways."

"Thank you?"

"Come on," Esteban said, "look, through the crowd. There appears to be somethin' over there. Let's see what it is."

I turned to what had gotten his attention. Among the mass of alien life, there formed a bubble of open space the crowd refused to enter. We pushed our way ahead, rubbing shoulders with exotic, two-headed environmental suits and red-eyed creatures in black robes with heads like cauliflower. The source of the disturbance became clear.

At the center of the open space scuttled a trio of upright slugs, each as large as a horse, their dark skin like an oversized burlap sack draped over a thick, squirming mass. Several of the species strolling at the edge of the cordon gestured with their hands as if attempting to communicate with them. The slugs pivoted their eye stalks, regarding one after the next, then made a hissing sound, flailing the hardened forelegs extending from their chests. Some standing nearby retreated at the sound, yet others moved closer. The slug-people came to a halt near a stall of umber tubers and vermillion stalks, casually inspected what was on display, then turned to face me, all six of their eyestalks focused.

For an instant I thought I heard the word *human* in the back of my mind, but then it was gone, a quickly fading memory in a sea of overstimulation.

The one at the head of their group approached me, and I realized in horror that it did not touch the ground. Beneath its mass, it was supported by a swarm of thumb-length, winged insects, a trail of dead ones left in its wake. From a pulsing gland near their base, fresh slave insects were secreted, their tiny spines put to the test under their master's weight, a skittering sea of cockroaches.

I wasn't sure how much more weird my stomach could take. I had no memory of insects at all, and yet it seemed that the universe at large had a great need for them. I took a step back and felt Esteban rest his palms on my shoulder.

"I'm here, *amigo*," he mumbled. "I'm here."

The leader of the slugs closed the distance between us. I didn't know if I should stand my ground or flee. Perhaps it would have answers, it had taken an interest in me the others had not.

A tentacle extended from a hidden pocket of flesh below its forelegs. I felt compelled to reach out my hand and shake it in greeting. It only seemed polite.

"Hello," I said. "I am Milo Hughes." The crowd backed away from where we stood, the Exchange becoming quiet for an instant.

The tentacle shot out and wrapped around my wrist, sending a shock up my arm into my shoulder. I fought to pull away, but it had taken hold. Esteban rushed in, attempting to push the creature off so that it might let go, but he might as well have tried to push a house over. The slug did not budge.

Numbness filled my arm and chest, filtered into my neck and stomach. My legs began to go weak. I collapsed to the street.

"Let him go!" Esteban shouted, then slapped at one of its eye stalks.

It let out a screech, and the tentacle receded into the slug's body. It retreated from us, calling for its compatriots to follow. At least something was vulnerable.

"You okay?" Esteban asked as he watched them go.

"I don't know," I rubbed at my tingling wrist. "It burns like hell."

The crowds of the Exchange resumed their activities as if nothing untoward had happened. Just another pair of aliens who had had a strange encounter. Curious, yes, but nothing more.

"Hey, Foundry!" Esteban called out. "Hey. Foundry!"

There was no response.

"I'll be fine," I said, more for my own confidence than his. "I don't think they were trying to hurt me, they were just trying to understand me."

"Yeah, and sharks explore the world with their teeth." Esteban let out a sigh. "I'm getting tired, *amigo*, all the walking. We're gonna have to face facts. We needs a place to crash and something more than what we got in our pockets to eat. I don't see this being a place for that, not unless we got some scratch."

I rubbed at my arm, the skin inflamed where the thing had touched me. "Right."

"Hang in there and we'll figure it out. I don't think the Foundry brought us all this way to die. I still believe humans are here."

"Me too," I replied, thinking back to the word I thought I had heard in my head.

Whatever these slugs were, they knew what humans were. It had reached out and touched me just to be sure.

CHAPTER 22

The word *human* echoed over and over in my mind. That filthy creature, that slug, had said the word, I was sure of it. They were here somewhere, or had been, but my resolve was weakening. Every turn of this mission seemed to present another challenge, another roadblock between us and its completion.

It was strange that hope had been the spark of this mission. A hope that we might find help and save our world. A hope that others might have found a better way to exist and grow. A hope that we might be part of a wider universe full of possibility and new mysteries. On an intellectual level, I carried this hope with me. Trouble was, hope isn't intellectual. The more time that passed from the destruction of the *Vasco Da Gama*, the emptier my stomach became, the more this hope became an indulgent dream.

Cynosure was a remarkable collection of Foundry machines working in harmony beneath a dome orbiting a mighty gas giant. It was teeming with life from all over the galactic neighborhood, driven by commerce; and as I started to pay better attention, I realized, driven by communication and conversation between the species. Not all spoke using words as we did. Some used their hands, others what seemed to be systems like our implants. But by the way they carried themselves around one another, nods of heads, hand gestures, flexing muscles and folding sections of skin, it was clear a dialogue of some kind was occurring. I only wish I understood a sliver of it.

Esteban and I wandered for what felt like days, though it was likely only hours, briefly taking naps in the doorways of great skyscrapers as if we were vagrants, unable to enter these edifices even when others exited. Within the buildings, gold and silver robots waited, acting as bouncers. They placed their metallic hands gently on our shoulders and escorted us back into the street whenever we attempted to enter. We began to wonder what it took to have access, and could not come up with an answer. Cynosure was built for alien species to congregate and remain for long periods of time, yet there were no diplomatic quarters for the humans? Were we being slighted?

Where were the rest of the *Vasco Da Gama's* crew? The Foundry had said they made this choice, came here themselves. How would we find them? I needed to know. Were Mom and Dad okay? Was Shelly alive?

We stood before a building, our sentiment defeated, its surface studded with flashing white lights running in sequence, and I felt something splatter on my neck. The street around us was empty. I looked up.

Water fell from the sky in drops.

We were inside an artificial dome latched to a chunk of rock orbiting a gas giant, and it was raining. Raining…

"Damn," Esteban mumbled and pushed himself up against the building. "Didn't see that. When's the last time I felt it sprinkle?"

I couldn't recall what it was like, and as a result I stood in the middle of the street, water soaking my jumpsuit.

"*Amigo*, under here, no place to dry off." He took hold of my arm and pulled me under cover. "First rule of fighting in the field, ya? Keep your clothes dry, especially your socks."

"Why socks?"

"Because if they get wet, you get sick." He shook his head. "Time to rewrite the training books for exploration. Looks like ours made by a bunch of ignorant geniuses. It's okay, not your fault. That's why you have me."

"I'm thirsty," I said, reaching into the falling rain, droplets running over my fingers. "Is it safe to drink?"

Esteban cupped his hands into a bowl and collected some. He put it to his nose and gave a sniff, then downed the contents. "Taste like water. I think it's safe, falling rain is usually safe."

"Less contaminants?"

He nodded.

We drank the rain as best we could, but what we could collect with our leaky hands wasn't enough to sate our thirst, the excess pouring between our fingers and palms. Still, it was good to have a drink.

A moment earlier, it might have seemed strange to rain inside the dome, but the purpose soon became apparent. While many of the species fled indoors, retreating to their various buildings and supposed living quarters, others began to appear. From between the gaps in the street, segmented worms emerged into open air, their heads reaching dome-ward, their clawed faces opening to collect the bounty of the artificial sky. Among them were other creatures that seemed marine in origin, bumpy orange starfish with six points, bulb-shaped anemones festooned with flowing tentacles which pulsed as rain wicked off them, bioluminescent flickers running through their bodies. Somehow these actions came across like a pleasurable smile, a sigh of relief, a joyous conversation.

I wiped the excess moisture from my lips and marveled. Now that the streets were calm, I felt able to truly process the moment. Afraid or not, I was in an alien place surrounded by beautiful wonders.

The rain slacked and the strange creatures slinked back into hiding. The streets remained quiet, if not empty.

"Come on," Esteban said. "There has to be a place for us."

We roamed the various districts of Cynosure in the hope we might see a sign that said 'Human' or maybe 'Vacancy'. It was strange that the Foundry was so determined to meet our needs aboard the station, and yet so absent here. We were missing something; I was sure of it.

"Oh shit," Esteban said, and pulled me around a corner of the nearest building. "Shit."

"What? What is it?" I brushed his hands off of me.

"Isoptera, *amigo*. Two blocks down."

Why, oh why, had the Foundry taken our weapons? I poked my head out and took a look. He was right, there they were, a group of six Isoptera. A cold shiver ran down my spine, images of what had happened fresh in my memories. Of course they were here, but was it for us? From this distance, they looked to have no weapons, at least none in the variety of energy rifles or spatial compression grenades. This group was dressed in diaphanous robes of red and blue, their trains hanging just shy of the damp streets.

"We have to move to the edge of the city," Esteban declared. "They look important. See, they're talking to the others, ya?"

"What will we find at the edge of the city?"

Esteban gave a halfhearted shrug. "Less attention. Places others don't like to go."

"Does that apply here?"

"One way to find out. Always a bad part of town, and the rent is cheap."

"Do we have another option?"

"Stay around here and have the termites eat us, ya? Fall asleep from exhaustion?"

"What if we can find a building to get into? Maybe there's food inside."

"Ain' found it yet."

"Okay," I said and gave him a pat on the back. "So long as it gets us away from them."

On Esteban's instincts, we hurried through the crowds away from the center of Cynosure. His confidence was about all that kept me from freaking out in the moment. What the Isoptera had done aboard the *Vasco* was far too fresh in my mind. The smell of their carnage too raw. I couldn't tell how big the city was, but from the position of the planet overhead and the time that it took to cross, it had to be a good ten or fifteen miles. A map would have been nice. A greeting as we got off the ship to offer a little direction. Maybe an instructional pamphlet—*Ten places not to miss when visiting the Foundry!* We looked to be the only confused species dumped in this cosmic melting pot.

To my surprise, the further we traveled away from the center of activity, the less maintained the city became. Buildings began to show signs of wear. Trash lined the streets. We even came across the occasional corpse of what we could only assume had been sentient life. None of this gave me solace. Isoptera might not be here, but what was? What would find this an acceptable haunt?

"They're all the same," Esteban said as we entered the new district.

"What are?"

"Places like this." He gestured at the forgotten buildings, pieces of damaged fascia hanging from rusty eaves. "Universal. When you don't have anything to trade, you come here."

"I wouldn't know."

"Rich boy grew up in the suburbs," he replied, giving a wink.

"I don't know about rich, but yeah. I think they called Whispering Pines a planned community."

"Count yourself lucky, *amigo*. Baby Esteban didn't have that luxury."

"Neither did *minha avó.* "

"Que?"

"What's it in Spanish again… Abuela? Grandmother?"

"Oh, *si. Abuela.*"

"She was from Rio de Janeiro, lived in the *favelas*. I wouldn't call them slums, but they weren't exactly the best part of town."

"That the place with drug lords an' no law, kind of random lookin' houses, ya? No slum you say."

"Yes, and no. It's weird. She always spoke fondly of it, even though she was glad she moved to the United States. It had its dangers, sure, but there was a liveliness there too. People used what they had to get by. Art was everywhere. Music and dancing and food and laughter. She referred to her community as one of creative survivalists." I sighed and for the first time in years, missed Earth. She was long gone, just a vague memory in my heart, mostly Mom's words. "Anyways. It's a pretty scary place where people live on the edge. I did not have that kind of upbringing. I was insulated. Despite my mixed skin, the place I grew up was vanilla as hell."

"Necessity be the mother of invention," Esteban commented.

"No arguments there."

"Don' forget, *amigo*, not all that is beautiful shines."

"What about you," I asked, "where did you grow up?"

He paused, peeked around a corner, then waved to keep moving. "Lots of places, no real home. Most places around Madrid."

"Spain?"

He nodded. "It was okay for a long time, just me, *Mamá*, and an uncle down the street who fixed old clocks."

"So, a long time but not forever?"

"Nothin' is forever, Milo. Uncle Pepe caught a bad fever one year and couldn't shake it. When he passed, it was hard on *mi mamá*. She worked to make ends meet, odd jobs and all the hustle business that people got into those days, cloud driving, deliver groceries an' take-out. Economy got weird, flipped on its head, and people had to do anythin' to put food on the table."

I felt a stab of pain in my chest in anticipation. "What happened to her?"

He scratched at the back of his neck, stopped in the middle of the street and turned towards me, eyes on his feet. "She took a late-night rider during drunk surge hours, when playing taxi paid the most. A guy had too much and got aggressive. She said no, he said yes, next day I had police knocking on my door. I was just a fifteen-year-old kid, alone."

My jaw went slack. "Esteban, I—"

"It's okay, *amigo*." He raised his eyes to meet mine. "Haven't talked about her in long time. Seems fitting. She was a good woman and I miss her, ya? Wish she was here to see it all. She would have found this remarkable."

"What happened to you?"

We started walking again, heading deeper into the slums, dodging trash and other interplanetary detritus. There was no longer any sign of the Isoptera. At the end of the street, we spotted a building with open doors and made for it.

Esteban continued, "The state took me. I ran away and looked for *mi papi*."

"Your dad?"

"*Sí.* I knew he was out there, but for all I knew he lived in a place like this." He gestured towards the abandoned structure ahead. "Got bad on opioids after a work injury and ended up on the street. *Mamá* kicked him out when I was young. Everyone wants to know their *papi*, good or bad. I found mine, and he was a disappointment."

"Just as your mom had told you?"

"And worse. Turns out he had somethin' like six kids and wasn't enough parent for one. Still, you wonder why *papi* don't love you, it becomes personal."

I gave a sigh at that, then followed him into the dark building. Esteban removed a hand terminal and flicked on the flashlight. It wasn't a large structure, but it had a door we could barricade and a space to lay down. It was dry and as far as we could tell, empty.

"Here," he said. "Help me push this thing in front of the doorway. Maybe we can get some real sleep."

We lifted the broken door, laid it against the portal, groaning, then moved a square, desk-like piece of furniture across the room to press up against it.

The two of us found seats along the near wall and Esteban laid his hand terminal face down so that its light could act as a stand-in campfire.

"Did the state take you back?" I asked after a while.

He shook his head. "No. I found a way to forge my papers and joined the service. If *mi papi* couldn't give me direction, I hoped my flag would."

"Did it?"

A silent moment passed as Esteban considered his answer, eyebrows crowding the center of his face as he thought. "Being a soldier is no easy. You do as you told, and you learn discipline. Some good things happen, some bad. I stand for my country, my flag, my people, but I was asked to do things at times… well… A soldier doesn't get to choose his path. A soldier follows the direction of his leaders."

"Have you killed anyone? Humans, I mean."

Esteban hung his head and nodded. "It's no glorious. People just people." He let out a sigh and gave a crooked grin. "Enough memory lane, we're safe for now. Get some proper sleep, find answers tomorrow."

"And find something to eat," I mumbled while resting my hands on my empty belly.

"Wait till it rains again, maybe we eat worms."

"I don't think they'd appreciate that."

"I don't appreciate starving to death."

"Fair."

"I take first watch, *amigo*. Close your eyes. I'll put a timer on the hand terminal for six hours."

I gave a nod and laid down on the hard floor. For a moment I wanted to ask Esteban if it was okay to put my head in his lap, being that a leg was a more comfortable pillow than this cold slab, but then decided that might be weird. We might be becoming fast friends; but acting like girls having a sleepover was a bit much.

Sleep came without my assistance. My eyes fell shut and that was that. I had dreams of home, of the halls of the *Vasco Da Gama*, of delicious protein bars and of the faces of Shelly, Mom and Dad… Of James and the captain, Mary and Perry.

My leg itched and so I reached down to scratch it. As I did something sharp poked me on the tip of my right index finger and I snapped awake. It took a moment for my eyes to adjust in the unevenly lit room. Gathered around my feet were a dozen or more furry, black-and-white-striped mammals no more than two feet in height. Their eyes were massive, the light of Esteban's neglected hand terminal reflecting nocturnal, yellow tones. I had seen these creatures in the street earlier. The closest analog I could remember from my studies was that of lemurs, but that wasn't right either. These had not just little hands, but razor claws and long teeth, canines which protruded from their black ringed mouths like daggers.

They paused at my awakening, chittered among one another, then resumed their practiced task of tying my arms and legs. I struggled against their efforts.

"Esteban!" I called. "Wake up. Esteban! They're trying to take me."

My friend was fast asleep, snoring loud. Could someone be that tired?

"Esteban! Wake up, damn it."

One of the mammals broke free of the group and rushed my face, pulling my mouth wide and stuffing it with something spongy and wet. As I fought to scream, I bit down and released whatever liquid was contained in the medium. It was sour and rank, its taste gagging me as it tried to go down my throat.

They lifted me off the ground, taking me away from Esteban. As they swung me around, I tried to kick out and wake him up but missed. To silence me, several of the sadistic mammals dug their claws into my leg, puncturing my jumpsuit and the top layer of skin. My heart quickened and I felt hot all over. No matter how hard I struggled against the bindings, they would not budge.

I was out on the street, without my only friend, being carted off God knew where through the slums of Cynosure. What did these creatures want with me? It was clear their intentions were not friendly.

My teeth squeezed down on the sponge as I began to scream, its liquid dribbling over my lips, running down the side of my cheek and neck as if I had a hole in my mouth. No matter how hard I fought to make a sound, all that escaped was a muffled cry.

I didn't know what to do. I had been taken.

CHAPTER 23

There was no breaking the cable the furry little assholes had bound my arms and legs with. Trash lay around the neighborhood, and they had opted for a low-tech, low-cost solution in keeping me restrained. My ankles and wrists were hot as if someone had cut them, pain increasing as I fought to free myself. I wasn't giving up, even if the struggle was wearing me out.

What did these things want with me? Were they like the Isoptera, curious about what I might taste like? Or did they just want to rob me? It would have been easy to say this was the most terrified I had been in my life, but that might be a lie. Given all that had happened in the past few days, weeks, years, however long, I had been in constant danger. Was this just how it was living outside an interstellar craft? Was Earth this scary? How much had my parents sheltered me from?

They carried me in the opposite direction from which Esteban and I had come in the debris-strewn slums of the city. It was night, or what passed for a Cynosurian night, so the sky above was dark but for a glimmer of gold orbiting the gas giant. I focused on that single light for a moment, allowing myself to be distracted from my predicament. My eyes adjusted, and I swore I saw a golden ring in orbit. The scale of the object had to be incredible, a structure at least as large as the Foundry's facility at Barnard's Star 3. But what was it? Why did I care?

A flurry of terse conversation cut in and out over my implant channel, drawing me back into the moment. I bounced in the grip of the damned furbags and was taken into a dark building with open spaces, crates and boxes within. It was a warehouse, a storage facility.

Laughter skittered at the edge of my augmentation, the noise of my captors. One of them looked at me, its right eye black instead of yellow, and I watched as its expression scrunched like it had sucked on a lemon. It fiddled with a slip of glass the size of a hand terminal and the voices went away, my universal translator jammed.

They laid me on a table at the center of the dank warehouse and freed my hands for a moment, only to bind them to a metallic surface. The same was done to my legs. Despite my protests—words screamed through the sponge, punches and kicks given at any possible instant—they proceeded as if I were totally ineffectual. The crowd of lemur people strapped me to the table, arms and legs splayed, back spasming with pain. I turned my head to the right, cheek brushing cold metal, and saw a second table. Upon its surface lay a fly covered lump of meat, a series of gleaming silver objects jabbed into it. Beyond, a cable was strung between a set of crates like a clothesline, its length burdened with organic material of various shapes and sizes. These could only be alien organs, intestines, lungs, and liver. The implication drove me to renew my struggle, no matter the stress the bindings had placed on my worn ankles and wrists.

Liquid oozed out the sides of my mouth, the sponge choking me as I lay on my back.

The creatures gathered around me, gesticulating with their hands. Conversation began to bleed into my implants, this time taking the form of actual words, their tone nasally and staccato.

"What color inside?"

"Hard to say."

"We find out."

"We always find out."

"I say green."

"What reason green?"

"Green comes from its face. Thing it sniffs with."

"You think that life?"

"Might be life."

"Might be sick."

"We no get sick."

"Me knows this."

"Go get tools. All sharp?"

"Always sharp, me do work."

"Good, good. I cut first."

"No, I cut first."

"No, I!"

"It hears."

"Off, off."

Black Eye leaned towards me and removed the slip of glass once more, pushing buttons on its surface. The voices went away. Whatever it was the thing carried, it was blocking the Foundry's ability to translate.

It was clear what these creatures intended. I had to get away. How would Esteban find me before it was too late? Normally he could ping my implants so long as they were within range, but whatever device these creatures used, it blocked those signals.

A furbag appeared on my left with a curved blade nearly as long as its arm. One of its companions slapped the object from its hand, sending it clattering to the floor, then gave it an instrument with a finer edge. I fought to understand the words they were saying, screamed through the gagging sponge to communicate, but nothing came out. Again and again I made my best effort to no avail.

To my shock, something responded to my implant's desperate queries, and it was not the sadistic furbags. A shock of excitement hit me, and I found myself smiling. Deep in my right jumpsuit pocket, the nanofluid Perry and I had cooked up back on the ship pinged green, ready for instruction.

I pivoted my head left, then right, assessing the location of all my assailants, the back of my skull grinding against the table. They were caught in another argument. I could only guess it was over where to cut me first. Though my options might have been limited, at least now I had one.

I had two options before me, maybe three. I could use the nanofluid to cut my bindings and try to snag one of their blades before cutting the others holding me down. Or I could rush the jamming device, putting my faith in Esteban waking up and running to my aid. And if I was certain I might die, there was always revenge. I could at least take one of them down with me. A belly full of nanoscopic machines ripping you apart one cell at a time seemed pretty scary. But was I so malicious? Could I do that to another living thing, even if it had hurt me?

My deliberations didn't take long.

While the furbags argued over what instrument to use, I closed my eyes and mentally reached for the nanofluid. It wasn't an easy connection. The machines were useful for what they were, but not the best when it came to signal strength and processing. They were designed to be used within the web of a robust data-rich network, and yet these poor things only had my brain to power them.

I took hold of the material within my digital reach, its will a slippery eel gripped with shaky fingers.

The tube vibrated in my jumpsuit pocket and burst, its quicksilver contents oozing through a hole in my pants leg. Now that it was free of the glass tube, it was an effort to get it to move, every machine its own mind. I wished for a moment that I had designed these nano machines to work differently, created an ad hoc network they could have used in sequence instead of this peer-to-peer connection, but there was no time for that. I needed them to cut my bonds before these sadistic creatures cut me open.

On the other side of the table, the furbags settled on something long and slender with a barbed end. They tested it on the bare flesh of my left arm, leaving a gash of red just past my elbow. It was surprising that I felt no pain at all. The blade must have been more than razor sharp.

I swallowed and tried not to focus on the blood welling up from my arm, but rather on my means of escape. The quicksilver pool of nanofluid crawled its way along the side of the table beneath my back and out of sight, moving one, two, three centimeters at a time. Sweat beaded on my forehead and my mouth tasted of copper.

"Bleeds red," the words cut in over my implants and I broke concentration, the mass of nanofluid coming to a stop inches from my right restraint.

"Why red? Red strange."

"Of course, red, oxygen breather. Red."

"We are not red."

"We are part red."

"Argue this I will."

"Want me show your life fluid next?"

I sucked in a deep breath and struggled to refocus, blocking out their argument. The fluid started to creep once more, until it reached the edge of the table where the restraint was secured. It oozed over the edge to a hoop of metal and wrapped itself around the base. I gave the tiny machines instructions to dissolve whatever material they came in contact with, dismantling it on a microscopic level. Focus was all I needed. Keep focus.

A shock went down my left arm and I twisted to see what they had done. The furbags were pricking my skin with silver needles, shaking wires sticking out of my flesh.

"See how quick it bleeds."

"Don't want quick death."

"No. Slow. More interesting."

My lip quivered and my eyes watered. I bit down once more on the sour sponge and let out a moan.

There was a snap to my right as the metal hoop broke. My right arm was free. Before they could realize what was going on, I twisted on the table, clocked the one holding the bundle of needles in the face, then snatched the curved blade from its friend.

The gathering of furbags backed away from me in shock, hands over their mouths in a gesture of speak no evil.

"It fights."

"No giving up."

"It might be angry."

"Might kill us."

"Must take care of this."

"Must take care."

I tested the bindings on my left arm to see if the blade would cut them, sawing as quickly as I could. The furbags rushed in and I was forced to lash out. Black eye took a gash on the arm as he shielded against my attack, another along its right shoulder. My movements were limited with three of my four appendages still strapped to the table.

Realizing my handicap, a second group came around the other side. I tried once more to cut the cable, but for as easy as this blade had sunk into flesh, it would not sever my bonds.

They came at me from all sides, jumping in, my weapon clattering to the floor. Though it might have taken six or seven of them to pin me down, they had numbers and leverage. I screamed in impotence and watched, wide-eyed, as one of them leapt onto my chest with a fresh blade in hand. The creature flashed what reminded me of a smile, its teeth as razor sharp and sociopathic as the knife it held.

I fought against my assailants, but I wasn't going anywhere. The nanofluid gave no response. My head was a mess, it was too hard to concentrate.

The furbag on my chest leaned forward, ready to make the first of many incisions. I was destined to end up like the other sentient creature on the table beside me, a collection of flesh and organs to be studied by an alien conspiracy.

"Let us look inside," it said.

"Yes inside," its friends agreed.

I squeeze my eyes shut and struggled against them, digging deep for strength that did not come.

From out of view came a series of deafening bangs of metal on metal, then the pressure on my right arm subsided. The furbag sitting on my chest hopped away. With my right hand free, I reached in my mouth and removed the sponge, spitting its contents out onto the ground.

"That's right, shit bags!" a man shouted, voice echoing across the open space. "Go ahead and fucking run, ya?"

It was my friend. My only friend.

Esteban rushed towards a group of three furbags, a gleaming metal rod raised in his hand. One lashed out with a knife and he sidestepped, then swung his rod like a bat and clipped it on the jaw, sending it skittering back onto the floor, teeth scattering like dice. The furbag recovered and scurried back, left its instruments and limped away. Its companions followed suit and an instant later, the warehouse was empty.

"Esteban!" I shouted, the word escaping my mouth. It felt good.

I twisted around on the table and was met by a cluster of glossy eyes hanging from a set of spider-like legs. The contents of my stomach, what little they were, bubbled up and out onto the table.

Esteban rushed to my side. He gave me a pat on the back and smiled. "Damn, *amigo*. Is bad, ya? Let's get you free and patch that arm." His eyes moist as if he had been crying. "You're here. Everthin's okay. You're here. Done leave me again, *amigo*. Can't be alone. I can't."

"Didn't plan on going anywhere," I replied. "These things had made other arrangements."

The spider thing that accompanied Esteban reached out with its front legs and unwrapped my bonds. It helped me sit upright as he ripped a sleeve off of his jumpsuit and produced a flask of water. It was hard to tell individuals of other species apart without clear, identifiable marks like Black Eye, but I had a feeling I'd met this particular creature in the market.

"Thank you," I told the spider, and it gave a nod. "How did you find me?"

"Gi'vor here," Esteban replied, sticking out a thumb. "He knows the city inside and out. Let's say he's very familiar with these assholes." He poured water over my cuts, eliciting a painful hiss from me, and tied the broken sleeve over them to soak up the blood. It wasn't pretty, but it would work for now.

Gi'vor gave a shiver. "Yes. The Frendol are an odd species, even for Cynosure. They are curious of the insides of living things. Many of my hatch siblings have been taken by them."

"I am sorry to hear," I said.

The spider lifted its body and lowered it. "You must have safe quarters?"

"We've been trying," Esteban replied. "Nowhere in."

"No welcome?" Gi'vor queried. "Guide on disembark?"

"What welcome?"

"The Foundry gives welcome, place to stay. There is food, drink, safety."

Esteban put a palm over his face and dragged it downward. "Now we find out."

"You mean to say we didn't have to wander?" I asked, feeling absently at my makeshift bandage with the tips of my fingers. I knew that shock was likely given my injuries. We needed help and soon.

"Damn."

"Maybe the rest of the crew has found quarters," I suggested. "They could be there waiting on us."

Esteban gave a nod. "Seems like good plan."

"Can you help us find help?" I asked Gi'vor.

It lowered itself again, eyes gleaming in the dim light. "Yes. For the common good."

"So, question?" Esteban ventured. "If the Foundry protects life, how in hell does it let this happen?"

Gi'vor twisted around and inspected the room. It thought about this for a moment before answering. "I believe this place is broken."

"Broken?"

"Yes. The Foundry is powerful, but simple at times. It cannot help where it cannot see."

"Yet we can talk to one another," I offered. "Is that not proof the Foundry has influence here? Pretty sure I don't speak whatever language your people do."

"Translation is localized," it said. "Security is different."

"Okay." I slid off the table onto my feet, Esteban steadying me. Blood seeped around my injuries. As we limped away, I caught a glimpse of the nanofluid, its mass spread out along the floor like spilt mercury. I fumbled in my pockets for something that might hold it and turned up with a resealable plastic bag. "Might need it again."

"Good move, *amigo*," Esteban said.

"Worth a try."

The nanofluid flowed into the flimsy package and I slipped it into a pocket.

"Let us go find your housing," Gi'Vor said, leading us back out into the streets.

CHAPTER 24

We found ourselves in the crowded city center of Cynosure, in an open square with a glass obelisk not far from where we disembarked. The fact that we had missed it, and hadn't been directed to it, made us both angry. The obelisk's display instructed us how to operate it and communicate with the Foundry's directory. Away from its orbital facilities, the Foundry was not as forthcoming and conversational. It was a distributed system and it appeared that the majority of its higher intelligence was clustered elsewhere. The obelisk was merely a functionary. An alien information kiosk.

Human quarters were marked on the map and within just a few minutes we were safe inside one of the skyscrapers, our new friend tagging along at our request. The spider thing had made me exceedingly nervous, my hindbrain expecting that we would become its dinner at any moment, but we had little choice. It, Gi'Vor, knew the city, and we knew nothing. It knew how the Foundry worked and perhaps what it was, and we were blind. Esteban and I hoped beyond reason that the rest of the *Vasco's* crew would be waiting for us inside. Maybe have a cake and some fine wine. A song ready to sing.

We entered our assigned quarters to find a comfortable space similar to what we had had abord the *Vasco Da Gama*, only scaled up to accommodate several dozen families instead of one, tones neutral but for a few splashes of color, umber and burnt orange on beige. There was an open-concept living room / kitchen with a massive black monitor along one wall, a sectional couch capable of comfortably seating twenty facing it, complete with end tables decorated in flower pots. Along the edge of the kitchen was a bar with stools, bottles of wine and clean glasses positioned at its center, a silver tea service at one end, a coffee maker at the other. There was a stove, an oven, and a fridge set against the wall, with a backsplash of graduated blue tiles over a deep sink.

It was a home, and a well-appointed, well-stocked one at that. Only one problem. No humans.

"This is how you like to live?" Gi'Vor asked, his tone curious. "It looks sterile. It is very dry."

Esteban crossed his arms and rubbed his stubbly chin. "Not bad."

I limped my way around the room, running my fingers over the various surfaces. It was real, but short of ripping this idea straight from someone's mind, how had they known? There were too many details, tasteful abstract art, contemporary lighting fixtures, blankets draped over the backs of couches for getting cozy during a movie.

The rest of the quarters were just as quiet as the living room. Halls of empty rooms with well-tucked beds and vacant workspaces, desks and reading chairs, bathrooms with glass-fronted rainwater showers and evenly lit vanities.

While it was a beautiful place to stay, safe and welcome in our predicament, no one from the *Vasco Da Gama* could be found, and this fact, while not surprising, was nonetheless disheartening. At this moment, though, I was too tired to freak out. Too many days without food and rest had left me a husk.

Once I was satisfied that we were alone, I went back into the living room, where Gi'Vor was questioning Esteban about the value of having plants on end tables.

"Are there first aid supplies?" I asked. "I need to tend my arm."

"Yes. Call a service." Gi'Vor gestured to an open patch of carpet in the center of the living room. "That looks like a good place."

I went to the spot and spoke, "First aid."

A chair oozed from the floor like the one aboard the Foundry had. I took a seat. Nano machines, just like on the orbital facility, oozed up my leg and into the wound. They numbed the pain and knitted the skin together, before disappearing back where they had come. Within moments I already felt better, the physical pain from the Frendols' encounter erased, if not the mental pain.

"I feel better already."

"You still need rest," Gi'vor said.

I gave it a shrug and stumbled as soon as I took a step; my fall arrested by the spider creature. "I got this," I said, waving him off. "We can go looking for them in just a moment."

"Rest."

"Hungry?" Esteban asked from the kitchen, his arms overburdened with goods. "I can cook us somethin' quick. No going to look for our people without some food on our stomachs."

"Fine," I growled.

"Got some steaks, cans of beans, cheese, anything we wants, ya? The Foundry knows how to hit the local mart."

"I'll take anything. I'm starving," I said, and took a shaky seat at the bar, not sure if I was hallucinating from blood loss or if this was real. It was all a bit too perfect. With exhaustion layered on top of it, reality was tenuous and malleable. Humans were out there somewhere, and we were taking a break for a steak dinner. It wasn't right. "Thank you Gi'Vor. I could not have made it without you."

The spider put the flower vase it had been inspecting back on the table and skittered over to me. "The common good is always good."

"I get it," I reached for one of the bottles of wine and turned it over, "and yet so many don't make the effort." I uncorked the bottle and poured two glasses, one for me and one for Esteban. Drinking had never been a motivation for me, but given what we had gone through, I think I deserved some chemical calm. "Want me to look for a third? I'm not sure what you drink. I'm not even really sure what you are."

"Eipren," Gi'Vor supplied. "This is what we are called. What is in the bottle?"

"It's called wine," I replied. "It's a drink made of fermented grapes."

"What are grapes?" It inspected the unmarked bottle from several angles. "Is your species mechanical?"

"Why do you ask?"

"Fermentation creates alcohol, does it not? And alcohol can be used in combustion?"

"Humans are strange," Esteban said and gave a chuckle.

"You are the same Eipren from the Exchange, right?" I took a sip of wine and reached for a bowl of peanuts I didn't recall being there a moment earlier. Esteban may have been cooking, but I needed something on my stomach. The mixture of sour grapes and salty nuts was divine, a combination of flavors I had never experienced aboard the ship.

"I am from the market," it replied. "We have met before."

Esteban flicked a switch, and the stove came to life, a solid blue flame burning in open air. He tossed a measure of oil into a skillet and unwrapped a steak from a plastic sleeve. It was all so surreal. The Foundry had gone to painstaking detail to make us comfortable, even including what packaging we used back home to allow us the full experience of preparing our food.

"It was all I could think," Esteban said and flipped the steak with a fork. "Open my eyes in that flop and no Milo. Little furbags were fast and quick, had you out the door without a sound."

"The Frendol are dangerous," Gi'Vor interjected.

"Frendol," I repeated, then tossed another handful of peanuts in my mouth.

"Found our new *amigo* here," Esteban went on. "Begged for help. He had a good idea on your location. How do you like your steak?"

"Excuse me?" I asked.

"How do you like it? Medium? Rare?"

I shook my head, not understanding what he was asking. Wasn't all food either cooked or not cooked? Again, I hid my ignorance. "Whatever you think is best."

"Medium rare. A little pink good for everyone."

There were so many questions rolling around in my head, it was hard to focus on such an empty stomach. The wine began to relax my muscles as well as my stress. The echoing screams from those on the *Vasco Da Gama* quieted. Dad's last words, a loop running in the back of my head, became a whisper.

I rubbed my face and forced a smile. "So, I guess our people aren't here?"

"Guess not."

"Then where are they? Are they dead?"

Gi'vor made a throaty noise and leaned towards Esteban's untouched glass of wine. "I do not believe your people are dead. Are you sure you are not mechanical?"

"Biomechanical," Esteban shot back.

"Why do you think they are not dead?" I pressed.

"I smell something here. It is faint, but it is like you. It was here when we came in. Humans have been here."

"That would explain the elaborate setup." I raised my hands and gestured at the room. "I wonder whose fantasy this was?"

Esteban pointed a finger at the far wall, where a picture of the Second International Space Station hung. "I have an idea."

There was only one crew member aboard the *Vasco Da Gama* who had served in low Earth orbit over many missions. "Captain Williams?"

"Would make sense."

"But where are they now?"

Gi'Vor cocked its body. "Hard to say, Cynosure has much traffic."

"*Que bueno!*" Esteban said an instant later, then sat a plate with a steaming steak and a helping of black beans before me.

"Do I put sauce on it?" I asked. "Dip it in something?"

He scowled at me. "You a heathen?"

"I don't think so?"

"Then no. Eat the damn steak, feel better. You had enough now." He bypassed the glass of wine I had poured and took the bottle instead, tossing it back for several seconds. A moment later, he set it back on the counter and wiped the excess from his lips with a sleeve. "Good shit, ya?"

Gi'Vor glared at Esteban. "Does it not thin your blood?"

"One can only hope."

"Dangerous."

"That too."

I ate my food with care, taking my time so as to not puke up everything he had cooked. I had never felt the effects of starvation, and we had come close to the edge. Each bite made my stomach quiver.

"Can I gets you anythin' Gi'Vor?" Esteban asked. "Must be a good host."

"No," it replied, several of its half-dozen eyes blinking. "I am not required to eat often."

"Do you eat for pleasure, or nutrition?"

"I find it strange that you have heated your food. You are not alone in this custom, yet we do not."

"You eat it raw, still alive?"

"Only partly," it said, and paused, looking for the words. "We eat greengums. They grow from the ground."

"A plant?" I asked between bites of my steak, juice running over my tongue and between my teeth. Hunger was quite the flavor enhancer. The experience near transcendent.

"That is close enough of a word. My home is very wet, it is almost all water, deep as would come to your waist. It is why we evolved as we did, grew tall, many things in the water like to eat Eioren hatchlings. Over the ages we grew taller, and our mature legs are too hard for dragoeels or snap jaws to hurt us. And while they might eat our young, we do not eat them. Greengums grow taller than us, have long arms and stand tall, thin fingers reach from their arms and flitter in the wind."

"So, they're like trees?" I asked.

Gi'Vor paused then shook its body. "Yes, but not trees. Not. Plant. They have spores, no seeds, these grow better in the deep thicket. Greengum comes from the thicket. When fresh, it is alive."

"Mycological," Esteban offered. "Mushrooms."

"Mycology has always appeared alien to me," I said. "Doesn't match with anything else that grows on Earth, and the spores can survive in a vacuum."

"Mushroom?" Gi'Vor offered.

"Yes. Mushroom."

I took another bite of steak and considered this moment. It was tragic that our mission had gone down the way it did. This was what first contact should have been, conversation over a meal about home. Another observation I made was that the more we spoke to Gi'Vor, the easier it was for me to understand. Words that were skipped began to be filled in as if the Foundry were writing fresh translation scripts as we spoke.

Esteban took the stool beside me and set down his plate. His eyes were wide, and he was licking his lips. "So is your planet blue?"

"No," Gi'Vor replied. "It is green. We breathe oxygen, just like you. Ours comes from the water, the algae. It grows like a film upon the surface, bright green and sometimes red. Only dead water from the barren sea is blue."

"And your people travel through space?" I asked.

Gi'Vor vibrated. "For more than six hundred cycles, we have explored our system and beyond. We have made contact with four Foundry facilities in this time."

"Do you know how many there are?"

"Hundreds. Thousands. The Foundry is everywhere, and with the wandering gate, its influence spreads ever more."

I blinked at the mention of this.

"Wait, what's this wandering gate?" Esteban asked before taking an oversized bite. "Like a door?"

"You look into the sky of Cynosure," Gi'Vor said, "you will see it. It orbits Ligonas-7, as we do, a golden ring which burns in the light of orbital dawn."

I nodded. "I saw it when I was on my back being taken away by the Frendol. It has to be big."

"Ten thousand Eipren ships could pass thought it side by side and have room for more."

"What is it?" I leaned in. "Where does it go?"

"Where it exits changes by the moment." Gi'vor reached out one of its legs to scratch at another. "Excuse me if I speak beyond your knowledge, I do not know much of human experience."

"Go ahead."

"The ring operates much like all the Foundry does, creating different types of elements from base particles. It is why you can eat your rare steak, why I can get greengum in my quarters. The Wandering Gate exists in a state of quantum entanglement, so that when something enters it in our local star system, thousands of light years away it will emerge."

"But how is that possible?" I mused, thinking back to my classes on advanced physics. "Does it transfer the matter between the two points?"

Gi'Vor paused, then shook. "No. The entrance to the wandering gate on our side works like a molecular scanner. It records the placement of every particle that your body, ship, clothes, and food are made of, then transmits that information to the other side. When you reach the gate, you are broken down into your base components, then stitched back together with a new set of components in exactly the same combination at the other end."

Esteban and I gave each other a worried look.

He spoke first, "So, are you still you on the other end?" Esteban wondered. "New particles and all, would I be the same me? It's weird, ya? I mean, what about the soul?"

"I do not know," Gi'Vor stated. "We too believe in a spiritual essence. I would fear losing it, for one. I do not wish to be absent from the Day of Enlightenment."

"Do you go somewhere on that day?" Esteban probed. "An afterlife?"

"Yes. To be part of the All. You cannot be part of the All without the Sien, my spiritual being."

"That gate is a long way away," I began speculating, "how did it get there? If they are entangled, then they most likely began at the same point."

"It wanders."

"I don't understand."

"The gate at the other end is moving, it never stops. Where it is today, and where it is tomorrow or a thousand years from now, will be different."

"Moving as in, with a will, or just randomly?"

Gi'Vor shook and said nothing.

Esteban raised a cube of steak with his fork and stared at it. "They make these portals, ya? Keep one still, then shoot the other off into the black? It just keeps movin' and movin' with nothin' to stop it. Would increase their range, allows them to spread all over the galaxy."

"It does," Gi'Vor said.

"Why they no use them at every facility?"

Gi'Vor lowered itself and one of its legs twitched. "Could be too expensive to produce. Could be they are as scared to use as we are. My people do not know."

"Would our crew have gone through the gate?"

"It is unlikely. The only ones I see use the gate on a regular basis are the Gene Brokers and the Foundry."

Each answer brought forth more questions. I shoveled beans into my mouth and washed them down with the last of my wine. "Who are the Gene Brokers?"

"You have met them already."

I scowled. "What? I have?"

"Yes. They took hold of your hand. Touched your bio map."

Esteban and I stared at one another, blinking. I pushed my plate away and gave our new friend my full attention.

"Who are they?"

"The Gene Brokers?"

"Yes."

"They are like the Foundry."

"And how are they like the Foundry? Do they create facilities which summon burgeoning species?"

"No. They protect life, in their own way. Different ideas, same goal."

"Elaborate."

Gi'Vor shifted where it stood, reaching what must have been a more comfortable stance. "I cannot say if the Foundry is more than a machine, but all machines were made by someone. Still, it has a belief, an objective. The Foundry is helping the Universe along. In its view, the Universe is alive, intelligent and conscious, and all life is only a part of that higher life. To help the Universe become self-aware, life must be protected, life must be guarded. The more life, the more aware, the more connected the Universe is."

"A universal mind," Esteban offered.

"Yes, but more than that. If you look at a model of our Universe, and my own brain, they would be similar. There are nerves and neurons, connected in a web. What if this was more than spirituality? What if the Universe was itself a being who lives in a different reference of time than we of limited lifespans can comprehend?"

My mouth fell open. This idea felt right, familiar. "And each of us was simply a neuron in this great mind?"

"You understand."

"They protect life that there will be more neurons? So that the brain will be healthier."

"So it is said."

Esteban rubbed his temples with his fingertips. "I think my own brain is about to explode, ya? *Cogito, ergo sum.*"

"You said the ones who grabbed my hand," I said, "the Gene Brokers, that they had a different perspective. What does that mean?"

"They too believe the Universe can become self-aware," Gi'Vor went on. "And so they help life along."

"What do you mean help it along?"

Gi'Vor lowered itself and twisted slightly. "They trade genes."

"And do what with them?" Esteban asked. "Go on card battles? Maybe play mad scientist?"

"Who can say? Build new species? Manipulate others? I have heard stories of the Gene Brokers' dealings, but how can I know what is true?"

"It knew what I was," I said, rubbing my arm where it had touched me. My impression of them was not good. My instincts told me to be cautious. "It said *human.*"

"So what now?" Esteban asked. "Our friends, they're not here. I don't see no sign. I don't mean to be selfish, but I'm tired, ya?"

"You need rest," Gi'Vor said. "I will leave you for now. Come find me, if you need me."

After receiving our thanks, for which it did not understand the need, Gi'Vor left Esteban and I alone in the quiet human quarters. We finished our meals and polished off several more glasses of wine before taking showers and changing into fresh clothes. It felt good to be clean, as well as a little drunk. Being a touch inebriated helped bring this surreal place into context, or at least lower our inhibitions enough that we could allow ourselves to accept it.

"We'll go out and look tomorrow," he told me and took a place on the couch. "Let's take a break, ya?"

I furrowed my brow and scratched at the back of my head. "I feel guilty relaxing when our people could be in danger."

"You think they felt bad relaxing when you were bein' cut apart by spider monkeys?"

"Lemurs, not spider monkeys."

"You think I'm zoologist?"

I was too tired to argue. I found a place on the couch and propped up my feet, laying back with my head on a pillow.

Esteban pinged the monitor and to our surprise, we found several movies we knew on stream. Where the Foundry had procured these was hard to say, I didn't recall titles like the Matrix, Avengers, and Skyfall being available aboard the *Vasco Da Gama*. Had these films been beamed out into space years earlier and placed in storage for just this event?

It was strange, given our situation, our missing people, how easy it was to fall into distraction. We had a warm, dry place, familiar food, and alcohol. I don't remember what movie we watched that night. I'm pretty sure I fell asleep before the introduction finished rolling. At some point, I woke up, a blanket draped over me, the room dark but for the glow of a table lamp. I had been dreaming, but everything was mashed together, details unclear, anxiety rampant. James. Dr. Reed. The captain. They were telling me something, but I couldn't understand.

Esteban sat in the corner, staring off into space.

"*Amigo*," I said. "You okay?"

He shook his head and pivoted in my direction. "What?"

"Are you okay."

"Yeah," he said, wiping the moisture from his eyes. Had my friend been crying? "I'm good." And before I could say a word, he sprang up and bolted for the kitchen. "Let's get some breakfast going."

We spent the next few days recovering from our ordeal. Danger or not, it did our friends no good for us to go mad. The Foundry had been smart in creating these mental bunkers that species, assuming the others got the same treatment, could retreat to and be more at ease. Being in these quarters, I didn't feel we were in an alien city light years from Earth. For all I could tell, we were aboard another spacecraft, and yet wasn't that what all planets were?

Several days, or what we thought of as days, went by in a blur of rest, food, old movies, and more wine. Esteban and I did not talk much, the weight of everything that had happened too great for the moment. We gave ourselves time to process. I used the Foundry's service to summon a journal and began writing daily, chronicling our experiences, even though I was unsure if any other human would ever read them. Did that matter?

After several serious hangovers, which made me wonder why people drank at all, and fully recovering from the incident with the Frendol, Esteban and I decided to venture out and look for evidence of our friends. We had a base to work from, a safe place to return. This was enough for now.

A week of this resulted in nothing but conversations that went nowhere with creatures we could hardly comprehend. We spoke to bi-peds with heads that looked like cauliflower wearing black robes festooned in shimmering gems. We spoke to knee-high worms with mouths made of bundled tentacles who sang every word they spoke in harmony. Some of these were friendly, some were dismissive, all of them were near incomprehensible. Each day we returned exhausted and more confused than the last, lacking any leads. Our people were lost, no doubt about it, and with the chaos of life in Cynosure, they were not memorable.

I spent the following evening journaling in bed, pen in hand, book in my lap. It was nice to write on paper, the first time I had done so in years. Had it been the day we made paper planes in detention? Yet was this really paper? If we were to break down the materials and look at them on a microscopic level, would it be made of something else?

My pen flipped out of my fingers and bounced off the nearest wall. I gave a chuckle, set down my journal, and leaned off the bed to recover it. As I was reaching for the pen, I caught sight of something beneath the bed.

"Esteban!" I shouted. "Come here."

I retrieved the object and sat a journal identical to my own on the bed and flipped it open. "Are you coming?"

"Hold your horses, *amigo*," he replied, appearing a moment later at the door, his eyes heavy. "Shit man, what? What you want?"

"I found this."

"And?"

"It's not mine."

"Oh." His postured shifted immediately, and he leaned forward. "Ohh… Who then?"

I flipped through the pages, scanning over what had been written. It took some time to figure out whose it was, but once I did, there was no doubt in my mind. This was from a member of the *Vasco Da Gama*. A man who was physically blind.

"It's Perry's journal," I said, and my heartrate increased. "Perry's journal."

Esteban took a seat beside me on the bed. "What's it say?"

I flipped to the back and read as quickly as I could. "They've left Cynosure."

"And went where?"

"Where indeed."

The following morning, Esteban and I woke early and hurried to the Exchange. If one person could help us with the information we had uncovered, it was our new friend. The city had shown us time and again how fortunate we were in meeting the Eipren merchant. It could help us find our friends, find Shelly, find my parents. I wanted to throw my arms around all of them so bad, they ached. Apologize for not coming sooner.

This early in the day, the Exchange was quiet, only a few persons in evidence. Gi'vor was unpacking goods and putting them out for display.

"Good morning, Gi'Vor," I said.

It turned and regarded me for a moment with its black eyes, then shook. "What is 'morning'?"

"When the sun comes up over the horizon."

"Oh."

Across from Gi'Vor's stall, one of the cauliflower heads and a green mass which strode on a dozen tentacles began to argue. The merchant, which appeared to be the cauliflower head, was holding up a pressure container and was shaking it. A tentacle creature reached out and tried to pry it from his hands, one of its companions rifling through the trade box in the stall, retrieving a set of crystal shards it had used as payment for the item.

"What's going on?" I asked.

Gi'Vor twitched. "The Kiben put word out through the market it had fourteen dram of gaseous fullerites. It wanted to trade them for crystalline oxygen, something Leprin have naturally on their world."

Esteban narrowed his eyes. "Leprin the tentacle folk, ya?"

"Correct."

"Crystalline oxygen?" I marveled. "How is that even possible."

"Rare."

"They disagree on price, ya?" Esteban asked.

"Bait and switch," Gi'Vor replied.

I shook my head, not understanding. "Excuse me?"

"Material in canister is not gaseous fullerites. It is likely a stable isotope, and in small quantity with a seal to mask from easy probing. Still useable, yes, but not worth that weight in crystalline oxygen. Kiben hoping to vanish after exchange. Leprin were smarter."

"Bait and switch," I said, turning the statement over. "It's a scam."

Gi'Vor stared at me, its many eyes blinking. I think it was confused.

"They lied about the goods."

"Yes."

"We think we found where our peoples went," Esteban cut in.

"This is good news."

I opened the journal and pointed to a place on the page. "I'm not sure if you can read this, even with the Foundry's assistance. It is a journal, something we use to keep track of what we do and how we feel about it."

"Localized organic material memory augmentation," Gi'vor said, eyes blinking in sequence.

"Sure, you could call it that. Anyways, one of our people wrote that they were moving to a new colony, a place to call their own. It is on the fifth moon of the third planet in this system."

Esteban smiled. "Can we get there? You know how? Can the Foundry take us?"

"Yes," Gi'Vor said, words slow and careful. "I know how to get there. It is a place the Foundry will not take you. We must act quickly, enlist help. There will be a price."

"What kind of price?"

"The Jalek will tell you," Gi'vor said, and by the tone of his voice, he seemed almost afraid. "It will tell you."

"Who's the Jalek?" Esteban scratched his chin.

"You will see."

CHAPTER 25

Our Eipren associate proved yet again to be a valuable asset, and a possible friend. It was hard to know how relationships worked in other species, but it was offering us help we desperately needed, and was not asking for anything in return. This sounded like friendship to me. The other humans had been here, now all we had to do was find our way to where they went. The Foundry, at this point, would be unwilling to transport us or grant a ship from scratch, and so that left us at the mercy of one of the most powerful persons in all of Cynosure—the Jalek.

Time was a relative concept, but relative or not, Cynosure had been here for centuries. Whatever the Jalek was, it had been one of the first to find the Foundry network and arrive on this rock. It had worked as both a proponent for the Foundry's agenda, and an agitator, an agent of chaos with unclear motivation and objectives. What information we were given about it was mostly hearsay. The Jalek had never traded with Gi'Vor, or any of the Eipren for that matter. They were too young a species, too immature for an all-knowing entity of ages and eons. And yet at times, and serendipitous ones at that, it was necessary to state your case before this being, no matter your species' age.

We entered one of the tallest structures on the far end of the city and were led inside. Instead of traveling up into the towers as I had expected, we entered a golden lift as large as the living room in our quarters and were taken down into the rock which made up the asteroid. Esteban and I exchanged worried glances, eyes continuing the conversation we had before entering the building. There was no other option that we could find, so we had to throw ourselves at the mercy of whatever this thing was and hope for the best.

"The Jalek is old," Gi'Vor told us. "What it wants, I cannot say. But there is a something. It always wants a something."

"What kind of something?"

Gi'Vor's body shook. "A something."

The doors to the lift opened, and I felt a wash of throbbing, rhythmic noise press against my chest. We stepped out into a dark room filled with multi-color flashing lights, and I realized what had hit us was music. It was unlike anything I had ever heard before, instrumentation slow and complex, frequencies tingling at the corners of recognition, melodies uneasy yet present. I can't say if I enjoyed it, given my current state of disquiet, but neither was it bad.

Gi'Vor led us into the dark, and when the lights flashed again, I realized that the room was filled with species of every variety, less diverse, but no less interesting than the streets above. We squeezed between their gyrating forms. On my left were a pair of worm-like creatures coupling, their bodies connected by a pulsing lattice of flesh, while on my right, a trifecta of mammalian bi-peds rubbed pelvises as if attempting to start a fire by friction alone. The air was thick and damp, a dense fog filling the spaces between exchanged conversations, chittering, screeching, and droning words. Some of the alien creatures drank from cups as varied as their means of locomotion, liquids every color of the rainbow, while others crammed shards of crystalline dust up their respiration organs, producing physical tremors and tear-jerking exclamations.

"Holy shit, *amigo*," Esteban said under his breath. "We've found our asses in like—an underground club."

"Because we are under the ground?" I asked, confused.

"No, no. From the looks of it, these things doing illegal shit. Mating on the dance floor, takin' drugs, not that there's rules for all that here. Unless there is? Underground just means out of, like, public eyes. *Policía*. Who knew *la fiesta* was universal? *Movida la vita*."

I felt something stumble and fall against my leg. It pivoted, dropped its glass, then glared at me, the contents of its drink running down my right boot. A short, furry creature looked up at me, one of its eyes rimmed in black. I took a deep breath and straightened my back, making myself appear taller. Anger filled every inch of my body. Black Eye, the Frendol who had nearly vivisected me in the warehouse, stood stock still as if an apex predator had discovered its hiding place, and remaining frozen was its only hope of avoiding detection.

Just as I was about to throttle it, throwing every bit of anger I had into a single punch, Esteban held me back. Gi'Vor urged us in another direction.

"Not here," Gi'Vor said. "There are other venues."

"Not here, *amigo*," Esteban echoed.

Reluctant, I followed my friends and did my best to tamp down my fury. Cynosure was created by the Foundry to protect life, and yet it walked this line in perfect dichotomy, hypocritical as most ruling institutions.

"Fuck him," I growled.

"Yeah, yeah, fuck him," Esteban echoed.

We reached the end of the room where a pair of thorny shrubs covered in thick slime stood sentinel beside a cavernous doorway. Gi'vor went first, lowering his mass until his eyes nearly brushed the floor.

"State your business," one of the sentinels said, its words resonating within all our implants.

"The humans desire an audience with the Jalek," Gi'Vor offered.

"The Jalek will soon hibernate," one said.

"Which is why we have come now, rather than during the next cycle."

"The Jalek does not have time for children," the other said, and I found it strange, how even though they were translated by the Foundry and sounded the same, I could tell the difference between the two sentinels.

"Others of their species have come before. They only wish to follow."

"They smell," first said.

"Yes." Gi'Vor turned to look at us and gave a shake. "They smell."

"Their smell will leave," the second suggested. "It is too… natural."

"Yes, natural," the first responded.

I moved to interject a word or two in protest—to me they smelled just as bad, just as sweaty and rank and acrid as I'm sure we did to them—but then the door opened, and a tiny, pink figure no taller than my ankles, back hunched and body like a hairless gorilla, waved at us.

Esteban and I gave one another an uneasy glance and stepped forward.

"No," the sentinels said as one. "Only one may go."

"I'm not going in alone," I protested.

"Then all of you will remain here."

"Is okay, *amigo*," Esteban replied, raising his hands in supplication. "I trust you. You got this."

I leaned close enough to him no one could hear. "What if it's a trap?"

He smiled. "Then we have one more time to get it right if I'm here. We both go in, and you know, die, it's over."

"Fine."

"Come back though, please," my friend said, his words almost a plea. "Don't care to live alone."

"I plan on it."

I turned to walk through the door and was swallowed by darkness, a lump in my throat. My confidence was nowhere near what Esteban's was. This did not feel like a trap in the traditional sense, but a creature who had never even met with our new friend, or any of his species, had welcomed me with little protest. Something wasn't right.

The cavernous passage widened, and a light appeared at the end. I found myself in a circular chamber with walls made of stone. Its floors were covered in strips of red and gold, rows of garish pillows stitched with geometric patterns starting at the center and spiraling out to the edges. There were metallic shelves covered in bottles and boxes, open containers of powder and hunks of metal, raw and refined, a collection of goods and culture, statues and artwork, idols and fetishes. One could spend a lifetime studying all that was here, fitting together the puzzle pieces of existence and cultural development on different worlds.

There was no time to marvel.

At the center of it all stood a fleshy, humanoid creature the size of an ape. It appeared like a man hunched over, body draped in strips of cloth, hands and feet both used to stand, their angles not quite natural, somewhere between forward and hind. Its too-large head bobbed, with a face like an undefined mammal, smooth cheeks, and forehead vaguely human, with nose, mouth, and eyes, proportions exaggerated to cartoonish lengths. Along a knotty spine and down its arms ran a series of thorns, black and hard, their tips gleaming in the shifting amber lights of the den.

"You must be one of the humans," it said, and from the shadows a half-dozen bundles of pink limbs no bigger than a cat climbed onto various positions along its body. They anchored into place, taking hold of the thorns and positioning over footholds, dark fossa and antrum I had not seen until that moment. It glared at me, peering down the length of its hooked nose.

I took a deep breath, patted my jumpsuit, and replied, "Yes, I am human."

The Jalek's nostrils flared as it sniffed the air. The creatures hanging onto its thorns regarded one another. "Are you so sure?" it said after a moment. "You smell of travel, of recycled air. Do you even know what it is to be human? Human is more than just genetics, I would say."

I scowled. Why in the hell did this nightmarish lump of pink think it was okay to talk down to me? How would it know what it was like to be human?

"I am as human as any other human," I said, fighting to keep my voice even.

The Jalek pulled a silver device from a pocket in its robes and punched several buttons. "Ah, yes. That's the word—Earth. Do you remember your Earth then? Can you describe the place you grew up? The place in which you were born? What did it smell like? What did the food taste like? Did you go swimming? Was there a lake? A… playground?"

My eyes fell from the Jalek onto my shoes. What color were the walls of my living room? What was my room like? The memories were jumbled together, but were they real? Of all things I thought of Jasper, of the fast-food toy under the kitchen stove, of Mom throwing her cell phone out the window as we sped away from a normal life. These memories were as difficult to hold in clarity as water was in cupped hands. Were they even mine? Or did they belong to someone else? Did I borrow them from my parents' stories?

"You are thinking about it," the Jalek went on. "You are an adaptable species, but not one of good memory."

I raised my eyes and stepped forward; fists clenched. "I remember enough. I remember my life aboard the *Vasco Da Gama*."

"That frail sailboat you used to reach the Foundry?"

"Look, was I allowed to meet with you so that you could mock me? Or am I right to assume that you know why I came?"

The Jalek gave a shrug. "I know many things."

"Can you help me get to where the other humans went?" I said through gritted teeth. "I am tired of being talked down to."

The Jalek made a noise I could only classify as a laugh. Its body shook and the fleshy, miniature versions of itself raised their tiny arms and waved. "Your people have no idea, no context of what the universe truly is. I'll be curious to see how long you survive. My collective has been among these stars for tens of thousands of solar cycles. We know of species who have seen the galaxy turn. Why did you travel to the Foundry?" It paused to scratch at its side. "I will guess. You grew too fast, used energy sources that put your fragile biome in danger? Maybe war. Mostly greed. Shortsighted greed motivated by fear."

"Shut up," I growled, not realizing how furious I was becoming. "I'll ask again, can you help me get to the other humans?"

"I might if I cared," it said. "Come back when your species has matured beyond infancy." The Jalek turned to leave.

No. This wouldn't do. I was not leaving without the thing that I wanted. We were going to find the remaining crew of the *Vasco Da Gama*, and this lump of flesh was not going to stand in my way. "I was told you wanted something, and that you would help me if I got you this something."

The tiny Jaleks regarded me even though their master had turned its back.

"You would get me that?"

I swallowed and gave a nod, unsure what I was committing myself to. "Yes."

A moment passed in which the tiny Jaleks conferred with one another. It was strange to watch, as if each of the creatures was another aspect of the same mind. I could not understand their words, but their body language communicated urgency, interest, and reservation.

"I will give you passage if you bring it to me," it said.

"You will give me and my companion passage."

"I will give *you* passage."

"No," I said, my word even as still water. "I go nowhere without him."

The Jalek chuckled again. "Fine. You amuse me with your hubris. Bring it to me, and I will give you both passage to the place you will die. Either way, it does not matter."

"Why would it not matter?"

It paused. "If you fail me, you will die either way. Failing the Jalek is terminal."

"Are you saying you'll kill me?"

A throaty chuckle crawled from its throat. "No, human. If you return without the *something*, I won't have to." It turned to face me, eyes cold and black. "You will die of radiation poisoning for coming to see me and have no means to recover."

I felt for my chest and swallowed. Was it messing with me, or was this true? I had no way of confirming if this was a bluff.

"You're a bastard," I said.

The Jalek shook its head. "Different species have different needs. Find the *something*, and I can help you." It exited through a back door without another word, leaving me alone among its treasures with absolutely no further instruction.

I made my way back to Esteban and Gi'Vor, who were waiting for me by the sentries. Before I could open my mouth and voice my concerns, such as honestly having no idea what the something really was, a tiny hand tugged my jumpsuit leg. I turned to see what had requested my attention.

It was one of the smaller Jaleks, a slip of paper in its hand. I took the paper and it scurried off back down the cavernous tunnel towards its master.

"What happened, *amigo*?" Esteban asked, his arms crossed. "The paper has the key, ya?"

"I've been dosed," I said, and looked the paper over. It had a simple drawing of a tank filled with liquid, its outer construction clear and contents undefined. To the side of it lay something roundish in shape with the texture of grey matter. "Not sure what variety of radiation, but the Jalek, or its room... Its radioactive."

"What?" Esteban's mouth fell open.

"I have radiation poisoning."

"*Ay ya, hermano*." He put a hand on my shoulder. "I'm so sorry."

"I'm not dead yet," I replied, giving a half grin. "I think it's why it asked me to go in alone. It can cure me, but I have to bring it this." I turned the paper over so Esteban and Gi'Vor could see.

Gi'Vor lowered its body as if sighing. "That is a Phantamorph."

"Hey, *amigo*," Esteban said, "that's the thing on the street you tried to talk to on day one, ya? The marine eyeball thing."

"I think the Jalek wants me to find this in its tank." I pointed to the organ-like object on the paper.

"It is the memory gland," Gi'Vor said. "Or so I believe. The stories must be true."

"What stories?"

"The Jalek seeks experiences. If it is indeed radioactive, it must limit its exposure to most species. If the Jalek can acquire the memories and experiences of other species without being around them, then it would be like—"

"Traveling," I supplied.

Esteban's eyes went wide. He spun around, taking in the underground alien club as if seeing it for the first time. "This a human memory."

"What?"

"The reason this place is so familiar," he went on. "This is an experience that was given to the Jalek. No telling whose experience, but this reminds me of downtown Barcelona or Ibiza."

"Did someone have to die to give it up?"

Esteban shrugged. "Hope not."

We exited the club and worked our way back to the street. By the time we were above ground, I was feeling feverish and nauseous. Esteban steadied me as we walked.

"I guess there's not a lot of doubt," I said. "I was hoping for a minute it had been bluffing."

"We gots to hurry and find this thing."

Gi'Vor went ahead of us. "I know where one will be."

"Will it give this thing up willingly?"

"Would you give a piece of your brain willingly?"

"Guess not."

"We will have to trap it."

I stopped to face Gi'Vor, the busy streets full of life rushing around us. "This organ of a Phantamorph, will removing it kill it?"

"I am not a doctor," Gi'Vor replied. "I only know what I have read, what I have heard. My understanding is that it is a place that memories are stored. As for if it will kill it, who is to say? Phantamorphs are symbiotic colonies, exceedingly complex organisms."

"I don't want to kill anything," I responded, and put a hand to my mouth, my stomach doing flips. Esteban tensed and I raised a hand to signal I was okay. "I don't want to kill."

"That thing lives in a big tank," Esteban said. "Surely that's not the one thing it needs to live, ya?"

"We know next to nothing about it. The brain stem is a small part of our bodies, but if it snaps, we die." I took in a deep breath and went on. "Besides, how are we going to keep the Foundry from killing us?"

Gi'Vor's body vibrated. "Leave that to me." It produced a small slip of glass from a pocket on its body I had not realized it had. "Your Frendol friend still carried it."

Seeing the jamming device made my heart quicken. I was angry, not at Gi'Vor, but of the whole experience with the Frendol. I wanted to snatch it from his spindly legs and shatter it on the street just like mom had her phone.

"You swiped it?" Esteban marveled. "I like you, Spider-Man."

"What does that mean?"

"Don't worry about it. That's a compliment where I comes from."

"I see," Gi'Vor replied.

"I don't want to kill," I repeated.

Gi'Vor took the lead, navigating us through the crowd. "Then let us hope the memory gland is not needed for it to stay alive."

Sometimes having a conscience could be a nuisance. What other choice did we have but to see this through? We needed passage to wherever the rest of the crew had gone, and only the Jalek could provide it. I needed to be cured of this sickness it had inflicted me with, either intentionally or as a biproduct of how it lived. The answers to both lay at the bottom of a hovering fish tank. Like it or not, my hands were tied.

"I don't want to kill," I mumbled, the words meant only for myself. "I don't want to kill."

"I know, *amigo*," Esteban said, patting me on the back. "I know."

CHAPTER 26

We waited on our target, crouching low at the corner between the Exchange and the Aquatic District. Gi'Vor informed us that the Phantamorphs, of which there were only a half dozen in Cynosure, passed down this street like clockwork once every day-night cycle. The streets were quiet this early, a few cauliflower heads and a group of lanky, mask-wearing figures in silver scales milling about. The Foundry's enforcers were out of sight. I wasn't sure if the Foundry would interfere, as I was essentially planning on climbing inside the body of this creature and removing one of its organs. What would it do to me if I got caught? Would it punish other humans, or just me?

To say I was conflicted over this choice was an understatement. Never in my life had I set out to harm another living thing. I had distant memories of my cousins burning ants with a magnifying glass under the bright sun and being horrified at their actions. Those tiny things did not deserve to die like that. Yet here I was, about to steal the organ of a living thing, just to save my skin and return to my friends and family. It was selfish. Self-serving. But was this just the story I was telling myself? Did we even know what this would do to it? For all we knew, the tank was just a tank, and we'd be removing a sea sponge from the silt at its bottom. There were only two choices I was aware of: do this for the Jalek, or die.

Esteban put a hand on my shoulder. "You okay, *amigo?*"

"No," I replied. "But I am going to have to be."

He gave a nod. It pained me to know that he understood. He knew my thoughts and would follow my lead.

"It comes," Gi'Vor said, then stood tall on its many spindly legs, black eyes flashing along its mass in the light of morning. "I will delay it."

Our spider friend moved swift yet casual into the street. The massive tank which held the Phantamorph skimmed the surface of the pavement, making little noise but for small burbles of air in water. The murky blue of the tank swirled with life, tentacles and flowing fronds.

Gi'Vor took position before the Phantamorph and attempted to start a dialogue. The tank came to a halt and a glossy, circular panel mounted in front, its diameter wide as the center pane of the *Vasco's* cupola, illuminated with scarlet. The eyes within the murk advanced to the side at which Gi'Vor stood and regarded him with curiosity.

Esteban and I held our breath, waiting on our friend to make a move. For the longest time, they appeared to stare at one another, not a word of gesture exchanged. Gi'Vor waved one of his arms and began to walk in the same direction the Phantamorph had been traveling. The tank resumed its course, following the lead. We followed them at a safe distance, hoping that the Phantamorph did not have eyes in the back of its tank. We came to another crossroads and Gi'vor halted, as did the Phantomorph's tank.

"Looks like they just havin' a chat, ya?" Esteban mused.

I scratched at my cheek, what little stubble I had on my chin fast becoming a scraggly beard. "I don't hear anything, do you?"

"No. Must be all implants."

"Think that's why we couldn't talk to it? The longer we are around Gi'Vor, the easier it is to understand it. Why not that as well?"

"Hold on." Esteban threw out an arm and stopped me in my tracks.

The ground began to rumble, bits of dirt and gravel vibrating against the gilded streets. Esteban and I gave each other a look and threw ourselves against the nearest building. A tide of flesh and bone and churning hooves came hurtling down the street. Gi'Vor vanished among the crowds a moment before the wave crashed against the tank. The Phantamorph made no sound of alarm as this stampede of six-legged mammals, bodies like cows from the back only, heads monstrous and large, jagged teeth and eyes the size of dinner plates, threw their bodies against its tank. Liquid sloshed out the top of the tank and down its side. Dozens of this cattle species, the Brelaps, tripped over one another, trampled their friends, then scurried up and readjusted.

The stampede died down, the Brelaps hurrying off down the next street, vanishing just as swift as they had come.

An instant later, the tank ceased hovering and crashed onto the pavement, water sloshing over the lip upon impact. Esteban gave me a look and we took off running towards the back of it. Standing at the rear of the tank we realized it was much taller than our short-term memory had approximated, at least ten feet. I was a tall guy, sure, but that was too much to climb when the glass was smooth.

"Here, step in my hands," Esteban said, and linked his fingers together. "I'll toss you up."

I put my palms on the outside of the tank and set my left foot onto Esteban's hands. He gave a gesture with his chin, and I moved my right foot up onto his shoulder, before stepping up with the left. Shakily, he stood tall, and I walked my hands up the side of the tank. Once my outstretched hands were high enough, I took hold of the lip and Esteban pushed me up onto the precarious edge, which was no more than six inches wide.

"There ya go," he said, then fell forward, hands on his knees and catching his breath. "Go get 'em."

The tank rocked as it attempted to reinitialize its systems and hover once more. I nearly lost my balance. I took a pair of swimming goggles from my pocket we had had the Foundry 3D print and slipped them on my head.

"Now or never," I mumbled, then fell forward into the murky waters. For good or bad, the choice was made. I only hoped it could be forgiven.

I wasn't sure what I was expecting, but the water was hot and dark. Intermittent flashes of blue light found their way through the mire, fronds of organic material brushed against my arms and legs. I sank to the bottom of the tank and began to search for what had been on the Jalek's picture. There was almost nowhere to step within the space, the bottom of the tank was covered in coral and teeming with spiked urchins. I would take a step and the urchins would anticipate where my next move might be. I found myself treading in place instead of walking. Trying to move was awkward and unfamiliar. Swimming was not something I had much practice with. Nor was holding my breath.

After several fruitless moments, I felt the tank begin to move again. It gave a shift, and I sank onto a patch of urchins. Several of their spines pierced my jumpsuit and drew blood. I winced and jerked away, swimming upward. My nose and mouth broke the surface, I took a sharp breath, then something pulled me back beneath the water.

I spun to see a collection of slender, garishly colored tentacles clasping my right ankle, their lengths festooned with rows of polyps. They were bound to an undulating, amorphous mass of black, which appeared to be anchored at an invisible point in the center of the tank. I struggled against this grip, but it would not budge.

A light flashed off to my right at the bottom of the tank, something like a cross between a bioluminescent fish and a snake, and then I saw it. The *something* the Jalek wanted. The memory gland, whatever it was. I kicked at the base of the tentacles, and for an instant they let go. This was my opportunity. I swam for the *something*, hoping the light would remain long enough that I could put my hands on it. As I reached for it, fingertips inches away, the polypy mass of tentacles took hold of my ankle once more and began dragging me back into the center of the tank. Urchins gathered beneath me, their spines glowing red in anger, macro-scale antibodies intent on battling a foreign threat. I twisted and swam toward the surface but could not get myself free. I was running out of air. My vision blurry. Every defense within the tank was alive, intent on protecting the host, just like my own body during an infection.

Despite my struggle, there was no breaking free of the Phantomorph's grasp. In that moment, I realized I should have brought something sharp, but I had not expected this creature to have such a robust defense system. From the outside it looked like no more than a floating aquarium, yet within it had an arsenal of restraint and torture devices.

A distant splash brushed my ears, sound enhanced by the liquid medium. Was it a Foundry enforcer come to take me out? This seemed most likely. Desperate, I twisted and reached for one of the urchins at the edge of the group, attempting to grab its base. Several of the spines along its edge pricked my fingers, a sensation a series of white-hot hammer strikes against skin following. I fumbled and held it with the tips of my fingers. As everything started to go black, my chest seizing from a lack of oxygen, I stabbed at the mass of tentacles. They instantly withdrew, withering like a plant exposed to sunlight or a slug covered in salt.

Now free, I shot for the surface and took in several deep breaths, then dove again, heading straight for the *something*. Once I was halfway to the object, I saw that the Phantamorph had taken hold of something else. I squinted my eyes for a moment, then felt panic rush through me. The truth of the situation became clear. On the other side of the tank, Esteban was caught by several groups of tentacles. He was unresponsive, fast being lowered onto a bed of urchins. The flash of light came again, catching my attention for a moment, and there was the memory gland.

I closed my eyes, willing this world away, seeking focus. My chest and shoulders felt tight. I clenched my fists and ground my teeth. The protective organ on my left began to unwither. Did I have enough time before the other mass of tentacles recovered? Why couldn't anything be easy? Why did it have to be so goddamned hard?

Steeling my resolve, I reached down and took hold of an urchin, careful not to be pricked, fingers around its base. With both feet on the side of the tank I pushed off towards Esteban. I brandished my urchin and pricked the various tentacles around his arms and legs and watched as they fell away. Esteban was unresponsive, and so I shook him hard as a I could. Given the water resistance, that wasn't much. His eyes snapped open. He gave a nod. With an outstretched finger, I pointed to the surface and swam back for the memory gland, unwilling to leave without our prize.

A moment later I broke the surface, taking in deep breaths of air with an appreciation I had never known. Esteban helped me out onto the lip of the tank, and we lowered ourselves down onto the street before anything within could retaliate. In my left hand I held a spongy, ochre ball with the texture of grey matter. Gi'vor appeared and took a glance at what we had recovered.

"This is it?" it asked.

"I think so," I replied, then turned, hearing the screeching sound of metal against the street.

The Phantomorph's tank had ceased hovering once more, crashing in place. The running lights along the outside began to dim. The murky waters cleared.

"We need to go," Esteban said, leading me away. "Come on, now. Before the cops get here, ya?"

As we walked away, prize in hand, I felt a deep sense of regret. It had not deserved what I had done, but what other choice did I have? It was my life, or its life. I needed to find my people. We had a mission to accomplish, Foundry Intent – Contact and Save Earth. This had to be done to get us back on track. Would it have done the same in my place?

My eyes became blurry. Esteban did not press me with questions, he just led me with an arm around my shoulder and let me be.

Upon returning to the Jalek we found no club, no underground party under the streets. The building was empty, nothing but the sentries waiting for me. They waved me inside and I presented the prize to the ancient creature alone. It waited for me, a glass of something blue in one hand, a strip of brown meat in the other.

"I have your *something*," I told it, my mouth sour.

It took its time chewing the pitiful strip of meat, regard fixed on the memory gland in my hands. The tiny Jaleks wandering around its body conferred with one another. One ran down its arm and took a sip of the blue liquid. The Jalek gestured for me to lay the object on the ground before it. The curious part of me wondered how it would acquire these experiences, these memories from such a varied set of biology, but that was clearly what it did. Would it scan them with a piece of technology and download them into its brain? Did it consume the memories like food? Had it killed one of our crew to get the memories of a nightclub? A terrifying thought.

Once it had finished chewing it spoke, "Good work. This will do just fine." It gave a wave, and the tiny Jaleks shimmied down its body to the object. For a moment, I thought they might pick it up and carry it somewhere, but to my horror, they began to pound on it with their tiny fists. Within an instant, the memory gland was a lump of ochre pulp on the floor oozing a viscous, black fluid.

I took a step back, my breath catching.

"Do not worry," the Jalek said, and took another slice of meat from a bowl beside it. "The Phantomorphs are, to put it in your words, assholes."

"You had me kill it for nothing," I said.

"They murdered and enslaved several Dei'charin colonies."

"You had me kill it for nothing!" I said again, this time laced with venom.

"And?" the Jalek tossed the meat into its mouth. "There are more of them."

"But it had thoughts, feelings, a life. You had me take those away."

The Jalek chuckled. "Did you not fire on the Isoptera who boarded your ship?"

"That was different."

"Oh, is it? Life or death, that is what existence is. You had a choice, do as I asked, or die."

It reached into a pocket and tossed me a glass vial. I caught it with my right hand and looked it over. "What is it?"

"It will cure your radiation sickness."

I looked at the vial, contents thick and scarlet, questioning if it was telling the truth. "Why did you have me do it?"

"Because it was fun?" the Jalek mused, watching its smaller selves circle the pile of pulp, a couple of them pulling at the crushed matter with their unsettlingly tiny fingers.

"I don't buy it. There's more. You are an ancient creature, I can't imagine you're entertained in such a way."

"Now in that, you are wrong." It called its tiny selves back onto its body with a cooing sound. "I am far more cruel than you can imagine, and I get great pleasure from it. Still, you are part right. Survival outside one's home world takes cunning and cruelty. You will be forced to do things, to give things up in order to survive."

"I am good," I said, and thumped my chest with a fist. "I am not a killer."

"If you wish to survive, you must become a killer when the time is right. As it turns out, Isoptera find human flesh very tasty. If they were to come to Earth, they might turn your world into a farm. Would you not kill to keep that from happening? Yes, yes, self-defense is a moral high ground you keep standing on, but survival is brutal. There is a time to be kind, and a time to be cruel. There is a time to remain as you are, and a time to transcend."

A question which had been dancing at the edges of my thoughts dared to be spoken. "Who are you? Who are you really? This isn't how you began, is it?"

The Jalek gave a crooked half-smile, its oversized, not quite human face forcing my stomach to do flips. "No. If I were to take you through the ages, the many forms I have had, you would not believe them. I have adapted to survive in many different environments, and I now persist with the barest hint of what the Universe originally made me to be."

"Where did you come from?"

"A distant place, hundreds of light years away, a planet now cold and dead, a people not too unlike yours. We failed to adapt quick enough, war, disease, hunger. I came to the Foundry determined to survive. I came to the Foundry determined to help it in its mission."

"To protect life?"

The Jalek gave a slow nod. "It did not specify what life."

I let that thought sink in. I sure hoped we were favorites.

"I want to see my people," I said.

"And you will. When you leave this place, my guards will take you to your transport. It is not far away." The Jalek stood with a groan. "Now go."

I turned to leave, not sure how to feel. There was still so much unknown. I only hoped that once we reached the colony, we could figure it out. I hoped my parents were okay. I hoped Shelly was there. So much hope in a land where hope was such a fragile thread to dangle from.

"And one more thing," the Jalek said.

"Yes?"

"Do remember to take your medicine. It would be a shame for you to die after all that moral conflict."

CHAPTER 27

We stood at the docking platform beside the deep space transport waiting for the Jalek's pilot to arrive, going through our backpacks again and again ensuring we had everything we needed. Our packs were filled to bursting, almost too heavy to carry, and yet it still didn't feel like it was enough. What sort of situation were we headed into?

The craft we waited to board was a gilded, scorpion-shaped vessel that rested in near silence, its arms a pair of clawless nubs, its tail without a stinger, plumes of gas oozing from the joints near its shoulders. A soft, white light traced patterns along the angles of its exterior, revealing centuries of wear and hard use, scars from micrometeors and solar flares. It took me a moment to realize that the ship was not resting on the ground, but instead was hanging from a magnetic hook on a rail, its belly covered with arrays of antenna and other delicate equipment that were unable to support its weight. Even though it appeared sturdy, I imagined it to be as fragile as the *Vasco*, remembering the Jalek's insult. The void was an unforgiving place where forces beyond comprehension were commonplace. One wrong step, a minor miscalculation, and even one of the Foundry's creations could be destroyed by an errant asteroid or the crushing pressure of a gas giant.

We were not alone in needing to take a quick jaunt around this solar system. Several other passengers were gathered: a handful of cauliflower heads, a pair of Draeg, and a lone, aquamarine biped covered in cybernetic equipment. It turned out, most of the planets in Lignos were habitable in some capacity; either naturally, through a prolonged terraforming process, or the use of artificial structures such as Cynosure itself. It seemed most species didn't care to remain in the city for long, but those who did remained here forever.

Aware of our near-dawn departure, Gi'Vor came to show us off. It was hard to tell what it was thinking, given its dark body and black eyes, unfamiliar gestures and actions. I had mixed feelings leaving it behind. This alien owed us nothing, and yet it had helped us more than once, even saved my life. Was it a friend? Or had this been convenience? Were we just a curiosity? Did that matter?

"How do your people express gratitude?" I asked.

Gi'vor's attention fixed on me. "Gratitude?"

"Yeah, *amigo*," Esteban said. "Thanks."

"I do not understand."

I shook my head and took another approach. "We want to give you something intangible in exchange for your help."

Gi'Vor leaned forward, looking to our open hands. "How can you give me something intangible?"

"Is knowledge not intangible?" I ventured.

It shook. "Yes."

"Thank you," I said. "We would not still be alive without your help. We owe you a debt of gratitude."

It stood there for a moment, processing what I had said, the concept so foreign it didn't know how to respond.

Esteban flashed his pearly whites. "You're our little Spider-Man, ya? We appreciate what you did."

"Appreciate," Gi'Vor repeated. "This I understand. To recognize the full worth, full implications. Yes. I receive this appreciation, and for my part, I appreciate what you have done as well."

I blinked. "What did we do other than complicate your life here?"

"Broadened my experience. Allowed me to peer through a portal in space-time. I will never visit your home, and you will likely never visit mine, but we are better for knowing a little more of what is beyond our own gravity well."

"You're right. To be honest, when we first met I was afraid of you."

Gi'Vor leaned to one side, shifting on its legs. "I was afraid of you as well."

Esteban let out a chuckle and put a hand over his face, holding more back. "Of us? What? Why?"

"As a human, you are terrifying to look at. Those hands of yours are huge. You could crush my eyes with them."

"Gi'vor doesn't know what spiders are, ya?" Esteban patted me on the shoulder.

"No," I replied. "It wouldn't know."

"I have looked them up from your records," it added. "They are too small to be like Eipren. They have venom, oftentimes, we do not."

"This is true." I gave a smile, impressed by its curiosity, a trait many species shared, a desire to know more and just for the hell of it. I supposed this was the major driving factor in why we all made it here. Without that curiosity, that beautiful madness, we would have remained under rocks till the sun went cold.

"Look," I went on, "there's a quote I love from a writer on Earth, *'Travel is fatal to prejudice, bigotry, and narrow-mindedness, and many of our people need it sorely on these accounts. Broad, wholesome, charitable views of men and things cannot be acquired by vegetating in one little corner of the Earth all one's lifetime.'* What it means, is that when you learn more about others, fear tends to pass. Knowledge is anathema to fear."

Gi'vor dipped itself. "For my Sien to be part of the All, I must be willing to grow. You helped me grow."

"Goodbye, Gi'vor," I said.

"Stay well." Gi'vor shook in response.

The Jalek's pilot appeared, waving its hands, a cauliflower head dressed in robes with a red cape and broad shoulders. We boarded the ship after it. Esteban and I hefted our backpacks full of food and supplies through the hatch before climbing a short ladder. We had been informed that the food kept aboard the deep space transport might not be suitable for humans, and that it was best to prepare for this to keep from starving. I only hoped our destination was indeed the human colony. It would be unfortunate to arrive on a distant moon only to starve to death before we could manage any return arrangements.

Unlike the Foundry's typical designs, the interior of the transport was dark and a bit cold, its surfaces covered in pipes and nets. The pilot made for the forward of the ship, where an orb of blue liquid ten feet across sat recessed in the floor. It slipped out of its outer clothing and stowed it in a wall-mounted drawer before pressing a series of buttons at the top of the sphere. A clear hatch opened, allowing the cauliflower head to submerge itself completely. As it sank to the bottom, wires and cables snaked from hidden ports in the tank, connecting to various locations along the pilot's vertebrae.

"What in the heck is that?" Esteban asked, reaching out to grab the arm of the mechanically augmented biped.

The creature glared at Esteban, electronic eyes shuttering, blue and black, servos along its arms whining in consideration. "Star sphere," it said, voice crackly like a broken speaker.

"A what?"

"Star sphere," it repeated.

"What does it do?"

"The pilot is the ship. The ship is the pilot." The creature turned its back to us, making for another section of the ship.

"Amazing," I said, marveling at the sphere. "So, the pilot is given a direct connection to the functions of the ship. It would be like having a second skin. Can you imagine what that allows it to see?"

"A universe in colors," Esteban ventured.

"And inertia. G-forces."

"Ya. I bet the pilot can take this rig places that would turn us into spaghetti sauce without it. What, three Gs on take-off from Earth?"

"Right. I can remember feeling like my brains were on the back of my skull in the launch vehicle."

"Imagine a hundred, *amigo*."

"Splat."

A voice cut in over the intercom, "*Human passengers, make for room six, rear of the transport. We leave once you are secure.*"

"Come on," I said. "Let's buckle up."

We entered a room modified for humans. There was a set of acceleration chairs, big enough to eat us alive, and soft as pillows, an outside port on our right. Advanced technology or not, inertia was still an obstacle. Everyone had to strap in or potentially become a stain on the wall under intense acceleration; everyone other than the pilot in its star sphere. Once we were secure, harnesses and straps clipped, the pilot made an all call across the ship and began a countdown. I could feel the craft vibrate as we started to move, the magnetic hook transporting us to the outer dock.

Esteban gave me a grin.

"What's that look for?" I asked.

"It will be nice to see humans other than you, *amigo*," he replied.

"Tired of me already?"

"Damn right. Hoping maybe Miss Patton is still alive."

"Jennifer from Bioscience?"

He tilted his head. "We had a thing before it went down. Off and on. Maybe put it back on, everyone needs comfort and company, ya? I know I ain' the only one."

I felt my face turn hot, suddenly embarrassed like a schoolboy with a crush. "What do you mean?"

"Shelly, *amigo*. You're hoping she there."

"And my parents," I added, a palm caressing my warm cheeks.

"Sure. Sure. Blood and all that."

"I hope we get what we want."

Esteban's attention fell onto his hand terminal. "Me too."

There was a great deal riding on this journey. We hadn't discussed it explicitly, but we had spent enough time together I felt there was an understanding over what was at stake. We were leaving behind a land of comfort, an apartment with unlimited food and drink, shelter and space, on the hope that we would be reunited with our people. Cruel or not, I didn't believe the Jalek had lied to us. It seemed to keep deals in the same way a fae creature from a fairy tale might, holding to the letter the agreement if perhaps not the spirit. And yet, even if it had acted in earnest truth, a great deal could have happened. Maybe our people did leave for the moon. Maybe they fell into a trap. Maybe humans were still alive, but those not the ones we were desperate to see. These ideas were even more frightening than never seeing humans again.

We could have played it safe, stayed in Cynosure and lived out our lives in a land of constant wonder. Esteban and I had forged a friendship out of circumstance, and I now saw him like the brother I'd never had. There were worse humans to be stuck with forever.

"They'll be there," he said, leaning forward and putting one hand on my knee. "They'll be there."

The transport jostled and I shifted my attention to the window. Cynosure was sliding away, the vessel accelerating, the ship's exterior portal filled with swirls of stormy gas clouds as large as Earth, ribbons and eddies of scarlet and ginger twisting upon the surface of a gas giant at dawn. We banked away from the distant cloud tops into a ring of iceteroids I had been unable to see from the city. Among the glittering shards of fractal lattices, a golden gate appeared.

"That's it," Esteban said, leaning forward. "The ring Gi'Vor talked about, ya?"

"The Wandering Gate," I supplied, mouth going dry.

Our transport fired a set of thrusters, pushing us into a higher orbit. The Wandering Gate did not fall from view, we were instead able to get a better look. At this distance, about three quarters of the ring was visible, dawn's light reflecting off its gilded surface to reveal a complicated network of geometric machinery shot through with rivers of brilliant amber liquid, fuel or perhaps molten material. The longer I watched, I realized that some of the glitters around it were not from the ice in the ring, but drones tearing the city-size glaciers apart and returning them to the gate. The reason we had not seen both the ice ring and the gate near one another previously, was that it had repositioned itself to refuel. The scale of it all gave me a headache. It was quite possible that this was larger than the Foundry structure in orbit of Barnard's Star 3.

The moment passed and the window went dark, leaving nothing to see but distant pinpricks of starlight. I laid back in my seat and closed my eyes. The pilot made a safety call and accelerated us by several Gs, our bodies pressed deep into the soft acceleration chairs. The trip would take nearly a week, the first day a continuous burn to reach cruise velocity, then a ramping down to maintain thrust gravity. Esteban and I did our best to keep rested, to not dig too deep into our reserves, and to save our single bottle of wine for a special occasion.

With little to distract my wandering mind, I dwelled on what had happened on Cynosure, especially the death of the Phantomorph. I had willingly taken the Jalek's errand, and it had resulted in the cold-hearted murder of a sentient life. Maybe the marine creatures were assholes, but it had never done me wrong.

"You okay, *amigo*?" Esteban asked, his eyes narrowed. "I know that look, ya? A bit cold, a bit vacant. Too many gears turning round."

"I'm fine."

"Fine? Ya? You know what that means?"

"That I'm okay."

He shook his head. "No. You fucked up, insecure, neurotic and emotional. F. I. N. E."

I chuckled. "Oh. I see."

"Get it off your chest, it was pretty heavy what happened."

"I did what I had to."

"Still, all hard. Yous were backed in a corner. Shit deal."

"I don't want to talk about it."

"Okay then, can I tells a story?"

"Free world and all that, I think."

Esteban grimaced. "There was soldier that believed in his flag, in freedom, ya? Bad things came to world, bomb wielding idealists who been twisted to kill for economic reasons. War over oil. War over data. War over land not underwater. They say it's religion, but it's for money, power, resources, religion is often excuse. Hard times make hard people. Too many dollars at the top mean no dollars for the bottom. No dollars, no food; no food, no security; no security, people easy to coerce into evil. Understand?"

"Maybe."

"This soldier is given mission. Go with squad to take out leader of a splinter organization, the opposition. Charismatic man who leveraged social media to brainwash people. So you raid yellow house at the top of the hill to keep an attack from happening, attack that would kill hundreds. Soldier goes in with his friends, no one is there, just empty rooms and supplies for bombs. They sweep building, about to leave, then a boy stands at the end of the hall, package in hand. A boy, no more than thirteen. He looks at package, then at trigger sitting on table two steps away. Soldier locks eyes for a moment, then boy makes run for trigger. Soldier is given no other choice. In the end, little boy winds up on the floor in a pool of blood.

"What else was soldier to do, ya? If boy had taken hold of trigger, squad would be dead, attack may still happen. The right choice was made in the moment, but leaves a deep scar, ya? Breeds anger for those who hurt the boy. He did not deserve this. He was fed a diet of hate and lies. He had kind eyes, large and full of wonder. Now. He has nothing."

I sniffed and gave a nod, understanding. Knowing my friend's heart, this was something he did not carry lightly. "Esteban…"

He raised his hands to stay my reply. "Another life. Another person. Time will show you. We has a mission to complete, ya? What you say we drink that wine now?"

I nodded. "I say yes."

There was a choice before me, I just wasn't sure I could make it. This had been an impossible situation, and I had done what I could in the moment. Still, that didn't mean I had to absolve myself of all wrongs. If I were put in that position again, would I kill another to further our cause? To help complete the mission? At this point, saving Earth seemed so far away.

The wine went down fast, leaving us numb, and a little emboldened. When we were allowed to move freely about the cabin, we attempted to strike up conversations but got little in return.

It was no surprise that the Draeg spent most of their time soaking one or more of their leg-roots in a basin of clear water. They spoke almost the entire time, so long as we were not around, their words like creaking wood on a windy night, hollow and ethereal, branches moving in expressive patterns. I wanted very much to have a conversation with them, ask the kind of questions I had asked our friend Gi'Vor. What was it like on their world? How did a group of tree people develop technology and spaceflight? It was nearly impossible for me to conceptualize this for their species. The same went for the Phantamorphs. I could not imagine either race working with electronics or poring over schematics, building personal computers in garages or constructing intertwined, world-wide computer networks. Had they formed early space exploration organizations like NASA and the ESA? Sent capsules into space with a single shrub to circumnavigate their globe? Had international pressures and cold war pushed them into rapid innovations so that they might reach the nearest moon before their enemies?

So many questions. No answers. I took their silence as an insult for a while, just another race looking down at us humans like the Jalek had, but then I noticed they did not converse with the cauliflower heads, or the solo bio-hacker. Maybe it was just easier to keep to yourself and your own. Gi'vor had been afraid of us. Maybe they were too.

The pilot made its final call as we approached our destination. My stomach was a storm of excitement and nausea. I was unable to see the planet from this angle, and that bothered me. Did people flying across the globe in commercial airlines ever feel this way? Anxiety over not having the same view the cockpit afforded the pilot? At least window seats would give them a view of the ground, mine had given mostly empty space.

We hit atmosphere and the shuttle began to vibrate, its exterior hull heating as we aero braked. The view outside the window turned white then red, then blue as we fell towards the surface, the transport now gliding on airfoils. I could see clouds and distant mountains, lakes and scattered forests and open plains studded with rocks. The sight was breathtaking, an expanse of natural beauty stretching all the way to the horizon. This was the first time since I was five that I would set foot on solid ground. Artificial gravity and closed environments were all I'd ever known. This would be real.

The ground swelled within the window by degrees, every angle filled by red dirt and distant trees. The shuttle made a final rocking motion, and all noise ceased, engines shutting down, reactor cooling to a lower power mode. I waited for the all call, and when the pilot said it was safe, I unbuckled, the ship's orientation now perpendicular to what it was when we boarded.

"This a layover or the final destination?" Esteban mused, taking his heavy backpack from the storage rack in our room.

I gave a shrug. "I'm done making guesses."

We climbed a set of ladders to the exit hatch where the pilot waited for us.

"Air is safe to breathe," it told us, the sack near the base of its cauliflower shaped head pulsing. "Not so everywhere."

"How close is the colony?" I asked.

It opened the exterior hatch and pointed. "Beyond the tree line, could see on approach. Will not take you long."

"Thanks."

It gave a very human-like shrug and withdrew into the cockpit.

Esteban and I climbed through the hatch and down a long ladder. I hit solid ground and my feet began to tingle. I jumped in place, testing the surface to see if it had any give. My friend stared at me like I had lost my mind.

"You okay, *amigo*?" he asked.

I gave him a smile and stopped jumping. "I'm… Ready?"

"Ready, ready."

CHAPTER 28

We left the transport behind and ventured off into the forest. With no direction over the dangers of this world, we were left guessing as to what might could harm, or even kill us. Esteban's survival training from the service was valuable, yet even this only went so far. I found myself scanning the area near us for snakes and large insects, predators and aggressive plant life. To be honest, it was all a little overwhelming. Not only was this place alien, but it was also new, and exciting. A forest of real trees surrounding me, not a simulation.

The forest was dense, the plants mostly green, time having made them into something between jungle and deciduous flora, though it was lacking in a dense underbrush. Moisture permeated the air, and the ground was soft, covered in a fine carpet of triangular leaves and other organic detritus. Some of the plants were in bloom, brilliant blue-and-orange flowers with whiskery stamens protruding two and three times the length of the petals. It was all familiar, yet different. Evolution had taken a similar path to Earth on this distant moon, branching at only a few forks in the developmental road, not all of them.

Esteban stuck out a palm and held me back. I gave him a scowl and then realized he had kept me from running into a blackish frond as long and wide as the length of my arm. The alien frond undulated as if blown by a gentle breeze, then out of nowhere, it snapped at the forest floor, its blades lashing out at a fat beetle analog.

"How did you know?" I asked.

"Instinct. No everything here is friendly, ya? Can't be if it wants to survive."

"Yeah."

A sonic boom washed over us, rocking the canopy and scattering flocks of flying animals. I paused and turned my attention skyward. The transport's exhaust was burning through the sea of endless blue, its form shrinking with each passing second.

"Don' worry, *amigo*," Esteban said. "I think we're almost there."

"You sure?"

"Positive. I smell cookin'."

We pushed through the forest, up a gentle hill, then made our way down into an open valley of orange grass. Smoke rose from a scattered collection of geodesic metal structures ahead, dirt roads running between them, sunlight reflecting off of antennas and other heavy equipment in evidence. Our pace redoubled, and as we drew near, I could see people, real human beings milling about, talking, carrying gear, laughing.

"People," I mumbled.

There was a shout, and a man at the edge of the colony pointed to us and waved. Everyone within sight paused and turned our direction. Before anyone could speak, a woman broke from the crowd at a full run, heading deeper into the colony.

"Bugger me with a broomstick," the pointing man said, and I realized I knew him. I fucking knew him. I was looking at none other than Gareth Baker, a living crew member of the *Vasco Da Gama*. He was not alone. The edge of the colony was rapidly filling with other humans, the crowd dressed in a motley of dirty jumpsuits, overalls, blue jeans and assorted workwear.

Gareth gave us a welcoming smile. "Oi, it's Jackson's boy and the Spaniard comin' up out the brush. The hell you doin' on Creatus?"

"You sad I ain' dead?" Esteban extended a hand and Gareth gave it a vigorous shake. "Good to see another human. Milo is good company, but he makes for a small world."

"Hey, now," I replied in mock objection, and gladly accepted a handshake. "Good to see you."

"Likewise, likewise. Sure you two have a story or six."

The gathering crowd approached; faces I had known all my life filling my view. They were here. Alive.

"Where's Mom and Dad?" I asked Gareth.

He gave a sigh, then shook his head.

Just as I was about to ask for more information, Captain Tobias Williams pushed through the crowd and clasped me by the shoulder with a hand, his grip so hard it hurt. He looked a little older, moved with a slight limp, eyes tired and weary, in spite of the pleased expression on his face.

"Milo Hughes," he declared. "Damn good to see you."

"Captain."

"How in the name of all that is good did you make it here? The two of you look healthy."

"It's a long story."

"One we want to hear for sure."

"We were just getting to the part about his parents," Gareth supplied.

Captain Williams nodded. "I bet you have a lot of questions, and so do we. I hate to jump right into it, considering we have much to celebrate. But there's no easy way to say this, and no good time to tell you."

"Where are they?

"Milo, you have to understand."

My heartrate redoubled, my chest tense. "Are my parents dead?"

A moment passed as the captain chose his words carefully. He scratched at his stubbly chin, then replied, voice thin, "We don't know for sure."

"Did anyone see them die?"

"No. We have done our best to put the events back together in a timeline and… no. The Isoptera took a lot of us. We were outgunned and overwhelmed. Everyone did their best to get to the capsules and a good portion of us did, but not all. No one saw them die. And yet, Adriana and Jackson were not on any of the capsules."

"Henry B was our pilot," Esteban interjected.

"Did he make it?"

"No, sir, he did not."

The captain frowned. "That's too bad. Good man. I'm sure you know what happened to the *Vasco.*"

I shrugged out of my heavy pack and leaned onto its rigid frame. "It broke apart."

"Like a piece of splintering candied brittle. The Foundry reduced it to its base components, as it said, once all of us were free. We have always hoped there were other groups, but the Foundry is not forthcoming with certain information."

"Don't we know," Esteban put in, patting his chest with an open palm. "Bureaucratic runaround."

"I had hoped your parents were with you."

Everyone fell silent for a moment of reflection.

I set my jaw and swallowed. "Until I see a set of bodies, they are not dead." My parents were the heartiest, strongest-headed people I'd ever known. They weren't dead. They couldn't be dead. "I'm holding on."

"Fair enough," the captain agreed.

The dam broke and next thing I knew random crew members started patting me on the back and shaking my hand. They bombarded me with questions about how we had gotten here and what had happened. I saw George and Austin, Dr. Karen, as well as Mary and Perry. At the edge of the crowd, James lingered, a mixed expression on his face. Each time I tried to get closer to him someone pulled me away, and before I knew it, he was gone. Esteban was swamped just as I was in hugs and handshakes, smiles and people trying to catch up. I hoped Jennifer was here for his sake, but I didn't see her face.

I spun around to ask Perry how things had been, to tell him we had found his journal, when out of nowhere I was tackled. My back was thrown flat onto the ground, a pair of arms wrapped around me, a body lying over mine. I shook my head and reopened my eyes; I was looking at the sky.

"Milo!" Shelly said, her brilliant face inches from my own, her hips straddled across me. "It's you! You're alive!" She ran her hands over my chest and squeezed me again. "It's really you."

She was here, in the flesh. As quick as my brain processed this sliver of information, I felt a wave of excitement and nausea wash over me. My hands began to sweat, and I found it hard to speak.

"You okay?" she asked, a rye smile on her face. "Didn't mean to take you by surprise."

"Shelly," was all that I could get out. I coughed on the dust our fall had kicked up. "Shelly."

"That's my name." She let out a chuckle. "A lot might have changed, but that remains the same." She rolled off of me and stood up. "Here, take my hand. Sorry, didn't mean to knock you off your feet."

I couldn't believe it. It was her, standing before me, smiling back. Most of our lives I had only seen her in shipboard attire, a featureless white jumpsuit and boots, but here she was dressed in a form fitting grey t-shirt with a cropped leather jacket, silver necklace and black stone pendant, blue jeans with a knife strapped to her thigh, and high-topped work boots. Over her shoulder she wore a satchel of supplies. Her mop of curls was pulled back to keep them out of her eyes. She looked every bit the badass frontierswoman she had no doubt become.

"No, no," I replied. "Not at all." I felt my face brighten, the tension in my shoulders and chest over the news of my parents unwind.

"Wow, Milo. Look at you. You're here."

"It's what everyone keeps saying."

"Could use a haircut and a shower, that's about all."

"You saying my hair is too long and I stink?"

She crossed her arms and nodded. "Yes. Yes I am."

I averted my gaze and scratched at the back of my head. "Maybe you can help with that."

"Maybe."

For a second time she threw her arms around me, stink or no. It was great to be held. To be touched. I drew her close and we just stood there, her chest against mine, a warm cheek against my shoulder, the scent of clean, dark curls filling my nose. Could we stay here forever? Would that be okay?

After a moment she whispered in my ear, "I'm so glad to see you."

I was about to respond when someone shouted in our direction, "Shelly! Hey!" My heart gave a start.

Shelly immediately let go and took a step back. A guy my age with a thick beard and a mane of blonde hair made his way over to us. It took me a while to figure out who it was, given the drastic changes to his physical appearance. It was Lance Brittan, her one-time boyfriend.

"It is you," he said, taking a place to Shelly's right, a bit too close to be just friends. I didn't like these details. "Welcome to Creatus."

Well, this had happened fast, I thought she was done with the joker. It had hardly been a few weeks since we had left the Foundry facility, and she was already with someone else? Had we not shared a moment in the simulation before that attack? What of our unfinished business? I swallowed my feelings down and extended a hand, my stomach doing flips. "Thanks."

"Where you been?"

"It's a long story."

"I'm fucking sure."

"We're just glad you're safe," Shelly said, her happiness not dimming. "You're safe."

"Shelly," Lance said, his tone flat. "We've got some shit work to do on the other side of camp."

She spun and gave him a scowl, hands on hips for a moment, before letting out an amused chuckle. "It can wait."

"No, it can't," he insisted, his mouth tight.

"Yes, I'm pretty sure it can."

"It's for the—" His words cut off as his attention drifted to something over my shoulder.

I pivoted where I stood, knowing on some level that I wasn't going to like what I saw. From out of the tree-line came a half-dozen horse-size slugs propelled on beds of insects, their eyes-stalks bobbing, claws twitching. At their side walked members of the *Vasco Da Gama's* crew, engaged in deep conversation with them. Humans were working with *them. Them...*

"What are they doing here?" I whispered.

Shelly blinked at me. "The Gene Brokers?"

"Yes. Them."

"Who do you think brought us here?" Lance replied. "They've been helping us out."

"Don't trust them," I said, rubbing absently at my right arm.

"Why?" Shelly tucked curls behind her ear and cocked her head. "They've been great along the way. Helped us set up this camp, get our supplies in order. A few of us have even been sick, the universal inoculant not quite taking care of everything, and so they've treated us."

Something in what she said drew a thought to the surface. I was under the impression it had been weeks since we had first made contact with the Foundry, but this colony was well-lived in. Everyone was at ease as if in routine, clothes were worn, not from poor construction but hard work.

"How long have you guys been here?" I ventured.

"Two years, Earth time," Shelly replied, matter of fact. "Best we can estimate."

"What?" I put a hand to my mouth. "Two years?"

"Why?"

"I—well," I shook my head in an attempt to decant my scattered thoughts, "Esteban and I have had a hard time figuring out the exact time. We believe it has been no more than a month or two in our frame of reference since the *Vasco Da Gama* arrived at the Foundry."

We watched as the slugs and their entourage entered the colony and made their way past our group. I was given a few more hellos and handshakes by the escorting crew members as their group passed. For their part, the Gene Brokers ignored me. I was just another human.

"Two months," Shelly mulled this over. "Why didn't we arrive at the same time?"

"I don't know," I said. "Whatever method of travel the Foundry used to bring us to Cynosure must have had a margin. Maybe we traveled slower in our ship. How would we know how long we were in stasis?"

"Maybe." Shelly watched the Gene Brokers scuttle out of sight. "I often wonder how long it's been since we left Earth. Another eighteen years, decades?"

"Centuries?" Lance added. "There's no way for any of us to know for sure."

"There's no going back is there?" I mused.

Shelly shook her head. "I don't think so. At least, not as it was. I hope it's not been too long to help."

"Well, long time or not, Gene Brokers are bad news."

"But they are our patrons. They take care of us."

"Look, I had a run in with one in Cynosure. It grabbed my arm with this tentacle thing and burned me." I pulled back my sleeve to expose the fading red mark. "It hurt. I heard things. I've talked to others."

"They seek to do no harm," she pleaded, putting a soft hand on my arm. "They are like the Foundry. It must have been an accident."

"Yeah, yeah, they protect life. I've heard the line." I ran my fingers through my hair and sighed. "I'm telling you, that's not the whole story. The species we encountered in Cynosure were afraid of them. We made a friend with an Eipren and from his impressions they don't tell the whole truth. There's more to it."

"Eipren?"

"They're spider-looking people. Very courteous. Saved my life."

"Ah. And I suppose I owe them a thanks."

"Gi'Vor."

"What an interesting name."

Without preamble, Lance began to wander off in the direction the Gene Brokers had gone. "You coming, Shelly?" he mumbled over his shoulder, his tone brusque.

"In a minute," she said.

He paused for an instant, back going straight, shoulders tensing. "Whatever," he growled and stomped off.

Shelly flashed a weak smile in his direction and sighed. "Life," she mused.

The captain reappeared, giving me a slap on the back. "Milo, we have business to attend to."

"We do?"

"Yes." The captain waved at Gareth.

"Sir?" he asked.

"Get word over to Freda at the Post. Let them know we have arrivals and that I authorize the use of Deadly Force."

"Deadly force?" Esteban added himself to our huddle, fingers rubbing his chin. "What is this?"

"You heard me, soldier," the captain replied. "Homemade hooch isn't going to drink itself."

Gareth punched Esteban on the shoulder and let out a laugh. "An' it's cheap as chips, mate, a headache in a tumbler. Get ya right pissed in a couple swallows."

This made Esteban grin. "Best plan I heard all day. No better time to get pissed, ya?"

Shelly sidled up beside me and took hold of my arm. "Shall we?"

I opened my mouth to speak but nothing came out. Instead, I tipped my head and followed her lead. As far as I was concerned, she could take me anywhere she wanted, and it would be just fine. I only hoped Lance wouldn't be too angry at us, and well, you know, if he was angry—he could go fuck himself.

CHAPTER 29

Esteban and I were led through the flaps of a dome-shaped structure filled with aluminum tables, benches, and the moist smell of savory cooking. My stomach growled at the delicious aroma, even if I had no idea what was in the pot. The Post, as it was called, was large enough to seat about a hundred colonists shoulder to shoulder, dimly lit by rope lights and LED tracks, with an open kitchen and buffet tables at one end, and a gleaming copper machine as tall as the domed ceiling on the other.

It was interesting to me no matter where humans went, no matter what we did, there was always a desire to create a meeting place, a center of social activity. Aboard the *Vasco Da Gama* we had utilized the mess halls, observation rooms, and in many cases, the bridge. As us youths had gotten older, we had even made our own dance club in a set of empty quarters, a place where we could let our hair down and be kids in peace. The Post was no different, other than the fact that adults, as it seemed, required one thing kids did not—the opportunity to burn through brain cells while they flapped their gums.

In a place like Creatus, the name the *Vasco's* crew had given the moon as well as the colony, there was little opportunity to go off on holiday. It was for this reason that Mary and her brother Perry put their engineering prowess to work and built a necessity for human settlers. A copper still. It didn't seem to matter that this monstrosity churned out a beverage as similar to engine degreaser as it was to hard liquor. Its true product was something everyone needed at times. A vacation.

Perry led me over to the still, pulled a fresh glass mug from a nearby shelf, then drew a measure of hooch from a tap.

"From the reservoir," he said, his electronic eyes gleaming in the dim light. "Have a sip. Tell me what you think."

I took the offered mug and gave it a wary eye. I could already feel my eyebrows singe at the smell. "We sure this is safe? Positive this isn't hydrazine?"

"No, no, no," Perry replied, and drew a mug for Esteban. "Hydrazine smells like ammonia."

"An' you call this Deadly Force?" Esteban asked, sniffing his mug and twisting it in the light like someone inspecting both the bouquet and legs of a fine brandy. "How many folk gotten pregnant after this here?"

"Well," Perry smiled, "more than a few have tried."

I realized I was still staring into my mug, hoping the answers to everything might lie on the surface of the clear liquid. Wrong beverage. What idiotic things might I end up saying after this hit my system? Will I end up all over Shelly professing my undying love when she was clearly already seeing someone else? Would I show them how much of an idiot I truly was? There was only one person in this room I had truly let my guard down in front of, and for that, I now considered him a brother.

"It's safe," Shelly assured me, a smirk on her soft face. "I've had more than my fair share."

"I'm not so sure about this," I replied. "Experience in drinking isn't something I've earned yet."

"Not enough headaches?"

"Nope."

"This might help."

Esteban looked over at me and raised his mug. "Let's do this, *amigo*. We've been through worse, ya?"

I gave a long sigh and raised my mug in response. "Forged in fire."

"Que el camino se eleve para encontrarte en tu viaje!"

We downed the contents, and my throat caught fire. This was nothing at all like sipping on wine. My arms and back shuttered and I started to cough. Visions of cartoon characters sipping from clay jugs with XXX written on the side popped into my head.

My friend was not fazed in the least. He licked his lips and nodded at Perry. "Good shit, *amigo*."

Perry gave him a toothy grin, his optical headset gleaming. "Right?"

I blinked for about a minute, feeling as if the lining of my esophagus might have been ablated away, and soon realized that Shelly was patting me on the back. The coughing came under control and I stood upright.

"God damn," I muttered.

"What you think about Deadly Force?" Perry asked, wringing his hands in anticipation.

"Deadly AF," I replied, my voice horse.

At this, Perry's back went straight, and a smug, proud look took hold of him. He dusted off his shoulder and gave a harrumph. His sister Mary rolled her eyes at him and tossed back her rainbow blonde curls. She was older than I remembered, creases of skin at the corners of her eyes conveying a life of many smiles, a little softer around the middle. This made her no less pretty. Was her hair always different colors? How many times had she changed it over the years? Did someone ever truly grow out of that?

"I think that's enough for now," Shelly interjected, and led me over to a table. "How are you holding up?"

"I'm okay."

"You sure? I guess Dad told you about your parents."

My lips tightened, and a lump rose in my throat. "He did."

"I'm sorry, Milo."

"I'm not giving up on them. No body. No death."

She gestured to a bench where I could sit. "I'll stand by you in that. If there's a way to keep looking, we will. They aren't the only ones with a missing status."

"Thanks."

"You hungry?"

"Famished."

"I'll get you something to eat."

"That's okay," I said, standing again. "I can get it myself."

She raised her open palms. "No. I got this."

"I don't want to impose."

She spun on her heels and made for the buffet.

A clamor of voices rose over my shoulder and I saw the Post filling fast. The people entering were not mere crew members of the *Vasco Da Gama* stuck on a distant world. They were colonists. Creatus was no way station, people were settling in. Whatever duty shifts the day held were done, and everyone was calling it. Time to eat, drink, and be merry, for tomorrow we may be murdered by space slugs. Before the crowd could swamp us, the captain appeared and asked everyone to give us some room, that there would be time for this later. Appeased, they went to their own tables and he came to sit with us.

"Get some Deadly Force in you?" The captain took a seat across from me.

I tugged at my collar. "Yes, sir."

"A bit rough the first go. Gets smoother, I promise." He took an offered mug from Perry and sipped on the fiery brew. "Ahh. Good to celebrate. We're so glad you're here."

"Music?" Perry asked, and with a nod from the captain he pressed a few buttons on a hand terminal. The Post began to vibrate with soft, bass-heavy music, a mix of light-hearted 2020s electronic pop with drawn-out downbeats and catchy lyrics wrapping the room in a sugary cocoon.

"I'm glad to be here," I said. "We didn't think we'd make it."

Shelly set a pair of trays before Esteban and I then took a seat on my right. The plates were covered in green and yellow vegetables, varieties I could not name, and a stringy brown meat smothered with gravy.

"Always such a good host," the captain told his daughter.

"Mom raised me right."

"Yeah," he said, heaving a sigh. "Give it a taste, boys. All the food is native, safe to eat, thanks to our benefactors. The yellow roots are kasara, look like carrots and taste like potatoes, and the green bits, those are rapni. Kind of like turnips. Then there's the meat—"

"Your benefactors?" I interrupted.

"Yes. The Kabosai. Gene Brokers."

Shelly put a hand on my leg under the table and squeezed. I held my tongue. It was not easy telling myself that my personal experience may have been one-sided. I needed to make new judgments, not just those borrowed from Gi'Vor.

I took several bites of my food. It was good. Fresh ingredients were not something I was used to, having lived most of my life on the *Vasco Da Gama*. The vegetables had an earthy quality that was unfamiliar, and almost too much salt for my taste. Still, it was food, and it settled nice on an empty stomach.

"Perry!" the captain called. "Bring us another round."

"Ooo, I'll get a pitcher!"

I raised a hand. "Since when did one of the most talented engineers aboard the *Vasco Da Gama* become a bartender?"

"Don' you know, *amigo*?" Esteban cut in before shoveling food into his mouth.

"Know what?"

He swallowed everything down without hardly chewing. "All engineers secretly desire to tend bar."

"He's on to something," Shelly added.

I shook my head, not understanding. "How is this a thing?"

"Oh, it's a thing."

The captain nodded. "It's a thing."

Perry returned with a pitcher three quarters of the way full with Deadly Force. Just thinking of drinking it all made my head swimmy, made my stomach do flips. The captain poured us each a little more.

"Want to hear a joke?" Perry asked, bouncing on his heels.

Esteban rolled his eyes and put a palm to his face. "*Ay dios mio.*"

"Okay, okay, okay. So there's Frank, an aerospace engineer—"

"Because of course," Shelly whispered beside my ear.

"—and he purchases an old portable music player, not like a terminal or even a phone, a standalone player. He's in his office trying to get his newly acquired gadget to work when the janitor, Joe, walks into the office and asks, 'Hey man, what are you listening to?'

"Frank replies, 'Nothing yet! I can't get this damn thing to work! Can you help me?'

"So, Joe decides to give it a shot. He sticks the ear buds in his ears and presses a few buttons. After bobbing his head to a beat, really getting into it, he hands it back to Frank. When Frank tested it for himself, he heard nothing.

"He said, 'Damnit, Joe! This isn't rock, it's silence!'

"Joe scowled back at Frank and said, 'Well, fuck you! I'm a janitor. You fix it then.'"

We gave Perry a blank look, not sure how we should react. Was there a punch line coming? Perry sighed and dug into his back pocket, unfolding a large piece of paper covered in lines and scribbled notes.

Mary glared at her brother. "This is why you should never trust an engineer with graph paper."

"I'll bite," I said. "Why not trust them?"

"They're always plotting."

Perry slapped his forehead with the unfolded notes. "Oh, har har har, Mary." He gave a pause, pointed at something on the paper, then went on, "I have another. The optimist says, 'The glass is half full.' The pessimist, 'It's half empty.' What does the engineer say?"

"I don't know," I offered. "What?"

"It's twice as big as it needs to be!"

I gave an easy chuckle at just how bad the joke was.

The captain pointed a finger at Perry. "I think they're getting worse."

"They're definitely getting worse," Shelly agreed. "Hey, Dad, by any chance would you know any jokes about sodium?"

"Na," he replied, smirking at his daughter.

I suddenly felt like I was ten all over again. Was I surrounded by adults, or oversized children?

"Alright, alright," Perry went on. Everyone tensed. "Two theoretical physicists are lost at the top of a mountain. Theoretical physicist number one pulls out a map and peruses it for a while. Then he turns to theoretical physicist number two and says, 'Hey, I've figured it out. I know where we are.' 'Where are we then?' 'Do you see that mountain over there?' 'Yes.' 'Well… That's where we are.'"

"Kind of funny?" I commented, feeling bad for him.

"Christ on a cracker," he mumbled and folded up his graph paper.

"Good try, little brother," Mary said, and squeezed his shoulders.

"Look, if you're not part of the solution, then you're part of the precipitate."

The captain raised a mug. "You're a hell of an engineer, Perry. Can't be good at everything."

Perry took the moment to skip around his musical playlist, not quite liking what we were listening to. Mary snatched the hand terminal from his fingers.

"My collection, my choice," she said.

"Give it back! I'm tired of hearing the same old songs. Its all blap blap womp this, zig zig that."

"Then you should have thought to make a backup of your own collection to a hand terminal, like a smart person."

"Mine had movies."

"Which take up more bytes, numbnuts."

"Yeah, yeah, yeah." Perry grabbed his sister's shoulders and shook. "Wait, stop. I like this song."

"This song?" Her eyes went wide.

"Yes, yes!"

"Alright, what the hell?"

Esteban gave them a scowl as the song started. It was bouncy and light, like the rest of Perry's selections had been, yet I could tell it was far older. The quality of the recording was tinny and high, less bass and more Casio keyboard, a young woman singing about her wistful hope for all girls. I knew I'd heard the song at some point, maybe in an old movie trailer, a girl in a patchwork of fashion styles with teased red hair chewing bubblegum dancing to the beat, but I couldn't be sure.

The siblings began to sing to one another. I knew these lyrics. I knew them. A girl coming home in the morning getting scolded by her mother for having too much fun the night before. Then it hit me. Was this song, *Girls Just Wanna Have Fun* by Cyndi Lauper? Seriously?

I raised an eyebrow, and before I could take a shot at them for being so ridiculous, Shelly took me by the hand and led me out onto what was fast becoming a broiling dance floor. The room spun and a crowd appeared. Shelly hopped and skipped and would not let go of my hand. My mouth hung in a half-smile, my chest thundering. She looked back at me as we spun round and round, her eyes flickering with strings of light, curls bouncing with each awkward step, a smile wide enough to bridge the gulf between worlds having taken over her face.

The siblings grew ever worse in their singing, not bothering to stay with the key of the song. Shelly joined them.

I was pretty sure if you had called in experts to determine the aptitude of the *Vasco's Crew* for dancing, you would discover that we were about the worst dancers in the universe. It was likely Gi'vor had better moves, possibly even the Jalek. I imagined it doing kick lines with all those weird copies of itself. We moved like a bunch of sweaty teenagers up too late who had raided their dad's liquor cabinet. And you know what? It was perfect. No one cared. Everyone was free and unrestrained. We were at the ass-end of God knows where, but we had each other. We held a candle of humanity in a dark room, and for this instant, that candle burned bright as a star.

Although I didn't know all the words, the chorus was easy enough to sing along to. And so I did. And for as silly as I felt, my joy multiplied.

We all just want to have fun.

The song came to an end and everyone clapped. I leaned over on my knees and caught my breath.

"That was fun," Shelly said.

"Yeah, it was," I replied. "Fun."

"I had almost forgotten what it was like. So much… you know."

"I do."

The crowd dispersed and she gestured to my seat at the table. We took our places and swallowed down more Deadly Force. It got easier the more we drank. Shelly tidied up her curls and let out a sigh. She ran a finger along the rim of her mug and rocked her shoulders to the beat of whatever song the siblings had chosen next. We sat in silence for a few, just listening, taking in the vibes, enjoying the company.

Perry broke the silence. "I'm curious, did you see Isoptera in Cynosure?"

"Yeah," I replied. "A few. They were dressed differently. They looked important."

"I see. They have a small presence on Creatus, but they won't come near with the Kabosai around."

"Why's that?" Esteban asked, raising his eyes from his mug.

"I think they're afraid of them. The Kabosai are, well, they have resources. Somewhere up in orbit they have a ship, and I can tell you this, the Foundry didn't build it."

"Oh?"

"Yeah. It's not all sleek and gilded. It's a hunk of rock with engines strapped to it. I'm damned curious about what it looks like on the inside."

"They not bring you here in it?"

"No. It was another transport. The ship in orbit has too much mass. Far too big to enter a gravity well."

"A mothership," Shelly clarified. "Has to be at least three miles across."

I rolled my eyes. "Small by Foundry standards."

"Small," the captain mused. He reached for the Snoopy pin on his shirt's lapel and rubbed at it with his thumb. All this way and he hadn't lost it. "Sure. We could call it that."

I closed my eyes for an instant, imagining the enormous, asymmetric asteroid as it made eccentric polar orbits around the moon, the light of Lignos drawing it from darkness each full rotation, pockmarks of micro-meteor impacts across its skin. One end of the rocky, charcoal lump had a hole large enough to admit a hundred transports at a time; the other, a collection of six stacks as tall as skyscrapers, engines with enough delta-v to shift orbit and launch an object heavy enough to cause nuclear winter if it were to impact Earth. Fine details came into focus, machinery along its surface in a ring, pulsing orange lights within the maw of its open harbor, windows and hatches along habitation buildings and sections with symbols in more languages than I could ever comprehend. All was in perfect clarity. Too much clarity.

It hit me. This was not my imagination. The images were real, telescopic. Shelly had her hand resting on my leg. I didn't dare open my eyes. Somehow, she was beaming the image to me through her implants, a peer-to-peer network connection similar to what I had done with the nanofluid. Her fingers tensed and I imagined her knowing smile. She was being clever.

This wasn't all that came through. After a moment images of crew members flashed in my head, bodies and bloody messes painted upon the deck of the *Vasco Da Gama*. I doubt Shelly was aware she had transmitted them. Signal bleed. Whatever feeling of calm I had taken started to erode. There were things I needed to know.

"Captain." I opened my eyes once more. "May I ask a question?"

"Of course, Milo." He leaned forward on his elbows and clasped his fingers. "What is it?"

"I need to know. How many of us survived?"

His attention fell onto his mug, and for a moment he said nothing.

"Two hundred and ninety," he replied.

Esteban snapped out of his reverie; his eyes narrowed. "That's all?"

"Yeah."

"Deidrick?" he asked.

"I'm sorry. Confirmed to be taken by the Isoptera."

"Jennifer Patton?"

Shelly shook her head. "Sorry, Esteban."

His jaw set into a hard line as he downed the rest of the contents in his mug. Mary came around behind him and wrapped her arms around his neck, holding him tight. Esteban did not push her away, he raised a hand and touched Mary's arm. With a nod she called Perry back over, and he refilled Esteban's mug.

"We lost a lot of good people," the captain went on, tapping the table with a finger. "But we're here now, and we're alive. What else could we have done? I have gone over the events more times than I can count, and the result would have been about the same. Should we have raised a better security force? Would that have mattered? Would the Foundry have reacted in a different way if we had come on a ship armed with nuclear weapons?"

"We're blessed to be alive," Shelly added.

"I was hoping for more," I said, not sure how to respond.

"So were we," the captain replied. "Tell us, Milo. What happened? How did you two get here?"

"I hope you have a few minutes."

"All we have is time."

I took in a deep breath and shook out my hands, preparing to get this rock off my chest. It was time to experience it all over again.

"Okay…"

Over the next hour I laid it all out. I had expected Esteban to chime in or correct me if the details were a little off, but he had fallen into a silence over the news of Jennifer's death. I told them about our harrowing escape from the *Vasco Da Gama* in the capsule, the Foundry's lack of clear information aboard the station, and our transport to Cynosure.

It turned out that our fellow crew members had had a far easier time in the city than we had, not being homeless, not dealing with the Frendol, not having to make deals with the Jalek. They had found the monolith upon arrival and were escorted to the quarters we had later discovered. They had lived in luxury for nearly a year before the Gene Brokers, the Kabosai as they were called, brought them by transport to Creatus for reasons I did not understand.

"They protect life," the captain insisted. "They protect us. We needed to start over. No ship. No way home. Cynosure was not the place."

"And so, they offered to bring us here," Shelly said. "The Foundry has engineered many planets and moons in this system. It will take a great deal of time before our numbers outgrow this rock."

"Wait. Wait." I raised my palms in confusion. "Hang on. We intend on staying here forever?"

The captain shrugged. "It's the best plan for now. We have no industry to speak of, no ships. We are getting by just fine, plenty to eat, very little danger. And with powerful friends among Cynosure and the Foundry network, who knows? There's a bright future for us among the stars."

"What about the mission? What about FICSE? What about those suffering back on Earth? Humanity sacrificed so much for us to be here. Trillions of dollars. Almost a decade of work. And not to sound cliché, but we are the last, best hope to reverse the damage we did to our world. We have to make the Foundry help us, it has the power, we've seen it. My parents dedicated their lives to this cause. My life to this cause."

Shelly exchanged a knowing glance with her father. It was brief, but I could tell it was important. This was a discussion they had had before, and both of them had strong feelings.

"We'll cross that bridge later," the captain assured me. "The mission isn't over, there are just complications."

"Complications? This sounds like an excuse."

His expression became one of annoyance, his mouth slack and eyes narrowed. "Like, we don't have a ship and we don't know where we are. How do we even get back to Earth? How long has it been? Will it even matter by the time we return? There are many factors to consider, most of all, the safety of everyone here. The only thing we know for sure is we are alive."

The hooch was going to my head, making me feel safe in being mouthy. Even though I saw it happening, I couldn't stop it. Superior or not, I deserved answers. "So, you're telling me we're giving up?"

"Giving up?" the captain asked, his expression turning hard. "Milo, you have to understand, we are in an impossible situation where we have little or no control."

I stood up, my palms flat on the table. "I just went through hell and back, only to find out that the purpose of my life—which I had zero choice about, to literally save the fuckin' Earth—has been taken from me. Not to mention, my only blood, my parents, are lost. You're going to have to cut me some slack. It's a lot to take in at once."

"Milo..." Shelly reached for my arm.

"Is there a bathroom?" I asked.

The captain gave a sullen shrug and gestured towards one end of the dome.

Before anyone could say a word in response, I stormed off.

This was bullshit. They had given up far too easy. Mom and Dad had lost the bulk of their lives to nothing but a false promise. And for what?

I found the men's room and relieved myself, muttering my frustrations under my breath. As I was washing my hands afterwards, looking to give myself enough time to calm down, the door opened.

James stepped inside.

He froze as soon as he spotted me. The metal door slammed shut behind him with a ring.

"James," I said while using a towel. "How are you?" I extended a clean hand.

"Milo," he said, not taking my hand. He took in a sharp breath and began to cough, a hand to his chest.

"You okay?" I asked. It was a hard, dry cough. It didn't sound good.

He raised an open hand to quiet me as he regained control of himself.

"It's good to see you. I'm so glad you made it." I waited for him to respond. When he didn't, I went on, "You okay?"

"I—" he started, then paused. "What are you doing here, Milo?"

"It's a long story. How's your mom?"

"She's dead," he stated, deadpan.

"James, I didn't know."

"No. You didn't. She was killed by the Isoptera, and if I had had some… Never mind. Look, I'll go piss in the woods. Better that way." He turned on his heels and reached for the door.

I caught him by the shoulder. "Dude, I'm so sorry. Is there anything I can do?"

"You can let me the fuck go, that's what." He shrugged out of my grip and exited the bathroom.

What in the hell had that been about? James and I had always been close. I rubbed my temples and made my way back to the table, my neck and forehead sweaty. Shelly and Perry were the only ones still there, the captain, Esteban, and Mary having moved on.

"I'm sorry," I said. "I got wound up."

Shelly smiled at me. "It's okay. Dad went home. He's not mad at you, he understands."

"Esteban okay?"

Perry shrugged. "Mary took him to a set of quarters. Jennifer's death was hard on us all. To be honest, everyone's death has been hard. We're family, blood or not."

"Yeah," I said, hanging my head.

Shelly kept her eyes fixed on me. The Post was starting to empty, the music now a soft buzz in the background, only a handful of others besides us three in evidence. She glanced at Perry, then back at me, playing absently with her curls.

"Welp," Perry barked after a moment as if suddenly remembering something. "I best be off. Have a good night."

"You too," Shelly told him. She hopped over to me and took hold of my arm. "What do you say we get some fresh air?"

I nodded. "That would be nice."

"How about I show you the stars from Creatus."

CHAPTER 30

Shelly led us out of the Post into a pitch-black night. The star of this system, Lignos, had been high when I had entered the dome, but now… time had moved fast. For some moments I had a hard time seeing. Everywhere I had lived for the past eighteen years had been lit for convenience in one way or another. During night-mode on the *Vasco Da Gama*, the edges of the halls still had a glow. The same was true in Cynosure, where there were streetlamps to guide people at night. In the colony on Creatus, however, there were no lamps or lights of any kind, and the dark wasn't quiet. It was active with the sound of hooting animals and chittering insects. Life was busy doing what life did, surviving, mating, thriving. It was all so alien. Normal gravity. A sky overhead. Real plants. Crisp air and a gentle breeze.

My foot caught on a rock and I nearly pitched over on my face, my drink sloshing a little onto the ground. Shelly caught my arm.

"Milo?"

I sighed hearing her say my name. "Yeah. Just a damn rock."

"We don't have far to go. I'll guide you."

"Thanks. It has been a while here for you, two years to settle in. You still draw?"

"I do. I'll have to show you my sketchbook."

"I'd like that."

"I guess you're still interested in tiny machines."

"For sure. Especially when they help save my life from psychopathic lemurs."

"What a crazy thing to happen."

"Just glad none of you had the same experience." I scratched at the back of my head. "I know this is random, but how did you beam that picture into my head?"

Shelly lifted her shoulders in a shrug. "Whatever do you mean?"

"You know what I'm talking about. The Gene Broker ship."

"I have my ways."

"I see how you're gonna be. Can you show me?"

"Maybe, just maybe. Remember, I studied neural connectivity. I've been researching it more, even here. Better ways for us to integrate with systems and one another."

"You modified your implants?"

"Just a little."

My eyes adjusted to night about the time we reached a set of storage boxes with lids high enough to brush my belly button. She hopped up on one, leaned her back against the edge of the Post's structure, and patted the empty spot beside her. I handed her my drink and climbed up. The instant my backside hit the metal box, I tensed.

"Steel gets a little cold out here," Shelly told me. "If you sit here for a minute, your butt will warm up."

"I have goose bumps."

"Guess it doesn't take much does it?"

"Well, I, eh." I turned towards her, the clarity of Shelly's features resolving before me. "I've had plenty of reasons over the past few weeks to catch goose bumps."

"That so?"

"Yeah."

"Let me give you another." She pointed up.

I leaned back, turning my attention to the sky and gave a start at what was overhead. Half of the unfathomably open space was filled with an imposing world, a gas giant whose color was difficult to discern as Creatus traversed its shadow. At its northern pole blue lights danced, aurora skipping for thousands of miles as charged particles were dragged into its magnetic field, reaching higher states of energy. Beyond the borders of the eclipsing world was an endless black dome shot through with billions of pinpricks of light. The Observatory on the ship had been beautiful, but this, it was different somehow. The sky here was cold and clear, no dense atmosphere to block my view.

It was real.

Unfiltered.

"Wow," was all I could get out.

"Yeah," Shelly replied.

Her hand was resting on the box beside me. I reached out and clasped her fingers, and she did not pull away.

"I look at the sky and ask myself if this is what early man felt," she said.

"What do you mean?"

"We were young when we left Earth, but our parents weren't. With the exception of the astronomers on board who had access to certain remote locations, very few of them had the opportunity to look at the stars in a naked sky. There was so much light pollution on Earth, so much real pollution. Dad has always talked about how he looked up, as if by staring at the sky he would find the answers to every mystery. I think humans have always looked up. Sure, space is wonderful, but there is no up. We have spent the last eighteen years crossing the void, seeing naught but one world in the end."

"Space is a cold and empty place."

She looked at me for an instant and gave a smile. "I'm not so sure about that."

I took another drink, hoping it would calm my accelerating heart rate. It didn't work.

"I wonder what it was like to live aboard the ISS-2," I said, looking to fill the quiet.

"Dad said it was great." Shelly shifted where she sat, scooting closer to me, hip to hip. "It was a lot more cramped than the *Vasco Da Gama*, and for good reason. It was put in orbit in another era, a massive undertaking. Few people got to serve on the ISS-2 or Vega Station."

"Fewer people got to ride a nuclear candle into the black."

"True." She squeezed my hand and sighed. "You know, I like it here, but there's one thing I miss from the *Vasco Da Gama*."

"What's that?"

"Long showers."

"Is a five-minute shower considered a long shower?"

A mischievous look took hold of Shelly's face. "I might have had ways to get around the water restrictions. My dad is the captain after all. Takes a good hour to get clean and all my muscles relaxed."

"Privileged girl," I spat.

She gave a shrug. "What can I say, we're all just people doing our best to survive."

"Isn't that the truth."

In the distance an animal let out a caw, and a moment later, something similar returned the greeting. I wondered what all was out there and how dangerous it really was. "So, um, did they have long showers on the ISS?"

She shook her head. "Not even close."

"You know I've always wondered, what was it like for everyone else? Like their families. They didn't get to bring everyone along like we did."

"Well, it wasn't easy for those back home, which is why many of them are single when they go up. Mom was alone a lot. While Dad was orbiting the Earth every ninety minutes, Mom had two feet on the ground taking care of everyone. She had my uncle with autism, and my grandmother who had cancer. It was a lot, and for a while she felt as if Dad was running from all of it, rocketing off into the sky to leave these problems behind."

"Was he?"

"I don't know, I've never asked. I don't think so. Dad is driven by exploring the unknown, which is why we're here. Once he was back on the ground full-time, they worked it out. Took a while, but marriages aren't easy. Then came me." She gestured at the air with her free hand. *"Ta da!"*

I smiled. "And here came you. Geez, I'm sorry I haven't asked yet, how is your mom? She still whip up those awesome cheese snacks?"

Shelly paused at my question, her breath catching. It was clear I'd said something wrong. All sense of playfulness had evaporated like medical grade alcohol on bare skin.

"She's… well… Soon after we reached Cynosure—" Shelly let go of my hand and covered her face. She scrubbed fresh moisture from her eyes and let out a nervous chuckle. "I can't—She's gone."

"I'm sorry," I said, not sure what else to say. How many parents had been lost when the *Vasco Da Gama* fell? James's mom. Mrs. Williams. Mine? When *minha avó* passed in the floods. I wouldn't grieve Mom and Dad, not yet. They weren't dead. Not dead. "Shelly, I didn't know."

"It's okay." She pulled herself together and wiped her damp fingertips on her pants. "Not your fault. It was an accident. She was crushed by an Angore. It hardly even noticed she was there, and it was not inclined to talk about it after the fact. Foundry machines tried to save her, but it was too late. The facility was not equipped to treat that type of trauma. Humans are still new to the Foundry."

I put a hand on her shoulder, and she turned to face me. She folded into me and I wrapped my arms around her. We held one another under the stars; one human who had lost one of the most important people in their life, and another who just felt lost. She had let me cry on her shoulder once before. Time to return the favor.

After several minutes, she drew away, her face inches from my own. We stared at one another, frozen in the moment, her eyes reflecting the light of distant galaxies. A gentle breeze stirred her curls, and they tickled my cheeks. She licked her lips and swallowed.

"Shelly," I began, throat dry. "I—there's so much to say. I don't know where to start." Her amber eyes begged me to say more, to reveal all the secret, hidden places in my heart. "You and I—"

"Hey!" a shout came from over my shoulder, and it hit me like the crack of a whip. My back went straight and began to tingle. In an instant I was stone sober. Whatever spell this moment had cast over the two of us snapped like a dry twig.

"Lance?" Shelly said, peering off into the dark, her expression incredulous.

He took a step forward and I could just make out a stern look on the pretty boy's face.

"We have things to take care of," he said in a tone that brooked no arguments.

Shelly looked down and realized we were still holding hands. She jerked away and slid off the storage box. "Okay."

I wanted to ask if everything was okay, but the words did not come. While Lance was making me angry, his dominant presence had a way of cowing me.

"You okay, Milo?" Shelly asked.

"Yea—yeah," I replied, and hopped onto the ground. "I'm fine."

"Good. Look, Perry's house is two down on the left. Go grab him and he'll get you settled in."

"Thanks. I need sleep anyways. Long trip."

She gave a half-hearted smirk and waved. "Get some rest, Milo."

"I will."

"Come on, Shelly," Lance insisted, taking her by the arm. "We have to go."

She jerked her arm free and shook her head at him. "Fine, fine. Hold your horses."

I collected our empty mugs and took them back into the Post, my feet as heavy as my heart, toes of my boots cutting furrows in the dirt as they dragged along. I could only think about her. So many sleepless nights on Cynosure I had dreamed about her smiling face, the spark of light in her eyes. Now we were here, and she was beholden to another. I didn't know how to feel. Maybe I had indulged in too hopeful a fantasy.

"What in the hell do I do now?" I mumbled, making my way for Perry's house. Rest was what I needed. Shelly or no, my life was a state of constant change.

I closed my eyes and refocused my thoughts.

There was a mission to fulfill, and even if everyone else had given up, this guy hadn't. We were sent to make contact and save the human race. I wasn't letting go.

CHAPTER 31

I woke the following morning feeling far better than I deserved. There was no headache, no blurry vision, no excessive grogginess. I had downed more than my fair share of the local hooch, and it had left me feeling fine. I wondered if this had to do with the universal inoculant the Foundry had given us. Did it somehow correct my blood chemistry and prevent a hangover? It had to have done something. I had lost count of how much I had drunk.

Perry had gotten me set up in a small dome at the edge of the colony with Omar Tehrani. Without the time to prepare for our arrival, I wasn't given a proper bed, but they had been able to put together a comfortable cot. It was raised off the metal floor on cargo boxes, a collection of animal pelts and a mattress of synthetic fiber materials overstuffed with flock.

I couldn't have asked for a better drop-in roommate. Omar was an unimposing, quiet guy my age with walnut skin and squinty eyes. We had never really known each other on the ship, and with the captain's restrictions around religious expression, it made sense why. Shortly after dawn, I could hear him praying outside. Curious, I wrapped myself in my covers and poked my head out the door. Omar sat on his knees, hands on his legs, head to the ground, muttering words I did not understand, nor did the Foundry's translator.

Strange that I had traveled lights years through chaos and uncertainty, and yet I found one of the most alien encounters to be a human activity.

I went back inside the tent and got dressed, taking a few minutes to freshen up in the bathroom, get a proper shower. When I looked at myself in the mirror after I was done, I blinked. My hair was a mess, scraggly as a homeless man's, ragged ends hanging over my ears. My beard, long like a mountain man's. My eyes were bloodshot and moist. Hangover or no, I had not gotten any real sleep. Did any of us anymore?

"Morning, Omar," I said, stepping out of the bathroom with a freshly trimmed beard and hair slicked back. "Thanks for letting me crash."

He nodded. "It is my pleasure."

"Hope you don't mind. I saw you praying this morning. It was fascinating."

"Oh?"

"Yeah, I only know what it looks like from videos. I've never seen someone pray in person."

"What a shame," he said, putting away the roll of cloth he had used to rest his knees while he prayed.

"Why do you do it? What is it for?"

"It is to bring me closer to Allah. God."

"I'm not sure I know God."

Omar gave me an amused grin. "The fact that you are here on Creatus, alive, in the only human colony in an alien place potentially hundreds of light years away from Earth… You may not know God, but I believe God knows you."

"Fair enough." I went through my backpack, grabbed my hand terminal and a few other necessities. "What do we do about breakfast around here?"

He fiddled with a tea pot and filled it with water. "While we can make breakfast in our yurts, The Post is best. Less waste when we keep things centralized."

"But tea at home?"

"For me, tea is meant to be had alone." He reached for a shelf and removed a book, an actual book, leather bound with paper pages. I had seen notebooks from time to time, like Perry's journal, or mine. But this. This was something else.

"Is that a holy book?" I asked, curious.

He shrugged. "Huxley. *Brave New World.*"

"Oh. Not what I was expecting."

"Things are not always what we expect."

I nodded at the door. "I'm headed out to eat. Need anything?"

"No. Thank you for asking."

The morning, such as it were on this moon, was cool and damp, misty clouds sauntering overhead, the sky a mixture of amber and azure. Whatever passed for birds in this place were soaring about the expanse, flying in formations, diving about in groups of hundreds, paying us and our activity little or no mind at all. From time to time, one of them would peel away from the group and land on the top of one of the many white and silver housing domes. They were black and orange with wings set in reverse, the tips of which appeared to be dipped in red paint. They had no feathers to speak of, just glossy, leathery skin covering their bodies from their diamond-shaped tails to their spear-like heads. They would peck at the roof with their nose, looking for breakfast just like me, then shoot off into the sky and rejoin their flock. A cycle I saw repeated again and again.

As I watched, my mind drifted back to my parents and their missing status. I refused to believe they were dead, but I wasn't sure how to go about looking for them. At this point, I had no way to return to the first Foundry facility, nor did I have access to any networks I could send requests for information. I could ask around and see if anyone remembered last seeing them, but that would not likely do any good. I needed information that we did not possess. The Gene Brokers might have a way, but there was no way in hell I'd trust them. Could God help me find them? Maybe I should ask Omar to pray for them.

I shook my head and sighed. I was like Dad. I did not care for things to be out of place, events out of control.

The colony was a flurry of activity, people bustling about between the many domes and yurts as they focused on their tasks. It was clear there was no lack of work in a burgeoning colony like this. I passed clear domes full of hydroponic plants, machine shops running fabricators at full tilt, clicking looms spitting out bolts of synthetic fiber, and unfamiliar, greenish animal skins drying in the sun. Folk waved as I passed but did not break for more than an instant from their tasks. They moved with the purpose and urgency of those who had only today to complete their lengthy to-do list.

I found Esteban bent over beside the house he had been assigned, his face green, a palm against his chest. On the ground before him was a pile of vomit big around as a dinner plate.

"You okay, buddy?" I patted him on the back. "You look like shit."

He stood upright and nodded. "Now I am. *Ay dios mio*, no lie with that stuff, ya? Serious."

"Weird. I feel great this morning."

"Because you young. Wait till thirty and beyond."

"Yeah, yeah." I tossed a thumb over my shoulder. "Think you can eat?"

"I can try. Probably need to."

"Try not to puke it back up."

We strolled over to the Post, a cool breeze making the hairs on the back of my neck stand on end. At the edge of my view, a ground car propelled on six wheels half as tall as me returned to the colony, its cargo bed full of an assortment of metal scraps of all shapes and sizes. I wondered for an instant where they had gotten it from. It wasn't ours, so there had to be a fallen ship or an abandoned city nearby, maybe a Foundry dump.

"One man's trash," Esteban commented and said no more.

The line for breakfast wasn't long. We had slept in, it had seemed, but no one gave us flak about it, given our recent arrival. Reading between the lines of small talk, the colony had an unusual schedule to follow. Everyone kept bringing up the 'normal days' and the 'dark days' of the week. I just wanted a cup of whatever passed for coffee and a plate of food.

"*Maldición*," Esteban cursed as we took our seats. "So many early risers."

"Not a morning person?"

He rubbed his temples and eyes. "Not today, *amigo*."

I sniffed at the coffee analog they had brewing in a stand beside the buffet. It was bitter and dark, with an earthy smell much like the vegetables here. I took a sip and curled my lips, finding it sour and acidic.

"Yikes." I reached for the condiment box on the table. "Let's see if they have some cream and sugar."

We scarfed down our plates of cooked tubers and crunchy slivers of meat, offering one another little conversation in the meantime. The few who were slow at getting started with their days had vacated, and the Post was empty but for the two of us and the kitchen staff.

I pushed my finished plate away. "There we go. How you feeling?"

"Give me another hour or so. Take some water in. I'll be good." He took a drink and wiped his lips off with the back of his arm. "Last night go well?"

"What do you mean?"

"Shelly, *amigo*. Have a good time?"

I gave a long sigh at that. "Yeah, well… It could have been something great."

"What happened? Not so sweet no more?"

"No. It's not that. It's just, after I had my temper tantrum in front of the captain, she and I went outside and looked at the stars, just talked about life." I paused, thinking back, turning the events over and over in my head. "She's spoken for."

His eyebrows crinkled and he sat up straight. "What? Who?"

"Lance Brittan, the pilot's son. Couldn't you tell?"

"No." He shook his head and dusted off his palms. "I done think that is what you see. Not right."

"But twice now, in the same day, he shows up and insists that she follow him."

"Bruh, I saw how she acted around you, the puppy dog eyes, the hand on your leg. If she is with someone else, it's in name only."

"Whatever. It's over."

"Give up fast, ya? Willing to fight for the crew, the mission, but not her heart?"

"It's not about that."

"Then what's it about?"

I stirred the contents of my coffee absently, watching as the fatty oil that passed for cream mixed then separated again into tiny beads. "I don't know. We were on the verge of something just before shit went sideways. We had a moment in the Foundry VE. We were really connecting, not just feeling chemicals override our brains."

"Chemistry is good too," he put in.

And I couldn't disagree. "Look, we've almost kissed twice, I'm sure of it."

"Then done make it almost next time, ya? Almost is for second place and dead people."

I was going to protest Esteban's position, but before I could Mary appeared behind him, a pleased expression on her face. She came striding over, her steps playful, and slid up beside my friend.

"He lives!" she said, bumping him with her shoulder.

"Just barely," I told her. "Another couple shots and I think we might have been digging a hole out back."

She shook her head. "Bad idea. Can't do that here, the fauna in the dirt is, well, quite aggressive."

"Oh?" Esteban leaned back and glared at her. "How this?"

"Yeah. Let's just say, they might be carnivorous. Worms with teeth, rat-like things that burrow around like bad mothas. Mothers with an a, an a for asshole."

I glanced down at my feet, my toes and heel tingling at the idea.

"Don't worry, Mr. Milo Hughes. That's why we have metal floors. Besides, they only go for putrefied flesh, not the living variety."

"Good to know."

Mary hopped up and bolted across the room, pouring herself a cup of the coffee analog. She drank it black, without any cream or sugar.

"How can you do that?" I asked when she returned.

"It's an acquired taste, like raw oysters, haggis, kimchi, those sorts of things. You get used to it. The best part is that it does have a stimulant. Not like caffeine, per se, but it won't kill you."

I stared at my mug warily. My heart rate had begun to climb. "What do you mean?"

"Well, it's chemically closer to coca than caff."

Esteban snapped to his feet and went to pour himself a cup.

"You okay there, buckaroo?"

He licked his lips and smirked, his expression devious. "I'm thinkin' it's time to acquire a new taste."

"Comes in real handy on the back half of the week."

"I've been meaning to ask about that," I said. "I keep hearing people mention the dark side of the week. How does day and night work here? Seems pretty normal so far."

"Normal?" She barked out a laugh. "Normal isn't even close. This is a moon, okay? So, it gets a bit complicated."

"But last night was night, right? And now it's morning. Seems normal."

"Would seem that way. What you experienced was one of our many eclipses. And then, three of four times a year, we have several hours in which Lignos is blocked. It gets a bit difficult to track, if you feel me."

"I thought it was just hiding behind that thing." I pointed at the sky.

"Nope. It can get a bit disorienting."

"Okay so… I'm confused."

"Do you want to keep rambling or let me tell you?"

"Shoot."

She raised her hands and began to gesture. "Creatus makes a full rotation every twenty-seven hours. Unlike most moons, it is not tidally locked, which is good."

"We don't fry ourselves on one side while being frozen on the other?"

"Not the best way to encourage life. Now when we are on the light side of Lignos Three, like we are now, it's like living on a planet with long days. The trouble comes in another three days. You'll notice them getting warmer and warmer. For the time being it's a balmy fifteen Celsius, around sixty degrees Fahrenheit. By the end of mid-week, it will be thirty-two Celsius. You'll be shedding your clothes faster than you can say supercalifragilisticexpialidocious."

"Because of the sunlight?"

"This moon heats up, fast despite its size."

"What happens when we enter the dark side?"

"Goes from hot to balmy, to pretty damn cold in just a couple days. By the time we reach the day side again, we are at the edge of freezing. This has made for an interesting place to stay, and why most of us wear layers of clothing. The moon experiences the seasons not by the calendar year, but the day of the week. The flora here has adapted quite well to this unusual cycle by acting like evergreens. As for the fauna, it appears some feast in a fury for days, then burrow or hibernate during the latter half of the week."

Esteban rubbed his chin. "Cycles like that remind me of my first serious girlfriend, ya? Passionate fire grew hotter and hotter by the day, only to go frigid. About the time her heart was frozen solid, it would thaw, and we start all over."

I let out an involuntary chuckle at that.

"Look, boys," Mary pointed a finger at us, "I didn't sit down to talk orbital mechanics, that's Perry's expertise. I wanted you to know that I discovered something this morning I thought you might find interesting."

"What's that?" I asked.

She removed her hand terminal and set it on the table between us, a top-down map of the area on her screen. "See this ridge? I hiked my way up to the top yesterday and discovered when I do, my implants pick up a Foundry signal. It's not much, but it's like the connection on the station, not Cynosure."

My heart began to thunder against my chest. "Seriously? A connection to the Foundry?" Maybe learning more about Mom and Dad wasn't so hopeless.

"Yeah," Mary said, her expression brightening at my sudden interest. "They have equipment here. I have no idea what it does or what it is for, who can say, but I do know is that we can access it."

"And what does accessing it give us?" Esteban asked.

"I believe it's a data center of some kind, a high-availability cluster. The implant interface is weak, sure, and the connection breaks all the time like a hand terminal at the edge of network range. With how the interface comes across, I have a theory that most intelligent life have the same basic brain structure, on let's say, a software level. Meaning, that while our cultures and languages may not match up, we process the universe in the same basic way. This allows a connection to navigate the Foundry's network directly with our implants through a virtual, visual interface. Like the VEs we used on the *Vasco*."

A thought struck me. "Do you believe we can get around the Foundry's bizarre security measures this way?"

"Hard to say. If I was closer to the source, I'm confident I could find out."

"Do you think it's dangerous? Could the Foundry hurt someone connected?"

"I don't see how. I'll be careful either way."

"I bet the hub can tell me more about my parents' whereabouts."

Esteban pursed his lips. "Maybe give us a clear path on what they can do to save Earth too, ya?"

Mary raised her open palms. "That would be great. I bet there'll be information about all kinds of things. Thought you might find it interesting."

"I do. Thanks."

"Sure." She stood up and gestured for us to clean our table. "Now that you two are fed and full of cocaine, we should go find you some work."

Esteban's eyebrows raised. "Already putting us back at it, ya?"

She gave him a mock salute and flashed her pearly whites. "Work won't do itself. Besides, makes the days pass quicker. I'm sure Dr. Brennon could use a couple strong boys like you."

CHAPTER 32

I couldn't help but dwell upon the Foundry network link that Mary had discovered. It made me wonder if it was a way into the network that could get us behind its strange security protocols, and why something like this would exist in the first place. Was there information out there about the Gene Brokers? Maybe even my parents? Computer systems and networks may not have been my strongest subject, but I knew enough from programming the nanofluid. It was clear the Foundry was a distributed system. It only made sense the actual data surrounding their whereabouts could be accessed in this hub. Barring a faster than light means of communication from each of the Foundry's facilities, a constant feed would need to be open, updating the local data centers against parity values to the most current version like a cloud.

Maybe it would work; then again, maybe it wouldn't. I was getting ahead of myself. There was no telling how far we would need to travel from the colony in order to have a signal strong enough to find out. What dangers did this planet pose between here and that point? Did we even have vehicles capable of making the trip? Questions. Questions. One day at a time.

Mary led us to the medical dome where about two dozen people sat waiting under an awning to see Dr. Brennon. They murmured at our arrival, several of them giving offhanded waves. Like the rest of the people on Creatus, I knew them by face, if not by name. I was shocked to find so many in need of medical attention, given the nature of the nanomachines the Foundry had injected us with. At one end of the row of formed wire chairs, I spotted a pair of middle-aged folks coughing, hands to their mouths, the sound thick and mucousy.

"Not nice to stare," Esteban whispered.

"I wasn't staring," I replied. "Observing."

"Yeah, yeah. An' I ain' lusting when I peep a pair of ripe headlights."

"What?"

"Come on," Mary said, tugging on my arm. We stepped inside.

Three examination areas were within the dome separated by thin, paper curtains. There was a surgical room closed off to the side and a pair of doors at the back leading to a connecting dome. Dr. Brennon and one of her assistants were working with Paul Faraday from Resource Management, setting what appeared to be a broken arm. He winced as they put it into position, then wrapped it with a series of cloth strips before adding a layer that dripped with glue. The doctor gave him a pat on the back and closed the curtain before coming to greet us.

"Good morning, new arrivals," she said, flashing her laser white teeth. "Word is already getting around about your little adventure."

It had been years since I had seen Doctor Brennon, notwithstanding our objective frame of time reference, due to hyper suspension. I hardly recognized her at first glance. Like most of the adults from the *Vasco Da Gama,* she was in her early forties with a lean physique, a look of dreamy hope tempered by hardship in her eyes. She wore a white lab coat, red blouse and black slacks. Her hair was board straight, dark brown with greyish purple lowlights, pulled back into a neat bun held in place by a slender, metallic spike.

I reached out a hand in greeting. She took hold, placing her other hand on top of mine before shaking. This moment stretched out longer than I had expected, her eyes searching for an answer to a question I wasn't privy to.

"My memory may have been scrambled," I said, looking to break the strange moment, "but weren't you a nurse last time I saw you?"

She let go of my hand and shrugged. At a groan from her patient, she glanced over her shoulder before returning her attention to us. "An eighteen-year trip is a long time to stay in one profession. Truth is, I'd been studying to be a doctor for a long time. The unfortunate loss of Dr. Reed merely accelerated the process."

"We heard," I said, lowering my voice. "I'm sorry to hear it."

"Good lady," Esteban added.

"We were the best of friends. I can only hope I live up to her example." Dr. Brennon turned her attention to Mary. "Fresh helpers?"

Mary nodded. "They've got nothing better to do. Thought you could use a bit of assistance, taking out the trash, scrubbing the floors, that kind of thing."

"If they're new, they deserve to do something nasty first."

"Like what?" I asked.

"Milo gets yard duty, the leaves on these trees shed like crazy. Esteban, you're on toilets, and let me tell you it will be a job. Creatus's food does not settle well on the stomach. Gastrointestinal issues rank high on the list of concerns right now."

"I don't do toilets, ma'am," he replied, back straight. "With all due respect."

"All due respect," Mary mused, rolling the words around in her mouth.

"Damn." Dr. Brennon shook a fist in frustration. "Hard to get good help these days." Mary and Dr. Brennon looked to each other and gave a chuckle. "Look, it has been a madhouse around here the past few weeks. Free hands are free hands."

I crossed my arms and narrowed my eyes. "What's been happening?"

"Mostly dings and bruises. People are clumsy to say the least, like Paul there. He's been helping out in the motor shop, even though it's not really his strength. Knocked over a box of tools and fractured his radius along the anterior surface two inches above the styloid."

"Good ol' Paul," Esteban said. "How long till he recovers?"

"Six weeks or so. Till then, he'll be on light duty."

I lowered my voice and leaned in. "What about those coughing outside? I thought we couldn't catch viruses or be overrun with foreign bacteria because of the universal inoculant."

"It makes a difference," she said. "A big difference. Come here. Want to take a look?" She led me over to a series of microscopes on a lab table beside a whirring centrifuge. "Go for it."

"I'll leave you in good hands," Mary said, then squeezed Esteban's shoulders before turning to exit. "Bye, friend."

He gave her a wink in response. "Maybe cards later?"

"Anything is possible to those who believe." Mary left us with the doctor.

I leaned over the microscope and put my eyes to the lenses.

"You might have to adjust a little to get it in focus," she said, guiding my blind hand to the proper knobs. Her fingers were soft, pressure kind and reassuring. Images of Shelly and the other night flashed in my mind. "Don't turn too fast." Her hand fell away, and my heart gave a start at its absence. Human touch was another unfamiliar, alien thing.

The skittering blob I looked at came into focus. Though I could not make out features, the cluster's population too small to observe through the visual spectrum, I could see movement, color, purpose. The sample on the slide, which had appeared nothing more than a drop of liquid with the naked eye, was teeming with life.

"Whose sample is this?" I asked, pulling away and rubbing my eyes in an effort to force them to readjust.

"Mine, but it doesn't really matter. They all look about the same. What you don't see, is anything but the machines. When I drew that sample, I had had a small cold of sorts. There were foreign bacteria in my bloodstream. These tiny machines, tuned for just me, took care of them."

"So, they do work?"

"Brilliantly. That still doesn't help us with environmental and physical challenges. The cough is the result of, well, we aren't really sure. They aren't the only ones having issues. There's about thirty of us at a time, it pops up, and we clear it away. Our Benefactors help us treat them."

"Your what?"

She led us through the back doors into another dome, this one open, its outside edge lined with six examination chairs connected to all manner of equipment, cables and tubes draping from ceiling trusses, gimbaled bronze and triangular boxes lit by emerald light mounted to their arms. At the far end was a workstation populated by alien instruments, black machines that appeared almost organic, covered in knobs and dials, ports and red-lit readouts. Before these machines, three horse-sized slugs labored, their attention focused on this vast plethora of technical minutiae. They paused at our arrival and twisted to face us, the roach swarms beneath their masses facilitating this action. Their eyestalks blinked, insectile arms twitched.

Esteban tensed out of the corner of my eye.

"Milo, might I introduce you to three of the Kabosai." She motioned from left to right. "This is Lobas, Sinas, and Fidar, if I am right. Sorry to say, Benefactors, it is still a challenge for me to tell you apart."

The arms of the one in the center, Sinas, twitched. "You are correct," it said, its words not quite audible, a whisper in my ear. This gave me a chill. "I know you. We have met before."

"Cynosure," I mumbled, then began rubbing my right arm where it had touched me. Violated me. My palms began to sweat.

"Yes. Human. Natural."

"His name is Milo," Dr. Brennon supplied.

"Milo," it echoed, the word brushing against my ear like a nail file.

Dr. Brennon went on, "The Kabosai have been helping us adapt to this world. It has its challenges, a slight difference in atmospheric makeup from what we are used to, less gravity, though that is something we have learned to deal, with thanks to your mom. And of course, there are other factors too."

The doors behind us opened, and to my surprise, Shelly and Lance appeared, handled metal cases in hand. Lance shouldered past our group and made for the Gene Brokers' workstation without preamble, setting his case beside it. Shelly froze where she was.

"Morning, Shelly," I said.

She took a step towards me, an expectant look on her face. "Sleep okay?"

"Slept fine. Thanks. Omar's a good roommate."

"Glad to hear. Nice guy."

"Real nice."

"Shelly," Lance insisted, eyes wide. "The case? Come on. We don't have all day."

She shook her head and rushed to set her case down beside Lance's.

"I'll see you later, Milo," she said, and exited the room along with Mr. Golden Beard. My stomach had become a twist of knots. I felt the sudden need to be alone, if only that were an option.

Esteban gave me a look, his eyebrows raised in a question.

"Are we ready for the next trial?" Sinas asked.

"Yes, we are." Dr. Brennon stuck her head out of the room and waved those who had been waiting outside in. They took their seats as if by rote. The Gene Brokers turned their backs and returned to their workstation.

"What the hell is going on?" Esteban whispered.

"If you would," Dr. Brennon gestured for us to stand by the doors. "They will need room to work."

"Is this safe?" I pressed.

"Perfectly. It's not the first time we've been given gene therapy. It makes us all healthier. The Kabosai are experts."

"Not the first time?" I gestured for the doctor to step to the side. "We are letting aliens make changes to our DNA? This seems wrong."

"They are our Benefactors," she replied, and held her ground. "They saved us and set us up here. We pay them back by helping them with their projects. Besides, if we didn't have their help, this planet would have killed us already. How are they acting any different than the Foundry?"

"Do we know their intentions?"

Sinas and Lobas turned their eyestalks towards us, before going back to their work.

Dr. Brennon let out a long sigh and crossed her arms. Her back went rigid. "Do we know the Foundry's intentions? They say to protect life, just as our Benefactors do, but what does that really mean? They let the Isoptera tear the *Vasco Da Gama* apart, then kept our group separated from yours, as likely a few others we've been unable to find. Milo, I understand your concerns, we all had them, but the truth is we are now playing in a game where we hardly know the rules let alone have the skills to play. We're out of our depth."

"I just don't trust them," I said.

"Would it have anything to do with the fact that they aren't the easiest on the eyes? Does what you see as normal, or beautiful, have a negative bias on your view of them?"

"No," I shot back, a little too hard. "No." But I knew she was part right. It had taken my life being saved more than once for me to see Gi'Vor as more than a spider. These giant slugs were ugly, they moved around on insects secreted from a gland on their ass. Spiders were bad enough, but these were worse.

She squeezed my upper arm. "You okay?"

"I don't know."

"That's fine." She smiled at that, her posture relaxing. "Since they've started performing gene therapy on us, we have been able to adapt to the high levels of ammonia in the atmosphere, the aggressive pollen this moon has, and mercury in the soil. We wouldn't still be alive if not for them."

"Aggressive pollen?"

"With microscopic razors."

I felt a tickle in the back of my throat and fought the urge to clear it.

"We are ready," Sinas stated, a buzz in my ear.

"Very well." The doctor gave me a nod. "Milo?" I stepped out of her way and took my place as instructed.

The doctor made her rounds, connecting the cables and tubes on the examination chairs. Those receiving the therapy waited patiently for them to be plugged in, their arms restrained, IVs run, the various electronic boxes oriented so that certain sides faced their bodies. Several times she called out to Sinas, checking to be sure the setup was correct. It gave her commands for minor adjustments. It was clear this was not their first rodeo. They had a routine. Once all the adjustments were made, she took a place beside them at the workstation.

"Please close your eyes," she told those waiting. "Today's procedure may not be the most comfortable. The cough you are afflicted with is the result of silicate dust from the eastern deserts kicked up during the dark half of the week. Rain has been sporadic the past few months, so what gets blown over here settles into our lungs. You will be injected with a series of specialized viruses that will alter sixteen independent genes. This is a dormant sequence in humans, that if unlocked, will allow your body to encapsulate these silicates and pass them during your usual bowel movement. Questions?"

I had plenty, but the patients did not.

"Inject them with viruses?" Esteban asked me in a whisper.

I nodded. "It's a technique we used even on Earth. The earliest trials were meant to treat people with hemophilia who lack the proper proteins for their blood to clot. Free bleeders."

"I thought that was when ladies menstruated in public to protest."

"Um, eww. No. That's something else entirely. What in the hell would they be protesting?"

"The use of feminine products, I think."

"Yeah, no. Moving on."

"Time to get started," Dr. Brennon said. "Sinas, if you would."

"Yes," it replied, and I stuck a finger in my ear to scratch it from the inside. That voice made my skin crawl.

Sinas's eye stalks leaned forward, and the room went dim. A whining sound began to grow, a power source spinning up outside the dome. I watched as the silver boxes pointed towards the patients began to glow with aquamarine Cherenkov radiation. Beyond this, there was nothing. No invasive machines. No surgery. Everything about the procedure was happening on a nanoscopic level.

Several minutes passed, the doctor looking over the Gene Brokers' shoulders at the readouts. The overhead lights began to brighten. The whine of the generator tapered off.

Doctor Brennon clapped her hands together. "Alright. We're done." She made her way around the room and helped everyone get out of their exam chairs.

"That it?" Esteban asked me.

"Looks like it."

The patients cleared out and a fresh set entered, James among them. We exchanged uneasy looks as he made for the exam chair farthest away.

Esteban bumped me with his shoulder. "What was that about? Thought yous were friends."

"I have no idea."

Sinas turned to face me. "It is your turn, Milo."

I edged back towards the exit. "No. It isn't. I'm out. I can't do it, I won't."

"This moon is hostile to human physiology," it insisted. "You will become sick. Maybe die."

"I'll figure it out."

"Milo, come on," Doctor Brennon pleaded.

I scrambled back through the exit and made my way outside, Creatus's cerulean sky summoning a modicum of calm. There was no way in hell those things were going to manipulate my genes.

Esteban glared at the medical dome, lost in thought for an instant. "They lost their damn minds. Those thins ain' like the Foundry."

"Am I prejudiced?" I asked.

"What? What you mean?"

"Towards the Kabosai, or Phantamorphs, or Eipren, whatever. Am I prejudice?"

"It ain' prejudice if they're trying to kill you, ya? Hard to know truth. No context."

"But do we ever really know anyone's intentions?"

"No." He scratched at the back of his neck. "That's where trust comes in. But nature, *amigo*, it gives us instincts. Instinct says, they make me nervous."

"Me too."

"Keep them eyes open."

"Wide and awake," I agreed. "Wide and awake."

CHAPTER 33

It took me some time to adjust to the cycles of Creatus that Mary had outlined for us. There were four days with normal day and night, if a touch long, then three in total darkness. It set me off balance, the human body perfectly tuned to a twenty-four-hour circadian cycle, not whatever the hell you classified this madness as. I vacillated between extremes in clothing, going from t-shirts to heavy coats within just a few hours, depending on where I threw my effort for the day. It was strange, and yet liberating, not to wear the same outfit again and again. I was thankful that the domes were climate controlled, and so most often the outside temperature didn't much matter when helping out at the Post or in the machine shop. Yet if I threw my weight in at the motor pool or with the hunters for the afternoon, it was everything.

Four weeks at my back, and I had yet to find where my skills made the most difference. There was little need for my expertise at this time, especially when we had no means or equipment to produce nanofluid, so I was reduced to simple labor.

Despite the awkward situation with Lance, I made every excuse to be near Shelly. Most days she ran errands around the colony, went out on expeditions into the forest with our hunters to gather herbs and plants as they tracked destri, a furry herd animal that was easy to catch with plenty of tasty meat. On those days I volunteered to do the dirty job of cleaning whatever kills were brought back. This gave us a few moments to chat while Lance was at the scrap heap busy sorting through alien wreckage. The majority of my conversations with Shelly were small talk, catching up on the events of their days in Cynosure, the rest on random esoteric topics like philosophy and string theory, similarities between networks and cerebral architecture. The subject never mattered to me. We could discuss the shape of rocks and I would have been perfectly satisfied.

Gene therapy continued for several days each week, until darkness fell on the back half, and the Kabosai retreated to their shuttle. Either they needed time to regroup after terrorizing us, or they liked the cold about as much as we did. I suppose I couldn't blame them. 'Colder than a witch's titty', as Perry said one day, though his expression hardly did the weather justice.

Within my analog journal I kept note of those who had visited the Gene Brokers recently, to keep track of any peculiar signs of sickness or change in behavior. So far everyone acted as they always had. The only brand of mind control the Gene Brokers seemed to be exercising came through the ordinary variety of manipulation. Quid pro quo.

I snapped awake one pitch-black morning on the back half of the week covered in sweat, body shaking. My dreams had run away from me, a nightmarish gauntlet of memories and amalgamations of memories. My sheets went flying onto the floor and I rubbed my eyes with my palms to the point they began to ache. On my left, Omar sat up in bed watching my little freak out, a single desk lamp illuminating his half of the room.

"Are you okay?" he asked, tone concerned. "You have been tossing and turning for hours."

"I'm sorry. Didn't mean to be a bother."

"You're not. May I ask what your dreams were about?"

"No, it's fine."

"No, it's not. Your words say, 'It's fine'. Your body states otherwise."

"Well…" I sat there for a moment, collecting my breath. "I was back on the *Vasco Da Gama*. Esteban and I were fighting our way through the ship with Deidrick and James. My parents, they ran to me and were sliced in half by energy weapons. Then, I was unable to move. I had a gun but could not fire. The Isoptera pounced on my parents' fallen bodies and began to feast."

"Oh," he responded and got out of bed. Omar poured an extra measure of water into a teapot and began heating it up. "We will have tea."

"I thought you only had tea alone, and with a book."

He gave me a smirk. "I said that because I wasn't sure if I wanted your company. I do like my alone time."

"What changed?"

"Whether I want your company or not, I think you need mine." He waited on a stool beside the tea pot's heating element, eyes fixed on the spout. "We've all had the dreams, even those who did not lose anyone."

"I think they're still alive. My parents."

"You do? Any evidence of this?"

"Just a feeling I can't shake."

"Hope can be blind."

"Says the man who prays to Allah eight times a day."

Omar shrugged. "Hope and faith can be one and the same, or different. And just for the record, it is five times."

"Who did you lose?"

"Friends. One of my parents. I came out lucky. In truth, we all did."

"Did you watch anyone die?"

He took a deep breath and nodded. "Yes. Not really a friend, but a crew member. Yuri Popov. I sometimes close my eyes and see the look on his face as the Isoptera overtook him, hear the words he said just before he was dragged away. *'What about Saundra?'.*"

The room became chilly, the sweat on my arms and forehead freezing in place. I gathered my sheets back up and wrapped my body. "Will they ever go away?"

"Might be time to talk to someone. I had to do it. There's no shame in it."

"The ship therapist?"

"No. She was killed in the attack. The one to see now is Perry, of all people. He has studied counseling for the past two years." The water began to boil. Omar poured its contents into a pair of slender glasses with gold handles. "Careful, it's hot."

"Perry? Are you serious?"

"Right?"

I sipped at the tea, its flavor bold and sweet, warmth radiating from my stomach out into my bones. "Thanks."

"We're all in this together, brother. The dark half of the week is a struggle, going days without proper light, less contact with others. I wouldn't plan on venturing out today, the gauge reads twenty Celsius. The sun will be up again in twenty-seven hours."

"Mind if I borrow your book, then? Might be a good way to pass the day."

"Not at all."

"Have you read *1984*?"

Omar grinned as he handed me his leatherbound copy of *Brave New World*. "Finish that and we'll discuss how similar those two books actually are."

When the sun returned, I went back to work, a new sense of hope propelling my leaden feet. Omar had given me room to process my feelings and offered an unbiased ear. It had helped. There had been a great many changes in my life since the days of the *Vasco Da Gama*. I needed to give myself a bit of grace.

I followed Omar's advice and sought Perry, who for the day was working as foreman for the forage and survey teams. He stood at the eastern edge of the colony punching numbers into a tablet, the action a bit archaic for a man with electronic eyes and neural implants.

"Milo," he said as I approached, not breaking his attention from his work. "How are you?"

I stuffed my hands in the pockets of my parka and shrugged. "I'm making it."

He lowered the tablet and turned to face me. "I'm not convinced."

"You know my sleeping assignment. Omar is my roommate. He said that if I was dealing with some things and needed to talk them out, you might be the right person."

Perry gave me a vigorous set of nods, the silver on his visor gleaming in the morning light. "Yes, yes. I will say, there's a lot to do today. Short weeks and all. Want to go along on my land survey? I could use the help. We can walk and talk, *Law and Order* style."

"I'm not sure I know what that means."

"If you don't get the reference, don't bother. Now, if you want to watch a few episodes, I can drop them to you from my hand terminal."

"Maybe later," I replied, unsure. There were plenty of classics I enjoyed. Might be something to fill the dark days next week.

"Alright, let's go down this hill and over to that ridge." He punched a few numbers into his tablet. "There we are. I need to count the steps as we go. I need to get an accurate measurement of the topography of this valley as well as a count of local flora within the wedge. Steer clear of those fern-looking things."

I took a step to my right and squeezed between a set of trees, watching my footfalls. "That bad?"

"Can be. Poor Gareth had one grab onto his leg the first week we were here. Didn't get all the way through his pants but left a nasty friction burn. They are hungry, hungry." Perry led us down a hill through what I began to recognize was a trail. Humans had already begun to alter the environment of Creatus in subtle ways. He would take a few steps, look around, then punch a few more numbers into his tablet.

"Why are you using buttons and not your implants?" I asked. "We might not have a local network, but the headset works, right? You can see."

"Old habits die hard." He raised a finger and counted under his breath. "I'm no spring chicken, ya know? None of us but you kids are. Been a long journey."

The hill leveled off as we neared the valley floor and we hopped over a babbling brook. A wild breeze ventured down off the eastern mountains to rustle the tree-tops in the valley. The avia, what I learned they called the bird-like animals, began to shriek among the canopy.

Perry's shoulders tensed. "I'm not sure I'll ever get used to that damn noise."

"It is a bit startling."

He bent down and made a close inspection of a series of shrubs with hand-shaped leaves, his digital eyes making him appear twice as curious, an alien attempting to understand a new world. "Anyways… What's on your mind, friend? I normally like to take people somewhere private to talk, but I suppose this is about as private as it gets. Next survey team is a mile ahead, everyone else, they're around but far enough off. You'll have to get on without the couch."

I closed my eyes and rocked on my heels, steeling myself to go through it all over again. It had to get out, no keeping it in. "I'm having dreams."

"That so? What kind of dreams?"

"Nightmares, you could say. It seems to be only on the dark half of the week. I see my parents dying over and over. I see the faces of crew members torn to shreds, Isoptera ripping them apart and feasting."

"Is this a memory, or just a nightmare? I don't mean to pry, but did you see your parents die on the ship?"

"No. I was on my way to save them. They pinged me, and I ran to their rescue, but I was knocked down by the Isoptera. Esteban, Deidrick, James and I, along with squad two and three, fought them all the way through the habitation ring. We were buying time for everyone else to get out."

Perry tapped a foot on a patch of soft peat not far from the brook. "Will you do me a favor? Tell me how many of those trees with red leaves there are on your right within, say, ten meters or so."

"Sure." I did as he asked, coming up with fifteen.

"How does this nightmare make you feel?" he went on after recording my result.

"How the hell do you think it makes me feel?" I whirled on him with an anger hot enough to melt copper, crackling voice rising in volume, then froze, took a deep breath. The only thing to do was cover my face with my hands. "I'm sorry, that's not fair. You don't deserve that."

"This is a safe place." He gestured at the serene, alien forest, unaffected by my outburst. "Take a moment to appreciate that fact."

And I did. We stood there in silence; my eyes closed. The leaves rustled around us on a gentle breeze. The brook, now out of sight, burbled as the ice melted and flowed down to us from higher ground. The air was sweet, a hint of floral sugar and must, and at the edge of my perception, the smell of baking bread from the Post. I felt myself swaying, my body naturally inclined to fall into sync with the steady rhythm of this place.

"Okay," I said after a while, and opened my eyes.

Perry was looking at me, a curious expression on his face, even with his mechanical eyes. "Go on." He waved and we started up the opposite ridge. "Sorry, steep hill. I need to get measurements from the top. Tell me how you feel."

"About the hill?" I was careful to navigate the tangle of roots acting as forest floor. I didn't much care for spraining an ankle or busting up my knees.

"No, Mr. Musk. Stop deflecting."

"Okay. To be honest, I feel afraid. Anxious. Inadequate."

"Inadequate? In helping the *Vasco's* crew and your parents during the attack? How's that?"

"Because maybe I could have done something."

"Done something how?"

"Fought harder? Been smarter? I don't know. Killed more Isoptera."

Perry reached the top of the ridge and took hold of a branch, pulling himself over a tangle of roots to reach level ground. He spun and extended a hand to me. "Interesting."

"What's interesting?"

"May I ask what your parents did for a living?"

I glowered at him for asking such a stupid question. "You know what they did."

"That's not the point. Tell me what they did. Talk it out."

I found a moss-covered rock on the landing and took a seat, catching my breath. From this vantage I could see the other side of the ridge, the steam and smoke rising above the canopy from camp.

"Mom was a biologist," I said, "specializing in the effects of micro-gravity on human beings. Dad, an astronomer and astrophysicist."

"And growing up, what sort of skills did they teach you? Every set of parents have their own flavor. For mine, they were gamers and comedians."

"Why does that make so much sense?"

Perry took a seat beside me and gave a noncommittal shrug.

"Well," I said, "they taught me critical thinking. The scientific method. General computer skills. That was about it, they were not much when it came to interpersonal relationships."

"Ahh. I see. Did you have any other family that were close?"

"There were my cousins from Rio I used to see a couple times a year, we would do the whole midnight Christmas thing at *minha avó's*. Destroyed in the Illinois River floods. Another victim of manmade, environmental fallout. I also had an aunt I used to stay with, lived next door, but in truth I don't remember much about her, other than the fact that she thought digital devices were the devil."

"And they might just be," Perry commented. "Side note, when you guys did Christmas did anyone make *sonhos*?"

"I think so. Those are the Portuguese cream donut puffs, yeah?"

"Oh yeah." He rubbed his hands together. "Had a friend whose mom made them."

"Now I'm hungry."

Perry gave a smile. "So all in all, you had a fairly erudite set of parents, yes? An intellectual home life."

"Absolutely."

"Did either of them serve in the military?"

I raised an open palm. "No. Hell no. They were pacifists. They believed a military should exist only to protect a country's borders from other militaries."

"That so? Then it would be fair to say neither of your parents were militaristic? They were instead academics. Neither were the most physical either, were they?"

"You seen my dad? For a man who rarely drank, he sure found it easy to acquire a beer belly."

"Fair point."

I hung my head and turned my thoughts over. "I get what you're trying to say. Neither were one to raise me with those type of skills. We were not a military family. We were not survivalists, or whatever."

"Not that you would need an upbringing like that to be a fighter," Perry said, "because I can say with all confidence, Milo Hughes, you are a fighter."

"Yeah. Maybe."

"So, are you good at critical thinking?"

"I like to think so."

"Science?"

"Yes."

"Computers?"

"Good enough to program millions of tiny machines to do simple work."

"Then they did teach you something. What's really the matter here? I might be speaking out of turn, but I get the feeling you did not have the best relationship with your parents. I got to watch you grow up. Not many secrets on a ship so tight."

"Not the best relationship," I mused. "That's an understatement."

"Then why be so hard on yourself for losing an unwinnable scenario? By all accounts, none of us should be here, you included."

"I don't know. I don't know. Maybe, well, I said some things before it all went shit sideways."

"Yeah, I know. I was there. Do you feel guilty about that?"

I nodded.

"We all say things we don't mean at times."

"Yeah, but I need to make that right. My parents might not have been the best at times, but—" My eyes began to mist over, the world turning blurry. I scrubbed at them with my palms. "They're my parents, man. I think they were doing the best they knew how."

Perry put an arm around me. "As we all do. It's all anyone can do. Before you can move on with your life, you're going to have to let that guilt go."

"And how do I do that?"

"Well, brother, that's the million-dollar question. It's different for everyone. We can only live in the present, not in the past, not in regret. We all make choices, good and bad. Don't let your past mistakes keep you from pursuing joy in your future."

"It starts with acknowledging it, huh?"

"That it does. Get it out in the open. It's okay to feel. If you need to hurt, hurt. Just be honest with yourself."

We sat there for a moment in silence, enjoying the calm of the forest. In the distance I heard the foragers shouting commands back and forth to one another. Another survey group wound around the western edge of the valley.

"Thanks," I said, after some time. "No offense, but I wouldn't have expected you to be so good at this."

He gave me a smile, back going straight with pride. "Just wait, I'll be changing your opinion soon enough. I've been working on a few more jokes."

"God help us all."

"Indeed," he let the word draw out. "Indeed."

"Do me a favor?"

"Absolutely."

"Don't tell anyone what we talked about."

He slapped me on the back. "Wouldn't dream of it, good sir."

CHAPTER 34

After helping Perry wrap up his survey, I made my way back to the colony. Earlier that day, Esteban had sent me a ping to meet him at the hunting lodge that afternoon. I had to say, it was nice being within a normal data network once more, one that us lowly humans could use to communicate remotely. Some things you take for granted until they are lost. This was no exception. We might not have had the full integrations that the *Vasco's* network afforded, data rich and full of augmented reality, but the ability to send a short message through a bit of text was welcome.

The lodge was buzzing with those returning with fresh kills. While some of our game was captured by steel traps, our primary source of meat, destri, had to be hunted like deer. It required getting up early in the first hours of the normal half of the week and waiting for them to cross our path. Destri had a strong sense of smell and an even more adept sense of sight, and so remaining downwind in a camouflaged perch was critical.

"Here you go, Milo," Gareth said as I entered, gesturing to the corpse lying before him on the slaughter table. It was a squat, thick doe, its fur a mottled with black and dark green. It had six legs, each slender and reedy, while its body was powerfully built, muscle upon muscle cutting swirls and lines across its hide. "Make nice for dinner, that. The honor is yours."

"I think I'll pass this time. I've been honored enough this week already."

"Lazy tosser," he replied, reaching for his itchy forehead with blood-painted gloves.

"Gareth!" one of the other hunters called. "Giving him the business there? You're making me feel left out."

"Oh, you'll get yours, ya twat."

"That's a touch too far, mate."

Gareth pointed at him. "Mate? You ain' my fuckin' mate."

"Take that stance tomorrow when you need help dragging bodies back to the litter."

Esteban spotted me among the group and gave a wave.

"Next time," I told Gareth and scurried away. "I'll get you next time."

"Gots you a gift, *amigo*," Esteban said.

"Oh, yeah? Is it my birthday?"

"Who would know, ya?"

"True. Thanks anyways."

"Might not thank me later." He bent over and removed a black and grey rifle from a silver carrying case. "Here, all yours."

I took the offered weapon and looked it over.

"That there is a VP-214," Esteban began. "Jokers here, no offense to those been feeding us, okay, they been using an SL-9 Mauser pattern, fires .308 with five plus one capacity. Nothing wrong with that for hunting destri, but there other things out there, ya? Other nasties. I don't want a bolt action rifle in my hands if Isoptera come to chew on my legs while sittin' in a perch."

The rifle was black, light weight, its barrel long with a solid muzzle brake, and a scalloped, honeycomb rail assembly for attaching grips and stands. I wrapped my fingers around the hand grip and put the stock to my shoulder, its shape comfortable, profile reassuring, the stock of the weapon straight, its bend to comb non-existent for maximum scope efficiency if so desired. This was a weapon intended to be used in combat, versatile depending on the situation, and yet it looked more than capable of serving up supper.

"Ammunition?" I asked.

"6.65, decent range, good kinetic energy. Will do many jobs."

"And this one's mine?" I asked, grinning.

Esteban nodded. "*Claro, amigo. Es* all yours. Though it comes with heavy responsibility, must help out in fighting if get attacked."

"Sweet. Happy birthday to me."

"Maybe have some cake?"

"Damn I wish."

I looked the rifle over again, testing its weight, making myself familiar with the feel of it. It was a fine weapon, very different from the MJ-6 we used aboard the ship during the attack. I was pretty sure this was one of the options I had played with in the combat VE. While the idea of fighting again was not one I desired to entertain, it felt good to have a weapon if the day came.

The foraging party returned along with a throng of hunters, Shelly among them, a bulging sack of goods tossed over her right shoulder. I crouched down, setting my new toy in its case while watching her out of the corner of my eye.

Esteban gestured towards her with a flick of his head. I took a deep breath and stood, back straight.

"No fear," I told myself. "No fear."

"Milo!" Shelly said, and tossed her arms around me. "Have you had a good day?"

"I have," I replied, and it was true. I felt lighter for having talked to Perry. "How went the foraging?"

"Good. We found some plants we believe can be used as tea. Potentially some new herbs, spices. Nothing major but they certainly help out with quality of life. Soon as they pass the metabolic tests, we can have a try."

"Sure make this shite taste good," Gareth said, raising the bloody ass of the destri he was butchering.

"Anyways." Shelly rolled her eyes. "What about you?"

"Spent the morning with Perry. Needed help on the survey."

"What a piss job," Lance said as he stepped into the hunting lodge. His hair was wet with sweat, slicked back, face was covered in grease. "A real man puts in his time with a muck."

"Can't argue there," Gareth replied, then slashed through the destri's neck, allowing its blood to pour out the side into a catch basin.

"Survey work isn't easy," Shelly replied. "Besides, it's necessary if we are going to extend the camp down to the valley. Plenty of fresh water we can pump up here."

Lance glowered at me. "Just seems like he could be putting his weight somewhere valuable instead of drinking up our booze and eating all our food."

"Hey!" I raised a finger and pointed it at Lance, the hackles on the back of my neck rising. "I pull my weight."

"All two pounds of it." He took a step towards me. The two of us now an arm's length apart.

Shelly stepped between us, raising her hands. "Hey, hey. We got enough going on. No need in this."

"Whatever." Lance tossed a set of tools on the slaughter table. "Hey Gareth, there's the shit you wanted."

"Cheers, mate!" Gareth replied, grinning ear to ear.

"Come on," Shelly took hold of my sleeve and led me out of the hunting lodge.

Esteban shouted after me, "*Amigo*, what about your present?"

"Drop it off at my quarters?"

"Alright. Alright. I guess it's your birthday and all."

We stepped outside.

"Is it really your birthday?" Shelly whispered once we'd taken a few steps.

I shook my head. "Hell if I know."

Once outside, we headed away from the lodge. I hoped Lance didn't pursue. His blood was hot over me being back, and I didn't want to get into a brawl. Perry might have thought I was a fighter, but I didn't see myself that way, not in this setting.

Not far from the medical dome Shelly raised a palm, gesturing for me to halt. Up ahead her father, the captain, was in a heated discussion with our Benefactors. The three slugs stood across from him, their bodies shaking as their twitchy arms remained still. Shelly and I crouched beside one of the storage buildings and watched.

"This is becoming too much," Captain Williams said, the fingers of his left-hand scratching at his right arm. The skin had broken out in a red rash. A childhood stress reaction. "It's one thing to do minor adjustments, it's another to ask for limbs or bone marrow. Those are painful procedures for humans, and I know you might not understand, but we humans get sentimental about our appendages."

My arms and legs began to tingle at the mention of this. There was another alien entity who had once asked me for body parts. A donation, it had said. And now…

"Do you wish to thrive on Creatus?" the central slug, Sinas I presumed, asked the captain. "Though we excel in bioengineering, data is required to create a complete genetic chain."

"Can't you just scan us? You have machines we've never seen before. Hell, the Foundry has something you can use, I'm sure. With all the shit you probed us with, someone must know what the inside of my ass looks like by now."

"It is not the same."

"Well, that's tough shit. You aren't being this invasive. I'm not authorizing it."

"But what about our deal?"

"To hell with the deal. This goes outside the bounds of what we determine as ethical or moral."

"We are here to protect life. We must see it grow and flourish. The Universe will not awaken without its proliferation."

The captain pinched the bridge of his nose. "I still have no idea what you are talking about. The Universe, big U, is not alive. Just people. Just us, just you and me and the countless other species beyond this rock. Eating, thinking, shitting. What life does."

"You are wrong."

"Maybe I am, but a handful of humans giving up their body parts won't change that." The captain turned to leave, coughing under his breath. "I said good day, sir!" he shouted, then stormed off in the opposite direction.

The Kabosai remained there for some time, staring at one another as if in silent conference.

"What was that all about?" I whispered at Shelly.

"Nothing. Just an old argument."

"Over giving up body parts?"

Shelly shook her head and rolled her eyes. "We aren't giving up our bodies for alien science."

"I sure hope not."

The Kabosai began to make their way off through the camp, back towards their shuttle over the southern ridge.

"You hungry?" she asked, tossing a thumb over her shoulder. "Want to get dinner with me?"

"You sure? I don't want to cause any friction with Fancypants."

She glared at me. "Dinner. You and me. Maybe a bit of Deadly Force to top it off."

"Okay. Sure."

As we made for the Post, the wind began to pick up. Blue skies were turning grey. Trees were bending under the force of an incoming storm. Before I could remark on the change in weather, the sky went black and alarms in the camp, as well as within my implants, began to sound. I drew my shirt over my mouth and squinted my eyes, the whirl of the tempest intensifying.

"Milo! This way," Shelly shouted over the rush of wind. She was no more than a step from me, and yet it was near impossible to see her through a wall of dust. "Take my hand. I have limited AR. I know where we are going."

She led me through the tempest, each step deliberate, piles of dust gathering around our boots, until we reached the curve of a dome. We burst through the door and slammed it behind us, dust piling on either side. I wasn't sure exactly where we had gotten to in the camp, given that the storm had turned me around, but we were alone in a dimly lit storage building, shelves stacked with boxes in rows on all sides. At one end sat a pair of chairs with a table between them, a pair of half-finished cups of stale coffee left on top.

"Here, let me get that for you." She dusted off my head and back. "That stuff gets in everything."

"I'm gonna have sand in my ass for a week."

"Did you breathe it in?"

"I don't know."

"After it's over we'll be sure to see Dr. Brennon. These dust storms have fine silicates that can shred the hell out of your lungs. Best to keep a mask on you, just in case."

"That would have been good to know."

"Sorry. Should have said something earlier. It's been a while since, well, one of the gene therapies was a means to deal with these storms."

"Yeah. I think I remember the doc mentioning it."

"Can you get me?" She raised her arms over her head and closed her eyes. "Dust me off if you would, kind sir."

"Sure." I patted at her arms and legs, as well as her back, neck, and hair, the fine dust falling from her like baby powder. I knew full-well she could have done this herself, yet she asked me to do it. Asked me to touch her.

When I reached her chest, I patted her, then recoiled. "My bad, I'm so sorry."

She snatched up my hands and gave me a smile. "For what?"

"For. I mean. Your breasts. I didn't mean to."

"It's okay." She chuckled, breaking the tension for an instant. Her hands let go of mine and she began to twist one of her curls with a finger.

"This would be the time for a long shower, wouldn't it?"

"Yes." She gave a deep nod. "Yes, it would."

I shrugged out of my parka and set it on the back of one of the chairs. She did the same, her attention not leaving mine, our eyes fixed on one another. Her pupils had grown wide, becoming massive portals in the dim light of the storage dome. They invited me closer, and so I took a step towards her, closing the gap between us. She did not back away. In fact, she licked her lips and put her hands on my hips. I felt my heart begin to thunder its way through my chest. It was difficult to breathe. Was it the dust or something else?

There was no denying that hers was the most beautiful face I'd ever seen. It was what I wanted to see when I woke up in the morning. This voice was what I wanted to hear. This soft skin and kind soul what I wanted to open myself up to and become entangled with.

She started, "Milo, can I just—"

But before any other words could be spoken, good or bad, a spirit of fate, maybe blind optimism, overtook me. I leaned into her and pressed my lips to hers. She raised her hands from my hips and threaded her fingers through my hair, drawing me deep into our kiss. In that moment I lost track of where I was, what was going on. We were back in the VE inhabiting our incorporeal bodies, drifting above the Foundry, a torus of gold at our backs, dazzling beneath the eternal gaze of a crimson god. Like it had been under stasis, time was difficult to keep track of. It stretched out like a rubber band, each deep breath, each gentle brush of body against body, increasing the tension from which reality would snap back into focus.

After some time, we broke free and smiled at one another, nothing else, satisfied by the moment. I felt my knees go weak and I took a seat. Without preamble, Shelly positioned herself on my lap, wrapping her arms around me.

"Took you long enough," she said, matter of fact.

"What?"

"I've been waiting on that for a long time." She let out a chuckle. "I thought it might end up being forever."

I averted my eyes, cheeks going warm. "Me too."

"Why so long?"

"Can we clear the air on something?"

Shelly grinned, already knowing what I was going to ask. "Lance is not my boyfriend."

"Then why is he so possessive of you?"

She tipped her head to the side, staring off into nothingness. "Well, we dated once upon a time, and when we arrived here there was a period that we all needed comfort. He may have been that comfort. I told him that I didn't want that to be forever, and he has never let it go. He's a good guy, sure, and he fell hard. But he's not the man that I want."

"Oh?"

"Yes. There's only one for me, and it's a silly little boy who came and played in my quarters with tiny little toys, a boy who stuffed his face with chocolates and made fart jokes."

I felt my breath catch.

"You might know him," she suggested.

"I'm getting to."

"How does he feel about the little girl he used to play with?"

"She's all he ever thinks about."

"That so?"

"Yeah."

"And for how long has this been going on?"

"A long time."

"Why didn't he speak up?"

I took a deep breath. "Maybe he didn't feel like he was good enough."

"He's always been good enough."

"Then why didn't she say anything?"

"Maybe she had some childish shenanigans to get over."

The winds died down, yet the two of us did not move a twitch. We remained silent in the storage dome, holding on to one another. We had traveled billions of miles and gone through fire and hell to reach this moment. It was one to treasure, to cement in our minds forever.

When we emerged, we were not the same pair of explorers as when we entered. Shelly held my hand as she walked me back to her quarters. I wasn't sure where this was going, all I knew is that it felt right.

Despite the silica dust storm, the people of Creatus were getting back to work. A minor inconvenience. I even saw the Kabosai milling about. They locked eyes with us as we passed through the center of the colony, watching. What were they thinking? What did they really want? I couldn't be for sure. All I knew, was that I didn't trust them as far as I could throw their horse-sized, slimy asses.

"You okay?" Shelly asked.

"Yeah, yeah, don't worry. I'm fine." I paused and gave her a smile. "Maybe more than fine."

CHAPTER 35

"Morning sleepy head," an angel's voice whispered in my ear. It made me question for a moment if I was alive or dead. I had to be dead. One only gets a few get-out-of-hell-free cards in life. My hand was almost empty.

"Am I dead?"

"Not yet," the angel replied, "though I wouldn't be surprised if you had sprained a muscle."

"What?"

I sat up in bed, rubbing my eyes for a moment. Shelly laid next to me, the sheets pulled up over her bare breasts, my left leg warm against hers beneath the covers.

"So, it wasn't a dream?" I reached out and put my arm around her.

"If it is, this is a really good dream."

I glanced at the clock on the wall, realizing it was the back half of the week. Outside, the temperature was plummeting below freezing and I was closed in a tiny dome with a beautiful, naked woman. If that wasn't a dream, I didn't know what was.

Several days had passed since our initial encounter. The colony as a whole had said little when we were discovered holding hands at the Post that evening. Word must have gotten around quick, because Mr. Fancy Pants Asshole had decided to make himself scarce. I didn't look forward to dealing with him in the future, but at least Shelly and I had a few days alone to cement our long-pent-up feelings.

The moment to deal with Lance would come in time. I only hoped it didn't involve fists.

Shelly and I readjusted in bed, leaning back on our pile of pillows, her head coming to rest on my chest. I ran my fingers through her curls, feeling her warmth against me as she rose and fell with the rhythm of my measured breaths.

"Do you think we'll be here forever?" I asked. "No one seems to be in a hurry."

She took a long moment to reply, the question loaded. "On Creatus? I'm not sure."

"Why is that? We were sent out here to complete a mission, and it's almost like people don't have the will to finish it. The Foundry didn't tell us no. We just got sent off on a tangent."

"Life isn't terrible here. Sure, it's not what we're used to. It isn't what we're made for. But Creatus is a place to survive. I just don't know if it is a place to thrive. Then again, if not here, where would we go? I think people are just happy to be alive."

"There's a million billion worlds out there, but only one made perfect for humans. It's hurting."

She sucked in a breath. "You're right, Milo. We still have a mission. I know Dad is just doing the best he can for the crew, but we have to return to Earth one day. We have to bring them help, if its not too late."

"I still feel that the Foundry means to help us, that much is wrapped in the signal." I stroked her curls with my fingers, strands silky like fine threads.

"What if that feeling is a lie?"

"I spoke with the Foundry, face to face, and despite how things turned out, I get the impression whatever drives it is trying to do the right thing. Maybe this whole phase is a test. To see how moral or ethical our species is, or maybe what we'll do. I'm not sure. All I know is that I'm having a hard time giving up. This isn't just some grand frontier adventure. We were given a task. It's the very meaning of our lives."

"No choice for us?" she mused.

"None."

"I don't disagree. But we don't even know how long it has already been. Has it been decades, a century? We can't say. The world outside the rat race of Earth exists on a different time-scale."

"Like the Jalek."

"Yes."

"That thing has lived for thousands of human lifetimes. It has watched the universe from a cosmic perch, the ridge of the eternal mountains, able to see the passage of species."

"How poetic," she mused.

I smirked at this, face turning bright. "I have my moments."

"I often wonder how long we can live now. The universal inoculant alone would save billions on Earth."

And it was true. Which begged a whole host of questions all tied to the central theme. How long had it been? If we had a ship and burned back home now, would we even make it before humanity destroyed themselves? My earlier observations of human history played back in my head. Humanity had ever fought wars for resources. So, if we could give them the means to have limitless resources, would not that end war? Famine? Plague? Would it not usher our species into a golden age? What would become of Earth without death? Overpopulation? New shortages? We needed the help of those more advanced than us, ones who had driven down this road before, but perhaps even moreover, some of us needed to leave the cradle behind. There just wasn't enough space for everyone.

It was time to reach into the heavens en masse.

Questions upon questions circled around in my mind. At the end, I came to a sad conclusion. Mission or not, we did not have the answers to Earth's problems. Even if we had the will or means to return, all we might do is arrive just in time to watch them languish.

I closed my eyes and willed that thought away.

"But you know," Shelly said after a moment, "that old discussion, let it be for another day." She rolled over and put her hips across mine, bare flesh on bare flesh, sticky from sweat and pleasure.

"Another day," I agreed, and allowed her to draw me into a flurry of anesthetic kisses.

I would never give up on our mission, but Earth was a long way away, while Shelly wasn't.

The week began to warm again, Creatus having orbited back to the day side of Ligonas-3. Much to our regret, work continued. Shelly and I said our goodbyes for the day, giving more than our fair share of kisses and hugs, committing to see each other again that evening. I went back to my official quarters to check on Omar before heading off to help in the machine shop. The prospect of running into Lance wasn't a happy one, but it made more sense for my skills rather than the hunters or the mess, and there was no way I'd be part of what Brennon was doing with our Benefactors.

Omar was seated inside the dome, feet propped up on an ottoman, a cup of tea in hand. As I came in, he smiled at me and closed his book with a thunk.

"Tea?" he asked, excited. "It is time for more tea. Have a few minutes?"

"You must have heard."

"If I hadn't, you think I'd be smiling at my roommate who's been missing for half a week? I promise you I would have gone looking for your frozen corpse. Come on, now, tell me. Small colony."

"Small ship."

"Some things never change."

Once Omar had squeezed almost every last detail out of me, I headed over to the machine shop, a skip in my step. The colony was abuzz with activity, fresh sounds and rhythms of life I was fast coming to rely on. The shrieking avia made their calls above. Destri crooned in the distance. People sang. The wind howled and retreated. Every detail as clear in my mind as crystal.

For the time being, most of the machine shop was focused on taking scrap from the wreckage of an alien battle cruiser. The materials were various aluminum alloys, carbon nanofiber, limited quantities of steel, and of course, titanium. Metallurgy might not have been my specialization, but with the construction of the nanofluid on the *Vasco Da Gama* I had learned a lot. It appeared that many of these materials were lightweight with good tensile strength. Whoever's ship it was that we were chopping up for scrap was not Foundry made. Those materials were as yet beyond our understanding, and from conversations the crew had had with other species in Cynosure, we were not alone in our ignorance.

The machine shop was an open garage of junk and half completed projects, homemade forges, fabrication machines, 3D printers, and more tools than I would have expected a burgeoning colony to possess. Most of the models for these items had been stored on various hand terminals the *Vasco's* crew members had stuffed in their jumpsuits before the ordeal. To show their benevolence, our Benefactors had used their technology to adapt the 3D models and print the machines we needed to get started. Thus was the seed of our colony production, a handful of tools and structures built first by the Gene Brokers. It was no wonder we had been dazzled into blindness by their greatness.

Sometime around lunch, Esteban decided to join me, content with the number of destri he had dragged out of the woods that morning. We analyzed and fed hunks of aluminum into a crucible where they would be poured into molds and rolled into sheets for vehicle construction. What the colony needed at this time was another half-dozen land cars, but for now we had only a single truck.

"So, *amigo*. You did it, ya?" Esteban asked, tossing a length of silvery material into the brightly glowing clay pot.

"Yup."

He dusted off his hands and gave me a slap on the back. "Started to wonder about ya."

"How?"

"If you had the guts. Seen you run head long into battle but too afraid to pucker up them lips."

"Whatever."

Just as I was about to start the next stage of the process, calling for help to pour the molten contents of the crucible into molds, the captain stumbled into the shop. He made his way to the foreman but collapsed onto the ground just short of him. Esteban and I rushed over and helped him stand back up. The rest of those working in the shop held their breath, frozen.

"Are you okay, sir?" I asked, my voice shaky.

The captain coughed into his fist and clasped his chest. "I—I can't—" A wheezing noise came from his mouth and nose.

Esteban flicked his head to the side. "Come on, let's get him to the doctor."

"Please," the captain hissed. "No doctor."

I stared back at him, incredulous. "No doctor? Why?"

"I ain' havin' you die on me, sir," Esteban said.

We led him away from the machine shop to the medical dome.

The captain's body became heavier with each step, his legs going weaker. His skin was turning purple and pale, his breathing slowed. By the time we had reached the doctor he was nonresponsive.

"Get him on the bed!" Doctor Brennon ordered. "Nurse! We're going to have to tube him. Crash cart."

"Yes, ma'am."

"The two of you, get out."

"But," I protested. "I can help."

"Not here. Not now. Get out. Go!"

The nurse shoved Esteban and I out the front door.

Esteban took a seat in one of the chairs outside, his face falling into his hands. "*Ay dios mio.*"

Less than a minute had passed, and Shelly appeared, a terrified look written on her face. I hadn't even had the chance to ping her yet.

"Where's Dad?" she asked.

I reached out and took hold of her hands. "With the doctor."

"What happened? Tell me."

"We don't know. He just collapsed. Started coughing."

"Can I see him?"

"No. We've been told to stay out here."

"Shit," she mumbled. "Shit. Shit. Shit."

"Are you okay?"

"I don't know." She let go of my hands, then cut circles in the dirt, attempting to pace away her anxiety. "Damn it, Dad. Damn it."

I kept out of her way as she stomped around, saying nothing to fill the silence. What could I offer that would help?

"This can't be happening," she said. "This can't be happening."

Minutes crawled by; each tick of our implant clocks an eternity. Shelly's eyes were bloodshot from crying. She vacillated between tears and anger, wanting both comfort and solitude. Just as it was about too great to bear, the doctor reemerged.

"Shelly," she said, her voice quiet. "Your dad is quite a fighter, but in the end…" The doctor's hands trembled.

Shelly stood there, stunned, her fingers laced through her curls, tense, pulling at the roots. She took a deep breath, holding back a dam of tears and fury. "I need to see him."

Doctor Brennon nodded and led her inside. Shelly gave me a final glance before disappearing from view, her eyes sending me a message.

"They did it," I mumbled, my fists at my side, tightening as anger rose from my belly. "They fucking did it."

"What?" Esteban asked.

"The manipulating, slug bodied ass fucks."

He stood. "What you talking about, *amigo*?"

I burst into the medical dome to see Shelly at her father's side. I pulled the curtain close, giving Shelly privacy with the body of her dad, and called the doctor to me with a wave of the hand.

"Cause of death," I said, my words brooking no argument.

The doctor, for once, shrunk down at my question. "Acute respiratory distress."

"Has he been sick for a while?"

"No. He's been fine, that's the thing. We all get a cough from time to time."

"The silicates, I know. But that was resolved with one of the therapies, right?"

"It was."

"When was the last time he was given a treatment by the Gene Brokers?"

She crossed her arms and rubbed her chin. "Last Thursday, before it got cold again. Why?"

"That's what I thought."

I made my way out of the medical dome and stomped back to my quarters. My skin was as hot as if molten aluminum had been poured into my body through a hole in my head, sweat bursting from my eyebrows and face, teeth grinding against one another like a belt sander. Esteban followed hot on my heels.

"What are you doing?" he asked.

"Is my birthday gift at the house?"

"Yes. Why?"

"I think it's time to put it to good use."

Omar kneeled on his carpet just outside our quarters, praying. At our approach, he broke ritual and turned to look at us. "Something up?"

Esteban shrugged. "Don't know, man. But the captain's dead."

His body sagged. "Allah protect us."

I snapped open the carrying case of my new VP-214 and grabbed a set of fresh magazines.

"What are you doing?" Omar raised his hands in a pleading gesture.

"What needed to be done a while ago." I stepped around Omar and made my way through the colony, heading towards the last location I had seen our Benefactors. We were getting answers, and now. There was no reason this had to be done from the end of a barrel, but they had forced the issue.

The three Kabosai, Gene Brokers, Benefactors, whatever the hell you wanted to call them, were gathered not far from the medical dome, fiddling with what looked to be a generator or transmitter of some description. I approached them, pulled back the bolt on my weapon, then pointed the barrel at Sinas.

I shouted, "Answers!"

The three of them rotated towards me, motion smooth as vinyl records on a turntable, movement of their bed of roach slaves like liquid beneath them. They made no aggressive moves, merely stood there, eyestalks blinking.

"Why do you come with a weapon?" that voice again, a whisper right beside my ear.

A vein at the corner of my right eye began to pulse, matching the rhythm of my locomotive heart. I took a deep breath. "What did you do to the captain?"

"What is wrong with your captain?"

"Don't play dumb with me!" Saliva spewed over my lips, spraying empty air. "He's dead, and it was you. You did something to him last week. And you will answer for this."

"Have you come to kill us?"

"That depends on you."

"I see that you want something. Knowledge? Understanding? Retribution?"

"Why did you do it?"

The Gene Brokers turned their eyestalks around to look at one another in turn. Sinas went on, "We do nothing but protect life."

"Did you kill the captain?"

"Some always die."

"But why? Why did you do it?"

"To protect life."

"This doesn't make any sense. You kill to preserve?"

"We protect life," the others replied, reinforcing Sinas's words, a broken goddamned record.

"Protect life?" I growled, my patience running thin. "For what purpose?"

"The Universe must be awakened," Sinas assured me, his chest heaving ever so slightly as if taking a deep, frustrated breath while speaking a self-evident truth to an insolent child.

"I keep hearing this." My finger tightened on the trigger. "Again and again and again. But what does it mean? What does it really mean?"

"To think. To be. You think, and you are. We think, and we are. All things together, and more is awakened. Time expands. Enlightenment realized."

"Tell me how this involves us? We already think."

"The Universe is diverse and unkind. Not all life can thrive in all places. We must protect life. Give it a chance, the best chance. Make changes where necessary."

"But on what terms? At what point are the lines of goodness and ethics crossed? At what point will you reach into our genes and rob us of our humanity?"

Sinas reached out one of its arms and patted it against its chest. "A species will always be what they were in its mind. This was not our first form."

I thought about that for a moment, weapon slippery in my sweating, angry hands. The Jalek, the Gene Brokers, even the Phantamorphs, how did they begin? Their forms were not all created naturally, there were adaptations, changes, gross evolution or augmentation designed to give them the ability to survive in more than one environment. What else could these sorts of transformations accomplish? Were humans ready for this? How many of us had to die for us to find out? I wasn't waiting around to see.

Shelly came rushing out of nowhere and threw herself between me and the Gene Brokers. "Stop! Milo, put down the gun."

"I can't."

"Yes, you can. This will only make things worse. It's not the way."

"But—the captain," I pleaded. My words softened, "Your dad."

"I know." She scrubbed at her eyes with her palms and threw them down at her side, back straight. "Please, don't. Don't. He wouldn't want this."

The tactical rifle trembled in my grip before drooping back towards the dirt. I removed the magazine and tossed it to Esteban, then pulled back the slide and ejected the round seated in the chamber.

"Okay."

The Gene Brokers seemed to relax a little, their sags and folds lowering closer to the ground if only by a fraction of an inch.

Shelly stared at me, so many words in her eyes. I expected a ping from her to hit my implants, but it did not come.

"Apologize," she pleaded.

I took a deep breath and lowered my head, nausea nearly overtaking me as I did so. "Sinas, I'm sorry. I was angry, he was important to us."

The Gene Brokers paused, taking a moment to discuss my apology. "It is accepted," they said after some time. "Do you need assistance with the captain's body?"

"No," Shelly put in. "I know how he wanted to be buried. Leave that to me."

"As you wish," they said, and turned to leave.

The following morning the crew of the *Vasco Da Gama* gathered on the western edge of the colony along a high vista. From here you could see the distant silica deserts, the great forest, the river to the north and the flowery fields beyond. Delicate, garish insects filled the air in swarms, gathering and dispersing like aurorae, a hypnotic addition to such an important moment.

We stood in solidarity and silence. Few words would make a moment like this any less painful. At the front of our group lay a wooden box filled with soft lining, destri skins and synthetic fibers, the pallid face of our once-great captain turned skyward within. He looked like he was sleeping, arms crossed over his chest, content that rest from a long journey had finally come.

Shelly held on to me, her face buried in my shoulder, body shuddering. I fought back my own tears for her sake. This was a moment to be strong.

Mary strolled around the edge of our assembly, shaking hands and hugging necks as she went. We waited for her to take her place before the casket. She closed her eyes for a moment, rallying her will, then removed a small cue card from her back pocket and began to read.

"Today we lost a good man," she said after a moment, her tone even, measured, despite the gleam of moisture in her eyes. "He was the best of men. He led us across the great void with unceasing confidence, acting as a compass for our ship and hearts. Today, we honor him, taking up the lessons he gave us, as well as his mission. Though his body goes into the dark night, his soul lives on in us, in the lives he has touched. Tobias Williams, my old friend and teacher, you will never be forgotten."

She reached in her pocket and removed a silver pin shaped like a cartoon dog and placed it upon Tobias's chest. The Silver Snoopy gleamed in the afternoon light of an alien star, a sliver of metal representing a lifetime of exploration.

"Dad…" Shelly said, and buried her head into my neck. "Dad…"

CHAPTER 36

Little got done around the colony the following week. The death of the captain was a serious blow to the morale of Creatus's inhabitants. He was an icon, a leader, someone who for over twenty years had given us purpose and vision, and he was gone now. We were left to find direction on our own.

There was little I could do to console Shelly. She had lost her mother in the attack, and her father here. No one remained of her blood family. Grief was something new to many of us. We had lived in such a safe, insulated world, every basic need provided for us by the *Vaco*, the Foundry, and now, our Benefactors. But a pain of the heart could not easily be swept away. No amount of Deadly Force could fill the empty hole in our hearts. No amount of physical release could blind the mind forever.

I woke one morning to Shelly staring at the wall. She had clearly been doing this for quite a while, a pillow held tight in her arms, her expression blank.

"You okay?" I asked carefully.

"Yes."

I wrapped her up in my arms from behind and squeezed her, placing a gentle kiss on her head. "What can I do for you?"

"Just be here."

"Okay."

She took a deep breath. "Look, I need some time today. I know you want to help, but I need time alone."

Reluctant, I pulled back. "You sure?"

"I am. Come back later, please, but keep yourself busy for a bit."

"I can do that." I stood and got dressed. "Ping you later?"

She nodded; her attention turned away.

I plodded across the colony, my steps leaden, attention scattered. I wanted to make her feel better but had no power to do so. The loss of her parents only made me think more about my own. I hoped beyond hope that they were out there somewhere, safe, free from the reach of the Kabosai or something worse. I wished very much I had made different decisions, used different words when I had seen them last. Made an effort to be a better child. I had a hundred regrets on my shoulders, each of them heavy as a neutron star.

"Milo," Mary called, catching me just before I wandered out into the woods. "You okay?"

I shook my head vigorously, attempting to clear my thoughts. "Yeah, I'm fine."

"You look pretty dazed."

"I am."

"I think we all are." She drew up beside me and hugged my neck. I didn't realize how much I needed it until she was there. "In this together, okay?"

"Okay," I replied, fighting back tears.

"I have some strange news."

"Oh?"

"Yeah. Remember that signal thing I found?"

"I do."

"Well," she paused, finger against her full lips, "just come with me. I don't want things to get even weirder, but I think you'll find this of interest."

Mary led me to the Post where a small group was gathered around one of the tables. Perry, Esteban, Lance, and James, as well as one of our Benefactors were there. At my arrival, the Kabosai gave a gesture like a wave.

"Milo," it said.

"Sinas," I responded in greeting.

"I am not Sinas. I am Lobis."

"Apologies."

"Of nothing."

"Lobis has something to show us," Mary supplied, pointing to a sheet of paper laid out on the table.

It was a topographical map of the area in high resolution, various symbols sketched along one edge in what I could only assume was the Gene Brokers' language. At one end of the map, I recognized our colony, at the other was a ziggurat, a series of symbols beside it corresponding to the map's legend.

I cocked my head and squinted. "What are we looking at?"

"Maybe answers?" Esteban said. "Maybe nothing?"

"What do you seek, Milo?" Lobis asked.

I furrowed my brows. "What do you mean?"

"You are a truth seeker. What truth do you wish to unlock? Do you wish to save your home world? Find your parents?"

"What?" I gave those gathered a wary look. "What's this about?"

James and Lance exchanged an annoyed glance.

The bizarre tentacle the Kabosai kept hidden oozed from Lobis's body and tapped the ziggurat. "It is a data hub of the Foundry."

"I was right," Mary said, a touch excited. "We don't know at what level we can access it, but Lobis here has confirmed my theory. It is a distribution node for the Foundry."

"Much information can be gathered here," it added.

I felt my heart begin to race. "How far away is it?"

"Two days by ground car," Lance said, voice tight.

James crossed his arms. "But is it worth the risk?"

"My vote is yes," Esteban said.

"Mine too," Mary agreed.

Lobis retracted the tentacle and glared at me. "What about you?"

I scratched at my stubbly face and took a deep breath. It felt too convenient, all of it. Yet if there was even a chance of finding out what happened to Mom and Dad…

"Okay," I said, having paused for only a moment. "Okay. I'm in. What's the plan? What's the risk?"

"Ah, the risk," Esteban said. "Isoptera."

Lobis blinked. "You will be beyond our protection. Possible Isoptera scouts."

"Lovely," I replied.

"Just a chance for payback," James growled under his breath. "Give me some fuckers to frag."

"Or a chance to be eaten," Lance added. "Why you always so eager?"

"Maybe you'd feel the same if things went down for you like they did for me."

"Got to let that shit go, man. No sense crying over spilt blood."

"You're a dick, you know that?"

"I never claimed to be anything else."

Mary pointed to our camp on the map, then at the desert between us and the target. "The silicate flats will be hell on the land car. We'll have to clear it out of the machinery every day, and wear masks, but I think we can make it easy enough. We will drive in shifts to maximize our travel time. If the Isoptera crash on us, we'll shoot at them and run like hell."

"But what about the network?" Perry asked. "We have no proof it won't cook your brains. I don't care what you say, sister, I am going in with you."

"No, you are not, your place is here."

"The hell it is. I've lost enough family this week."

We allowed his words to wash over us without response.

A concern rose to the surface of my swirling mind. "What about the rest? Those we are leaving back. Will they be safe?"

Will Shelly be safe? This was not the time to leave the love of my life alone. She needed me.

One of Lobis's arms twitched. "We will care for those left behind."

"And how can I trust that?"

"Do you want answers?" It waited before going on, allowing me to fully digest the question. "There is no other way."

"Fine," I growled, my desire for knowledge outweighing my concerns in the moment. "When do we leave?"

"Tomorrow," Mary said. "It will be night, of course, but that will help with the desert fauna. They will not be active."

"Meet back here at dawn, ya?" Esteban said. "I'll start prepping."

I glared at Lobis, my hands sweating. "I hope you're not lying to us."

"What purpose would that serve?" it asked, and the meeting adjourned.

Against Shelly's request, I returned to her quarters, which had fast become our quarters. She was bundled up in a chair sipping a cup of tea, a pile of balled up tissues on the floor beside her.

"Milo?" she asked, setting her cup down. "What is it?"

"Something unexpected has happened."

"What?" She stood up quick, hurrying over. "What is it?"

"We have a way to maybe find out what happened to my parents, among other things. Our Benefactors have given us a map to a Foundry data node. Mary believes we can interface to it with our implants."

Shelly put a hand on my chest and gave a tired grin. "You have to go."

"I'm afraid of leaving you."

"Me?" She shook her head and let out a manic chuckle. "I'm tougher than I look at the moment."

"I know. I know. That's not it. I just feel uneasy. Something isn't right."

"How so?"

"I still don't trust them."

She took hold of my hands and placed her palms flat against mine. "We'll be fine," she said, comparing the length of her fingers to mine. "I'll be fine. I will take care of the colony while you are gone. I suppose, in lieu of Dad, people would expect it out of me."

"Are you sure you can do it?"

"Do you doubt me?"

"Not for a second."

"Good. Then do what you have to. The mission takes precedence. Find your parents, find the knowledge we need to save Earth."

"Okay."

"When are you leaving?"

"Tomorrow."

"Then that means we have one more night together." She took my hand and led me over to the bed. "Given all that has happened, I think we both need a bit of comfort."

"You sure that's appropriate right now?" I wondered.

She let out a long sigh and drew me into a tight embrace. "I can't think of a more appropriate time. It's like Dad always told me, 'Life is to be lived.'"

CHAPTER 37

With the help of the machine shop team, Esteban prepared the ground car for our night drive to the Foundry's data hub in no time. The truck was built with a decent-sized crew cab in front that seated three comfortably and had a flatbed rear for cargo. Because of this design, not everyone could ride up front, and given when we were leaving, those riding in the rear would freeze their asses off without modifications to the open bed. The team threw their weight together, and within just a few hours erected a bed topper that acted as a break against the wind. They bolted a few seats below the topper and mounted a portable heater to the corner of the bed. This meant that of the six of us, three would ride up front, three in the back.

The rest of us received a ping from Esteban when it was finished. We gathered the rest of our gear, weapons, food, medical supplies. I gave my sweet, slumbering Shelly a kiss on the forehead before letting myself out. She hardly stirred at the action, only a moan of something endearing slipping from her lips. I paused before opening the door to leave, gave her one last look, then stepped out into the dark.

"Everyone armed?" Esteban asked as we gathered beside the truck at the edge of the colony. It was the first day of the dark side of the week, and already it was uncomfortably cold.

"Can we get moving?" James insisted, his arms crossed and shaking.

"Only going to get colder, *amigo*," Esteban said, slapping him on the back.

"I'm up front," Perry called. "Wait… what did gramps call that? Riding shotgun?"

Mary pointed at him with two fingers. "I'm driving."

"Let's take shifts in back," Lance suggested. "James, since you're already cold, you go up first. We'll rotate in a few hours."

James nodded. "Don't have to tell me twice. I wasn't built for this."

"I guess it's just us in back." I turned to face Esteban and Lance. "A party waiting to happen."

"A fuckin' riot," Lance said, his expression deadpan.

"Let's roll out!" Mary shouted from the driver's window. "Anyone need to take a leak before we go?"

"No, *mama*," Esteban called back. "I went *pipi* before leavin' the house."

"Good boy! Good boy! Maybe you'll get a surprise from the store later."

"No foolin'?" He grinned from ear to ear.

"Do I lie to sweet little boys?"

We had one mission: cross the desert plains and infiltrate the data hub. I only hoped Mary and Perry would have the means to get us what we needed. This was a Foundry facility, and so far, the network had been less than forthcoming on important topics.

I climbed into the back of the truck with Esteban and Lance and pulled the door of the bed topper closed. It was warmer inside, no cold gusts of wind cutting through you like a knife, but it was not warm. I had hoped I could shed the parka once we were inside. That was not an option.

The truck got under way, its engine a low electric whine, gravel crunching beneath our wheels. Mary was driving half blind, the car's floodlights shining ahead and behind, following the trail marked out by our Benefactors. I only hoped it was complete. I hoped that there were no hidden pitfalls or fissures in our path.

Those of us sitting in back jostled around, each bump like a miniature explosion. The guys in the machine shop needed to pay more attention to the bed's suspension.

Once the trail had leveled off, Esteban pounded the back of the truck cab with a fist.

"Coffee?" he called, and there came three knocks in response. He went over to the heating element and placed a metal pot against it.

"Making enough for everyone?" Lance asked.

"Keep us all alert, ya?"

"How long will this drive take?" I asked, leaning forward in my chair, fingers wrapped around the barrel of my VP-214.

Esteban shrugged. "Twenty-six, twenty-eight hours or so."

"Why the gap?"

"Some of the terrain may be hard to navigate. Mostly flat, but it's still unfamiliar."

"And if we end up under attack, we tuck our tails and run?" Lance asked.

Esteban tapped the coffee pot and nodded. "Like the Devil's at our heels, ya?"

"I get tired of running sometimes," I said, feeling a little more confident with the weapon gripped in my fingers.

Lance sucked on his teeth. "There's a time to run. A time to leave well enough alone."

"Change isn't always bad," I replied.

"Depends on what changes, and to who."

I kept my eyes fixed on my boots. "Pretty sure things typically work out as they should."

"Same go for those who die?" A touch of venom in Lance's tone. "Found out about my dad, by the way, thanks for telling me. I knew he was gone, but it would have been nice to hear how sooner."

"He was a hero," Esteban interjected. "We'd be dead without him."

"Of course he's a goddamned hero." Lance shifted in his seat, his left foot tapping the truck bed. He reached in a pocket and fished out a tan brush, flipping it over in his hands. "I should have brought something to do."

"We could play cards, ya?"

"Let me rephrase. I should have brought something to do by myself." He began brushing out his beard, eyes focused on the roof of the topper. "This is going to be a long-ass ride."

And in that sentiment, Lance and I could whole heartedly agree.

Once the coffee was finished brewing, the truck came to a stop and we rotated, Lance and Esteban moving up front, James and Perry moving into the back. By this point, my toes felt like they were starting to freeze, and so I made sure to sit closest to the heating element.

Perry climbed in back, a smile on his face. "Milo, have you looked outside at all? It's just... Man. Come on."

"I haven't." I rotated my feet before the heating element, enjoying that they warmed up like crispy meat on a spit, one side at a time. "Shut the door! Get inside, you're letting the cold in."

He waved this thought away and pushed James into his seat. "Yeah, yeah. Here, check this out."

"Serious? Come outside?"

"Yes. For like two seconds. It won't kill you."

I drew my coat closed and glared at him. "It just might."

Perry tugged me outside by the sleeve. I swear my skin turned to ice the instant air brushed against it. We stood on the back bed of the truck, looking all around at the chilly, desert plains. I had expected it to be dark, the expanse we crossed a gulf of its own, but it wasn't. Stretching out before us for miles in every direction were random patterns of dappled, knee-high, bulbous flora that glowed a lambent aquamarine color, their short stalks rooted in the silicate soil.

I sucked in a breath; a bit shocked that there was anything else in this world that could take me by surprise. The universe, for all its horrors, truly had pockets of brilliant, tranquil beauty. Could this be the result of random chance? Of building blocks which just happened to fall into similar patterns again and again? Or was there more?

"Looks like these plants adapted the same as deep sea creatures," Perry said, pointing to what I thought was the horizon. "In the absence of sunlight during the back half of the week, they made their own."

"It's remarkable," I commented. "How do they survive out here in the dry and dark?"

"To quote Mr. Goldblum the sage, 'Life…uhhh…uhh…finds a way.'"

I gave a slow nod. "Wise words from a wise man."

"Come on. Let's get back inside. You know, Milo, you weren't wrong about the cold. I think my balls are gonna end up as cocktail coolers if we stay out any longer."

We retreated back into the warm topper and closed the door. James had taken my seat beside the heater. I sighed and sat across from him, rubbing my shoes to try and warm my feet again. Futile.

The ground car started moving, and from up front, music began to play. It was clear that they were diving back into Mary's collection, the sound of heavy bass and guitar power riffs no doubt echoing across the glowing plains. Perry nodded his head to the beat for a time, then leaned back in his chair and slumped over, asleep. James fiddled with his hand terminal, eyes not meeting mine. I couldn't take the silence any longer.

When I was good and sure Perry was out, his mouth wide, drool oozing over his lips, I spoke up, "Hey, James."

He did not respond.

I tried again, hoping the music had been too loud for him to hear me the first time. "James, you in there?"

He raised his attention and glowered at me. "What?"

"Thought you might want to talk. We have a long ride ahead."

"Why would I want to do that?" He continued to fiddle with his hand terminal.

"Because we're friends?"

"Since when?"

"Since almost our entire lives." I raised my hands, palms up. "Look, what's going on? Ever since I came back you have done nothing but avoid me and act like an ass. Be upfront, dude, what is it? Did I do something?"

"No," he stated, tone flat. "It's not what you did. It's what you didn't do."

"What's that supposed to mean?"

"Do you want to know?" His face turned hard, brows knitting, pupils narrowing. "Do you really want to know?"

"Yes. Yes, I do!"

"Fine," James spat, and despite the cold, his forehead began to sweat, a vein at the edge of his temple throbbed. "Mom is dead because of you."

I slumped back in my seat as if I'd been punched. "Excuse me?"

"You heard me, you elitist shit biscuit. Mom is dead because of you."

"I don't understand."

"He doesn't understand. For all his smarts, context evades Milo Hughes yet again." James covered his face with a trembling palm. "During the attack, Mom called for help. She was being overrun by Isoptera in the medical bay and needed assistance. I asked you to come with me and you didn't."

"Because my parents called for help, too. What did you expect me to do?"

"Anyone else in the world, and I might buy that answer. Your relationship with your parents was shit. You never stopped talking about how they weren't there for you and how we were your family. Mom was all I had, and you weren't willing to save her. Our relationship was worth saving."

"You think I should have sacrificed my parents to save your mom?"

"If I had had help, she might have lived! You went off on your own, and for all we know your parents are dead anyway."

"Don't say that."

"Dude, this is the reality we live in. I lost mom and I lost everything that mattered to me. I don't have some sweet face to come home to, I don't have a shoulder to cry on."

"What are you trying to say?" I leaned in, my chest tight. "That your mom was more important than my parents?"

James's eyes went dark. "Yes."

And this thought made me feel sick. I could understand that he was upset, but I wasn't the enemy. The Isoptera had shown up and screwed us all.

"Look," I went on, lowering my voice, "good or bad, my parents are my parents. Maybe they didn't deserve my love, but they had it, and as screwed up as it is, they still do. Would it help if I said I was sorry?"

"No."

"Okay then. Even still, I am." We sat there in silence for a while, neither of us looking at one another. Perry shifted in his seat and let out a long, dreamy sigh. "I really am sorry," I said after a bit.

"Sorry won't bring her back."

"No," I exhaled. "No, it won't."

"It was the last time I ever spoke to her," James mumbled, his nose scrunching up, his eyes closed. "The last time."

Our conversation came to a close. There was nothing else to say. I was getting tired, and so I made a pallet in the corner with a collection of skins and blankets we had packed, my front side warm, my backside ice cold. Sleep was hard to come by in this position. I had crazy dreams once again, though these were not violent. I was in the mountains of Montana riding a bike, zipping through switchbacks, a storm as expansive as the open sky at my back. Dad was with me, lagging behind, black clouds overtaking him. I tried to stop the motorcycle, but it wouldn't shut off. I kept thundering ahead, off into open plains and clear skies while Dad fell into darkness.

The truck hit a bump and I woke. All the lights in the back were off, and so I could only assume James and Perry were sleeping. A moment passed, I rubbed my eyes and resolved to stay awake, and then voices whispered in the dark.

I stirred, rubbing my eyes before peeking out from under the skins.

"Ooo, I like that spot," a woman said, her voice low and breathy. "My toes are going numb. Oh geez, that one shot down my spine. God, it's been a bit."

"That the spot, ya?" a man replied. "You ticklish?"

"Ticklish? Maybe."

"How about here? So nice and slick. Smooth. Freshly trimmed."

"Ohh, yeah, ohh, yeah that's it. Wait, your fingers are a bit rough. Hang on. Move them, right over. Okay, here, yeah that's it."

"I only aim to please."

"More men should learn to take instruction." She let out a guttural moan. "Goddamn, son. Don't stop. Don't stop. Bring your lips up here."

I rolled on my side, my back to the scene, and drew the skins over my head, stuffing my fingers in my ears, willing the world away. I had no problem with whatever Esteban and Mary did in their free time. I just didn't want to watch.

Or did I? I shook my head and forced myself back to sleep. It wasn't appropriate to eavesdrop.

There was no telling what we would face at the Foundry data hub. The best I could do to prepare was rest. Rest and put the conversation with James out of my mind. He was angry and hurt, and I understood, but I was not taking the blame for this. Dr. Reed did not die because of me. I did not order the Isoptera after her.

"Wake up, buttercup!" Esteban said after some time, his nose inches from mine, the topper's lights back on. It was no surprise that he smelled of sex and sweat.

"Get out of my face," I said, rolling out from under my blankets, pushing my friend back. "What is it?"

"We're here," Perry called from the doorway, rifle in hand. "I think it's high time we get some answers."

CHAPTER 38

It took me some moments to collect my wits along with my gear. Esteban had made coffee, and I swallowed down a few sips before exiting the car and braving the cold. It had been over twenty-four hours since we left the colony, yet daytime proper still was days away. It was no wonder life on this world had evolved in such strange ways.

I exited the truck and turned towards our target, expecting it to be nothing but a black lump against starscape. Instead, I was greeted by a solid, metallic structure lit by the glow of a thousand bioluminescent plants. The same bulbs we found sprouting across the desert had made their homes in lines up and down its façade, accentuating its shape like rope lights. As our Benefactor's map had shown, it was indeed a ziggurat, its square base wide, a good five hundred feet across, with ten additional levels connected by a single staircase, each tier successively smaller, culminating with a final cube at its peak.

"Time to get in some cardio," Mary said, fists on her hips. "This is definitely the place. I've been feeling the network signal get stronger for hours now."

Perry rubbed the front of his neck and paced. "Do we go inside or try and connect from here?"

"Inside, I think."

Esteban waved to Lance, James, and I. "Make sure your rifles are ready, you got fresh clips and clear heads."

"Plan?" Lance lifted his weapon and pointed it out into the dark. "They do the work, we just cover?"

"That's it, *amigo*."

"They better not let us down," James growled.

Perry raised his hands and shook them. "Show some faith, my brother!"

I stepped up beside Esteban and lowered my voice. "We might want to keep an eye on James."

"Ya?"

"He's a bit too eager."

"I think he's just hurt."

"I know, but there's more than that."

Esteban let out a long sigh and gave me a nod.

"This way, guys," Mary said, leading us towards the staircase.

Standing at the bottom of the ziggurat, the sheer scale of it was felt more than seen. For as much as was visible, something told me it went deep into the planet, thousands of feet. I might not have been as sensitive to signals and electromagnetic fields as Mary, but I could feel the hairs on my arms and neck stand on end as soon as my boot touched the first step. This place had power, unfathomable power, and we were intent on making use of it for a time. I only hoped it wasn't too much for us to handle.

We ascended the stairs, a blind vertigo coming over not only me, but also Perry. Esteban took point, leading us to the peak, while Lance and James covered the rear. Our vantage increased as we neared the top, but nothing of concern was on the horizon, the desert empty and quiet. Perry cycled through various modes on his visor to search for heat signatures beyond the visual range. We were clear.

We reached the cube at the structure's peak and found a door engraved with the symbols of a thousand languages, most of which were rooted in tight swirls and dots, circles and series of lines, fractals and Fibonacci sequences, their intricacy and eccentricity provoking deep thought and a sense of overwhelming insignificance. Staring at them made me feel powerful and yet small, as common as a grain of sand on a cosmic beach apt to be washed away by the next great tide into the endless, impartial nothing.

Mary scratched her head and inspected it closely.

"Alright," she said after a moment. "Now how do we open it? I don't see a handle or a doorknob. Anyone recognize the symbols?"

Esteban and I took a closer look. Nothing I had seen so far reminded me of any of this; not items from the Jalek's secure chamber, nor the symbols on the side of the Kabosai's hollow ship.

"How do you feel when you look at it?" I asked the group. Lance glowered at me in response. "I'm serious. How does it make you feel?"

"Cold," Perry said.

Mary tapped at her lips. "Curious."

"Lost." James sniffed and turned away.

Lance shook his head, expression hard. "Like it's saying, 'fuck you.'"

"Colorful," I mumbled.

"Tiny," Esteban admitted. "Really tiny."

"What if it isn't language as we know it?" I ventured. "What if, like Mary has already proposed, most intelligent life thinks the same? This might be a set of codes that operates different for everyone. A puzzle of sorts."

"A puzzle?" she mused.

"Yeah. On the Foundry, when it downloaded information to me from the implants, I felt like the world was pink. I can't explain how, but that is what it related to in my mind. Once I allowed myself to be comfortable with the idea, it came easier to me. Maybe our brains are like a big library with dozens of entrances."

Mary nodded. "We just need to let it in the right one."

"And that might be different for all of us. You said you felt curious, why not try and open it? That would be natural."

She turned to face the opening, closed her eyes, and reached out with her right hand. An instant later the door opened, revealing the space within.

"All I did was allow myself to be curious," she said. "It was like opening a door in my mind and shaking a hand on the other side."

Perry let out a whistle. "Could be literal. They do call it a handshake when two networks connect to one another."

"Why make a door like this?" James asked. "Why not just have a handle or something?"

Esteban took a step into the opening and panned his rifle around the side. "The Foundry only wants to admit certain intelligence, ya? Make it wired to that."

"Okay," Mary said, and went first. "Let's get a move on."

Before the last of us entered, Lance reached in a pocket and set a series of palm-size boxes outside the entrance. "Proximity detectors," he supplied.

"Good idea."

We entered the structure and the door shut behind us. That sense of ease I felt aboard the Foundry structure rushed back into me. I was not afraid of being stuck inside this thing for the rest of my life. I knew that we could leave whenever we wanted.

The interior of the ziggurat spread out, its immersive, internal space a maddening tangle of stairs set at impossible angles; some normal like the ones before us, some upside down or sideways, leading into doors which vanished into nothing. Various objects, jars or cargo boxes, sat at ninety-degree angles perpendicular to our position as if oriented to an alternative set of gravity. I had once seen a sketch by a 20th century artist who had portrayed 4th dimension concepts in such a way. Thinking of the inside of the data hub through M.C. Escher's lens was the only way I could make sense of the madness.

"Damn," Perry said, a bit uneasy on his feet. He wobbled, leaning a bit too close to the edge of our staircase. I reached out and took hold of his arm. If he had fallen, I had no way of telling if he would plummet to the black fathoms below, or drift onto another set of stairs, potentially out of grasp for geometric reasons I couldn't resolve.

"You okay?" I asked.

"Just a bit…"

"Overwhelming?" Mary suggested. "This is doing crazy tricks with my head. Which way is up? How do we orient?"

I swallowed the stone in my throat. "Are we close enough to connect from here?"

"I don't think so. Something tells me we need to find the node and make physical contact. I have no rational explanation for this, it's just a feeling."

"From the handshake?" I gave a smile, hoping to break the tension.

"Yeah. Exactly."

Perry took a seat on the stairs and started to bump his way down one step at a time. A strange memory rose to the surface of my mind, of me at my aunt's house when I was two or three, her instructing me this was how I needed to go down the stairs if she wasn't holding my hand. I nearly laughed at Perry, then as we descended into the structure, I realized he might not be completely crazy. The vertigo this advanced geometry summoned made my back tingle, the bottoms of my feet sweat. James gave Perry a curious look. Out of the fear of ridicule, mostly from Lance, I did not follow Perry's actions, but instead stood tall, eyes down, focusing on each footfall.

Moments later, we passed through an arch as a group. As we appeared on the other side, we found ourselves oriented to a new surface, our feet perpendicular to the previous wall on our left. The entrance to the ziggurat was now above my head and to the right. The occasional platform appeared off to the side of the many staircases, Foundry equipment placed in neat rows around its edges. Mary tested them to be sure they were not what we were after before we moved on.

"Come on Milo," I mumbled to myself. "Keep focused on your feet. Keep focused on your feet."

The deeper into the structure we delved, the more we experienced these shifts in perspective. It was soon difficult to even see the entrance.

"I have a theory," Perry said, bumping down another step. He was faster at this than I had expected.

Lance moved ahead then looked back. "What's your theory?"

"I believe that this is a means to maximize internal space. And now that we have gone a bit further, there seems to be a spiraling pattern."

"Not a spiral," Mary cut in, "but I know what you mean. Left, across, right, across, left, across, right, across."

"It's dark up there," Esteban added, attempting to look back where we had come. "Anyone have a rock or somethin'?"

"Hang on." Perry reached into his pants and handed a pebble to Esteban.

James scowled at him. "Who carries rocks in their pockets?"

"To be honest, I find it strange that none of you do."

Esteban inspected the tiny stone, turning it around in the light, then tossed it out into open space. The pebble slowed as it entered the center of the ziggurat, then fell out one of the sides onto a set of stairs we had already come down.

"Theory proved, ya?"

"We're close," Mary said. "I feel something."

"Me too," Lance echoed. "It's like a pressure."

James paused for a moment and gave a worried look.

"What is it?" I asked.

"I—I'm not sure," he replied, then drew his hand terminal from his pocket, flipping through a readout. "Nothing. Just a little movement outside. It looks like a false positive. Likely some avia or something."

"You sure?"

"No. No, not entirely."

Esteban raised his weapon, pointing back where we had come. "We stay alert. Mary and Perry, hurry down, we hold here. Milo, go with."

"Copy that."

We redoubled our pace and soon reached the bottom of the stairs. Why didn't this place have an elevator? Not only was the entrance several hundred feet away now, we'd also have to reverse our bizarre descent to get out.

At the base of the structure was a perfectly square room, twenty by twenty, with a series of gilded pipes and tubes threading in and out of the walls and floors, surfaces tiled much like the streets of Cynosure. At the center of it all sat a glowing pyramid, a half dozen prismatic lines bisecting its height. It didn't take a PhD to determine this was the data hub.

Mary made her way over the machine, unslinging the bags on her shoulder. I helped Perry stand, who, despite making it back onto solid ground, was still uneasy on his feet.

"You good?" I asked.

"No," he said, a hand on his stomach. "Whatever is at play in here is messing with my optics. It's worse now that we're in this room. Like Mom always said, puking in someone else's house is impolite, but projectile vomiting…"

"Is beyond the pail?" Mary finished with a sly grin.

"That's right, sis. Help me get over there."

"Sure."

She helped Perry take a seat beside the data node. He slipped off his headset and shut it off temporarily.

"Okay. I'm going in," she said, kneeling before the machine. "Here goes nothing." Her eyes closed as she placed her palms on its cold surface, the pressure in the room shifting for an instant.

Through my implant's local ad hoc network, I could feel that she was in, despite her silence as she navigated through the stream.

"Can we talk to her?" I asked Perry.

"I'm not sure. Her focus seems to be fully on the network. Let's give her a moment to process the information and make sense of it."

"Hey guys?" Lance called over our implants' comms.

Esteban replied, *"What is it?"*

"We've got movement outside the ziggurat. They're big and coming towards the stairs."

"How many?" I asked.

"Six or seven."

"Hang on," Perry said. "Let me see if I can reach the night camera on the ground car." He paused and put his visor back on. "There we go. Adjusting angle. Christ on a cracker, you guys better get ready for a fight. It's our favorite arthropods."

"What do?" Esteban replied.

"It's as we feared coming this far out. Without our Benefactor's influence, we've got Isoptera."

"Perfect," James growled.

"Three on six with a choke point," Esteban rolled over. *"They bleed, already proven. We can do this. Get to the top boys, we create crossfire from these crazy stairs, ya?"*

"Copy," Lance and James replied.

"Do I come up or stay here?" I asked.

Esteban milled that over for a moment. *"Take position midway."*

I took one look at Perry and his sister, the two sitting next to the data node. Perry gave me a wave and I took off up the stairs, entering one way and exiting the next, up and up and up, my guts twisting like a corkscrew.

Gunfire broke out from above, flashes of light in the dimly lit twist of stairs pointing up. An instant later, a body came tumbling down the space at the center, slow as it descended towards the bottom. A dying Isoptera twitching, its wings sheared off, ichor dripping from its thorax.

"Milo," Esteban said, my name spoken in singsong. *"Might be good to start shootin'."*

I knelt and pointed my gun upward, fixing it on the entrance. The Isoptera were attempting to force their way through the single door leading into the ziggurat. While they would have issues getting in through such a small entry, we would equally have issues getting out. If we made a run for it, we were dead.

"More contacts showing on our motion detectors," Lance reported.

James replied, *"Hold fire, I think I see one trying to pop its head in. Let's give it the chance."*

"Perry," I called down, then squeezed the trigger of my VP-214 just as an overeager Isoptera tried to force its way in. My rounds hit nothing but the gilded walls, the impact not leaving even a scuffmark. "Perry!"

"What?" he replied after some moments.

"Progress?"

"She's in but not finding what we need. It's too much data to go through, and there's security. If we had all day, maybe, but as it stands…"

"Can you help her?"

"I've tried, but for whatever reason I can't connect for more than a few seconds. I don't know what's wrong."

I fired again at the entrance. The door closed for an instant, then opened again, no insect in sight.

"They haven't fucked off yet," Lance replied. *"They're playing chicken."*

We had to do something and coming all this way could not be for nothing. Given that the Isoptera had come for us this time, even if we escaped now, they would be waiting here next time. I got the feeling no matter how much we begged them, the Kabosai would not help us out with this particular problem.

"I have an idea," I said, and abandoned my position, heading back down.

"Where you goin', amigo?" Esteban demanded.

"Mary needs help in the network. The faster we get what we need, the faster we can escape. I have some experience with my implants and networks. Dad and I did plenty of VE exploration, and then there's networking the nanofluid. I'm confident I can help her."

"Can' hold them forever, ya?"

"Won't need to."

I slid up beside Mary and set my rifle on the floor, took off my parka and rolled it up before me, placing my knees on it like Omar did when in prayer.

"Here we go," I said, taking a deep breath.

"Be careful," Perry told me.

"Careful." The word did not match up with anything we'd done.

As my hands met the cold surface of the machine, an energy filled me.

The physical world vanished.

CHAPTER 39

One moment, I was in an echoing space filled with screams and gunfire; the next, in an empty, black expanse. I focused my attention beyond the virtual environment, calling for a handshake. Off to the right of my noncorporeal form, a pink light appeared and grew larger, resolving into a hazy portal.

I passed through the opening and found myself in a maze of color and intention. Ribbons and threads of light shot out in all directions, prismatic flickers traveling along their lengths from here into infinity. Above me hung a thousand worlds, a thousand facilities, all connected by data streams. Facility 225 was fifteen light years from here, so its information was deemed to be set to a 4th degree time shift. Facility 596 had just made a full dump and though it was under a 7th degree time shift, it was a rarely visited facility, its information likely still up to date. Facility 447 had sustained damage relating to a hostile attack during first contact, but would remain operational, the situation partially resolved. This went on and on.

The Foundry network was massive, far beyond what I had ever imagined. Gi'Vor had told me it was expansive. I guess I just had to see it for myself. It controlled the known galaxy and was its most influential power. Questions nagged at me… Who created it? Who commanded it?

"Milo," a distant voice cut into the overload. *"Milo! You there, amigo?"*

My primitive grey matter was unable to process who this was.

I felt a familiar presence to my left.

"Mary?"

"I'm here," she replied. "I'm working on the security. There are layers." Mary was invisible, part of the network and yet not a part. I wished that I could see her physical body, so that I might orient myself.

"How so?"

"Shapes. Colors. Math," she said. "Damn, some of it is straight up quantum, more than I could solve without a lot of time and research."

"Like the entrance?"

"Like the entrance times ten. Take this for example," she said, and before me a square appeared, filled with numbers and notations. "It's a kind of shorthand, a code perhaps. I believe this is a trigonometry problem. Each symbol related to a variable. Each demarcation fractional or algebraic."

I stared at the problem for some time. Looking for patterns or solutions among the symbols. I was decent with math, but I felt the answer wasn't complicated. Something about it all seemed familiar, like a problem Dad might have had laid out on the kitchen table late one night, his mind set on solving it. Off to the side were two circles, the distance of these objects two or three times that of their diameters. They were connected by a lined shape much like an inverted triangle, though this triangle was missing its topmost face and looked more like a wide V.

"It's a parallax calculation," I mumbled.

"What?"

"Parallax."

"I'm not catching your meaning."

"It's how we measure the distance of an object by viewing it from two different angles and solving for the unknowns in the triangle they create."

"No, no. I know what trigonometric parallax is. But where are you seeing the relationship?"

"The circles. They're two points in space, maybe a star. I can't say."

"Okay," she said, mulling the idea over. "That makes a lot of sense, it's a measurement. And the distance relates to the coefficient of the next problem."

And like that, the next question appeared. I immediately made sense of small pieces of the equation.

"Fuel and weight ratio," I supplied.

"I daresay orbital calculations might be next."

"So, it's having us plot a course to gain entrance? That's the security code?"

"Seems to have always been the security code," she mused. "The Foundry is like a lock in itself, its location chosen to prove something of new species. Hang on, I'm working through it. A bit of nuclear fusion pencil whipping, a little orbital mechanics. It's a good thing interstellar space is pretty empty, not as much gravity at play. Wait. That's it!"

The mathematical problem vanished, and a passage appeared. I made my way through it, disembodied, only location and awareness. I found myself in a deeper place, this one filled with nodes and streams just like the other, though different. It was darker, the light of this room produced by the billions of flashing diamond studs of stellar mass that spread out around me. Where the other room had shown the network, this one had given me the galaxy.

"What now?" I asked Mary. "We don't have forever."

"I know. I know. God damned termites. Why couldn't they just leave us alone for a few hours? The Jalek told me they like how we taste."

It took her a moment to respond. "That's horrible."

"Yeah."

"Okay, I found something. Another security protocol."

An instant later, another problem appeared before us, this one made of shapes in an altered geometry much like the staircase we had descended. There was a room on the other side of a window, with rows leading in every direction that also bent back upon themselves. Colors flashed and moved across it, traveling one direction, only to appear somewhere else, the edge of each vertex connected to that of its fourth-dimensional partner. It was difficult to resolve, my brain designed to operate in only three dimensions that in themselves were being viewed through a two-dimensional frame.

I watched as sprites of data traveled down the various paths to different locations, tucking away what might be connected and to where. Instinct led me to reach out and pull one of the thread-like vertices as if it were the string of a guitar.

A vibration echoed through the environmental space, its frequency deep, unending. Before I could pluck another, a high frequency noise called back.

"That was me," Mary said. "I think we have to play a song of sorts."

"A song? Like what?"

"Well, I doubt it's by Cyndi Lauper."

"Then what would it be?" I wondered, looking for clues. All I had were the stars and the space between, the dimensional frame before me.

A crackly voice cut in and out of my head. *"Hey, guys?"* It took me a moment to realize that James was calling to us.

"What is it?" Mary replied.

"You need to hurry, like bad. We are running low on ammo. They've got several squads out there. I don't think we're getting away."

"We're almost in," I told him. "Just a little longer."

"Lance took a nasty burn to the arm. He's having trouble keeping himself upright."

"Just a little longer."

"Whatever."

"Maybe we should quit," Mary suggested. "Get out of here. It's not worth losing our lives."

"But if we do, we can't come back. They'll camp this place forever. No, we have to do this right now."

"How? I'm stumped. I don't know about any of this. It's almost as if The Foundry has opened a portal into a tesseract, and we have to make music. I bet someone could devote their dissertation to the study of this, and yet we have seconds to figure it out." Mary paused, as if an idea had just occurred to her. "Wait... tesseract, vibrations, hang on. It's a dark matter problem."

"What?"

"Dark matter vibrations. All theoretical, sure, we've not quite figured it out, but there is something that binds the empty space of the universe together. Dark matter is the medium, the vibrations, transmission. So, what would dark matter transmit by and large?"

I re-inspected the open environment, and the billions of stars shining down at me. I relaxed, allowing myself to perceive patterns. An instant later a red star flashed, then a yellow, then a blue, then a yellow. They blinked in sequence and started over again.

"Star frequencies," I answered.

"Exactly. We have to pluck the strings which match the frequency of those stars and in that order."

"How do we figure that out?"

"We'll have to guess. Red is a lower frequency. Blue is higher."

"Okay," I said. "I trust you."

"Here goes nothing."

I sat and waited. Sound passed over me, a low rumble followed by a slightly sharper ping, then a high note that came down and rested at the same tone of the previous pluck. Nothing happened.

"Try again," I said, and she did, attempting to adjust the frequencies, going a little high and lower. In rapid succession she made the attempt five more times.

"Nothing," she said. "Maybe we're wrong. Maybe that isn't what they are trying to get us to do." She kept up her efforts.

"No. I think this is right, we just have to find the correct frequency."

"Milo, we really need to—"

The world flashed, and I was projected into an existence of pure, prismatic light, divine and primordial. The Foundry's network firewall had fallen like a castle door. The universe lay out before me.

Information rushed into my mind as if a dam made of qubits had cracked in two, a thousand threads and lines of logic converging into a single, bundled node of nervous data. There were images and numbers and dates and reasons and theories and evidence and patterns, overwhelming, prime numbers in streams a thousand long, star designations in data tables, endless taxonomy of flora and fauna, *pain*, microscopic images of cell structure and active mitosis, practical intelligent designs and direction, algorithmic emotional analogs, analysis of spiritual rapture, the culmination of existential dread— then came—then came—understanding. A topic at a time, I started to see what it all meant. Pieces once disconnected, scattered, now became clear.

We were, *we are, we will always be* part of a bigger game. There was an infinite, timeless struggle with a single, clear objective—to protect life.

What that meant in practice varied greatly. The Foundry had not lied, it had protected the galaxy from interstellar war time and again through the influence of its network. It had given adversaries an even playing field, a means to communicate, a platform to air their grievances. Left to their own devices, many a species would have killed off their own worlds, or even taken to the stars to ravage one world after the next, seeking to replace the depleted resources of their mistreated homes. The Foundry was old, far older than anyone knew, having appeared at the same time the first starfaring species had crawled out of their own gravity wells in search of more. But who had created the Foundry? Not even it knew.

The Foundry was. The Foundry had always been.

It had a mission. Protect life. Awaken the Universe. It did its job, as it always would, calling those who could touch it, building machines, creating equilibrium. Indifferent equanimity.

And then came the Kabosai, Gene Brokers, Benefactors of Burgeoning Peoples. They were one of the oldest species, natural, adaptive, traveling into the black, nearly extinct. They modified themselves, changed, borrowed material from those they met, forced evolution, took new forms, not once, but many times. They breathed the void, listened to the dark, heard the silence, knew emptiness, found their cause. Not all species were natural. The rest are designed, pieces taken from many, twisted and turned, transformed and redirected. Natural is random, too slow, but strong; when modified, redesigned, a natural species can then know many worlds, their seed able to conquer the lands beyond the entropic horizon. Many species were designed, Degron, K'Val, Iltari, Breyon, and Eipren. More names. More and more and more, worlds behind the Wandering Gate and worlds far beyond.

Ages passed.

A pattern emerged.

Find the natural.

Make a deal, isolate and prepare for change.

Earn trust, increase quality of life.

Become ever invasive, influence social circles.

When tissue is required, ask for bone and hair, muscle and marrow. Good data. Better data.

Ask them to donate. Donate to survive.

If they become hostile, remove the strong, take them away, proceed to second phase.

New planet. New climate. Hope they are ready.

If fails, start again.

And again. And again. And again.

The Universe cannot awaken without help. The Foundry is too slow, relies on natural, believe it is already awake, will speak one day. Kabosai multiply, acting to give God a voice, acting to put life on all worlds.

I watched images scroll past, happening time and again, groups of natural species tossed into this genetic meat grinder, in the hopes that they would emerge resilient and powerful. Billions fell for the cause of creating trillions more. On paper there was a certain logic to this, but among those billions lost might be those I cared about, not just numbers. The ends did not justify the means.

I knew exactly where we were in the process. We were near the end of their cycle.

"Mary!" I shouted through the data network, not disconnecting.

"Yes, Milo?" she responded. "I can't see you."

"This was a trap."

"Because of the Isoptera?"

"No. Our Benefactors wanted to separate us from the rest of the group. We were a threat. They intend to steal everyone away. This is not the first time."

"What? What are you saying?"

"I'll wrap up a package and send you the data. We have to get back to the colony."

"But what about the rest of our group? Did you find out anything?"

"I'm staying in a little longer. Hold the enemy off."

I passed Mary the necessary data and continued to delve deeper into the bundles of information within the node. I couldn't leave without trying to find my parents.

"Milo," she replied, her voice trembling. "Lord save us from them. The Kabosai, they are not our benefactors, they are evil."

"I know…"

"We have to go. Maybe we can save the rest."

"Just a few more seconds. Just a few more."

"They're getting' real close," Esteban's voice cut in. *"We gonna have to break out soon, and that prospect no look good."*

I fumbled through the overwhelming madness and stumbled upon a facial recognition algorithm. Querying the microservice, I was able to trail its threads to a nexus at which it broke off into a thousand directions. Faces scrolled past my vision in a blur, a thousand shapes and configurations of life I had never seen. One in ten thousand was human, and those were already with us on the colony. I was just about to give up, having fallen into despair, time pressing upon me, when a dangling connection, weak and distant, drew my attention. I reached for it, mental fingers splayed, outstretched, taking hold.

The world went black, and a series of sleek star cruisers hove into view, their orbit synchronously fixed above a blue and red world. They were not Kabosai ships, they were something else. Not Foundry. They were of shadows and scales. I fell into them, through the hull and into its halls. Humans lined the inside, their faces tired and drawn. I knew some of them, they members of the *Vasco Da Gama*, others, hard to recognize as battered and beaten as they were. I inspected their faces one at a time, and then I found them.

Mom and Dad. Breathing. Alive. But where? And how? And when?

"Where is this location?" I queried the network.

In response I was given only an impression. *Beyond the gate.*

"Where? Where beyond the gate?"

The virtual world I was within began to vibrate and collapse. My implants lost connection. The vision split and faded away, and an instant later I found myself on the floor of the ziggurat, the data node to my right.

"Get up! Get up!" Mary said, reaching out her hand.

I took hold but found it hard to grip, my palms covered in sweat. "I found them. I need more time. I need more information."

"Too late, friend," Perry chimed in. "We have to go right now."

Machine guns rattled overhead; their fire was returned by the buzz of high energy weapons. Screeches of the enemy and shouts from our friends preceded a rain of stone bits, gunfire chewing into the structure's walls.

"Is there any way out?" I asked. "Is there another exit?"

Perry shook his head. "They've got the only door camped. I've looked for others, there's nothing."

"This place would have never passed fire marshal inspection," Mary said, looking up.

I spun around and searched for the Isopteran body that had fallen earlier. Much to my excitement, a black orb was strapped to its weapon's belt.

"I have an idea," I said, and took the orb in my hands. "Everyone run to the top. Esteban!"

"Yes, amigo?"

"I'm bringing them a present. Remember the hallway on the *Vasco?*"

"Hell yes. Bring that bitch up here."

Concern over falling off the stairs to my death on accident had faded away. I thundered back up through the multi-dimensional stairs, the orb in my hands, heavy as a bowling ball, light as a feather with as much adrenaline as pumped through my system. I passed Esteban and James, then came upon Lance, saw the discomfort on his face, the pain from his injuries, and pressed on. The three of them followed after me, pressing fire on the doorway, keeping the enemy occupied. Once I had hit the last flight of stairs, I felt for the trigger on the bottom of the orb and pressed it down.

The door of the ziggurat yawned open, a half-dozen insectile faces staring back at me. I screamed at the top of my lungs before hurling the ball straight at them, the button clicking into place.

I wasn't sure what surprise looked like on an Isoptera, but I was pretty sure that this was it. They shrank back and began to flee, their wings flittering wildly, antennae jerking. I was in the open and they didn't even bother taking me out.

"Get down!" Esteban shouted.

I threw myself onto the staircase, hoping I would be far enough out of line of sight, as a high energy whoomph came from outside the structure.

"Go, go, go!" I said, springing back to my feet and running outside, my VP-214 raised.

Isoptera or not, we had to get back to the colony. The Kabosai had plans for our people, and those plans didn't include us. This had been a diversion to get the strongest, most determined among our group away from those who were vulnerable.

We burst out of the entrance, the torn and singed bodies of Isoptera lining the ziggurat's face from the explosion. The air smelled of charred organic matter, like a sour roast left in the oven for hours too long. A few battered and dazed survivors took pot shots at us. Esteban, James, and I returned fire, sending them tumbling off the precarious edge and cutting a path through the chaos back to the truck. Mary and Perry brought up the rear, Lance's arms slung over their shoulders, his feet cutting furrows in the dust. He was in a bad way, having taken splash back from several near hits by the Isopteran weapons.

"Full speed ahead, don't slow down," I said as we hopped in back. We laid Lance down on the floor pallet. Esteban reached for a first aid kit and went to work on his injuries.

The truck's engine wined, reaching full power, and we screamed off into the dark.

"We made it, *amigo*," Esteban said, nearly falling over when we hit the first bump. "What did you find out?"

I hardened my expression. "That if we don't make it back quick enough, our friends and family are going to die."

CHAPTER 40

"I'm sorry, what the fuck did you say?" Lance asked, his voice labored and husky. The burn he had taken was bad, the skin along his right arm ashy and raw. He shivered. "Who would kill them?"

I took a deep breath to unpack all the information I had acquired within the data node. The truck hit another bump at high speed, and the three of us were airborne for an instant.

"Hey!" Esteban shouted up front. "Don't kill us, Jellybean." He went back to work applying burn cream, wrapping Lance's open wounds.

"What did you find out?" Lance pressed through gritted teeth. "You got any meds for this pain?"

"One sec, *amigo*."

"This is a cycle the Gene Brokers follow," I said. "They lure naturally evolving species into a trap of comfort and assistance. Then they start to modify them, change them so that they can live on other planets."

"Doesn't sound so bad," Lance said.

"You didn't see how far they twisted them. We see the Gene Brokers as massive slugs, but they weren't always that way. They used to be bipedal, though not very human looking. They had four arms, long limbs, massive eyes."

"But why slugs?"

"Their current state can undergo both high acceleration as well as null-g without sustaining damage or incurring bone loss. It's a more adaptable form, ugly as it is."

Esteban popped open a bottle of pills. "So, they want to make us slugs?" He tossed a couple into his hand and gave them to Lance. "Here you are."

"No. They have something else in mind."

"But why now?" Lance asked. "Wouldn't that kind of evolution take thousands of years?"

"Not with them. They are experts. Within a single generation they can create a new species. Esteban, Gi'Vor's people were designed by the Kabosai."

His eyes widened. "It what?"

"They were created by the Gene Brokers tens of thousands of years ago. After the Eipren world was seeded, they were left to their own devices and evolved on their own."

"Their gods the slugs, ya?"

"Creators at least."

"That's heavy."

"We have to make it back before they take everyone," I said. "I believe we are the strongest, and our group has been isolated. If they leave this world, we have no means of rescuing them. That's what this little side quest was."

Lance leaned back, eyes closed, willing the drugs to take effect as quick as possible. "Why put pills in a first aid box? Why not a fuckin' hypodermic?"

All I could think about was Shelly. I had left her in the camp with nothing more than a peck on the forehead. Maybe we weren't too late.

The truck thundered across the black plains, kicking up clouds of silica dust that could be seen for miles as daylight returned. It took what seemed an endless set of hours to return, far too much time for me to dwell over what had likely happened. When we came to an eventual halt, exhausted and restless, I didn't wait. I went bolting out into the colony, rifle ready, barrel raised. James and Perry followed after.

"Hold up!" James shouted. "Wait on me."

The colony was silent. No one was in sight, nothing disturbed. Everything appeared to be where we had left it. We came upon the occasional toolbox or personal belonging that had been cast aside, but nothing more. No sign of struggle or violence.

"Hello?" I called, scanning the empty streets with my weapon. "Anyone out there?"

James waved at me. "Over here."

He led me behind Perry's dome where Omar was laid up against the structure. His breathing was labored. Blood from a wound in his stomach had soaked through his clothes.

"Oh god," I said, putting down my rifle and taking up his limp hand. "We need to get you to the doctor. Now."

"No use," Omar coughed. "She's gone. Brennon."

"What do you mean?"

"They're all gone. The Kabosai came for us after you left and used, I don't know what, but they used something to disable us. Once everyone had fallen asleep, these creatures, with long legs and a dozen arms, they scooped us up and carried us away. They took them, Milo."

"Damn it!" I shouted, kicking at the dirt in frustration. "Where did they go?"

Omar pointed to the sky. "I tried to stop them. I tried." He started to tremble, his bloodshot eyes turning glossy. "I'm a botanist, not a soldier. I grabbed a piece of salvage, some bar with a jagged end, and fought. They swatted me away like a fly and one of them hit me with my own weapon. I couldn't do anything. I couldn't... stop them."

"It's not *your* fault," James told him.

"Why did they do this?"

"Because it's what they do," I said.

"But why?"

"To protect life..."

Esteban appeared an instant later with a medical kit in hand. He went to work on Omar, but once the clothes were cut away, it was clear we were only buying time. The skin was dark and inflamed, infection already having set in, and for whatever reason the universal inoculant was not fighting it off. None of us were doctors, and the Foundry could not help us.

"Will you get my prayer rug," Omar asked. I did not hesitate, hurrying back to what was once our quarters and recovered it.

We helped Omar roll onto his knees, screams bursting from his lips with each small movement. I had a hand rested on his back and was about to back away, to give him the moment he needed, when he shook his head.

"Don't go, friend," he pleaded. "Please don't go. Stay with me till the end."

I scrubbed at my eyes and swallowed. "Okay. I'm here."

Omar summoned what strength he could, focusing it on speaking with his god. I only hoped that when this prayer was done, the two of them would come face to face, a righteous soul united with his deity.

After some minutes, his body went limp, slumping deeper into his prayer position. Omar had passed beyond the veil of life and his soul was free to roam.

I remained there for a time, collecting my scattered emotions, then stood and turned to face everyone. They had been watching all along, not a word escaping their lips.

"He deserves a proper burial," I said, not knowing what else to do.

Mary gave a nod. "Sure. We'll take care of it."

James fumed at the edge of our group, hands open and closing, pacing. "This shouldn't have happened."

"But how could we stop it?" Esteban asked. "This is what they do."

"This is your fault!" James shouted, pointing a finger at me. "Every bit of it!"

I raised my open palms. "My fault? How is this my fault?"

Lance shifted in the chair Mary and Perry had set him in. "Yeah. This would have never happened if you hadn't held our Benefactors at gunpoint."

"Did you not pay attention to what the Foundry told us? This is their M.O., their modus operandi. If we had made a move or not, this would have still happened."

"Maybe," he gave a shrug, "but it would have been a long time from now. Years."

"Selfish fuck," James spat. "It's always about Milo and what he wants, no one else is taken into consideration."

"That's not fair," I said. "Don't put this on me."

"Life isn't fair!" James made a rush for me, white-knuckled fists at his side. "You did this. You!"

And that was it. I was done taking James's misguided shit over this or any other situation. This was not my fault any more than the death of his mother was. I shoved James back.

"And if I hadn't made a move, what then?" I growled in his face. "You would still blame me. All I have ever wanted is to protect everyone. I'm not taking this on."

"There you go again, avoiding responsibility."

"Stop!" Mary interjected. "Stop! Stop! This is pointless. Fighting among ourselves won't accomplish anything."

Perry gave a slow nod. "We're all hurting. I don't know what to do, but getting angry at what the Benefactors… seems stupid to call them that now… being angry at one another for what the Gene Brokers did is foolish."

I turned and walked away, lip quivering, crestfallen. What I needed was time to think. Time to consider the next move. Too much had happened too fast, and I couldn't process it all. I was tired of hurting, tired of feeling alone, tired of feeling like a failure. For a brief time, I had felt complete, real, and now… How do I go on?

But I was a failure, I had always been a failure.

I didn't deserve a good life.

I was a worthless *thing*.

I would never be what everyone wanted me to be.

I would always let those I loved down.

My knees struck hardpack and my eyes clouded over with tears. There was nothing I could do to save those I cared about. We were trapped on this distant world, and the Gene Brokers had taken everyone. It was over. The game was finished. We lost.

"Shelly," I hissed, her name near impossible to voice. "I did this. It is my fault."

Maybe I should just go off into the woods and live alone. I wouldn't be anyone's problem anymore. All I did was bring pain and destruction. I should stay in my place and keep quiet.

The air began to rumble, pebbles beside my hands vibrating. A distant roar scattered the avia. Even a few destri came shooting out from the woods. I shifted my gaze to regard the brightening orange sky and saw a pillar of fire falling towards the ground. My heart gave a start as the object on its tip resolved into the shape of a scorpion.

"It's come," Esteban said, putting a hand on my shoulder.

"It's come back for more pleasure," I replied.

"Pleasure?"

I stood, hand shielding my eyes from its brilliance. "Yes. Pleasure. Pleasure in the form of cruelty."

PART III

CHAPTER 41

There's a common question that surfaced out of the murk of my earthen childhood memories, one which I could not recall ever being asked aboard the *Vasco Da Gama*. A question a teacher would ask their students.

"What do you want to be when you grow up?"

I was sitting at the front of my class at Whispering Pines as my teacher, Mrs. Plumb, a slender woman in a blue summer dress with blond hair and bright blue eyes, asked us this question. Most of the kids shouted out at the same time, making it hard to follow. For myself, I sat at my desk, hands in my lap, nervous, silent.

"Firefighter."

"Ballerina."

"Author."

"Lawyer."

"Pirate."

"Teacher."

"Babysitter."

"Hair cutter."

"Teacher!" Again.

"Pilot racer dad."

"Actor."

"Catch bad guys."

"Dancer."

"Car fixer."

"Computer guy."

"Teacher." Yet again.

Mrs. Plumb smiled, handing out sheets of rainbow construction paper and crayons as we went on. She asked us to draw what we thought a typical day might be for a person in that role.

What sort of things would you do?

What would you wear?

How would you help your community by doing that job?

My classmates were so excited, their thoughts translated in a flurry by handheld sticks of paraffin and pigment. As for myself, I sat there, staring at a blank, cerulean colored page. It left me feeling empty, and a touch sad. Part of me felt I should draw an astronomer looking through a telescope, or a biologist analyzing Punnett squares, but neither felt right.

"You okay, Milo?" Mrs. Plumb asked while kneeling beside my desk.

I gave her a shrug.

"Having a hard time thinking of what to draw?"

"A little."

"What do you dream about when you close your eyes?"

I considered this for a moment, a tiny finger pressed against my bottom lip in thought. "I don't know." And it was true. My mind was blank. My heart, uncertain.

"You know," Mrs. Plumb said after a moment, "don't worry too much about what you'll be when you grow up. Often-times, that part comes naturally. We find jobs or roles that fit our skill sets and we're drawn to them like a moth to a porch light in summertime. Why not try thinking about *who* you will be instead?"

"What do you mean?"

"Our *what* might not always be under our control, there's plenty of things I could have done with my life but being a teacher always felt right. Our *who*, on the other hand, that is in our control. We are the choices we make. They affect the lives of those around us. Plenty of successful people do the *what* of their jobs very well, but their *who*, their purpose, is empty. They are like robots, acting on instinct without a thought for how they can effect change."

"Okay," I said, not understanding. She gave me a sly grin before moving on to the next student. I was five years old, knowing on some level that things weren't right in my life, but I couldn't articulate this. It wasn't till we boarded the Jalek's shuttle that this all came rushing back.

I had not been given the choice as to what I would become. Mom and Dad had seen to that when we broke onto the launch platform and violated federal law. But I did have the opportunity to choose who I would become. *What* referred to the tasks I would be required to do, whereas *who* was my identity. Both were intertwined, sure, but they were not the same. My identity was connected to my choices, not my situation, not just my role. Captain Williams had not been a leader because he was the captain; he had been the captain because he was a leader.

Choices were before me, and I had to make better ones.

If I was a failure, that needed to change. I could make the choice.

I would be a person who stood up for what was right.

I would be a person who supported those who had supported me.

I would be a person who was willing to look beyond the pain of the situation and find the objective solution.

I would be a person, a human, who would give everything to save his people, even if it terrified him.

My hope at that moment was that the Jalek had summoned us for more than just entertainment.

The Jalek's pilot welcomed us aboard its scorpion shuttle, now empty of additional passengers, without a word as to where we were headed or why. It screamed out of Creatus's gravity well and into orbit. Jets fired in hard vacuum, adjusting the ship's attitude before the main drive initiated, throwing the six of us back in our acceleration chairs at a minimum of five Gs, the synthetic material of our cushions hissing as they absorbed our body's kinetic energy.

"We are in a hurry," the pilot called over the intercom. *"Discomfort will be temporary."*

My companions vibrated on my left and right, their fingers white knuckling the armrests of their acceleration chairs. Everything had been rushed. There had been no time to sift through our personal belongings before departing, given the chances that we would never return. No time to mourn the loss of Omar, only a shallow grave and a handful of words before departure. He deserved more.

"Where are we going?" I asked, my words labored under the weight of acceleration.

"To see the Foundry," the pilot replied.

"Where is your master?"

"Waiting for you."

The Jalek had given me the means to reconnect with my people, only for that to be stolen away not long after. I had a good feeling it had known the probable outcome before we even left Cynosure. The Jalek had come from God knows where, lived for thousands of years, played its games of manipulation, and to what end I couldn't say. Now it had called me back. Whatever its purpose was, I had one too. If it was going to use us, then I was going to use it. I had to rescue our people. I had to rescue Shelly, and if it gave me an opening to do this, I would take it gladly. It was calling us to a Foundry facility. This could mean only one thing.

"It's waiting for me?" James asked the pilot.

"No. The Jalek waits for Milo Hughes. You come as passengers only by my master's good grace."

"Bullshit," James mumbled, and I could feel his sidelong indignation even though I wasn't looking.

The pressure against our chests did crazy things to our heads. I could have sworn I was lying on my back at the bottom of an elevator shaft. Part of me wanted to unbuckle myself, stand up, and climb my way up the perpendicular floor to the top so I could look down.

"I'm having trouble breathing," Mary said.

Esteban strained for her and rested his hand on her lap. "Relax. Tensing makes it worse, ya?"

"I know. I can't stop."

"*Estás bien*. Just breathe."

"In, out," Lance added, "in, out, slow."

"The good news is, it takes twenty Gs to pass out," Perry offered. "You should be fine."

Mary scoffed at him. "Not as young as I used to be, little brother. I can't make it through the night without two or three trips to the bathroom."

"Yet you're young enough to change your hair color every time a new boy kisses you."

"Hush up, snot for brains."

"*¿Que?*" Esteban asked, curious. "What this 'bout kissing? *¿Besos?*"

"You didn't know, Este?" Perry said.

Mary growled, "Shut up, Perry!"

"It's true," he said.

I called up to the pilot and requested a virtual interface to the external sensors. The cauliflower head within the Star Sphere opened up a link that the six of us could connect to with our implants, allowing us to track our progress as well as see what was nearby, an augmented reality overlay of vector tracking and other detailed navigational information. Creatus soon disappeared into the distance, a green rock swallowed by the darkness of Lignos-4's night cycle. As it vanished, sighs came from my companions, dreams and wishes now lost to time, a home never fully realized.

Our course was locked. It would take five days for us to reach the Foundry's facility, and for the first full day we would have to remain in our acceleration couches burning hard. I found that I spent most of that time sleeping, emotionally drained from the events of the last few days. I had little to say, feeling as if I was stuck between states of rest and action. Once the shuttle had reached cruise velocity we got up and moved around, took meals and explored the ship, stretching our legs.

Before we knew it, we were being called to strap back in for the deceleration burn. You would think, after having gone through it on the way out, five Gs would be easier to deal with coming back in. You would be wrong. My muscles ached at the pressure. Lance fought through the discomfort by cursing under his breath again and again. Perry told jokes until we voted he shut up. James dug furrows in his armrests. I was pretty sure Mary and Esteban squeezed all the blood out of one another's hands.

Several days later, a golden torus blossomed in the augmented navigational view. This was not just any Foundry facility. It was as I had hoped, one of the actual foundries, a copy of the great ship building structure that we had burned nearly two decades to reach. Docked around its donut-shaped circumference were a hundred vessels, each hundreds of meters in length, their features delicate for their size, spurs and sharp edges, skyscrapers mounted with antimatter engines.

The pilot brought us in to a small dock, external hatches closing behind us, the bay pressurizing to that of a single atmosphere. Safe for humans.

"You may disembark," it said over the intercom.

"Thank you," I replied and unbuckled.

"Give your gratitude to my master."

We gathered up our backpacks and climbed out of the shuttle. The craft did not leave like it had on Creatus. It remained here, engines cold, no doubt waiting on its master to finish conducting its business.

"What a fascinating ship," Perry said as we walked into the warm, white halls of the Foundry. "Nothing like what the Gene Brokers bussed us around in."

"No?" I asked.

"No. There wasn't all the gilded material all of the Foundry seems to be made of. Its hull was dark, black mottled with red, its construction solid and well-worn. Sure, the Jalek's shuttle has seen time in the void, that's clear, but even with that wear, and this scorpion shape, I can tell it is of the same make. Foundry make."

Lance rubbed at his beard, wincing at the pain in his arm. "Agh, I thought everyone was forced to adopt the Foundry's ships?"

"So did I," I mumbled. "I guess we still don't know all the rules."

"Not sure there are any," Mary added.

"There are rules," Esteban said. "Trust me on that."

"But it all seems so random. Arbitrary. One group is given favor over another."

"But do we know that for sure, ya? Little humans peeking through windows into the eternal."

Lights appeared on the floor, guiding us to a predetermined destination, so we hiked our way along the path down a series of featureless halls until we reached a gilded door inscribed with designs, similar to the one at the Data Node.

Before I had the chance to solve the images, the panels of the door retracted and admitted us inside. There it was, the Jalek, crouching in the middle of a domed chamber, flanked by silver machines of organic design, its pink skin covered in strips of synthetic, ivory cloth, with black eyes gleaming, exaggerated face expectant. Along its body, the tiny versions of itself gave a greeting, hands waving, noses wrinkling.

"Damn," Lance muttered under his breath. "It's ugly as fuck."

"Shh." Perry placed a finger on his lips. "What happened to your manners? Don't offend it."

"What? Beauty is in the eye of the beholder an' all that, but geez, there are limits."

I held out an arm signaling my companions to stop.

"What gives?" James asked.

"The Jalek is too dangerous," I told him.

"Yeah, so? I'm sure it's clever. Well, I got news for it. So am I."

"No. Physically dangerous. As in, it gives off radiation, or uses it to survive, I'm not really sure which. What I do know is that if you get too close, you might be dosed. Happened to me once already."

James tossed up his open palms and took a wary step back, bumping into Perry. "Well, shit. Never mind. I think I'm good."

"*Amigo*, you sure you wan' do this again?" Esteban put a hand on my shoulder. "We can take turns."

"It called me. I have to go."

"*Vale. Vale.*" He lowered his head and gave me a weak smile. "We're right here. Careful, *amigo*."

"As I can be."

My companions stood sentry by the door we had entered through, watching as I approached the Jalek. The expression on its face was conflicted. It was hard to read to begin with, but I swore it looked both angry and morose, as if struggling over long forgotten memories brought to the surface by chance.

It had summoned us to the Foundry, and there could be only one purpose. It planned to make a deal of some kind.

"Are my companions safe where they stand?"

"From me?" The Jalek looked shocked. "Whatever for?"

"Yes, you. The radiation. Your food or what you give off, I don't know."

The Jalek waved a hand. "They are safe, and you have been inoculated."

I gave a nod, satisfied with the answer, and went on, "Why did you send for me?"

Its eyes blinked and its body shook, the tiny versions of itself throwing their heads back and spinning around. "Because you needed help."

"That's crap. You know I'm not that dense."

It gestured in the air with one of its hands. "You are smarter than most, Milo Hughes."

"Did you know this would happen? Did you know what the Gene Brokers had planned from the start?"

"Yes."

"Why didn't you tell me?"

"It was not part of our agreement. I find it curious how others deal in, well, certain situations."

"So, you wanted to see us squirm."

"Only a little."

"You're sick," I growled. "Twisted."

"What a narrow perspective."

"A perspective I'm not likely to change."

It shook its head. "Your loss. So much pleasure not experienced."

"What is your game here?" I pointed a finger at it. "What are you playing? Did you come to rub our face in something else? Show us that the big bad Jalek is better and all knowing?"

"I did not."

"Then why?"

It waited a moment before responding, taking several deep breaths as if collecting its thoughts. The miniature versions of itself climbed down to hide behind its arched back, disturbing the strips of cloth that hung from its pulpy, pink body like Spanish moss.

"I would tell you a story," the Jalek began, its voice turning cold. "Thousands of years ago there was a natural species known as the Gan. They lived on a pale blue dot in a system of ten planets that revolved around a yellow dwarf. They were a bright people, clever. They learned to harness fire, steam, then electricity, split the atom, and one day, fuse it. They made art and had culture, they made war and then had peace, though more were always lost than ever saved. They mastered their bodies and made medicines capable of prolonging life far beyond what any natural Gan could have ever evolved to be capable of. And so, they thrived, growing ever numerous, ever fatter, ever complacent, wallowing in decadence and pleasure. Their world reached a tipping point where the resources available were not enough to meet the needs of their exponential growth."

"And then they heard from the Foundry?"

"Oh yes. They heard from the Foundry. They departed in a fleet of a hundred starships of bronze and black, painted with the stripes of their proud nations, all set for the great, ancient structures. The Foundry gave them its assistance, forged new ships for them. But their hearts were not in the stars, not most of them. Their hearts were on Dran, their home world. They needed to save their people, needed to find a way to turn the tide of self-destruction set to crash on this cosmic beach."

"Who came to help?"

"In their hearts, the Gan knew the Foundry would help their people one day, but not now. Only one species appeared in the moment, and they had a price."

I sucked in a breath. "The Kabosai."

The Jalek hissed at this, its long face flooding with red. "Don't speak that word in this place. It is filth." The miniature creatures reappeared, their tiny faces burning, fists shaking in fury. "The Gene Brokers offered the Gan assistance in exchange for the preservation of their species. What they did not tell the Gan, however, was that it would change all our people, not just a few."

"What?" My eyes widened. "The entire population?"

"Yes. They came for the natural with the intent of protecting life, propagating new species, populating new worlds, adapting for places of biological niche. They spliced and cut and manipulated genes making the Gan into creatures they were never meant to be. In the end, the Gene Brokers failed. A virus common among the Gan, one that had been benign to all since the dawn of their species, ran rampant through their population and wiped them out. If not for the Gene Brokers' intervention, they would still be alive today."

I let out a long sigh, my chest catching on what felt to be a stone in my lungs. "I'm sorry, Jalek."

It scowled at me. "I don't need your pathetic sympathy. What I need is revenge. I have been waiting for a moment to move, and I believe that time is now. The Foundry is willing to help your burgeoning species, and I have brought you here to make sure that happens. In exchange, you will punish the Gene Brokers for what they did to the Gan."

This was a lot to unpack. The Jalek's species had undergone the same challenges we had, reaching an apex in their society which was unsustainable. They had asked for help, just like us, and chosen to put their trust in the wrong people. It had known this when it first assisted me, and had taken some pleasure in that knowledge.

"Why not help us sooner?" I asked.

"You should know by now the Foundry has peculiar rules. I don't think you'd have been willing to pay the price until now."

"The price?"

"Don't play foolish." The Jalek gave a tip of its disproportioned head. "Donation."

My skin went cold. I suppose I had known the answer, but part of me had been hoping for another. Willingly allowing my own dissection, to a degree. "Donation," I whispered, rolling the word around in my mouth.

"I knew that you, Milo Hughes, would have to be brought to a point of crisis. I knew that the stakes would need to be high enough for you to be willing to make that sacrifice. Was I wrong?"

My mouth was as dry as if I had eaten a fistful of sand. All my bravado had evaporated. "No."

"Are you ready?"

I closed my eyes, thinking of Shelly and our time together, cold nights with her warm flesh against me, soft kisses on my neck, honest conversations about nothing and everything. I thought of the friends I had made on the ship and the lives of those still at stake, humanity's future. Images of my parents flashed before me, a night where I felt alone and rejected, and Mom had given me ice cream. The pure smile Dad had flashed when he saw me on stage playing the Scarecrow as a kid. There are scant things worth sacrificing everything for.

I nodded.

"I am ready," I said, knowing that my fear was evident.

This was the only way, the best chance we would have, yet I was still terrified. A donation: an arm, a leg, a piece of my brain given over to the great Foundry, and for what? That it might genetically engineer us, as well?

"Is the Foundry like the Gene Brokers?" I asked.

"Yes and no. They seek only to understand, help where they can."

"So this donation…"

"It takes samples to understand. Not to manipulate."

"Do you know where our people have been taken? How much time do we have?"

The Jalek's hands twitched for an instant. "You have time. Their ships cannot accelerate as quickly as Foundry ships. It will likely take decades in your timescale for them to reach their destination."

"Decades?"

"Yes. But within a Foundry ship, time in a single direction is near irrelevant. The Star Sphere will allow you to speed and slow your metabolism to adjust your subjective frame of reference. If you so choose, decades may go by in seconds."

"I see. Where have they gone?"

"Beyond the Wandering Gate."

"Beyond the gate," I mused, chewing at my bottom lip. "Will my soul be lost? My Eipren friend Gi'Vor worried about that."

"Who can say if the soul is even real?" The tiny Jaleks changed position on its body, swapping their locations. "Though if it is, I would assume it is part of the universe, just as the Foundry hopes."

"A universal consciousness."

"Yes."

"Have you ever traveled beyond the gate?"

"Never."

"Why not?"

The Jalek said nothing, made no gestures. This was its poker face.

"Okay," I said after an awkward moment, the word exhaled rather than spoken. I turned back to glance at my friends, then to the Jalek. "Let's do this."

"Good," it said, giving a wave towards the soft outline of a door to its left, one that I had not seen until that moment. "The Foundry will guide you."

"What about my friends?"

"They will remain here for now. They are not yet ready."

"Hey!" James shouted. "I'm ready as any."

Perry called after, "Where are you going?"

"I understand," I told the Jalek, then stepped towards the door as it irised open, heading down the hall where the Foundry was leading me.

"*Amigo*!" Esteban took a step forward. "You don't have to do this."

I couldn't look back at them.

"We used to be beautiful," the Jalek mused over my shoulder, raising one of its frail, pink arms in reflection. "So very beautiful."

The doors hissed shut.

"Milo Hughes," a smooth mechanical voice called to me. *"Please step forward."*

And I did just that.

CHAPTER 42

"Welcome back, Milo Hughes," said the featureless white walls as the entity led me towards what could only be a surgical suite.

"Hello, Foundry," I replied. "Your speech is better than it was last time we met. Less jerky and cold."

"We have come a long way in understanding humans."

"That so?"

"Between your time on the first Foundry facility, Cynosure, and on the moon you called Creatus, including your invasion into the data network and beyond, we have learned much."

"Sorry about that. Did we break any rules? Will we be punished?"

"No. There is no punishment required at this time. No damage was wrought to our data network."

"Good." I thought that over for a moment. "Then why allow us in? Surely you could have kept us out."

"You earned it."

"What do you mean?"

"You were able to break past our security protocols. We could make it impossible, but what would we learn? You are an intelligent and resourceful species."

"Thanks?" I said, chuckling.

The hall went on for what seemed a mile, more featureless walls and symbol-covered doors. I wondered what they were all for. Were they modular, able to be transformed into whatever the current need was? Or were they setup ahead of time for certain functions based on species? There were an endless number of ways a planet could evolve. Some of the rooms could have different atmospheric pressure or mixes of gases, moisture, maybe even airborne chemicals which acted like drugs. Some might even be friendly to aquatics like the Phantamorphs, filled with saltwater so that they could free themselves of their mobile tanks.

"Have any other humans been to this facility?" I asked.

"Not this facility."

"But others? You've been in contact with humans other than us?" I marveled at the idea. We had no idea how long it had been since we left Earth, the rest of the fleet could still be en route to their destinations, but it seems that at least one had made it.

"Yes."

"Where?"

"I am sorry, that information is not available at this time."

I raised my hands, palms up, frustrated. "Okay, okay. Do you know the ship, or ships' designation? Ours was *Vasco Da Gama.*"

"One moment," the Foundry paused, thinking the question over. *"Revelation."*

"Revelation," I hissed, rolling the word around in my mouth. It was another of the UEI vessels among our distant fleet. "What happened to them?"

"They came to the Foundry for help, just like you."

"And did you give it to them?"

"That information is not available at this time."

"Yeah, yeah, yeah. What can you tell me then?" We reached the last set of doors, and I came to a halt.

"They faced similar challenges to that of the humans aboard the Vasco Da Gama. *Their ship was destroyed, and so were the Isopteran invaders."*

I ground my teeth at that. They were everywhere. "Those assholes again?"

"The Foundry struggles with what to do with them. They are scavengers who prey on new arrivals at many facilities. We protect life, and so we cannot interfere."

"What a political answer. Did any of these humans survive?"

"Yes. One and a half."

"I don't understand."

"No additional information is available at this time."

There was no use pushing harder. Hitting logical security walls with the Foundry only made my head hurt more than it already did. We would have time to ask later.

"One more question before we start."

"Yes?"

"Why a donation? Why not just give me what I need?"

"Unlike the Kabosai, we do not manipulate genes. We believe in the natural evolving on its own, as well as their Designed. However, we cannot assist a species unless we understand its genetic makeup fully. Muscle, bone marrow, nerve tissue and brain matter are often the best samples for achieving this end. To protect life, we must understand it."

"So, you need this to help us medically?"

"And more."

"Like how?"

"That information—"

I cut it off. "Okay, I get it. I just wanted to be sure it was going to a good cause. Like I said last time, I've grown fond of my body parts."

"Are you ready?"

I took a deep breath and massaged my face thoroughly. The idea of allowing a hyper advanced alien entity to cut off parts of your body in exchange for something was insanity. In truth, I still had no clear idea what the Foundry was, who made it, or what its true intentions were. At least the Jalek had been honest, if not forthcoming. But what other choice did I have? Sinas and his cockroach-propelled slug buddies weren't going to commit atrocities on other humans, on our friends, on Shelly, not if I had anything to say about it. I would watch their hollow ships burn in the great black void, sending their souls or whatever spirit inhabited their twisted shells off into oblivion. If that meant donating part of my body to see it done, it was a worthy trade.

I'll save you all, I thought.

"I'm ready." My attention rose to the door ahead.

The Foundry admitted me into a room no wider than one of the domes on Creatus. A hip-high slab of gold and white much like an exam table was at its center, the base of which flashed with a radiant glow, urging me to lay down.

I crawled up onto the slab and laid back, peering up at the smooth ceiling.

"Will it hurt?" I asked the Foundry.

"No."

"Can I watch?"

"If you wish."

"I do."

I felt a small prick in my right arm, and my body went limp. Chilly numbness rushed up my elbow to my chest and down into my stomach, back, legs, and feet. My head became swimmy, as if it had been disconnected and tossed into the ocean, each wave of chemical suppression giving me a new perspective.

A signal path opened from within my implants and I found myself suspended above my limp body. The clothes Shelly had given me on Creatus were pulled away with great care by a half-dozen, multi-jointed mechanical arms. After only a moment of struggle with buttons and zippers, they slid away. Each article was neatly folded and placed within a metallic box, my body left bare under the Foundry's blinding surgical lights.

Tools appeared from the floor, nanoscopic machines resolving into instruments of medical precision. This was not the first time I'd been under the blade since abandoning the *Vasco Da Gama*. My heart began to accelerate. I had no reason not to trust the Foundry with this. But saying it, even out loud, and allowing it to cut your body apart, were two different things. I had to remind myself the Foundry was not the Frendol. This was no autopsy.

"I will now take your donation," it said, voice empty of emotion. *"Do you consent?"*

"Do it."

I wanted to squeeze my eyes shut, but within the virtual perspective this was impossible. The mechanical arms went to work on my left leg, applying pressure on my upper thigh before making an incision just a few inches above the knee with a silver blade. Blood oozed at its edges and to my surprise I felt nothing. There was no pain, only a bizarre fascination as the Foundry cut deeper, through skin and fat and muscle, until we finally reached bone.

As the detached limb was lifted away and placed into a slender box, its contents filled with a frigid liquid, other hands joined in, cauterizing the wound before it hemorrhaged. I had expected the Foundry's surgical hands to sew a section of skin over my knee and form a nub, but to my amazement, a new leg began to form at the end of the table from a mass of silvery nanomachines.

My biological leg was no longer part of me. In its place was a new one, made of a solid white material covered in a faux, organic flesh, its features gilded with golden symbols and characters. It took the shape of my old leg, mirroring my right exactly. If a layer of walnut skin had been stretched over the prosthetic, I would have never known the difference.

"Will it work like my natural leg?" I asked.

"Better, even."

The tiny machines flowed like mercury, forming the top section of the prosthetic to my amputated limb. There was no need for the Foundry to attach anything.

Next came my right arm, following the same process, though this prosthetic did not begin at my bicep, rather above my shoulder and across part of my chest.

"There is one more thing," the Foundry said. *"I apologize."*

Before I could consider its words, my vision winked out.

I awoke sometime later upon the table, the surgical hands retracting. Feeling had begun to return to my body. Every muscle was sore, the nerves in my right arm and left leg on fire. I gave a groan, squeezing my eyes shut to curb the wave of nausea fighting to overtake me.

"One moment," the Foundry said, and then my pain began to subside. *"Better?"*

"Yes," I said, sitting up. "What the hell did you do?"

"Your prosthetics have neural inhibitors and feedback mapping. They will counteract phantom pain, the result of your surgical operation, by giving your brain the signals it requires to feel them as if they were natural."

I raised my right hand to inspect it. It was shaped just as before, the texture of my skin, right down to the creases on my palm, almost indistinguishable from my natural hand with the one exception, it being made of white and gold. I clasped my hands together and it felt normal.

"So weird," I commented, then kicked out my left leg. "What a good job. I think. I suppose time will tell."

"We are grateful for your donation."

I felt at the lump on the back of my head with my new hand, then tapped the tip of my spine. Metallic plates had been placed in both locations.

"What are these?" I asked.

"Part of your brain was necessary for the donation."

"Have I lost any of my memories?"

"No. Nor function. It was a microscopic sample."

"Okay. What about the thing on my spine?"

"You will need it if you are to captain a Foundry battleship from within a Star Sphere."

"A battleship?" I asked, mouth and eyes wide. I had been expecting a ship, sure, but this… This was perfect.

"We have deemed it to be necessary for your mission."

"What about balance? What about protecting life? Seems a bit overkill."

"Anything less against the Kabosai would not be balanced."

"They are well armed?" I asked, even though I knew the answer. There was no way Sinas and his like had gotten along this many centuries doing what they were doing without having big guns.

"That is correct."

"Is it hard to pilot this battleship?"

"Within the Star Sphere, you will pilot the ship as if it were your body."

"What about my companions? Can they come along?"

"The ship is equipped to receive them with minor bodily modification, if they so desire. They too have Star Spheres, though only one may be in command of the battleship at a time."

I gave a weak smile. "Wonder what they'll do with all their time if I'm playing bus driver?"

"Proxy will show you."

"Who?"

"You will see once you are on board."

The boxes containing my limbs slid away into a self-sealing hole in the wall. I flexed my new hand as I watched them go. No going back.

"Let us guide you to your new ship," the Foundry said.

I stood and recovered my clothes. "I can't wait." I paused, thinking over the events of the past year. Two years. Who the hell knew how much subjective time had passed?

"Foundry?"

"Yes?"

"We came for help. Your signal summoned us humans from out of the safety of our gravity well. Wrapped in that signal of yours was a feeling, an emotion. You communicated that you wished to help our planet. To help our species survive."

"Yes. The Foundry protects life."

"Look, I know we've made mistakes. We've let policies and old ways of thinking cause our people great pain. We've warred over resources and hurt the very people we wanted to protect. The air will one day be unfit for us to breathe. The water, unfit to drink. It will be too warm for the animals of the land to grow and thrive, for our plants to crawl out of the ground and reach for the sky." I closed my eyes and sighed. "Was it a waste coming here? Or are you going to help us save our planet?"

A silent moment passed as if the Foundry were considering this, all the data about humans and the implications of giving us assistance potentially not gifted to others.

The walls flashed white, and the exit opened.

"Not yet," it said. "Not yet."

And somehow, on some level, I knew why the answer was given. There was no time to dwell on it. Our people needed us. Earth would have to wait when Shelly was in danger.

"Okay," I said. "Thank you, Foundry."

CHAPTER 43

By the time I returned from my operation, the Jalek was gone. My companions were there waiting, milling about the room, inspecting the alien equipment while exchanging nervous, idle chatter.

"*Amigo*!" Esteban rushed over. "You did it, you really did it."

I raised my right hand and flexed my new fingers.

"Holy shit," Lance said, his jaw slack. "What the hell did you let them do to you?"

"He's bionic," Perry commented, his tone amused. "I knew we could rebuild him. How does it feel? Does it hurt? I have so many questions."

"No," I answered. "There's no pain or discomfort. I can't hardly tell the difference between my prosthetics and the originals, at least far as feel."

"Prosthetics? Plural?"

"That arm is beautiful." Mary put a hand on my bicep and squeezed. Esteban gave her a cross look as she did. "It's solid. Where's the other?"

"They did my left leg too." I patted my thigh.

James narrowed his eyes at me. For having grown up with him and been friends all those years, it was strange him being an enigma. "Why? Why do this? You plan on punching the Gene Brokers in the face with a robot arm?"

"No. It was the cost for assistance. The Foundry doesn't work for free."

"And what assistance is it going to offer us?"

"You know why we here," Esteban said.

"To get their leftovers, I bet."

I gave James a sly grin. "Why don't I show you instead?"

And to my surprise, James gave an approving shrug of his shoulders. Maybe we were making progress. I sure hoped we could. There was no reason our friendship had to die.

"I'm curious as well," Perry said, smiling.

"Hold up a sec." Lance raised his open hands. "Before we go any further… Who put Milo in charge? Ever since we came back from the Data Node, he's been dictating our actions. It's not like he's Captain Williams."

"I'm not so sure," Perry replied, his words stretching out.

Lance cocked his head to one side then the other. "What's that supposed to mean?"

"Did you see our pilot in the shuttle?"

"Yeah, the veggie head. He was floating in that bubble thing. Makes sense, spreads out the pressure of G-forces."

"Milo," Perry turned back to me. "Do these modifications allow you to enter one of these space bubbles?"

"Star Sphere," I amended, diverting my eyes for a moment onto the floor. "And yes."

"You're the pilot?" Lance pressed. "Big whoop. Captain Williams had several pilots, my dad included. Just 'cause you can fly the damn thing doesn't put you in charge."

And he had a point. I looked around the room at my fellow humans, crew members, as well as children of the once-great *Vasco Da Gama*, each standing in staggered positions around me. I waited for a moment, but no one's body language gave a sign of stepping forward, a desire to fill this power vacuum. We didn't have time to pussyfoot around with this.

"Look," I said, choosing my words carefully. "I know I've made my mistakes, and I know you don't all fully trust me. The truth of it is, the Foundry gave me the ship because of what I donated. That was the price. Someone has to be the leader. I might not be the leader you would have chosen, but I believe I know how to save our people. Put your trust in me for once, give me the opportunity to prove to you that it won't be taken for granted."

"This is your argument?" Lance sucked on his teeth and sighed. "Just because the ship is yours, that makes you the captain?"

Mary put a hand on his shoulder. "Are you willing to make a donation as well? Just curious. They might have a second ship."

Lance jerked from her grip and scowled. "That's a stupid question."

"I don't think it is," Perry added, taking a step closer to me. "Sure, all of us have lost a lot. Friends. Family. Home. But how many of us made the choice to put ourselves in harm's way, or did it merely come to us?"

"That's not a fair comparison."

Mary gave her brother a knowing glance. "Nothing about this journey has been fair."

"What is fair?" James asked rhetorically.

"I'm with Milo." Perry raised an open palm in my direction. "Good or bad, this is our best course of action."

"So am I, *amigo*," Esteban agreed, raising his hand for a high five. "Whatever experience I have is yours." I left him hanging, not wishing to exacerbate the disquiet among our group.

"I don't want to do this alone," I said, looking to James and Lance. "I don't just want your help, I need it. The Foundry has prepared our ship to accommodate everyone within their personal Star Spheres. In the end, though, there can only be one pilot, only one captain. This is not like the *Vasco Da Gama*. The ship will be my body, not just an extension of it."

James rubbed at the back of his head and started to pace; his eyes fixed on the ground. "You really believe we can save them?"

I took a deep breath, steeling my resolve. If I was to be a leader, I needed to inspire confidence while not being false. I was terrified that we were already too late, but what would staying here do? We had to try, and even if we failed, we'd fail knowing we gave it our all.

"If there's even a remote chance," I replied. "It happens as a team."

"Is this what you all want?" Lance gave them each a look in turn and was met with a mix of nods and shrugs. "Fine." He raised his right index finger and shook it. "You're the captain. I don't like it, but I don't see any other fuckin' way. Don't let us down, Milo. I've had enough of that."

The tension in my chest eased a little. "I don't plan on it."

"You better not."

"Come on," I gestured towards the exit. "Let's go. Our battleship awaits."

"So exciting," Perry said, rubbing his hands together. "This is all so exciting."

Mary rolled her eyes. "Don't go staining your underwear."

"Would be worth it."

James scowled at the two of them. "The hell is wrong with you?"

"Maybe we're born with it?" Perry offered.

"Maybe it's stupid memes," Mary replied, her words like a song.

"Memes?" Lance scratched at his head.

Now gifted with Foundry modifications, I was able to tap into the local network on a more detailed level. I knew on instinct where we needed to go in order to reach the ship reserved for us. We walked down several featureless halls before hopping onto a tram of sorts, a tube with smooth white seats glowing with prismatic backlight. The tram took us down a tunnel several miles in length, bringing us up to an airlock along the outer circumference of the torus. There was little conversation as we made for the ship. My thoughts were already aboard, attempting to understand how this would all work.

From the docking bridge, we could see our ship through a gallery of clear panels that were each about ten meters in height. The Foundry's creation was awe inspiring, a colossal, skyscraper-shaped hulk reminiscent of a building I had seen pictures of in school called the Shard in London. The ship's body was hundreds of meters in length, with jagged edges and angles that made up its forward end. Along the faces of its hull, layered panels of gold and white glittered, jagged sections that appeared capable of sweeping back towards the mammoth drive system at the base. There were bundles of antennas and hard points along the outer vertices, rows of bay doors for shuttles, and odd collections of spheroidal bumps in contrasting obsidian tones. Its details amounted to a work of art dredged with precision from a flowing sea of conscious thought by the nets of a timeless machine intelligence.

Mary swallowed so loud I could hear it. "That's a big bitch," she mumbled.

None of us could disagree.

We reached the end of the bridge and the exterior hatch opened, allowing us to enter humanity's first interstellar battleship. To say that the interior was spacious would have been an understatement. From where we stood, I could nearly see the forward end of the ship several hundred feet up a narrowing catwalk. It was hollow, but not fragile, its superstructure a crosshatch of supports and heavy equipment. Mounted on its interior surfaces were diamond-shaped craft similar in size to one of our ascent vehicles, as well as enclosed areas, private rooms, kitchens, quarters, and storage, numbering in the hundreds.

Mary tucked a length of cotton candy pink hair behind her ear. "There's enough space in here for every human on Creatus, and then some."

"We might just pull it off, ya?" Esteban stepped over to a nearby panel and started to punch buttons. "Would be nice if it had a manual though."

"Why not download the pdf," James interjected, pointing at symbols on the screen as he leaned in beside Esteban. "What's this do?"

"No sure. What's the worst that can happen?"

Mary shrugged. "We all die?"

"Hello there," an almost-human voice said from out of sight. The six of us froze in place.

"Hi," I said, my voice a bit unsteady. "Is this the Foundry?"

"No. I am not the Foundry. I am Proxy."

Mary peered over the rail of the catwalk and around the interior of the ship. "Proxy, just where are you?"

"I am not yet formed. I currently exist within the ship's network. What form would make you most comfortable?"

"'Not yet formed'?" Lance turned to James, who gave him a shrug. "What do you mean?"

Proxy replied, *"The Foundry has found that when the ship's AI takes on a form familiar to the species in command, it makes communication more efficient."*

"So, you're not the Foundry," I said, "but an extension of it?"

"I was created by the Foundry, yes, but I am independent. Anything I learn or assist you with is closed off from the Foundry for security reasons. That said, there are certain guidelines that I cannot override."

"Like what?"

"Like entering into battle from within a nullified zone around any Foundry structure. This prevents unnecessary collateral damage to key assets."

"Hold on, let's get back on the subject of form," Perry said, tapping his chin. "You do mean body, yes?"

"That is correct."

"Well, what have others done before?"

"Some have chosen for me to look like their dominant species; others, like animals or pets from their home."

Perry leaned close to me and whispered, the front of his optics brushing against my ear. "Let's make it a robot."

"A robot?"

"Sure. Like one from 20th century science fiction. Those big, clunky things with blinky lights and spiny pieces, maybe a chest of glass that has a typewriter clicking away inside it. *Forbidden Planet. Lost in Space*. Heck, even *The Black Hole*. They had great ones."

"Perry," Mary said. "You're being an idiot again."

"Come on." He raised his open hands. "Seems like fun to me."

We paused for a moment, looking to one another for inspiration. After some time, Lance shrugged his shoulders and spoke.

"What about a cat?" he suggested.

I scratched at my chin. "A cat?"

"Yeah. Had a tabby when I was a kid. Can hardly remember her, but she's a big part of my earliest memories. Sparks, we called her. Furry little Sparks."

"Ferdie," I said, letting out a deep breath.

"What?"

"That was my cat's name. We stuck her out on the back porch before my parents... It's not important. Anyone object?"

They shook their heads.

"Proxy," I said. "Do you know what a cat looks like?"

"I do," it replied.

Lance gave a weak smile then turned his face when he realized he had been caught. Maybe there was more than an asshole in there.

"Does it matter what kind of cat?" I asked the group.

No one gave a response.

An instant later, a five- or six-pound tuxedo cat appeared, its body primarily black with the exception of an orange stripe running between its eyes all the way back to its tail.

"Hello," it said, taking a seat before us.

Mary put her hands over her mouth. "My goodness you are so damn cute. Can I pet you?"

"Of course. This is part of my function."

She bent down and scratched Proxy behind the ear. Proxy leaned into her and to my utter shock, it began to purr, actually purr. I shook my head and blinked. Not only did it look like a feline, it acted like one. The amount of data the Foundry could glean from our thoughts about our experiences, foods, music, smells, tastes, touch… It was too much at times. We were a long way from Earth, but here we had a talking cat who would help us fight an interstellar war.

"Do you wish to depart?" Proxy asked once Mary looked satisfied. It took a leap onto one of the catwalk's banisters and found a better place to sit, its tiny paws balanced on the precarious rail.

"Hell yeah," James said, raising a fist. "What do we need to do?"

"The five of you must follow me to your sections."

"Will we be able to speak with one another?" Perry asked.

"Of course. This way." Proxy turned to face me, whiskers bouncing as it turned its head. "Milo, if you would, please enter the Star Sphere at the forward end of the ship."

"Okay," I replied, and gave the others a wave before heading off.

Proxy hopped down and I made my way up the endless catwalk, marveling at the sheer scale of the craft. The entirety of the human fleet, *the Brilliance, Galileo, Star Stream, Revelation, and Vasco Da Gama*, not to mention the I.S.S. 2 and Gateway Station, could fit within this ship and still have room for more.

"I will lead the others to their Star Spheres," Proxy said, its voice echoing in my head. *"They will require minor bodily modifications."*

"Will it be painful for them?"

"No. They will enter the Spheres and the ship's system will interface with their nervous systems."

"Do we have any idea where the Gene Brokers' ships have gone?"

"The Kabosai have crossed the Wandering Gate. Beyond that, I have no solid information at this time other than what we can infer. It should be possible to trace their drive ions or make appropriate estimates as to their destination once we are on the other side."

"So we're going to have to brave the gate."

"I see no other way."

The ship narrowed as I approached the forward end, yet even here it made me dizzy. I kept my eyes on my boots until I had reached my destination, then climbed the ladder on the side of the Star Sphere and sat on the platform at the top of the liquid filled globe.

At the forward end of the platform a chest for personal belongings was mounted. I started to empty my pockets and spotted something familiar within.

"Jasper?" I pulled a plush dog from within. "Proxy, how… Where did it?"

"I am sorry it is not the original," Proxy said. *"However, the Foundry thought you might like it."*

I stroked Jasper's soft ears back and smiled. "Maybe I should have asked you to be a dog."

"Would you like for me to change?"

"No. No. Stay as you are." I gazed into Jasper's black, plastic eyes and saw my own reflection. How appropriate. Anything he had ever done was really me in the end. There had been so much uncertainty in that season of my life. Funny how it all comes full circle. "Tell the Foundry thanks."

"I shall," Proxy replied. *"If you are ready, place the remainder of your belongings in the box. I would recommend taking off your clothes unless you have a cultural aversion."*

"No cultural excuse." I unbuttoned my pants and slipped them off. "Just good 'ol modesty. Feels weird to be naked in an open space. I think I'll keep my undies."

"As you wish."

I finished undressing and closed the box of personal effects. A hatch at the top of the tank irised open. I stared at the bubbling liquid within, my feet dangling over the edge, toes brushing the surface of the warm water.

"There's no reason to be afraid," Proxy said. *"You will be able to breathe. I will not let you drown."*

"You sure?"

"You can trust me. I am here to serve."

"I don't like that phrasing."

"How about, I am here to help?"

"Okay." I took a deep breath and slipped over the edge, splashing into the tank. The hatch closed and trapped me within. For an instant I found myself starting to panic, until a series of connections snaked out from the bottom of the sphere. They clicked into a half-dozen points along my spine, arms, and neck. I flinched, expecting it to cause pain, but there was none, just pressure. My desire to breathe was washed away.

"Initializing," Proxy said, and my vision went black.

CHAPTER 44

One moment, I was sinking to the bottom of the tank; the next, I was floating in a vast, virtual space, my body just as solid to me as it had been an instant before. Information flooded into me, the space beyond our ship's location made of intricate star charts and streams of cosmic energy. I was not just looking at the universe, I was feeling it, experiencing it firsthand through a body three hundred meters in length. I could hear distant stars, their radiation warm against the hull of the ship like sunlight on a summer day. I felt the presence of other ships within the Lignos system, estimated their destinations and origins based on velocity and time, planetary orbits and alignment. Even the Jalek's ship was not beyond my detection. It was burning back towards the orbiting rock of Cynosure at nine Gs of acceleration, orientation relative to us five degrees Z axis, even Y axis, negative fifteen X, drive temperature twenty thousand two hundred and nine kelvin, frequency resonation of cones fifteen thousand megahertz.

I stretched my arms and back and felt the ship respond, systems reaching out like limbs. "Holy shit," I mumbled. "I—"

"It's okay," Proxy said, appearing beside me as the black tuxedo cat with its orange racing stripe. "This part is often startling. Would you like to learn about the ship's system as your companions come online?"

"Yes. Please."

"Your ship is an L-560 Foundry Battleship, capable of multi-function combat applications; ship to ship, planetary bombardment, and base cracking of hardened moons or rocks. It may also act as a self-sustained exploration vessel with the ability to support the lives of four hundred humans for an indefinite period without fresh reaction mass or materials. Mounted to the inside hull are sixty-four modular rooms which can undergo nano-reconfiguration to fill whatever function is required: crew quarters, gathering places, workshops, and so on."

"Wait, indefinite time? What does that mean?"

"A thousand years at a minimum, longer depending on use."

"Wow. We'd be dead before we have the chance to run out of gas."

"That may be true but is unlikely. Due to your modifications, within the Star Sphere you will have the ability to manipulate subjective time. If you so wish, ten years, a hundred years, can pass in the blink of an eye, or a second pass at the speed of eternity. You will have full control of your metabolism and frame of reference."

"A one-way time machine."

"Of sorts." Proxy paused. "Esteban Lucero DeCarlos Lopez has come online."

"Good. Tell me more. We can travel and explore and shift time in one direction…" I reached out and grabbed hold of several threads of energy flowing through the solar system, plucking at them with my fingertips in an attempt to understand. The threads harmonized like a musical chord. "What else?"

"The L-560 has twelve antimatter drives designed to push its three-hundred-meter structure at a sustained acceleration of five Gs, as well as up to one hundred Gs for short bursts of one year or less."

I gave a chuckle. "Short bursts. Funny."

"This acceleration may bring the L-560 to a recommended maximum velocity of seventy percent of light speed, though higher numbers could be possible."

"Because of general relativity?"

"Einstein was correct. Unless you wish to remain out of sync with your species for eternity, remain at or below fifty percent to reduce time dilation."

"Nice to know that not all humans are dumb." I smiled. "The ship is fast, that's good."

"Perry Stablecamp has come online," Proxy reported, plopping over on its back and rolling around on a floor which did not exist.

"Can you patch them in on the briefing? Leave them on mute, please. I'd prefer not to hear them screaming when they first connect. Might be distracting."

"As you wish."

"So, we can stay out for a long time, and we're fast. What else? This is a battleship. How can it fight? What are its, what's the word… Armaments?"

"The L-560 is equipped with a wide variety of weapons and defensive capabilities. Along the outer hull are thirty-six drone fighters armed with high-energy beam weapons, ten kiloton kinetic rail cannons, and a complement of antimatter slug launchers. The fighters may be launched autonomously, or under the direct control of crew members within Star Spheres, provided that they remain within the maximum signal delay distance." Proxy paused again. "Lance Brittan and Mary Stablecamp have come online."

"They can pilot the fighters so long as they stay close enough to the main ship?"

"Correct. Once the fighters reach a distance of nine thousand kilometers or more, a thirty to one hundred and fifteen millisecond ping delay, the internal systems will begin to take over, putting the drone fighter on ever-increasing autonomy. By three hundred thousand kilometers, the delay will have reached over a thousand milliseconds per command. At three million kilometers, the delay will be so high the fighters become over forty percent less effective. It is recommended you keep them within this range. The Star Sphere may correct for some delay through subjective reference and predictive algorithms, but not all."

"Makes sense." I felt an itch on the back of my head and I gave it a vigorous scratch. "The speed of light is the limit."

"James Reed has come online," Proxy said, and settled into a seated position.

"Alright. Bring them in."

The rest of the crew appeared around me in a circle, our bodies floating, dangling their legs just as Shelly and I had when we entered the VE of the Foundry all that time ago. Each and every one was feeling their arms and legs to see if they were solid. Perry was without a visor.

"Can you see, Perry?" James asked.

Perry glared at him. "Why in Orion's ball sack do you think I'd need my visor in a virtual world?"

"Alright, feisty britches." Mary rested her fists on her hips. "Salty much?"

He rubbed his face and shook his head. "Hell if I know. I'm stuck somewhere between exhausted and excited."

"These fighters," Lance asked Proxy. "Is there a way we can practice with them before we arrive?"

"Like a combat simulation?" James added.

Esteban crossed his arms. "Good idea, *amigos*."

Proxy gave us a feline bow. "Yes. As soon as we are underway, I will provide the necessary combat simulations."

"Okay," I said, cutting back in. "So we have fighters. What other weapons are available?"

"The primary armaments of the L-560 include four ballistic antimatter slug launchers with a ten-thousand-kilometer blast radius per shot," Proxy said. "You also have a compliment of piezoelectric bombs able to disrupt electronic systems with EM radiation, up to and including fusion reactor systems. These directed waves of energy occur when their crystal lattices collapse under hyper-spatial conditions, radiating out in a sphere. Thermonuclear auto cannons, ten kiloton yield per projectile. And of course, the Para Lux array, a series of high-energy, ablative pulse weapons."

"Got a kitchen sink you can throw in?" Mary asked. "I am going to have to figure out how this ship ticks. The energy required for either the manufacturing of those weapons or their upkeep is. Well…"

"Staggering," Esteban said, and reached for her hand within the virtual space. She took it and nodded.

"As you may have assumed," Proxy continued, "the Kabosai will have many similar armaments. Most of these weapons can be diverted or countered with the L-560's systems. The hull of this ship is swarming with nano machines which may make repairs in real-time and reconfigure sections entirely. You may deploy effulgencent screens if the Kabosai lock energy weapons onto you. You may engage them in electronic warfare over their computer networks. The hull of the ship is also constructed of ablative materials and has moveable reactive points if kinetic weapons or explosives are used. These are not your greatest defense."

"If not armor, what is?" I asked.

Our view went from navigational to a bird's eye view, angle looking down on the hull of our ship docked with the Foundry below.

"Milo, please burn to a safe distance of at least ten-thousand kilometers from the station."

"Okay. Here goes nothing."

The movement took no real instruction. I thought about where I wanted to be, and on instinct the ship began to move, uncoupling from the Foundry facility, burning soft towards a point in space. After we cleared the first few kilometers of safe distance, the drive ramped up and pushed us towards our target.

"That was easy," I said.

"As it should be," Proxy replied. "We are now at a safe distance. Milo, extend your arms."

"What?"

"You will feel a new connection. Extend your arms. Do not fight against it."

"Alright," I said, spreading my arms wide. From the skin of the ship came a swarm of thousands of reflective, spheroidal black shapes. They took formation around me in a rough estimation of the positions of my arms. I lifted my right hand, and a collection of them followed. I lifted my left and got the same result on that side. I curled my body into a ball, and they retracted, drawing close to the ship, making it impossible to see us from our distant, overhead view. "What the hell are these things?"

"This is the Mercurial Integumentum, a second skin made of nano machines locked in place by a magnetic field within the heart of the ship. It will protect you against most weapons fire, so long as it is deployed in the right place at the right time with the right density. It may become diffuse for wide band energy weapons, and dense to counter ballistic or explosive attacks.”

“That’s pretty damn cool,” Perry said. “Can I have some too?”

Proxy stalked over to Perry and rubbed against his leg with its shoulder. “For what?”

“Do the fighters have it too?”

“Only the primary ship.”

“Meh.”

“We might actually have a chance,” Lance said, pointing to our ship. “I had my doubts, I guess I still do. Dad would have died to pilot this ship.”

I let go of the connection and the Mercurial Integumentum returned to a rest state along the skin of the ship. Or was it the hull? The armor? No. It was skin, my skin.

“Looks like it,” Esteban said. “Far as we know, they got only one ship and we faster than it. All we gots to do is run it down and disable it. Done wanna hurt our people, ya? I’m sure this thing got shuttles too.”

“It does,” Proxy replied.

Lance bent down and called the cat to him with a rapid click of his tongue. He gave it a scratch and picked it up. Proxy nuzzled against his chest and rubbed its chin on his arm. “We just get ready to support. Sounds like the ship itself has far more weapons than we need to take out the Gene Brokers’ hollow ship.”

“Is it possible to board their ship?” James asked.

“There is powered armor available on board,” Proxy answered. “However, it cannot be used from within the Star Sphere, due to electronic warfare. It is too easy to jam a control signal.”

“Good to know.”

I raised my hands to draw up a virtual whiteboard of sorts. A marker appeared in my palm. I began to outline the plan as we talked it through, facilitating discussion rather than ordering. My leadership position was borrowed at best, so I didn’t want to rock the boat by making demands. Mom and Dad had curried influence in their work through collaboration and mutual goals. It was time to draw on at least one good example.

“Okay,” I said, writing as I spoke. “We leave here and head for the Wandering Gate. En route we can each run simulations to get familiar with what this battleship is truly capable of. We pass through the gate and get a course for the most likely direction the Gene Brokers went. We burn hard to catch up, do what we can to disable them, maybe use the piezoelectric bombs or something else. Then we fly in with a couple of shuttles and powered armor and break them out of whatever hold they’re kept in.”

Lance set Proxy down and approached the board. He summoned a marker of his own and stroked his beard in thought. A moment later he circled the lump of the Gene Brokers' ship I had scribbled on the board, then drew two lines leading into its mouth. "How many soldiers do they have? If we have to be in the powered armor, that leaves only a couple of us to break them out."

"We know they have at least three," Esteban said. "I don' think they'll be expectin' it, ya?"

"Probably not," I agreed. "It's a start of a plan. We can refine it later. I think it's time we get moving."

"Agreed," Lance said, and made a flourish with his hand, the marker disappearing. "A good start."

I gave him a weak smile and turned to face the rest of them. "You know your places, then. I'll get us pointed in the right direction and we can get underway. We can save them if we work together."

"Wait, wait!" Perry said, raising his hands. "We forgot one big thing, one damn big thing. We can't go any further."

"What?" Esteban asked, his bottom lip poked out in thought. "What we miss?"

James lowered his head and sighed. "Everyone knows the ship needs a name."

Perry shot a finger gun at him. "Bingo bango, brother."

They were right. This was a big deal. Oftentimes the name of a ship gave purpose and personality to its crew and mission. A name could be remembered for long past its life, evoking inspiration and wonder for all who spoke it. We had been explorers on the *Vasco Da Gama,* a name taken from a historical explorer if not a great person, and so had the rest of the fleet. *The Brilliance, Galileo, Star Stream, and Revelation.* There had been other ships of exploration in history, *the Nina, the Pinta,* and *the Santa Maria,* as well as *the Mayflower.* There had been ships of war, *the Arizona, the Monitor, Yamato,* and *Dreadnought.* Science fiction had given us a thousand more, *Enterprise, Defiance, Galactica, Jupiter 2, White Star.* But for the life of me, I did not know what to call our L-560 Foundry Battleship.

The six of us remained in silence for a time.

Perry waved his fingers at the air and a white, red-striped mug of steaming coffee appeared in his hands. "Helps me think. Anyone want a cup?"

"Me." Lance waved. "How do I?" A mug appeared in his own hands, though his was white with the yellow, orange, blue and red insignia of a *futbol* club.

Esteban raised a hand. "Go Barcelona."

Lance raised his mug as if giving a toast.

"What about *Fidelas?*" Perry suggested. "Among my other hobbies, taxonomy, film, element collecting, and extreme ironing—"

"Extreme ironing?" James interrupted. "I have so many questions."

Mary shook her head. "Don't ask."

"Look," Perry went on, "I took Latin as a child. *Fidelas* means faithful. That's what we are, faithful."

I summoned myself a cup of coffee and looked at each of my crew in turn. They considered the word, rolled it around in their mouth, and began to nod.

"Welcome aboard the *Fidelis*," I declared, and in that moment something shifted. We were no longer just a collection of humans making the best of a bad situation. We now had an unshakable purpose, a mission, a just cause to stand behind. We would be faithful to those we cared about, faithful to humanity. The faithful never give up.

"This could be a suicide mission," Perry mused.

Lance nodded while sipping on his coffee. He gave a swallow and wiped the leftover brew off of his lips. "Yeah, could be."

"Setting course," I said, and we began to move. It was as simple as walking in my own body, and it felt wonderful. The power behind my every motion, the sense of acceleration, the shift in perspective. There was nowhere the *Fidelis* couldn't take us and I knew it, balls to bones.

I pointed the nose of the ship towards the orbital path and leaned into it, burning us towards the Wandering Gate in orbit around Lignos-5. Though it took days in objective time, within the Star Sphere I found myself toying with subjective time. In a matter of minutes from my reference we had crossed the solar system, passed Lignos itself, and were now curving towards our target, thirty AU crossed faster than you could eat a microwaved breakfast burrito.

The swirling red gas giant which had been our sky on Cynosure towered into view, its ice belt glittering in starlight, a field of a billion shattered glaciers. In that vista, the Wandering Gate was a speck of gold growing to encompass my entire view, a ring inlaid with flowing rivers of crimson. As we neared its mouth it activated, its once empty center becoming a vortex of purple and white energy.

"Is this gate dangerous?" Mary whispered, her arms drawing up to cover her chest.

"We don't know." Esteban took up position beside her. She reached for his hand and they stared at one another, eyes searching. "Gi'vor told us all about it, ya? How when you enter, you don't really teleport across space an' time, but you are, eh, deconstructed and rebuilt on the other side."

"Quantum entanglement?" Perry asked.

"Yes," I supplied. "The gate on the other side is entangled, or at least part of it. It never stops moving, thus it increases the range of the gate on this side. Thousands of light years crossed in a flash."

"But wait, wouldn't that mean it kills us and remakes us? Not teleporting us?" Perry reached out and brought the shared image of the gate closer. He inspected the details running along the inner edge where the energy vortex began. "Have to be honest, guys, that's a bit of a disturbing idea."

Lance hmphed. "We have a better option?"

"Not that I'm aware of."

"Killed and remade." Mary made the sign of the cross over her chest. "It begs the question, what makes us who we are? Is the soul something more than our memories? Will we even be the same person on the other side."

Esteban cocked his head at her. "I did not know you were religious."

"I'm not," she said. "I mean, I grew up Catholic, but had a hard time buying into it after I went to college. Science and religion didn't mix for me. Still, there are times since we left Earth, like now, where I just don't know anymore. God may not be what they taught us at St. Mary's, but God is real, even if He, She, It, whatever you want to say, is just the unknowable."

"Then we should go with God, ya?"

She began massaging her clavicle, a hand across her chest in an attempt to calm herself. "I think we already are, my pretty boy."

"Are you guys ready?" I asked, the ship slowly drifting towards the center of the gate. "There's time to change course, but not much."

"Let's do it," James said. "You know, if the soul dies with this gate, then our people are already dead, and maybe we deserve the same fate."

Perry put a hand on his shoulder and leaned in. "A bit grim, Mr. Reed, don't you think? How about a little positivity? You want a session with me later? My schedule is open."

"Shut up, Perry."

"Your loss, friend. I'm here to help."

"Heroes don't back down," Lance added. "And I don't plan on being a coward. Dad wasn't a coward. Neither am I."

Proxy twisted its head. "The Wandering Gate will not harm you."

"Will it take our souls?" Mary asked. "Can you answer that?"

"No, I cannot." Proxy began to lick the top of its paws. "As I do not have a soul, I cannot say for sure."

"Alright." I turned ahead. "Here we go." I willed my body into the gate, momentum carrying us into the mouth of what could well mean our destruction.

"May we say a prayer?" Mary asked, her voice small.

Esteban licked his lips and scratched at his arm. "What do you suggest?"

"*Our father, who art in Heaven,*" she began.

"*Hallowed be thy name,*" Perry picked up, joining his sister. "*Thy kingdom come, thy will be done, on earth as it is in Heaven.*"

Esteban joined them, "*Give us this day, our daily bread and forgive us our trespasses, as we forgive those who trespass against us. Lead us not into temptation but deliver us from evil.*"

James and I exchanged a confused look, not sure what to make of this. We had lived our entire lives aboard a spacecraft on which religion was effectively banned. This was as alien to me, to us, as Omar had been kneeling on his rug, as Gi'Vor twitching instead of nodding. Still, it gave me an unaccustomed sense of comfort, community, belonging. I only wished I had known the words to be part of this moment. Did I lower my head and pretend to mumble? Did I gaze into the void in quiet reflection? If there is a God, I hope he forgave the ignorant.

"For thine is the kingdom, the power, the glory, for ever and ever."

"Amen," Lance said, his head down.

The gate tore the forward end of the *Fidelis* into pieces, breaking it down an atom at a time. Brilliant light originating from the portal flashed over me and was gone. I felt existence go blank, yet somehow a thread of consciousness persisted. I was in a place between Lignos and the Wandering Gate's destination, without a body, without a mind, and still, my thoughts persisted if on some small level.

I could see Mom's face the night she asked me the question.

"Milo, have you ever dreamed of touching stars?"

"No," I should have said. But even that would have been a lie. I had known it then, and I certainly knew that now.

Another bright flare blossomed in my perception, and I was back in the virtual space of the Star Sphere, a fresh set of constellations before me, the ship's systems calibrating to map them. The *Fidelis* was intact. My friends, my crew, were breathing.

"We made it," Mary said, relief in her voice. She mumbled another short prayer under her breath. "We really made it."

Perry felt his arms and chest. He went to summon another cup of coffee in relief, then let it go, the contents vanishing into nothing. "Umm, guys?"

My attention snapped ahead. We were drifting away from the gate at breakneck speed, traveling at several dozen kilometers a second in relation to the gate. To our port and starboard, two blips had appeared on our local sensors. Instinct screamed for me to deploy the Mercurial Integumentum, my nanoscopic second skin. I threw my arms wide, and just as I did, the *Fidelis* rocked, having taken several broadside hits from the explosive weapons of two asteroidal vessels.

"We're under attack," I said. "Powering up the weapons."

"To the fighters, ya?" Esteban called. "Go, go, go, *amigos*. No time for simulations."

I was left alone in the virtual space, nothing but the ship's sensors and orientation control. I reached out and scanned the attacking ships, able to identify that these were not the same as those in the vision Shelly had pushed into my head through the implants. These were smaller, but there was no doubt who they belonged to.

Sinas and his friends had bet that we would find a way to follow them. They had been waiting for us.

"Trial by fire," I said, powering up the Para Lux Array. "Let's hope our guns are big enough."

A dazzling bar of light blossomed along the port-side hull of the *Fidelis*. Warmth filled my shoulders and arms, cascading out and into my fingertips as I struck.

The battle for our people had begun.

We weren't ready.

CHAPTER 45

The audio channel binding the six of us together was chaos, everyone groaning and cussing and talking to themselves as they rushed into their respective virtual environments while under fire. Fighters detached from the exterior hull, a squad of five forming up and heading towards the Kabosai ship to our starboard side. The pair of enemy ships hurled projectiles in our direction, and on instinct I let go of my critical Para Lux charge, casting a widening ribbon of energy into the black. For a split second, I had created a barrier that kinetic weapons could not pierce, a band of heat intense enough to atomize all incoming fire. The timing of such a defense was unfathomable, a nanosecond earlier or later and it would have missed entirely, and yet it didn't. Not a single shot from the enemy ships made it through.

"We're rushing in too fast!" Lance shouted. "Don't fire at them. Not yet."

"*Por que, amigo*?" Esteban called in.

The names of the fighters' pilots appeared in my Star Sphere's virtual interface, the diamond-shaped crafts screaming at thirty Gs towards the enemy, guns hot. At our rear, the Wandering Gate receded, our distance from the golden ring multiplying. We were now outside the Foundry's weapon nullification zone, traveling faster than when we had entered it in the Lignos system, no time to contemplate the fact that we were not the same people. Every atom, every molecule in our bodies had been copied and replaced, and yet I didn't feel like a copy.

The fighter on the far right, James's, let off a volley of ballistic gunfire that missed the enemy entirely.

Lance growled, "I said hold!"

"Why?" James replied.

"What if our people are on board?"

"Proxy," I queried. "Is there any way to tell if there are humans aboard those ships? Like a bio-sign scanner?"

The cat blinked at me as if I'd gone crazy. "Like in your science fiction?"

"Yeah. Why not?"

"Such devices do not exist, Milo. I can, however, deduce the likelihood of that possibility through other means."

"Like what?"

"In almost all known cases, the Kabosai place their client species in hyper suspension while traveling to their final destination. These hyper suspension units, like those the Foundry employs, create a certain frequency of thermal output that leaves an infrared footprint."

"Do you see evidence of one?" I previewed the dappled red and blue heat map Proxy projected onto my heads-up display within my virtual environment, colors overlaying both ships.

"I do not. While there are plenty of hotspots along their hulls, none coincide with the information we have on hand. It is possible the sections are being shielded to mask this signal."

Another volley of explosive weapons screeched through the gulf. I increased our acceleration, attempting to thread the *Fidelis* through the twenty-thousand-kilometer gap between the ships. I stretched my arms out beside my hips, then threw one up, and the other down. The Mercurial Integumentum rippled out from my body in waves, gathering up into two densely populated discs each a kilometer in diameter, the electromagnetically bound nanomachines absorbing nearly all the incoming explosives. Nearly. A single shot slipped through the defensive barrier, striking me just forward of the docking bays with what felt like a kidney punch delivered by a bareknuckle boxer fighting dirty.

I groaned through white-hot pain as the ship provided neural feedback, an entire section of hull breached, my eyes squeezed shut to block out the sensory overload. I felt for the injury with my right hand and smoothed it over with an open palm, gathering the swarms of nanomachines to begin repairs. Within a moment, the pain began to recede. I had expected tactile feedback, given how the ship felt to pilot, sure, but not like this. The ship had become my second skin.

"Is there anything else we can go on?" I hissed. "We need to act quick. I don't want to kill our people by accident."

"From surface level scans, it appears that these rocks are made of a mixture of iron, nickel, iridium, palladium, platinum, gold, and magnesium. None of these materials are effective at protecting against harmful cosmic radiation."

"Then if it's not well-shielded, it likely doesn't have our people on board?"

"Correct." Proxy paused for a moment as if analyzing a vast amount of data in just a few moments, its glowing, feline eyes staring off into blank space. The battle raged around me, a thousand data points, vectors and blips provided to give context within the combat theatre. "Lastly, these ship configurations are in our database, and they do not correspond with known Kabosai transformation vessels. It is always possible they have repurposed a design, though unlikely."

"It looks like a hunk of rock," Mary said. "How can we tell the difference between this and another ship?"

"It isn't the shape of the 'rock,'" Proxy went on, "it's the systems along the outer surface and the overall size from which I draw this opinion."

"You believe our people are not on these ships, but can't be for sure?"

"The chance is greater than fifty percent that there are no humans aboard this pair of Kabosai ships."

"I don't think I like those odds," James said. "Not much better than a coin flip."

"We have to take action, ya?" Esteban acknowledged. "I know how you be feelin', *amigo*, but can't keep flying circles round them. Guns on the surface be lookin' twitchy."

The starboard Kabosai ship gave off flickers of light around the open maw of its forward end. An instant later, a dozen contact warnings appeared on my sensors, backward-swept crescent moons made of charcoal matte metal having poured outward, each soaring on incandescent points of thrust.

We were caught between two enemy ships and a wing of fighters. Battleship or not, we had to fight back or die. The *Fidelis* might have had impressive defenses, but those meant nothing if we didn't use them.

"I'll take responsibility if this move is wrong," I said, sucking in a deep breath. "You guys form up and attack the starboard ship. Chew through their fighters, rip them up. I'll focus our main armaments on the other one."

"Copy," Esteban said, burning his fighter towards the opposite ship. "Form up on me."

"We're with you, Lopez," Lance responded, and I felt a sigh of relief. I hadn't thought to appoint a wing commander in the heat of the moment, but this made sense. Pilot or not, Esteban had led soldiers.

I recharged the Para Lux array and focused it on the port Kabosai ship. They launched another volley of explosives at me, and I blocked them with the Mercurial Integumentum. The array approached critical mass and so I let its energy fly, its beam cutting a molten furrow in the rocky, slate colored surface of the hollow ship. I had expected more damage from the energy blast, but at a range of twenty-two thousand kilometers the focus was diffused, rendering it less effective against a hard target like the surface of an asteroid.

"Got to use something heavier," I mumbled, loading slugs from safety storage up into the antimatter cannons.

"They're everywhere," James reported, his fighter banking to the right, shooting only a few hundred meters over the surface of the starboard ship. "I've got two on my ass."

"Coming in," Mary replied. "I've got a good angle, I think." Her fighter let loose a machine gun barrage of sabot rounds. One of the fighters on James's rear was shredded in two while the other turned away, cutting a ninety G turn that would have rendered an organic pilot into a chunky red paste along its interior walls. "Damn they're fast. Still, I would have expected these fighters to be harder to pilot. It's like it knows where I want to be and goes there. Boys?"

Their chatter fell into the background as more immediate threats arose. The port Kabosai ship returned fire at the *Fidelis*, radioactive ballistic shells pelting against the M.I. grid. I was able to block ninety nine percent of them, however one got through, turning a section of the forward end of the shard just a few dozen meters from my Star Sphere into slag.

Proxy cut in, "Removing atmosphere from interior in case of hull breach."

"Thanks," I said, and we were hit again. This time one of the explosive pellets broke through and impacted the middle of our port side. One of the machine shops was breached. "Come on… Load, weapons, load."

"Good shot, Lance," Esteban cheered, drawing my attention back to the fighter wing. They had managed to turn about a fourth of the Kabosai's crescent-shaped craft into twinkling collections of super accelerated scrap. "Perry and Mary, pull up and come around."

"Pull up?" Perry replied. "This is space, dude, there's no point of reference."

"Pull up against the elliptical."

"But we're not in a star system!"

"Your interface can do it," Lance growled. "Just imagine a circle bisecting the enemy ship like they're floating on water."

"I can't find the option."

"Oh, for God's sake. Figure it out on your own, there's no time to call I.T."

"Proxy?" Perry called. "Can you help me?"

The feline disappeared from my virtual space, vanishing to assist Perry personally. For as smart as the guy was, there were times he struggled with even the smallest things. I could relate.

"Little brother, you've got one on you," Mary cut in, and her fighter banked to the left and flipped, hull tumbling end over end, weapons roaring, nuclear rounds cutting a neat line in the path of the enemy fighter. She clipped its right wing and sent it spinning, though not disabled.

The starboard ship's power readings blossomed within my awareness, a prickling on my arms and along my back. Point defense weapons along its hull spun up and began casting lead into the black.

"We need to get further out," Lance called. "Can't take the fighters and cannons at the same time. They'll shred us to pieces."

"Pull range," Esteban ordered. "Put us in a better position, ya?"

"I see a way through the fire to one of the weapons emplacements." James's fighter dove towards the enemy ship.

"I said pull range, get out, is too hot, *amigo*."

"I can get this."

Lance let out a stream of words but all I could make out was, "Don't be stupid, James."

"Shit, shit, shit!" James shrieked, and his fighter came apart, its hull littering the surface of the Kabosai ship with debris. For an instant I thought I was going to fall apart, one of my long-time friends having fallen in battle, but then I just got angry. Really damn angry. He wasn't dead, not in the least, his body was floating a few hundred feet from mine within a Star Sphere. All he had really done was waste a precious resource by being reckless.

One of the reserve fighters detached from the *Fidelis* an instant later. James was away once more, just as eager to fight, judging by the speed with which he departed.

"Extra lives," he said.

"We don't have an infinite supply of those," I told him, frustration overtaking my tone. "Damn it, James, we need to be careful. No quick save. No continue."

"Don't be so touchy, bruh," he replied.

"You're not the one whose body is being pelted with radioactive materials."

"You mean the ship?"

"Whatever."

The port Kabosai ship began to burn away from my position, putting range between us. I turned the *Fidelis*, aiming the drive flame towards the second enemy ship, and began to burn into an intercept vector to close the distance to my target. Green lights came up on the antimatter cannon and I fired, letting loose a series of fifteen slugs, each about as big as an oil drum. With a precision I had not expected, the Kabosai ship employed a grid of defensive energy weapons, igniting my slugs in a dazzling, incandescent display so bright it left me blind. For several moments I couldn't sense anything from the instruments, the explosions too close to my current position for its signal noise to disperse.

I struggled to find my bearings through the static for several agonizing moments, then everything returned to normal. The Kabosai ship had taken almost no damage from my assault, just a few scars along its rock face. I could have used those weapons to turn half the cities on Earth into dust. Here, however, their blasts were almost inconsequential.

Before I could attempt to use the next weapon in the *Fidelis's* arsenal, the enemy returned fire. A bright light appeared near the mouth at its forward end, cutting a line down one side of me. There was a pause, and in this space, I was able to deploy an effulgencent screen. It launched from my left flank, a canister the size of a small shuttle with contents coiled under extreme pressure. After traveling a short distance, the canister exploded and a disposable reflective shield fifteen kilometers in diameter appeared, covering one side of our ship. Given the size of the original canister, the shield itself could be no thicker than a few atoms.

The Kabosai fired again, and the beam struck the reflective surface of the screen, deflecting its impotence into the void.

"Hell yeah!" I shouted, and realized I sounded a lot like Dad screaming while we rocketed up out of the Earth's gravity well all those years ago. "Proxy, I need something harder. Something to break that ship's shell."

Thin as the reflective screen had been, it began to deteriorate, its materials dissolving in vacuum.

The cat appeared on my right and stared off into the battle. "Yes, Milo. I will power up the rail guns. If you can bring yourself closer to the enemy, I believe we can break through the surface and use the Para Lux array. That should give us an opening to their vital systems."

"Anyone feel that?" Esteban asked over the open channel, his voice shaky. "My fighter here a little sluggish, ya? Last little bastard almost got me."

"It's lightspeed lag," Lance replied. "Getting a little too far out from the *Fidelis* for quick reaction. Proxy was right, we can't break physics."

"I'm fine right now," James said, his fighter making several barrel rolls as it rejoined the battle.

"Because you're still on your way back to the fight, numbnuts," Mary told him. "You're still almost on top of the ship."

"Hey!" Perry chimed in. "I thought I was the only one you called numbnuts. My feelings are hurt."

"Fine. Numbnuts One and Numbnuts Two. You feel better now?"

"No. Not really."

"Stay focused, team," Esteban said.

"Milo." Lance brought his fighter around the Kabosai ship, threading it between a series of three enemy fighters. "Why are you moving away?" The fighters bore down on him and he flipped his ship around, burning the opposite direction, shifting his momentum by three hundred and sixty degrees before opening fire. Two of the ships following him were torn apart, and the last screamed past, unable to produce enough acceleration in the moment to compensate.

"Keeping up with the other ship. You'll have to adjust."

He let out a sigh and his fighter formed up with Esteban and Mary. "Okay." As a group they cut a line through several more fighters, dodging rounds from the primary ship's point defense weapons like flies avoiding a thousand swatters.

"I see an opening," James said, rejoining their group. "There's no fighters anywhere close. I can fire down the mouth of the mothership. That has to do more damage. Wait… oh shit."

"I see them," Esteban said, increasing his acceleration to intercept one of the fighters crashing onto James. Nuclear sabot rounds danced around the enemy as it twisted and turned, taking evasive actions. "Pull out, James. Don't go for the opening."

"I'm locked in. I don't think I can pull out of this so easy. This fighter's ass keeps getting heavier and heavier."

"Time delay," Lance reminded him. "Are you not listening?"

James approached the maw of the enemy ship and let loose the fighter's payload of thermonuclear pellets. Hundreds of tiny nuclear weapons entered the opening and began to explode like crackling popcorn. His fighter approached the explosions at several kilometers a second. If he didn't change his direction, he'd frag another one of our precious fighters. He turned himself perpendicular to the hole, throwing every bit of delta-v the fighter had available into redirecting his momentum.

"Form up on his rear," Esteban said. "I see an opening for reals. Let's take it down, ya?"

"Their reactor is exposed," Proxy reported. "Increasing levels of alpha, beta, and gamma radiation are leaking into local space."

"Let's give it all we got."

James's fighter continued to accelerate, thirty, forty, fifty Gs of force. The opening drew closer, now forty kilometers away, thirty-eight, thirty-five, thirty.

"Get out," Lance said.

"I'm trying, I am. I'm having a bit of trouble changing my trajectory."

The *Fidelis* rocked, connections going black. A few moments later the ship began to reboot. I had no idea what hit us, but whatever it was it had left me groggy and sluggish. The port ship was preparing to fire again. I threw auxiliary power into the drive and increased our acceleration, narrowly escaping a combined barrage of energy weapons and ballistics.

Out of the corner of my perception, James's fighter bounced off the exterior hull of the starboard Kabosai ship. I only hoped it wasn't destroyed. Esteban and the rest had taken up a diamond formation and were headed towards the opening at the front of the enemy ship, dodging a hail of point defense and fighter weapons. Mary took a hit, but her ship kept going, half of one side missing.

The battleground beyond the Wandering Gate was littered with the debris of destroyed fighters and chunks of rock dislodged from the Kabosai ships. Lost munitions among the debris ignited spontaneously like forgotten fireworks, their fuses lit before being tossed into space with abandon.

"We have to take them out," I groaned. Everything was so hard to do right now. What had that attack damaged? Were we okay? "How do I stop them?"

"Accelerate around to the front of the Kabosai ship," Proxy supplied. "If you can hold off their attacks for about a minute, I can reroute power and bring the rail guns online."

"How do I hold them off?"

"Focus on the M.I."

"Okay." I closed my eyes and placed my hands before me, palms open, seeing the ship in my head as my body, a shield of obsidian before me. The Kabosai fired again, and I swiped my hands into open space, shifting the position of the M.I. barrier, using its location and momentum to deflect the incoming weapons fire. The Kabosai were relentless, constantly deploying new sets of weapons, throwing anything and everything they could at me.

One barrage after the next, I sent their weapons' fire scattering off into space or crashing against the M.I.

The barrier weakened with each moment, becoming less and less dense.

"Fire now," Esteban said. "Give them everything."

I let my attention drift for a moment onto my companions, and a shot hit me in the gut. I doubled over, not sure where the damage to the ship had been sustained. The M.I. faltered and several more ballistic rounds made it through. I spat into the virtual space, blood on my lips.

What the hell did this mean? Were we dying?

"Hands up," Proxy said, its voice stern. "Now that I have been given life I would prefer not to die. Hands up, Milo. Keep the barrier between us and them."

I drew my body into the fetal position and shut my eyes, the M.I. contracting around the *Fidelis* in a protective cocoon.

A wave of energy, light, and heat washed over my back. The other Kabosai ship vanished from my perception. They had gotten it.

"Weapons hot, Milo," Proxy said. "Hit them, now. Now!"

My eyes flashed open, and I could see the target. There was a spot within the maw of the enemy ship just a few meters wide. I focused on that point and fired the rail guns, a pair of super accelerated slugs hurled down a set of electromagnetic paths, reaching nearly three quarters the speed of light in under a second.

They struck the weakness in the Kabosai ship, and their kinetic energy was converted into heat. An explosion greater than ten thousand nuclear weapons flashed along the front of the enemy ship, its rocky armor sloughing away to reveal its soft insides. I didn't wait for suggestions from Proxy. I charged the Para Lux array and began to fire, intermittently reloading antimatter slugs, sending them down the same path.

The Kabosai ship began to bulge and crack until its reactor core went critical. A flash of light blinded my perceptions again, and then there was only rock and dust scattered into the void.

The battle was over, and there we were, drifting among a sea of wreckage. Though I felt like trash, we were alive. We had survived our first engagement.

"We won," Mary said, her voice thin.

"Feels good for once," Lance replied.

Proxy went to work deploying collection drones, gathering up what materials we might use to reconstruct fighters and repair the ship. Nothing went to waste in the vast reaches of space.

Everyone except Lance reappeared in my virtual space, haggard looks on their faces.

"I have confirmed that these were not the ships containing your human counterparts," Proxy said after a few minutes.

"Thank God," Mary exhaled, hands covering her face. "I don't think I could have lived with myself if they had died at our hands." She crossed her legs where she floated and Esteban came up behind her, massaging her back.

Lance reappeared, a frosty pint of beer in hand. "So, what now?"

Perry joined him in this affectation, summoning a brew of his own. He took a long sip and gave an appraising smile. "IPA?" he asked, foam stuck to his upper lip.

"Yeah. Something dad used to drink back on Earth. This one was called *Hail to the King, Baby.*"

"Not bad." Perry smacked his lips. "Not bad at all. Yo, Proxy, can we track the larger ship?"

Proxy leapt onto an invisible shelf before a growing star map. It looked upward, drawing our attention to several locations in our galactic neighborhood. "There are three star systems within fifteen light years of our position. From the data we have gathered from Foundry probes, the most likely system is Ph0nx, a yellow-type star system with eleven planets, two of which are within the habitable zone for liquid water and cool enough for humanoid life."

"Anything else to go on?" I asked, then summoned a beer of my own out of curiosity. After a sip of the sour, hoppy brew, I let it go and replaced it with a stemless glass of sweet, red wine. Beer just wasn't my thing. "You mentioned ion trails."

"Yes. Those are present, but difficult to sort from background radiation due to the pair of Kabosai ships that were waiting on us."

"How many lives did we take?"

The crew turned to me.

"I want to know, Proxy."

The feline lowered its head. "Approximately five hundred and sixty Kabosai were killed in the destruction of these two vessels."

"Okay," I let out in a sigh. "Okay…"

Perry swallowed down the rest of his beer without a word. Lance stared at his, lost in thought. James hung back away from us, picking and biting his nails.

That was a lot of death. I had already killed more Kabosai than there were ever humans on the *Vasco Da Gama*, even before the Isopteran attack. What right did we have? I was determined to save our people, to save Shelly and our friends, yes, but how many other sentient lives had to die to see this end? The Phantamorph was the first. It wouldn't be the last. The Jalek had told me survival required one to be ruthless, cruel. I wasn't sure I had the stomach.

"We head for the most likely system," I said after collecting myself. "We press on."

Esteban turned his head around to me and nodded. "Only way is ahead, ya?"

"Ahead."

Proxy recalled the salvaging drones and I turned the *Fidelis* towards Ph0nx, ramping up the main drive till we were accelerating at five Gs. If our estimations were correct, it would take about twenty-one years to reach our target. We would overtake the Kabosai at the edge of Ph0nx, and win or lose, this would be over. If today's battle was any indication of future events, we had a lot of training to do. Twenty-one years was a long time to prepare. A long time to rest. A long time to consider the worst.

"That fight was sloppy," I told the crew, and no one disagreed. "Let's get to work and be better. Let's show the Gene Brokers that they messed with the wrong fucking species."

CHAPTER 46

One battle was behind us, yet another greater one was ahead. What the outcome would or would not be, I couldn't say. As I began to peruse the Foundry's files on the Gene Brokers, I came to realize the ships they had left behind to cover the gate were relatively small. They were colony ships of a sort, as were all of their ships, but these were meant for more hostile territories. They were meant to stand up against heavy assaults like ours, and so were the transformation ships we pursued. The Foundry had no hard information on the actual weapons they used, only supposition. Though some of the Gene Brokers at one time had asked for Foundry ships, the majority of their fleet kept its distance from the network to maintain their own technology. This left a wild card among the galactic deck, which never sat well with the Foundry. How could it protect life, if one of the very things it was protecting would not play by the rules? The Foundry was not overbearing in the matter. It did not actively force those who kept their distance to adopt its systems. This was an enigma I could not quite resolve. How had the Gene Brokers gotten around the gravity tractors or nullification zones? How had they visited Cynosure in ships not constructed by the Foundry?

As we put distance between ourselves and the Wandering Gate, the *Fidelis* began to do something strange I had not expected. Proxy had said it could reconfigure the interior rooms based on our wants and needs, but this was not what it was doing. My skin began to tingle as nanomachines moved from compartments deep within what felt like my belly to the exterior hull, forming lattices hundreds of meters in length that shaped themselves into lanceolate panels, their surfaces reflective and porous. It was mesmerizing to watch, as if this new equipment were being coded into existence, 3D printed from the bottom up. The two dozen panels formed and attached themselves near the aft of the ship, forward of the drive by only fifty feet. Once their tips had tapered to a point, the panels began to fan out, hinged near the aft, as if the *Fidelis* were a jagged flower whose petals were blossoming.

"Proxy," I said after some time, breaking myself from the spell of its transformation. "What is this for?"

The cat turned its black and white face to regard me. "There is more energy in the universe than you are aware of. We have but to reach out for it."

"I don't understand."

"Stellar bodies are great distances apart. Even if the net energy is not in large quantity, or must be collected over long periods of time, it is there, and we may use it. There is solar energy, and background radiation, but there is something else, something that binds all existence together. When we stand between stars, we may tap into this."

"Dark energy?"

"You could call it that, but you would not be entirely correct. I'm sorry, Milo, but this might be beyond your understanding at this time." Proxy paused then hopped up into my lap, nuzzling its nose against my chest. "Are you ready to begin the training simulations as we approach cruise velocity?"

"How long will that take?"

"At five Gs of acceleration, we will burn for forty-nine days."

"No getting up to walk around, huh?"

"I would not advise it."

I turned to face the group. "Are you ready to train?"

"Are we going to run simulations for twenty-one years?" Perry asked, his tone uncertain.

"I would not advise that either," Proxy said.

I stared at the cat in my arms. "Why?"

"None of you are immortal. Subjective time will still force you to age, albeit at a slower pace within the Star Spheres."

"So you saying, the longer we exist here," Esteban said, "the older we get, ya?"

"Precisely. When you reduce your metabolic rate to shift your frame of reference, your aging slows considerably. Each of you has the ability to do so independently."

Mary gave Esteban a curious look, then reached out and squeezed his hand.

"I just want to get this over with," James said.

Lance gave a nod in his direction. "You and me both, but it's clear you aren't ready after that shit show."

"Way to call me out, bruh."

"Get over it. How long do we train?"

"Until we're ready," I said.

"This is the combat portion, sure," Mary said, crossing her arms and rubbing her chin. "But how are we extracting them? We can't just blow up the enemy ships and hope that our friends and families survive."

"I've been thinking about this," Lance said. "Proxy mentioned powered armor and shuttles. We'll have to use them."

"And did you consider how many guards they might have? Last I checked there's only six of us."

"An' not all six can go, ya?" Esteban said. "Got to be out of the Star Sphere to use, leaves the *Fidelis* open."

I sighed and gave a nod. "And there's no telling how much security the Gene Brokers keep on board."

"The powered armor is superior to most military ground units," Proxy said. "While I cannot speak with certainty, it has been highly effective in boarding the craft of various species. Esteban is correct, though, whoever is using the powered armor cannot do so from within the Star Sphere. It must be worn physically."

"We wear them down," Lance continued, rolling one of his hands in the air. "Knock out some of their weapons. Keep them busy. Two or three of us rush in on a shuttle and tear the inside of that ship apart till we find our people."

"I may be able to offer assistance," Proxy rolled over and looked up at me, its slitted eyes reflecting the false light of our virtual space. "If you can gain access to a console on the Kabosai ship, I might be able to tell you where the captured humans are on board."

"Perfect," I replied. "We find them, wear them down, create a distraction, recover our friends."

"I'm taking point on the rescue OP," Lance told us.

I had no good reason to argue with him, and so I held back any smart remarks. Still, there was a part of me that did not appreciate his dominant nature.

He produced a wooden comb from his pocket and began to brush his beard, his attention focused someplace else. "I'll take James and one other."

"You'll need a wheel man," Perry said, speaking in a silly accent I didn't recognize. "Only way we'll get away with the goods before the coppers turn up."

"This isn't a heist," Mary said, pointing at her brother.

"Oh, but I disagree."

"I'm the pilot, born and raised," Lance said. "The wheel man stops here."

Perry pursed his lips and shrugged.

"Look, guys, we only get one shot at this. Let's do our best." I let Proxy hop down out of my arms. "We have as good a plan as any, it just needs practice."

"To the fighters!" Perry said, pointing a finger skyward before vanishing.

The rest of the crew winked out, following his example and transferring into their own virtual spaces.

"Okay," I said, taking a deep breath. "Proxy, give us a simulation based on what we know of the Gene Brokers' ships. Create a battle theater that's an analog to Ph0nx."

"Program ready."

"Initiate."

We appeared in a simulation within our current simulation, the *Fidelis* fifteen light years ahead of its current position, two massive Kabosai ships within visual range. Like the ones we had already encountered, these were great hulks, their hulls made of repurposed asteroids whose interiors had been scooped out and filled with the guts of interstellar transformation ships. They were armed to the teeth with point defense cannons, energy weapons, ballistics, fighters, and God only knew what else.

"I have programmed the simulation with ten levels of difficulty," Proxy said. "I will start you off with level one so that you may become familiar with the systems."

"Weak," James said.

"You may feel different before this is over." Proxy paused for a moment. "Simulation has begun."

Like in our last encounter I focused my attention on one ship while the rest of them broke off into a squadron of fighters and assaulted the other. Before they could intercept the first of the Kabosai ships, warning alarms went off and the *Fidelis* was down, after I missed a wave of incoming fire.

"Again," I said, and the simulation started over.

I had to get my head in the game. I had to focus on what was important. There was far more data in this engagement than there was in the initial attack. There were celestial bodies to consider, planets and planetoids and asteroids and comets, hundreds of gravity wells that could distort or redirect distant incoming fire. There were close range engagements of just a few thousand kilometers, and ones in which we took potshots at one another from over twenty A.U. away.

We tried a hundred different strategies, each for a different situation. There was no telling how the enemy would show up.

Each time we failed, I saw Shelly's face, the faces of my battered parents on a transport somewhere beyond the Wandering Gate, Omar's eyes as he begged me not to leave him. Anger overtook me, fueled me.

"Again."

We got a little better. When we were succeeding in three out of four attempts, we would move to the next level of difficulty. After eight or nine hours, we would break and take whatever passed for sleep when your body was plugged into a life-sustaining acceleration sphere, then started again.

A week passed.

"Again."

Two weeks.

"Again."

Three.

"Again."

Four. We had to become perfect at this. No failures. No mistakes.

"Again…"

A month and change. We started over, became better.

"Again!"

We started over, transforming into a death machine driven by the will of human minds.

"Again! Again! Again!"

And over…

"Milo," Mary said, appearing in my virtual space. She put a hand on my shoulder and frowned. "It's time to rest. We've gone long enough. We're tired."

I closed my eyes and reached a hand to touch hers. "I can't fail them. I can't fail her…"

"You won't." She paused before speaking, her silence doing the heavy lifting. "Let's rest."

Everyone agreed. It was time.

"Fine," I conceded. "See you on the other side."

They vanished from within my virtual environment, retreating to the safety and comfort of their own, except for one. Lance lingered for a while as if he had something on his mind.

"You okay?" I asked.

He crossed his arms and peered off into nothing, his attention focused on the three-dimensional model of Ph0nx before us, a collection of colored planets and concentric circles, an orb of yellow burning at the center. "Why didn't you tell me?"

"Tell you what?"

"About my dad, about what happened when you and Esteban escaped the *Vasco Da Gama*. I had to hear it from someone else."

"I—well, to be honest, I don't know." Proxy looked up at me and vanished, sensing that Lance wanted our conversation to be private. "I don't know, maybe it had something to do with being overwhelmed in the moment, maybe it had to do with awkwardness over Shelly. I can't say."

"Even on Creatus she didn't let go of you." He kept his eyes averted but began to stroke his beard in an absent gesture. "Her heart wasn't with me."

I took several deep breaths. Even if they weren't real, the action helped to calm me. "Look, I'm sorry. I never tried to get between—"

He raised an open hand to cut off my apology. He wasn't interested in talking about Shelly and our relationship. "How did he die? Dad."

"He was injured before we got onto the pod," I replied. "Isoptera had cut him with a knife or a claw, something. I wasn't conscious for that part of the attack. He put on a strong face and didn't tell Esteban how bad his injuries were. His only objective in the moment was to save us, get us out alive, touch us down on the Foundry. And he did. Your dad was a hero. I wouldn't be here if not for him. You should be proud of him."

Lance's brows furrowed. "I am. I always have been, always will be."

"Then what is it?"

"I guess I just needed to hear you say it. Despite everything we've been through, not all of us are as self-possessed as you are."

"Self-possessed?"

"Yeah, Milo. You always seem to have a purpose. We're not all like that. Some of us are still trying to figure out what we are supposed to do with our lives. Some of us have lived in the shadows of great men and women."

"Some of us?" I chuckled.

This forced a smile out of Lance. He raised his attention to me, his expression returning to a neutral place. "She was never meant for me, I know that, but I had a life on Creatus. I had friends, family even. Mom is still alive, far as I know. Let's save them."

"I wouldn't be here if I didn't think we could. Cynosure would have been a better place to live out our days in comfort."

"Yeah." Lance nodded in agreement. "Get some rest."

"You too."

"See you in a few years, Milo."

Lance vanished, and I felt one of the many stones in my chest soften.

I dismissed the endless starscape and replaced it with a familiar setting, my quarters aboard the *Vasco Da Gama*. The space was quiet and empty, the door to my parent's room shut. I retired to my bed, mentally and emotionally exhausted. Proxy appeared on the floor and curled up at my feet, warm and reassuring.

As I allowed myself to sleep, falling into a time reference in which months passed each second, I began to dream. From my subjective frame of reference, it had not been all that long since the Gene Brokers had taken our people. Not long since I had held Omar's hand as he passed on to the other side. A little longer, and I had felt Shelly's soft, bare skin against mine. I missed her terribly, wanting nothing more than to put my arms around her and say how much she meant to me.

That's why it came as no surprise that when my dreams began, I saw a man and a woman dancing to old pop music. They spoke no words, but their body language was clear. The two of them spun in circles, chest to chest, hands resting on each other's hips, palms clasped. I could not see their faces, such as dreams were, and yet they were familiar. Was it me? There was no way to tell. Dreams were strange like that, random details processed and contextualized before being placed into long-term storage.

She placed her cheek on his shoulder, and he smiled, giving her head a kiss.

They dipped and rocked to the slow beat of the song, content in the moment, not wanting anything else but one another, each and every loving thought communicated through gentle touch.

The two of them were eating dinner, sitting in a kitchen with red mosaics on sandstone walls, him frying up a pair of steaks, her chopping lettuce and pouring drinks. Once the food was ready, they sat across from each other at a dark oak table. They stared into the other's eyes, the meal taken in its own time, smiles on both their faces, laughs exchanged.

"My rose," he said, and her cheeks turned bright red.

The two of them stormed down a hallway of steel catwalks and distant spaces. She raised her hands, frustrated, then pointed at him. Her expression, though I couldn't make out all her defining features, was angry, eyebrows tilted in, nose scrunched up.

He crossed his arms and grit his teeth, setting his jaw in a hard line.

She waved her arms around as if saying, 'Unbelievable. Why did you do that?'

He cocked his head and licked his lips, rubbed his face with an open palm. 'How would I have known?' his look seemed to say.

She patted her chest with open palms. 'You should have known.'

It was a fight over nothing. A fight over everything.

We were now in a dark room lit only by a single candle, my body positioned above hers, the two of us drenched in sweat, our heat trapped by ivory sheets.

She was a part of me. The scent of her musk filling my nose, the taste of salt in my mouth, the feel of her silky skin against mine and the brush of tangled hair across my face. We moved together, our minds focused on an elusive moment of completion, each action part of a dance which moved closer to climax, then farther, then closer yet, a spirit of trust interwoven, making each step just as rewarding. Soon the climax was no longer the objective, but a biproduct, our melding of body and mind all that mattered. A moment arrived, and the world went white with elated static.

We explored the world, the universe, together, places I had never seen or been, every moment different. There were great cities on continents surrounded by the bluest water, spires of ivory and green casting shadows on the shores. Buildings floating like fortresses upon the sulfurous clouds of Venus, life existing in a place no one ever thought possible. Forests growing in the deepest reaches of the ocean beneath domes of glass a dozen feet thick, oaks taking root in volcanic fertility never meant for a Quercus.

A thousand, thousand conversations were had and forgotten, the only words that survived were, "My rose."

Why would I say a thing like that? Why would I call Shelly, 'My rose?' It was a flower, right? Maybe? I believe we had a bush, maybe two on the *Vasco*, but my memory over that was hazy.

The dream began to fade. My time to rest had come to a close. The ship had reached cruise velocity long ago, so it was safe to move about. I woke within my Star Sphere, not the virtual space, and decided to climb out, cables disconnecting from my arms and spine as I broke the surface of the amniotic liquid.

Proxy appeared on the lip of the sphere in full, physical form.

"How far away are we from our target?" I asked, reaching for a towel to dry off.

"Three light years," Proxy replied.

I gave it a scratch behind the ear and smiled. "Still plenty of time."

"For what?" it sounded genuinely curious.

"For another good dream after I take a walk. My body's been in that hot tub for too many years."

"The Star Sphere will protect it from decay."

"I know. I just want to feel normal for a little while. Normal as I can be."

"As you wish."

It was nice to get up and stretch my legs, even if one of them was mechanical, a fact that would take some getting used to. I walked up and down the catwalk, flexing my ivory arm and articulated fingers, perusing the various machine shops and living quarters. All the time we had been on this ship, and I still had not really taken a look around. When I was the pilot, my body felt large, sure, yet no bigger than I always was, but walking down its halls and through its many rooms, I realized just how wrong that perception was. It was a goliath, and I was its pilot. If you had asked the little boy who had been woken in the middle of the night if this would be his fate, he would have thought you were crazy.

Though I had no need so long as I entered the Star Sphere again soon, I was compelled to fix something to eat. My stomach was rumbling, and I swore I could smell something savory cooking nearby, even if everyone was asleep. I made a stop at a large kitchen and dining area capable of seating hundreds, proceeding to rifle through the cabinets and fridge. In true Foundry style, it was stocked with familiar precooked foods and plenty of ingredients. Other than what little Esteban had taught me in our free time back in Cynosure, though, I had no experience cooking. I went for the fridge and searched for something premade. Nothing seemed to fulfill the craving I had.

A random childhood memory came to the surface, and in response, I could smell something sweet over my shoulder. I turned to see a red plate piled high with fried balls of cinnamon-covered dough.

"*Sonho*," I said with a Portuguese accent like Mom would use when imitating her grandparents. I plucked one of the balls from the stack and took a bite. The outside was crispy and sweet, the inside soft and fluffy.

The taste transported me back to the last Christmas I had spent on Earth. Mom, Dad, and I were over at a distant relative's house with lots of people, loud music, and a table full of food. Everyone was dancing and laughing, telling stories, eager to say *olá* to little Milo Hughes. I wondered if they, too, were now underwater. Did they survive the floods?

"How are they?" Proxy asked, hopping up on the counter.

"Who?"

"The snack."

"Oh, delicious," I replied. "But do me a favor, don't get hair on it."

"I don't shed."

"Well, isn't that great? The perfect pet."

"Does this make you miss them less?" it asked, curious.

I swallowed down my bite and sighed. "Not really. Whatever memory this is tied to is so old I can't attach much emotion. My life happened aboard the *Vasco Da Gama*, not on Earth. The child who first tasted these is like another kid who happens to live inside a corner of my head."

"Would you prefer protein cakes instead?"

"No. No. No," I protested, reaching for another *Sonho*. "I'll take these, thank you very much. It's so quiet in here."

"Yes. The Foundry ships are quiet."

"The *Vasco Da Gama* wasn't at all. It vibrated all the time. You could always hear the air circulation, the recyclers and engines. This… It's a bit weird." I sighed and plucked two more from the pile before heading off. "It's too quiet. I think I want to go back to sleep, but I'm afraid."

Proxy hopped down and walked beside me. "Afraid of what?"

"Afraid of what might happen when we reach Ph0nx."

"You have done your best to prepare, have you not?"

"I'm not so sure." I finished off my snacks and climbed the ladder down into my Star Sphere. "Maybe just a few more attempts at the simulation. Can't hurt."

Proxy nodded up at me. "As you wish, Milo Hughes. Loading program."

CHAPTER 47

Twenty-one years had passed, and I was still young. Earth was lost and aging, our original mission unfulfilled, a new mission having taken its place.

I never thought time could be such a slippery thing. All my life people had said off-handed things like, *'Time flies when you're having fun'* or *'That day dragged on and on'* in reference to how engaged or bored a person was with the events around them. As far as I knew, a second was always a second, a minute always a minute. But were they really? Were they somehow unequal, our passage of time controlled by the number of thoughts we had during a measurable period? Was this phenomenon like the quantum universe, where time only truly existed when observed? There was either time or no time. Schrödinger's cat, alive or dead.

The Star Spheres afforded us the ability to slow our metabolic rates so that our body would do less over a given period, shifting our subjective perception of time so that it seemed to move quicker. What was this perceptive change but a personal reality? Does this shift in perceptions not make it true? The ship gave us control of time in a single direction, and all the gaps between, the moments my neurons did not fire, or my heart did not pump, that my cells froze during stasis in ceasing mitosis and respiration, was there no time at all? Had those gaps been edited away like clips of raw footage not suitable for the final, feature film?

Does consciousness dictate time?

I pulled at this thread and wondered what the opposite was like. If my brain and body would allow it, could I process information quickly enough to cheat fate, to become nearly immortal? If I had infinite capacity for simultaneous thought, could I cheat death?

"The Foundry," I whispered in a moment of clarity, alone but for Proxy in my virtual space.

The cat looked up at me, then rubbed its face with the back of a paw. "You're starting to understand."

"It protects life."

"Yes, and time is running out. We must make more."

"But how is this possible?"

"I think you already know."

I gave a nod and returned my metabolic rate to that of a one-to-one setting, a normal flow of time, and when I did so, the others began to rouse from suspension. One after another they appeared in my virtual space, dressed in a motley array of clothes from James in combat fatigues, to Mary in a black and red star pilot's uniform, complete with slacks and fitted leather jacket with a futuristic emblem across the back, as well as James, Lance, and Perry with combinations of jeans and graphic t-shirts. Mary had once again changed her hair color, yet now it was a pure shade of silver instead of pink. Esteban too had affected his look, adding stripes of white to his black hair and half-trimmed crop of stubble on his chin.

"Everyone sleep okay?" I asked.

Lance raised a mug of coffee, clicking it against Perry's. "Like a baby."

"What a nap," Perry mused. "Anyone have crazy dreams? I had crazy dreams."

"A few," Esteban said, giving us a shrug. "Nothing too strange, ya? Just some trips around the world. Bit of futbol."

Mary squeezed his shoulders and smiled, a genuine expression of contentment on her face. "Just the usual. Dreaming I wasn't here, and yet thankful that I am."

I pressed my lips together and did not respond.

"Looks like we've arrived," James said, pointing to the growing star system in our navigational view. "We know what we're up against?"

"Data coming in," Proxy said. "I took the liberty of firing several veiled probes ahead of the *Fidelis* to get clear readings on the system, map out its orbits, and scan for ships."

"Very kind."

"I am here to serve."

"What's the word?" I recalled the information as it came in.

"As the earlier reports had shown, Ph0nx is a yellow star system with eleven planets. Four of which are mostly rock with either heavy atmosphere or no atmosphere at all, two hydrogen-helium gas giants, and two more with ammonia or methane as part of their atmospheric mix. Near the sun we have one planet, mostly ocean, which appears habitable."

"Is that where they were planning on taking us?" Lance asked.

"Hard to say. I would need to review in detail the various genetic modifications the Kabosai have given you."

James rolled his eyes. "Does it matter? Are they here? Are our people here?"

Proxy lowered its head in a bow. "Yes. They are here."

"Sinas?" I asked. "Its ship?"

"Yes."

I felt my heart skip a beat. This hadn't been a wild goose chase after all. The last twenty-one years and all the extensive training we had put in during our trip hadn't been for nothing. Our people were here. We could save them.

I'm coming for you, Shelly. Hold on.

"Sinas, however, is not alone," Proxy said. "There are four Kabosai ships. Two on our general trajectory approximately forty degrees against the axis. We will likely encounter them as we pass the eleventh planet. I cannot speak to their capabilities, given they are not of Foundry design, but this pair is different from the ones we have already encountered."

"How so?"

"They have a smaller signature and are far more open interior design. The shape of the asteroids used to construct them are different as well, less ovoid and more, what is the word, cigar shaped."

"Cigar?" I wondered, looking to my companions for assistance.

Esteban reached into the air and plucked a brown, paper tube from out of nowhere. He proceeded to light it with a flame that danced on the end of his finger before drawing a breath from it with his lips. He blew smoke out of his mouth and then licked his lips.

"What the hell?"

"Smoking," he supplied. "People still do it back on Earth, bad for the lungs and gums. Cancer and all."

I shook my head.

"So," Mary pointed at the crude ship signatures, "there's two enemy vessels we don't know much about. That's alarming. What about the others?"

"The transformation ships are here," Proxy said, and the room around us shifted, drawing us closer to the star at the center of the solar system. "An asteroid belt is scattered between the fourth and fifth planet. They hold station here."

"Do they know we are coming?"

"Almost certainly. Our deceleration burn is as bright as a star in its own right. It is difficult to mask such a radioactive signature when it is even visible to the naked eye."

"Fair enough," I said. "That means they have the advantage. No sense hiding."

I closed my eyes and reached into the ship's systems, extending dozens of antennas and multiband arrays.

"Sinas," I called across the system on an open channel. "Respond." A moment passed, time dialed back up to 60X to allow for lightspeed delay.

The rest of the group said nothing. I tried again. "Sinas. I know you're out there. Respond, please. Respond."

"Nothing," Proxy said after some time had passed. "No neutrino signals or transmissions on any other bands. It appears that Sinas does not want to talk to you."

"Well, let's see how it feels when we shove a battleship full of antimatter down its throat."

James patted me on the back and smiled, the first real smile I'd seen out of him in a long time. "I like this side of you, Milo."

"Always troublemakers, aren't we?"

"Always."

"To the fighters, ya?" Esteban asked, a hungry look on his grizzled face.

"Hell yeah."

My companions winked out and I was again alone with Proxy, the Star Sphere's virtual environment reconfiguring to give me a part navigational, part tactical view. Despite the tactile feedback that the ship could give me directly through my body, I enjoyed a visual interface for some of the ship's operations. After my sleepwalking episode, I had gone back into the simulations for a time and worked out what systems were best for me personally. It was time to put those to the test.

"Everyone ready?" I asked, and the fighter status indicators began to come back green.

"Ready," Mary said.

"I'm ready as a teenage boy on prom night," Perry responded, sounding perhaps a bit too excited.

"You know, little brother, that one was actually good."

Esteban cleared his throat. "Ready."

"Let's grind them up," James growled.

"Hey, Milo," Lance called just as I was settling into full interface immersion. "Don't fuck up and get us killed."

"You either," I replied, then let the ship's controls integrate fully into me.

I was no longer just in the ship. I was the ship. The ship was me.

"Here we go," I said. "I'll adjust our subjective time reference to skip us ahead until we are just a couple light seconds from the eleventh planet. You can then deploy the fighters and start giving them hell."

I ramped our subjective frame of reference up again, not accelerating the ship, but from our perspective it felt as if I had. Time whipped past at a hundred times the normal rate, more than a minute and a half passing every second. The eleventh planet began to grow in my view, the swirls of blue and purple which made up its atmosphere becoming ever clearer. The smaller, picket ships were nothing but yellow boxes floating in space to my left and right. As we changed position, so did they, moving into different orbits around the blue and purple giant until they broke free and matched our course and velocity.

Alerts went off, forcing me to slow our subjective rush through time. Fighters were swarming out of the picket ships, not just a dozen, but a hundred. I sucked in a breath and powered up the weapons.

"Oh damn," James said.

"Let's go boys and girl," Esteban called out, and our fighter wing burned ahead towards the incoming waves of enemies, the diamond-shaped crafts forming a symmetrical V.

I dug my open hands through the space beside me, gathering up the Mercurial Integumentum and holding it in my closed fists. The enemy fighters crashed onto our wing. Esteban and the rest broke formation to engage, unleashing streams of nuclear sabots to thin the swarm. There were a few lucky shots, bogeys down, but nothing more than a handful.

Lance's fighter went dead.

Mary's fighter went dead.

Though severely damaged, Perry's trudged on for a bit then winked out.

They hopped into fresh ships and rejoined the battle.

It was a challenge to keep the M.I. Barrier poised in the right position. The enemy fighters had become a swarm of wasps, stinging at me wherever there was even the tiniest opening. They began to chew through sections of the outer hull, and I felt a sensation akin to being eaten alive, a thousand tiny claws peeling at soft flesh.

I reconfigured the Para Lux array to cut in a wider band and began to lance out at the fighters, catching those careless enough to come within its reduced range. The point defense cannons worked nonstop. There were just too many of them. For every fighter we took down another three seemed to take their place.

"This isn't working," Lance said. "There's too many."

I looked for anything I could use to fight them more effectively. Our trajectory was within a few degrees of an orbital slingshot from planet ten to planet five, but how would that help? We were in the open with nothing but the M.I. to keep us alive.

Four more of our fighters went down. Esteban was the only one who had not reshipped. We had lost fifteen of our thirty-six spare fighters. If this was a battle of attrition, there was no doubt who would be the victors.

"Sections four and five have sustained severe damage," Proxy reported.

"I know," I snapped back at it. "I can feel it."

Esteban cut in, "Boss, can we keep throwing ships at them?"

"I don't see how." I powered up the rail guns and fired at one of the picket ships keeping distance. The shot went wide. I ramped up the drive and pushed towards it, and it matched speed again. Closing the distance was going to be a challenge. It was the only way I could rip them apart with what we had. "Proxy, did you say the probes you sent ahead were veiled. Does that mean cloaked? As in, undetectable?"

Proxy bowed its head. "Near to it."

"How does that work? Is there a way we can use the M.I. Barrier to function however it is the probes did to keep themselves cloaked?"

There was a pause before Proxy replied. "We have never considered this."

"Human ingenuity," I said, tapping the side of my head. "Esteban, you guys come back. I've got an idea."

"Copy that."

As the fighters returned, I drew the M.I. up against the *Fidelis*. The ship's main drive gave a flash and we pushed ahead at fifteen Gs. The nanomachines which made up the Mercurial Integumentum began to reconfigure themselves, taking on the qualities of the probes' skin, a thin composite capable of absorbing electromagnetic radiation and light. While this material was less effective at stopping incoming weapons fire, it would make us harder to detect.

The effects of this reconfiguration were almost immediate, the enemy fighters having a harder time keeping a lock on us. All they had to follow was our drive flame and the occasional sensor ping.

After several minutes, I cut the drive off and dialed down the power systems within the *Fidelis*, reducing us to a ballistic projectile several hundred meters in length. Enemy fire ceased. There was no telling how long this would last.

Subjective time was adjusted. Seconds passed for us; weeks of objective time vanished.

In freefall, we dove towards the gravity well of planet ten, allowing it to partially capture the *Fidelis* and change our trajectory, hurling us towards planet five like a spear. With what little detection equipment we could use while cloaked, I could see our distance to the picket ships was narrowing. They had chosen a similar course. They had drawn all their fighters back into their bays.

"Two hundred thousand kilometers to the enemy," James reported. "One ninety."

"Just a little more," I whispered, attempting to will the situation into our favor. "Just a little more."

"One hundred."

"Fifty-six."

"Thirty-five."

"Almost there." I balled my hands into fists and released them while taking several clarifying breaths. All we needed was to get close enough. Just one good shot.

"Fifteen thousand."

"Now, now, now!"

I threw my arms out and reinitiated the main drive, a sun coming to life in a flash. The M.I. exploded from my skin and began to reconfigure itself into more solid materials. Esteban and the rest of the wing shot out from their docks like missiles through holes in the thickening defensive barrier.

"Break formation," Esteban ordered. "Hit 'dem hard an fast."

"Don't have to tell me twice," Lance said, and he and James peeled out of the formation, taking the picket ship from the opposite side as the rest.

I powered up the Para Lux array and loaded antimatter slugs. Before the enemy could launch a single fighter, I unleashed hell. The high energy beam of the Para Lux sliced across the forward end of one of the craggy, cigar shaped ships, fusing launch bays and spine-like communications equipment and weapons hard points. When the slugs landed a few seconds later, just aft of my initial assault, the fighters rushing to take off were vaporized along with those stored beside them.

Waves of radiation were cast back towards us, sections of the M.I. going dead. Antimatter weapons weren't meant to be used this close to the enemy.

"I can't feel anything. Half my body has gone numb."

"Rerouting nanomachines for repairs," Proxy reported. "Standby."

"Fighters back up," Esteban said. "Went dead for a sec. An EMP or somethin'."

"You all okay?" I asked, checking the fleet status reports.

"Still here," James said. "A few got off. Running them down now."

Once the sensor noise had subsided, I could see the damaged picket ship was still alive, though limping. Power readings were inconsistent, heat was building up inside, fires breaking out, systems failing.

"Goodbye," I said, firing the rail guns. The hyper-accelerated slugs cut through the aft end of the ship, their transfer of energy a brilliant white flash, leaving what was left a shattered mess of red-hot, tumbling rock.

The remaining picket ship began to burn away towards Ph0nx's star, launching only a few fighters to keep Esteban and the rest busy. Our wing made quick work of the fighters then headed back within range of the *Fidelis*, keeping their lightspeed lag low.

"I have again located the transformation ships," Proxy reported. "They have begun to move away from the asteroid belt towards the center of the system."

"Are they on the same vector as the last picket ship?"

"Negative."

"Okay." I turned around and readjusted the trajectory of the *Fidelis*, plotting a course that would allow us to intercept the transformation ships. Proxy tagged the ship that Sinas was aboard.

We burned away from planet five into the asteroid belt, ramping up our acceleration to twice that of the transformation ships. The distance began to close. I checked the status of the picket ship and could see it was lagging behind our flank by several hundred thousand kilometers. We couldn't afford to take them all at once.

"Esteban, do you think you guys can take out the picket ship?"

"*Si, claro que si.* We got it."

"Range is a bit rough," Lance said.

Perry chuckled. "No harder than taking a piss while standing on the other side of the bathroom while your sister jumps out of nowhere and tries to scare you."

"Perry!" Mary shouted.

"That is not a childhood memory to share," James said.

"Childhood?" Perry mused. "Oh no. This was back on Creatus. I was—"

Lance interrupted him, "Look, all we need to know is if you pissed on the floor."

"I did not," Perry replied, his tone smug.

The fighter squad screamed away from the *Fidelis* towards the picket ship, avoiding the scattering debris from the destroyed Gene Broker vessel.

I leaned in towards the asteroid belt and began to burn, changing our trajectory so that we could thread our way through the field of rocks. The transformation ships began to burn away.

"Several contacts detected," Proxy reported as we entered the belt, a worried tone in its voice.

"What, where?"

"Mounted on asteroids. Energy weapons. Milo, defensive procedures now! They're powering up."

I closed my eyes and deployed Effulgencent Screens to cover all sides and angles of the hull. A dozen beams struck their surfaces and were deflected, though those weren't all. One cut across the aft of the ship, leaving a deep scar near a fighter bay that disabled two more of our reserves. Another bore a hole through the *Fidelis* and came out the other side.

"Damn it," I growled, summoning swarms of nanomachines to repair my burning flesh.

"That was close," Proxy said. "The last beam nearly came in contact with antimatter storage."

"At least we would have all gone out together."

"Not advisable." Proxy paused for a moment. "I have locks on the enemy turrets. They are within Para Lux range."

I powered up the arrays and began to tear the Gene Brokers' trap apart. It felt good to punch back after the pain they inflicted on me.

"Alright, they're headed for the sun," I said, vectoring the angle of our main drive to match trajectory. "Ramping up to ten Gs to intercept." The asteroid belt slipped away, the field of rocks rushing past to fall at my back.

"Incoming transmission," Proxy said. "Looks like Sinas wishes to speak now."

"It's about time."

CHAPTER 48

"Why do you fight us?" Sinas asked over an audio only communication's channel, its alien voice as cold and even as it had been on Creatus. The distance between us narrowed, and yet there was lag, several seconds from sending to Sinas receiving and sending again. Before I could make a comment on how disorienting the experience was, Proxy somehow compensated for this lag using the Star Sphere to make it seem as if we were talking in real time, face to face.

"You know the answer," I replied. "Those humans are my people. My community. My world. I care about them and their well-being."

"Is it the woman? Is that why you do this?" The line crackled for a moment as we neared Ph0nx's star. "The mating directive? We all experience it."

"Shut up," I growled, angrier at myself than Sinas. It didn't deserve to have the satisfaction of knocking me emotionally off balance. I was in control of myself. "I do come for her, but not just her."

"We must protect life," its voice echoed.

"By destroying it? I know what you did to the Jalek's people. It's abhorrent."

"The Gan?" Sinas mused. "There was no good in them. They were warlords. They found purpose only in inflicting death and suffering."

"And you destroyed them."

"We sought to give their natural genes new purpose beyond war. We protect life."

"And yet you failed. The Jalek is all that is left."

"Not true. The Jalek, it manipulates, creates falsehoods. The natural, the Gan, they did perish, but genes were repurposed. Gave birth to a hundred new species."

"Liar!"

"What purpose to lie?" Sinas asked. The transformation ships increased their acceleration. I leaned in, ramping up our drive to catch up. "We protect life."

"I'm tired of hearing this line. Shit, I'm tired of hearing it from you, I'm tired of hearing it from the Foundry. Do you truly believe the Universe is alive? That by seeding a million worlds with your, *designer species*, that you will somehow reach a divine level of enlightenment and awaken a god? Reality is what we have here and now. This place. This is reality. This!"

"You so sure? You not sometimes see beyond from within? We are travelers in our mind. You not heard the whispering voice of existence? You not have ideas and wonder where they came from, how you could think the same as someone across stars could think and at the same moment? There is something that binds us, that binds even you and I together. The Universe. It is one mind. We are a piece of it."

There was no denying that the Gene Brokers were cultists, born to a specific doctrine in which the ends justified the means. It was okay if a species was eradicated, so long as a hundred more took their place. It was okay to take those against their will and impose your own.

"Look, I get it," I said, attempting to soften my edgy voice. "We all desire to be part of something bigger, and I'm sure that's true no matter what species we're from. Call it God, call it the Universe, but coming close to that higher power is not worth the price you are paying. It's wrong. They were not given the choice."

"They took our help."

"Bait and switch," I said, recalling Gi'Vor's words about market tactics. "You didn't tell them the whole truth."

"We awaken the Universe. All will be one, and one will be all."

"Not today." The *Fidelis* was nearing the edge of weapon's range. I popped my fingers and felt the rail guns and antimatter cannons load, my arms becoming strong as if I had fists of iron to punch with. I rolled my shoulders and the M.I. shifted in tandem. "Give us back our people and we might just let you live."

"Human. You are outnumbered and outgunned."

"Hasn't stopped us yet." I charged the Para Lux array and began to mark weapons hardpoints upon the rocky, pocked surface of Sinas's transformation ship.

"Don't you wish to know where your parents are?" it asked.

I hesitated, my posture faltering for an instant. "What did you just say?"

"Your parents. Your immediate progenitors. We have information."

My teeth began to grind against one another. "Don't play games like this."

"Please, Milo Hughes, cease pursuit. In exchange, we will give you the location of your parents as well as other humans. People from Creatus are not the only ones who have traveled past the Wandering Gate."

"What is it talking about?" Mary cut in.

"It's like I said back at the data node," I replied, not broadcasting my words back to Sinas. "There are transports with humans."

"But how?" Lance asked.

"I don't know."

"*Hermano*," Esteban said, his tone regretful. "I—I don' know what—"

I shook my head and increased our acceleration. "It doesn't matter," I told them. "It's like you all said at one time or another, you and the people of Creatus are my family. I can't let them win."

Sinas severed the communications channel, my sudden silence taken as an answer.

Esteban and the rest of our wing reached the remaining picket ship and engaged the enemy fighters. I readjusted the M.I. and began to shield us from a hail of explosive projectiles launched from the transformation ships, Ph0nx's star just over its edge a few million kilometers ahead. The barrier went white-hot as the nanomachines gave their short lives to keep us from being ripped apart by hundreds of thermonuclear reactions.

My interface blinked red as thirty-two fighters shot from the jagged mouths of the transformation ships and started heading straight for us. They came from multiple vectors, from the left and right, above and below, making it ever more difficult to manage the M.I.

"I'm going to neutralize the weapons," I told the rest. "Soon as I do, we'll need a distraction to get you in."

"Milo," Proxy said, rubbing against my leg.

"Yes?"

"The transformation ships are altering course. The trajectory of one is aimed out past the star, towards no destination I can determine. Sinas's ship is making for the star itself."

"What?"

"Go for Sinas's ship," Lance said over the channel. "That's the ship that was over Creatus, I recognize it. The other one is the wrong shape."

"We let the other one go?" Perry asked. "Scot free?"

"I don't have any way to stop both," I replied. "Vote?"

"Sinas's ship," James said.

"Same," Esteban replied.

"Sinas," Mary added.

"Okay," I said, swallowing down my fears. Fifty-fifty odds. I hoped we were right. "We are going to board Sinas's ship. Initiating maximum acceleration. This is going to get pretty hairy."

As the *Fidelis* ramped up its main drive, the enemy fighters fell behind. For as quick as they were, I was amazed to see that this golden skyscraper of a ship could accelerate faster than them. The second transformation ship began to fall out of effective range, and I was left with only Sinas's vessel firing at us. The craggy black ball flashed again and again as additional projectiles were hurled against the M.I. From this approach vector, there was little Sinas could do to get around our defenses, though at the rate the nanomachines were vaporizing under the assault, I began to wonder if the leader of the Gene Brokers might win the long game.

Holes began to appear in the M.I. barrier, letting the occasional missile pass through. They struck along my belly and back, sending cascades of pain throughout my body, tactile feedback reporting severe damage. Staying ahead of the fighters or not, Sinas was tearing me apart.

Why not overwhelm us with both of the ships? Something wasn't right.

A lance of energy cut its way from fore to aft, snapping one of the shards at the *Fidelis's* prow, leaving a furrow along the hull, tanks of compressed noble gasses hissing and pushing me the slightest bit off course. I compensated and began to fire back blind, casting beams of Para Lux energy into the black ahead, hoping to intercept some of Sinas's assault.

Two more minutes and I would be close enough to melt some of its weapons' hardpoints, and hopefully neutralize it for a time.

"Almost in position," I told everyone. "We need a distraction, and quick."

"Ideas?" Perry asked. "I don't think my jokes are going to do the trick."

"I would advise burning away from the enemy ship," Proxy reported. "We have sustained heavy damage to the secondary power systems. Environmental controls in four out of six sections are inoperable. Nano vats five, seven, and nine are not responding. This will slow our regeneration of the Mercurial Integumentum drastically."

There had to be something we could do. If I fired antimatter weapons this close, we would no doubt disable the enemy, but we would be taken down as well. The thermo nuclear pellets would do little more than pepper the face of the rock. I could fire the rail guns and crack them open, but we still had friends inside.

Sinas did not waste this opportunity, the enemy ship pelting me with spreads rather than heavy concentrations of the explosive projectiles.

"L5 antimatter cannon is offline," Proxy reported. "Nuclear pellet storage leaking radiation into interior."

Options were running out.

"Wait!" I shouted, an idea rising from the murk of chaos. "Didn't you tell us about some sort of bombs when we first got the ship. Piezo electric E.M.P.s. Would they do anything at all?"

"Piezo electric bombs are better against munitions and smaller craft which are not as well shielded."

"How many do we have? What if we use all of them?"

Proxy considered this, its feline head cocking. "They might neutralize the systems of the Kabosai ship for a short period of time. No more than a few minutes."

"Loading now," I turned to check on Esteban and the rest of the squad. "Do you guys have a plan?"

"Got the picket thinkin' we all still in fighters," Esteban said. "Daisy chained Lance and James's ships to follow us. Locks good, ya?"

"They'll never know," Mary added. "We are in formation."

"Milo," Lance cut in. "I need you to slow acceleration so James and I can get to the powered armor and prep the shuttle."

The *Fidelis* rocked. My eyes closed, the pain overtaking me for an instant.

I felt blood ooze from my left arm, pneumatic fluids leaking from servos on the lateral Para Lux array. I ran my fingertips through the expanding crimson blot. I knew it wasn't real, but it didn't feel that way.

"I—um—", I said, fighting to shake the experience off. "That will leave us open to the fighters."

"Sorry, but I doubt the human body will survive forty Gs outside the sphere."

"Dropping speed. Move quick."

"Didn't plan on dragging ass and stopping off for lunch on the way."

I watched James and Lance scurry through the ship in a pair of pop-up displays, taking routes which avoided the sections that had been damaged to the point that atmospheric compression was impossible. The enemy fighters drew close, beginning to fire again. As soon as they were within range, I activated the point defense system and began to take pot shots with the Para Lux array. We were in a bad position, caught between Sinas's barrage and the fighters.

"We're in the shuttle, suited up," Lance reported. "It's time."

The *Fidelis* turned at an oblique angle against the transformation ship and our entire stock of the crystalline, piezo electric bombs were launched. The fighters immediately turned, attempting to burn away, but it was too late. The collection of milky shards began to compress, micro-hyperspatial singularities collapsing pockets of spacetime at their cores. As the crystals squeezed into these miniature black holes, the pressure forced their molecular lattices to release wave after wave of electromagnetic radiation. I placed the M.I. barrier between us and the enemy, making it as thick as I could despite all the attacks.

The twinkling lights of the drives on the enemy fighters winked out, the electromagnetic pulses temporarily disrupting all of their systems. The waves of energy persisted, striking the transformation ship and doing the same. Power readings from Sinas's ship disappeared as if we had flicked a light switch. Even the fusion reaction at the core of the asteroid had ceased.

"Go! Go! Go!" I told Lance.

The shuttle rocketed out of its bay towards the open maw of the transformation ship, no one the wiser but for us. They entered the opening less than a minute later and found a place to land.

"We're on board," Lance reported. *"Searching for our people."*

James took a series of deep breaths. *"You should see it in here. This isn't like anything I've ever seen. It's like the machines they had in Creatus, sort of, tubes and pipes and everything inside organic. I swear some of the machines are made out of, well, organs."*

"No time for sightseeing. Their power is coming back up. Lights are flickering."

"Find a console," I said. "Let Proxy help you."

"Headed for one now."

As power was restored to the transformation ship, some but not all of the enemy fighters powered back up. I took the opportunity to eliminate as many as possible, firing antimatter slugs towards those at range, as well as slicing those nearby with energy weapons.

"The picket ship is coming back around, *amigo*," Esteban reported.

"Damn," I growled and began to redistribute the M.I. barrier. "Can't we catch a break."

"The transformation ship's reactor is back online," Proxy said. "Their drive has reinitiated, though they are burning slow."

"Okay. We need to figure out—"

The power aboard the *Fidelis* shuttered and nearly winked out. The M.I. grid collapsed, its mass becoming grains of black dust scattering in space. My connection to the virtual space became hazy for a moment, perception flashing in and out of the amniotic tank, then reconstituted. As systems came back online, I felt my body on fire.

"What was that?" I asked Proxy, my voice husky.

"Our secondary reactor was hit. I have redirected power, but we must make repairs. With the loss of several nanovats we cannot keep up with this level of assault. We need to run."

"We can't."

"Then we will die."

"I'm not abandoning them after we've come this far." I closed my eyes and searched my heart for something, anything to push me through this moment. My resolve was holding on by a thread. I was afraid. I didn't want to die, but I saw no way out but through. "How are we doing, Lance?"

"So far they haven't tried to stop us. Only seen a few of the Gene Brokers roaming the halls, and those avoided us. We found a console and are hacking in."

Before I could gather the M.I. barrier up, the *Fidelis* took another heavy blow. One side of my body went numb.

"Wait. What the hell?" Lance called in. *"There's no one here. Not a damn person. Shit, not even that many Kabosai. Fifteen maybe?"*

"What?" I stared off into space. "How is that possible? The ship is huge. Where are they?"

"Looks like our people were here at some time, maybe, but there's been a swap. Slug faces made a swap."

"What are you saying?"

"The other ship has our people and most of this ship's crew, the one burning like hell to get out of this system."

"Bunch of cowards," James added. *"We've got to go after them."*

"Fuck," I spat, balling my hands into fists, screaming within my mind. In a fit of anger, I unleashed a barrage of antimatter slugs in the general direction of the incoming enemy fighters. There came a flash of white light and static. Half were vaporized.

Sinas's weapons came back to life, hardpoints for the explosive turrets recalibrating and focusing on us, on me.

"Those bastards! Those fucking bastards are going to—"

CHAPTER 49

The *Fidelis* began to reboot. Whatever it was that hit us had taken several primary systems offline. Three of the five redundant data processing cores were fused into blocks of gold and copper and metallic hydrogen, transistors and control pathways destroyed. I was heavy on one side of my body, as if someone had tied a series of free weights to one hip and asked me to race towards a finish line.

"Lance," I called over our open channel. "Get out."

"Already headed that way. We've got resistance."

"Nothing we can't handle," James added. *"Give us one minute."*

"We might not have a minute. I'm powering up what weapons we have left." I reached for the rail guns and antimatter cannons, channeling energy and ammunition into place.

In the distance, Esteban and Mary's fighters cracked apart and exploded. They reshipped and headed back out, no more reserve fighters to take on the picket ship. The ship that had our people.

"Are you holding?" I asked but knew the answer. None of us were holding. The lines were broken, we were scattered, the enemy had their blade to our throat, waiting for the moment to thrust the tiniest little bit and end it all.

"Take that bastard down," Mary said, and her fighter screamed ahead of Esteban's. They met the last of the oncoming fighters, spinning and twisting, cutting ribbons of ions with their drives, angrily tearing into the enemy ranks.

There were too many. No matter how ready they were to fight, they would be overcome.

The *Fidelis* rocked from end to end, Sinas having hit us with something hard, a rail gun blast or shockwave reaction. Several more warning alarms went off. I seemed to have collected the whole set. I gathered up what was left of the M.I. and placed it before us to catch the blows that followed. It felt as if the Gene Broker himself were standing over my kneeling body, relentlessly assaulting me, pieces of my skin scraping off with each impact.

I had had enough.

The M.I. broke for a moment as I spread my arms wide. I hurled one projectile after the next at the heart of the transformation ship. One rail gun shot landed just north of the maw, cracking the asteroid down the side, casting black rock and superheated metal into the void. Another landed near the opposite end, burrowing into a collection of obsidian spires, a wave of heat from the impact traveling along its surface in every direction, scouring the exterior features away, leaving it smooth and glossy.

Sinas's weapons flashed. I raised my arms again in defense and felt myself physically pushed back as if my feet were anchored in sand and a force were pressing down on me.

To my right, the star of Ph0nx burned bright, flares of solar energy lancing out into space, E.M. interference scrambling already-damaged systems. I felt myself lean to the side as if ducking a punch and went to Sinas's belly, a left hook, then a right, flashes of antimatter energy igniting on the underside of the transformation ship.

My left shoulder was struck and part of it shattered, debris scattering away.

I did not stop fighting.

I transferred every bit of power I could to the main weapons. Recharging the rail cannons and striking again. More of the transformation ship cracked. The M.I. began to scatter. The last of Esteban, Mary, and Perry's fighters went dead. Something struck me in the left ribs, and I looked briefly to see the remains of a Kabosai fighter jammed into me like a curved shiv.

"Enough!" I screamed and let loose my last volley. A coordinated strike of rail gun shots and antimatter slugs tore the front end of the transformation ship off as if I had taken hold of its mouth and snapped its jaw back.

"Power readings are fading," Proxy reported, a hint of relief in its voice. "The transformation ship is down."

I put my head in my hands and let out a sigh. "Is it over?"

Our reactor was having trouble keeping up with the power demands of the repairing nanomachines. A thousand systems were broken or destroyed, and with all the noise over the internal data network, it was hard to tell what needed priority. My extended body was bleeding, and I was the only doctor it had.

"Milo!" Mary said, her voice uncertain. "Come quick. Please, come quick."

I left my virtual space for the first time and followed her thread back to where she was within the network. The trip was clunky and indirect, as I was forced to route through several systems not designed for this sort of traffic.

I appeared in Esteban's virtual space and knelt beside his floating body. It took a moment to realize what was going on, and I again felt the pain of the enemy fighter who had stuck me in the side.

Esteban's Star Sphere was located at the impact site.

The external cameras gave me a view of the damage to the ship and how it extended deep within me, Esteban's sphere cracked, a carbon nanofiber strut having stuck it through the middle yet somehow not having shattered it. The strut pierced his chest just above the sternum, blood oozing from around the wound, the water within the sphere turning ever more crimson.

"Esteban," I whispered, returning my attention to his virtual space, my bottom lip trembling. "You can't die on us."

He gave me a warm smile. "You make it fine without me, ya? Big kid, all grown up. I'm gettin' old. Kind of slow."

"No." I shook my head. "You're the brother I never had. You are my family. I can't get on without you."

"I'm not the only family. Never alone, Milo." He coughed, letting go of my hand and clasping his chest. "Never alone. None of us are never alone."

"Esteban," Mary said, taking him in her arms. It was strange to see this great, muscular man held by such a small woman. They met each other's eyes. "You gave me life."

He reached up and brushed back her silver hair. "My rose," he said, that tone so familiar. "My rose..." His eyes fell shut.

A wave of realization washed over me. The dream I had had during our journey wasn't a dream at all. In fact, it wasn't even mine. It was theirs. I should have noticed that they had aged in subtle ways since we departed, the streaks of grey, a few wrinkled lines even within our virtual projections. They had used this time to live a life with one another while they could, before facing our uncertain fate. They had chosen love, in all its good and bad, and had found happiness in the end. What else could any of us want?

Esteban vanished from the virtual space and Mary fell onto her knees. Perry went to his sister's side and wrapped her up in his arms as she sobbed.

The virtual space flickered and buzzed, the ship's network having a hard time keeping up with our collective bandwidth.

"Sinas is powering back up," Proxy reported.

My jaw went slack. "What? That's not possible."

"Minimal power. Forward projectile cannons. Milo, you need to raise the Mer—"

CHAPTER 50

I opened my eyes to find myself suspended in the Star Sphere, tubes and wires snaked into connection points along my spine and arms. From beyond the curve and distortion of the liquid and glass, I could see explosions up and down the interior of the ship, coruscating flashes of red and orange and white. We were dying, not me. We. The *Fidelis* was no longer a body, it was a giant lump of metal lost in space.

With the atmosphere pumped out of the ship I was trapped in the sphere, breathing what oxygen was left in the pressurized tubes. I had no idea how long this would last without power.

We had burned through the Wandering Gate and fought against unspeakable odds, and they had won. They had tricked us into going for the easy target and escaped with their prize. I could only imagine the smug look on Sinas's face as he fired one last time. They had once again *'protected life'* by snuffing out a group of weary travelers looking for help. That's all we'd ever been. A genetic soup. We had left Earth hoping to find a way to save it, to treat the systemic sickness that was overtaking the cradle of humanity, and in the end all we were given was hardship and death in kind. It was no wonder God had left us behind to fend for ourselves. As a whole, we weren't worth the trouble.

I swam to the edge of the Star Sphere and pressed my forehead against the glass. It was cold, and soon the water I floated within would be too. No more amniotic bliss, just a shivering, unremarkable death.

I don't know if there's anything truly out there, I thought. *But if there is a higher power, God, Universe, whoever or whatever you may be, I could use some help. I don't want to die here if it serves no purpose. At least give me the strength to save the ones I love. I want my life to have meaning.*

The tank burbled and I floated in place, waiting. No response came from on high, not that I had expected any. I shivered, the liquid frigid. The air in my respirator became thin, the line's residual pressure running out. My heart rate slowed. Maybe I was thankful that the water could hide my tears. Who knew you could cry while submerged?

We failed.

We failed.

We failed.

The enemy had been too great for us to overtake. Now everyone who had been on Creatus would meet a dark fate at the hands of those manipulating monsters. They would have their bodies twisted and turned, their genes extracted and resequenced, their lives not just lost, but dismantled. This cast my mind with a profound sadness, but what regrets could I have? We had tried. We had been given one of the most powerful ships in the galaxy and it wasn't enough. That wasn't our fault.

What kind of life would Shelly and I have lived if this hadn't happened? Would we have had children? We were not genetic matches, scientifically destined to be with one another, but did any of that matter now? What did a perfect life look like beyond the Wandering Gate? Beyond the knowledge of the Foundry? No white picket fence. No perfect lawn or homeowners association. Pretty sure a perfect life would be having her in it, and she had been for a time, and that would have to be enough. I had to believe it was enough for Esteban and Mary, for Mom and Dad.

I watched the star of Ph0nx burn through a gap in the shattered hull of the *Fidelis*. The glass of the Star Sphere gave my eyes just enough protection to look almost directly at it. It was bright and beautiful, full of energy, a life-giving font of heat and change. Incandescent flares gathered and leapfrogged across its surface, electromagnetic fields containing raw, natural fusion.

My right hand began to tingle. I lifted it up and saw the skin of my mechanical arm glow. Power was feeding into it from somewhere. I reached out in front of myself and felt the electromagnetic field of the star.

It's not possible, I thought, then closed my eyes and reached out with my mind.

In the corner of my thoughts, like a flashlight with a dying battery kicked under a dusty old desk, I could see a flicker of light, a flicker of wistful energy. I approached the source on my digital hands and knees, crawling till I could slide my arm through a narrow gap in the network.

I took hold of this hope, and my entire body began to tingle, power returning to the Star Sphere, respiration activating again, my breathing coming under control. Awareness, though weak, began to flood back into me. I could feel subsystems coming back online, a trickle of power all that was needed to become aware again.

"There has to be more," I reassured myself, and searched every unmarked door, every dark hallway.

Just as I found the reactor controls and began to bring it back online, I was thrown back into the Star Sphere, nothing but life support still active. There wasn't enough power to get us jumpstarted again. All this side quest had achieved was give me an awareness that the *Fidelis* was not dead in space, but rather freefalling into the star. Two days, and we would reach temperatures that would begin to melt the outer hull, that is if I didn't freeze to death within the sphere first.

"We're dead," I said, breaking in and out of my virtual space. "Proxy?"

No response.

My muscles ached and my heart felt as if it might give out any moment. The vital signs report showed my blood pressure dropping as my heart rate increased. I couldn't feel my toes.

I flexed my fingers, hoping to will them back, and felt something on the exterior of the ship move. Out of nowhere, one of my earliest memories surfaced, its true meaning overtaking my thoughts.

"Milo, have you ever dreamed of touching stars?"

And then there was Mom, sitting before me, speaking with her warmest voice, holding my hands and leaning close, our noses almost touching. We were in the kitchen of our house back on Earth. Ferdie was rubbing against my leg. Mom's dark eyes were wide and glossy, the skin around the edges red with fatigue. Dad stood behind her with his arms crossed, a smile on his face.

Something was different. The memory had changed. What had once been a source of anger and resentment was now, well… I think I understood. I think I knew now why they did it.

"Have I ever dreamed of touching stars?" I mused, reaching my mechanical right hand towards Ph0nx's star. To my surprise, the damaged array the ship had deployed during our interstellar journey began to spread wide in response, its cracked and shattered crystalline panels unfolding along the *Fidelis* like a blossom come late in the season.

"I can touch it. I can touch stars."

My hand covered the light of the star, fingers wrapping around it. I now held it in the palm of my hand, a billion years of solar, nuclear energy—and more. I wasn't burned, but was energized, exhilarating tingles traveling all along my nervous system, a million thoughts, existence itself, passing through my mind. My soul was elevated, taken from my physical form and placed on another plane of reality. Everything was clear. I could see beyond the galactic horizon of time itself. I could hear the voice of the Universe speak to me, coaxing back to life parts of my extended body I thought dead.

"I made your dream true," I mumbled.

Radiation and light from the star flowed through the busted blossoms of the *Fidelis* into critical systems, repair routines kicking in, tiny machines furiously working to rebuild with what materials they could salvage. My body, my real body, became weak and weary. The star became hazy in my natural vision, focus fading.

"No," I said, holding onto the star as long as I could, the warmth, the awareness. The Foundry. The Universe. In that instant, I understood everything. It was alive. We were it. It was us. "No. Don't. It's not—It's not time. It can't be."

Perceptions faded to black, Ph0nx slipping from my tenuous grasp.

I had reached out and touched the face of creation.

I had lived a good life.

It was time for me to surrender to darkness for good.

Time for me to become part of the All.

CHAPTER 51

Nose to nose, cheek to cheek, the whiskers of a black and white cat with an orange stripe tickled my skin. It sent shivers down my face into my spine. Feeling began to return to my arms and legs, awareness trickling back into my mind one byte at a time. Was I alive, or was I dead? It was hard to say.

"Milo? Can you hear me?" the synthetic feline asked, and I opened my eyes. It stood inches before me; head cocked to the side.

"Did I finally die?" I asked. "Is this the afterlife?"

"Afterlife?" Proxy mused. "In a sense, perhaps it is. The life you once lived is over, knowledge and experience having forged a different path."

I roused myself into a sitting position. I was back within my virtual space, stars surrounding me in an endless sphere. "Way to get philosophical, Proxy."

It gave me the equivalent of a shrug. If a cat could shrug.

"Where are we? Is everyone okay?"

"Other than Mr. Lopez." There was a pause. "Yes, everyone is safe and alive. It took quite some time to repair the ship, we sustained damage to ninety two percent of all systems. We are now en route to 75-DFX."

"What? Why? 75-DFX? Did I order this?"

"No."

"Then why?"

"After you were able to jumpstart the *Fidelis's* drive with the battered solar collection array, I awoke to find the lot of you having succumbed to exhaustion. Knowing the mission you desired to execute, I placed each of you in a medical stasis till your bodies could repair themselves. Tracking down the transformation ship was not hard. They had made no attempts to cloak their escape. Once we were able, we burned for many years, attempting to close the distance between us."

"And?" I leaned forward. "What happened?"

"It was clear that the range between us and them in interstellar space left certain capabilities up to imagination. You have to understand, by the time you made your final assault against Sinas's transformation ship, the *Fidelis* was holding on by a thread. You had taken it to its designated combat limits and pushed beyond. It is quite remarkable, to be honest."

I shook my head. "Where are our people?"

"The transformation ship has broken away, changed course and I have let it go. Before you worry, it let loose a large section of its ship and cast it off into the void. Seems that the Kabosai had had their fill of the *Fidelis* and its capabilities. The section that was ejected had the thermal signatures of hyper suspension chambers."

"Shelly and the rest of our people," I hissed.

"Yes. However, they were intercepted by another craft before we had the opportunity. You do not need to worry. They were no Kabosai. A Melcorin explorer ship, as it seems, had been tracking our progress for many years. Their ship designs make them nearly impossible to find, shadows in the dark. We would have missed them, except during the capture of the hyper suspension pods, they gave off a familiar energy pulse."

"Melcorin? Who are they? Do they have our people?"

"The Melcorin are peaceful. I have contacted them, and they are taking your people somewhere safe. They are ahead of us by about one and a half light years."

"So they have our people?"

"They do. From past experiences with the Melcorin, I see no reason to distrust them. They are dedicated to the Foundry's mission."

"To protect life," I mumbled.

Proxy made the approximation of a smile. "Yes. Protect life." The expression made me uneasy. It was not natural.

"Why take them to this system?" I asked. "What planet are they bound for?"

"They take them here so they will not be alone."

"What does that mean?"

"Humans are already living there."

My jaw went slack, heart giving a start. "Wake the others. We have a date with destiny."

Mary, Perry, Lance, and James woke from their medical suspension and I brought them up to speed. We discussed Esteban and what had happened, both laughing and crying in almost equal measure. As malleable as the Star Spheres made reality seem, it was hard to believe he was gone and not just trapped somewhere on the network. My brother deserved a proper memorial, and we would give it to him when the time was right. Proxy had been able to preserve his body for that time. We would honor a true hero, our family.

Each of us made the decision to increase our subjective frame of reference. We wanted to reach our destination sooner, rather than later. Time rushed past, stars and nebulae and black holes, stellar anomalies and collections of cosmic radiation, shifting by degrees until we were falling into orbit around a blue and green world one and a half times the size of Earth. There came radio and neutrino chatter from the surface, a sign of active intelligent life. If this were not enough proof that familiar life was near, a massive, golden starship greeted us from orbit. One similar to my own.

"It's a Foundry ship," I said, inspecting its diamond shape from prow to stern. "Who are its pilots?"

"They are on the surface," Proxy replied. "Would you like to go and say hello?"

"Does a cat have an ass?"

Proxy twisted its body so it could check.

I placed the *Fidelis* in a stable low orbit and exited my virtual space, dressing as I left the Star Sphere in fresh jeans, grey t-shirt and a black, military style jacket. The others met me at the shuttle bay, and we headed down, leaving Proxy to care for the ship in our absence. This world dwarfed Creatus, the only rock bigger than Cynosure I had ever set foot on, its scale dizzying.

The shuttle hit the edge of the atmosphere and began to burn bright red, a falling star shooting its way through a thick expanse of puffy, white clouds.

We were jostled around in our acceleration chairs, my fingers digging into the arms, my teeth gritted. After being in the Star Sphere for so many years, it felt strange to be a frail little human again, my life at the mercy of a few air foils and a pair of liquid fueled engines.

At the edge of the horizon, there was a settlement of some kind, with squat, grey-and-white buildings of smooth stone, no more than a floor or two spread out for miles in a lush valley of green grass and tree analogs. I ordered the shuttle to put us down at the edge of town near the foot of a mountain, where scree met level footing.

The shuttle came to rest and we hiked towards the settlement just over the grassy knoll. Humans were gathered at the crest waiting for us. Among them were faces I had never seen in all my life. Their features were different, many lighter skinned or with deeper hoods on their eyes than what I was used to, but there they were. *Human.*

"Good to see other people," Lance said first, tipping his head back in thought. "Starting to believe we were the only humans ever made."

"Hi?" James added, waving a hand at the crowd. "We come in peace?"

"Pleased to meet you!" Perry ran up to the nearest person and took hold of their hand. "Name's Perry Stablecamp. Engineer. Therapist. Part-time aspiring comedian."

"Don't believe him," Mary said, letting out a sigh.

It was strange to see human faces I did not recognize. These truly were other people. Where did they come from? How did they get here? From the look of the settlement, they had been here a while. Built a city.

"You guys ever hear about the one where oxygen and magnesium got together?" Perry asked, then paused, allowing the stunned crowd to soak up his words. "O.M.G."

"See?" His sister gave him a smirk and squeezed his shoulders. The crowd did not respond. They were dumbstruck.

"Who are you?" a woman just a few years older than me with long, black hair asked. She had severe facial features, a sharp jaw and hawkish brown eyes, but was pretty in a hard sort of way. As she worked her way through the growing crowd, I could see that her left arm was mechanical just like mine. I had a good feeling that beneath her pants I'd find one of her legs was just the same. "You're human."

"So are you," I said.

"Is that, a *donation*?" she asked, fiddling with a collection of silver bracelets on her arm.

"Yes."

"Wow," she ran fingers through her hair and let out a chuckle. "Proxy said another Foundry ship had entered the system, and one with humans. I thought maybe there was a malfunction, ya know? Two ships in just a few months of each other is a lot of traffic out here in bum freak nowhere."

"Two ships?"

"Yes. You and the Melcorin."

My heart thundered in my chest at their mention. "Are you from the fleet?" I offered my mechanical right hand in greeting.

She smiled and took it, shaking so vigorously the bracelets on her arm jingled like a ring of keys. "We're from *the Brilliance*."

"*Vasco Da Gama*."

"Holy shit." She covered her mouth with both her hands. "No lie? This is perfect. Oh, man. This is perfect."

"The Melcorin brought our people here?"

"Yes. Oh, hell yes. The Melcorin are good people. Explorers. Egalitarian. Post-war thinkers."

"My Proxy told me about them."

"*Your* Proxy. How interesting. Yeah, yeah, turns out not every species is made up of dicks." She pointed to the clear, blue sky. "You and I have a lot to talk about. We are the only human ship captains here, after all. And while this place is pretty amazing, there are still some serious concerns out there."

"The Gene Brokers?"

She nodded. "Kabosai, yeah, we've had our brushes with them, but that's not all. Heard you guys crossed the Isoptera."

"That we did."

"Bastards are hell-bent on turning humans into cattle. Don't make for good company either, had one as a guest for a few days."

"You what?"

She shook her head. "Don't you worry your pretty little head about it."

"Is that why you guys didn't turn back to Earth after getting your ship from the Foundry? The Isoptera?"

"What? No. No. No." She shook a hand. "Long story. I hate to say it, but there's even worse things out there than the Gene Brokers or Isoptera. We decided we couldn't risk leading certain elements back to Earth, at least not yet. Besides… don't exactly know where Earth is. Big galaxy out there, and the Foundry isn't being loose lipped about it."

"We have to go back one day," Mary said. "We have to. We owe it to them."

The other ship captain pointed at Mary. "Oh, you're right, sister, and we intend on it. Most of us at least. We just have some things that need doing first."

"Like what?" Mary gave me a questioning look.

Lance shook his head and massaged his arm. "I don't think I want worse."

"Later! Later!" the ship captain said. "We have plenty of time for all that. Shit, how long's it been for you guys since you first reached the Foundry? Subjective time that is."

"Five or six years."

"Damn. Such babies." She gave a wink. "Oh! By the way, I'm Karianna Torlen."

"Milo Hughes," I said. "This is Mary Stablecamp, Lance Brittan, and James Reed. The loud one on the end…"

"Perry," she ventured, sticking out her bottom lip. "Yeah. I've heard about him. Hard to miss."

"You have?" he gave an approving smile. "See? I'm famous here already."

"No offense, bruh, but the head gear thing makes you stand out pretty good." She paused for a moment, then slapped me on the back with her mechanical arm, knocking the wind out of me. "Wait a second, Hughes. No freakin' way. Damn, this is going to be such a great day. Come on. This way. Hurry!" She gave a flourish of her hand and bowed. "By the way… Welcome to Novae. A place of starting over."

She led us through the settlement, its streets hemmed with white brick buildings, the space busier with humans than any place I had seen in all my life. Between the people of the *Brilliance, Star Stream,* and *Vasco Da Gama,* there were hundreds of people milling about, from people my age to elderly. Some were working with electronics or sewing clothes, others cooked over pots or tossed bits of savory meat around in oil filled pans. There was even a section with people trading objects they had found on this world, alien things made of colorful materials. Music found its way out of several homes, deep rhythms that changed the way I walked so long as I heard them. Was this what early human life had been like? Novae was so much more than Creatus. This was a city, bustling with life and culture, not just a camp. Hell, even my implants found an active network, AR integration and data ports awaiting commands, even if they were a little buggy.

We hit the edge of the main drag where a brick building stood several stories high. Karianna led us through a set of automated doors into a well-lit hallway and down a series of steps. The air cooled as we descended into what appeared to be an underground meeting place, an ovoid room painted in stripes with hundreds of chairs that lined the room's edge, all facing a central podium. At this time, the assembly space was near empty, except for one or two people.

"Milo!" Shelly leapt over a row of chairs to meet me. She took hold of my face and kissed me on the lips, pushing me back against the nearest wall more on accident than purpose. "You're alive."

"This knocking me down thing is becoming a habit," I said, chuckling.

She pressed her lips against me once more and I swore I heard Perry making wooing noises at my back. My feet went numb, but this time, it was for a good reason.

Karianna waved a hand and the rest of the group peeled away, leaving Shelly and I alone.

"What happened to your arm?" She caressed the skin of my prosthetic. "It's like Captain Torlen's. It was the Foundry, wasn't it?"

"It was."

"Did it hurt?"

"No. Neither did my leg."

"Oh, Milo."

"I missed you," I said, and we held one another tight, not wanting to let go. This was real. Really real. "When we left the colony for the data node, I didn't think that—If I could have stopped—"

She put a finger to my lips. "It wasn't your fault. You warned us. We believed their lies."

"I—I love you," I whispered in her ear, my heart aching as I said it.

"I know," she replied. "I love you too."

We kissed again, just to be sure.

"So, you have a ship now, like Karianna?" she asked, her head against my chest.

I nodded. "The *Fidelis*. We came to rescue you and the rest of the crew, well, colonists."

"Of course you did."

"We did not succeed, not really."

"We're still alive."

"No thanks to us. The Melcorin found you."

"And we're thankful for that. Milo, it was terrifying, those last few moments before we were unconscious. I didn't know what was happening, but something told me we were dead."

"The camp was so quiet when we went back."

"You're here," she whispered. "You're alive."

I sniffled, then swallowed. "I'm alive. You're alive."

"I'm not the only one."

"What? What do you mean?"

She gently pushed away, moving us to arm's length. "I have to tell you something though."

The tone of her voice made my heart catch. "What?"

She shifted her attention, and I followed her gaze, spotting a man and woman in their mid-sixties working their way down a set of stairs at the back of the meeting hall. It took me a while for my eyes to adjust, for me to realize just what and who I was looking at. Then it hit me, and I felt my body go weak.

"Mom? Dad?" I said, and they smiled back.

The two of them rushed over and squeezed me between themselves like cheese in a sandwich.

"I'm so sorry," I said, words hard to vocalized as choked up as I was.

"So are we," they replied. "So are we."

Mom wiped the tears from under my eyes with the back of her hand. My parents were clean and healthy, nothing like what I had seen in my vision at the data node. They were older than the last time I had seen them by a good many years, but that didn't matter. A few wrinkles and streaks of grey did not diminish their strength.

"We heard what happened at the Foundry and Cynosure," Mom said.

"So much has happened since then."

"I'm sure, and we're so proud of you, *meu lindinho filho.*"

I smiled at the two of them. "I don't think I turned out to be anything you wanted me to be."

"No," Dad said, a glint of moisture in his eyes. "You became something more." He fished in his pocket and recovered a silver pin of a dog in a space suit with floppy ears, just like the one I had seen Captain Williams wear. Dad pinned the Silver Snoopy to the lapel of my jacket and brushed it with his fingers. "Looks good there."

My heart skipped a beat.

"Hey-o!" Karianna howled, jumping into the middle of our little gathering. "No tears but tears of joy on Novae. We live in the land of second chances, new lives. We made it here through good and bad. Only one way but forward, that's the motto here."

I took Shelly's hand and gave my parents a nod. "No way but forward."

"Forward," they agreed, and as a group we made our way up the stairs within the meeting hall into the light of our new sun.

Music spilled out onto the hillside, a stereo turned up loud. People were laughing outside a row of bone-white homes, cups in their hands, talking to a collection of squat, blue-skinned bi-peds with leathery, flat-topped sections of flesh shaped like dinner plates sitting atop round heads. Melcorin. The rescuers.

"Will we go back?" I asked Mom.

She nodded. "We have to, they need us. But not today."

Dad agreed, "Not today."

Mom and Dad walked on my left through the city, Shelly to my right. I had dreamed of being here, but had not believed it would actually come to pass. I had started to believe that hope was for fools and politicians, religious leaders and idealists, but maybe, just maybe, the Universe wasn't done with me. The fleet of human explorers set to make contact with the Foundry had suffered through extraordinary times, and we had endured. Through fire and pain, we had reached for something higher and asked for help. It had responded only with, *not yet*. All was not hopeless, and there was much to prove.

I paused and Mom and Dad went ahead, Shelly running up beside them to answer some question. A cool wind rushed over me, rustling the grass at my feet, pushing my hair back, air smelling of bread and flowers. My arms blossomed with goosebumps.

Karianna stepped up beside me, her eyes fixed on the sky, a thoughtful smile on her face.

I turned to the ship captain. "I have a question."

"Yeah?"

"You said there are worse things out here than Gene Brokers."

"I did."

"What are they?"

She sighed and let go of her smile, losing a foot of height as her posture sagged. "Why not go have a few drinks and relax. We can discuss that another day." Her eyes trailed across the colony to a point in the distance where hunks of metal lay in a pile. I stared at what she had put her attention on for a moment, then realized what I saw.

Between the implant network and what data Proxy could beam down to me from the *Fidelis*, my augmented reality interface informed me that this was the wreck of a battle cruiser of unknown origin. It had fallen, yes, but something told me it was just the first of many.

"We're not safe, are we?"

Karianna nodded. "The galaxy is no quiet place. Even some among us just wish to see the world burn."

"And what does that mean?"

She chuckled. "Now that story, there's a five-drink minimum."

Shelly sidled up beside me, a satisfied look on her face. I took hold of her hand and squeezed.

"Five drink minimum, you say?" I furrowed my brows at Karianna. Shelly's eyes widened at the prospect.

"Five drinks," Karianna confirmed.

"Then we better get started."

"I'm going to have a headache tomorrow, aren't I?" Shelly asked.

Karianna ran her mechanical fingers through her hair. "Seems like it, toots."

"You wouldn't happen to have any Deadly Force, would you?" I asked as we worked our way into the crowds of distant humanity, Mom and Dad eagerly waiting up ahead.

AFTERWARD

First of all, I'd like to say thank you for coming along on this journey. This book, this series has been a lifetime in the making. Writing is something that isn't just an activity done when sitting at a keyboard, it's a refinement of ideas the subconscious mind works through every day of your life. As I am writing this, no doubt in the back of my head there are other stories being spun, new pathways of thinking unlocked. This is not because I am special, but because I am human, as are you. We were born to be storytellers, to be explorers of thought and consciousness. This is how we express ourselves, how we make sense of the world around us.

I hope you enjoyed this book. Ever since its release, I have asked myself a thousand times if the opening act was the right choice. You no doubt had certain feelings about it, watching a kid in a space opera grow up in real-time instead of the standard sweeping montage that ended in a boom—then he's an adult. But I felt as if Milo deserved more than a few bullet points in his upbringing. It was a choice I made as an artist to do something I hadn't seen before, and it either makes readers curious, or turns them away, but it's a choice I made. Could I have sprinkled this through the rest of the chapters? Yes. May we see a future edition like that? Maybe. This is for now what it is. To put this book in a wider context, the series overall is a kind of coming of age for not just Milo, but humanity itself. It is an awakening. A realization. A shift in universal perspective. So, if you felt lost at the start, and were in unfamiliar territory for the genre, you were not alone; you were with Milo himself seeking identity and acceptance. So many of us are Milo, or have had childhood experiences like him.

But when I was a child, I thought like a child, acted like a child, and when I became an adult, I put aside childish things. It's time for us to grow up, but in doing so, let's not lose our sense of wonder, of curiosity. The Universe calls to you; it calls to us all.

Welcome to the journey, Cosmic Traveler. It's good to have you here.

J Fitzpatrick Mauldin, March 2025

BOOK ONE OF THE FOUNDRY MIGHT BE AT A CLOSE,

BUT THERE'S MORE TO COME…

**IF YOU ENJOYED THIS BOOK, BE SURE TO LEAVE A
RATING/REVIEW.**

Unlock the Mysteries of The Foundry

Extras: Maps, Original Music, Stories, and more.

THE FOUNDRY

NOVELS AND SHORT STORIES

J Fitzpatrick Mauldin is a science fiction writer based in Atlanta, Georgia, best known for the hard science fiction first contact series The Foundry, which was featured in Kirkus Reviews. A technology expert and nationwide business leader by trade, he serves thousands of professionals in achieving their dreams while nurturing an insatiable passion for world-building and fiction. A father of two, husband, and lover of role-playing and strategy video games (though he's terrible at Baldur's Gate), he is also an amateur scientist with aspirations to pursue a PhD in an undefined, esoteric field. His fiction aims to offer readers immersive worlds to escape the noise of everyday life and inspire them to see the best in their fellow humans who ride alongside on this cosmic journey.

GET YOUR FREE E-BOOK & AUDIO BOOK, SIGN UP FOR OUR EMAIL LIST: www.jfitzpatrickmauldin.com
"A cunning young girl comes face to face with an interstellar threat when her mother and grandfather are murdered aboard their ship while making contact with a mysterious entity. Alone, and with no way home, Bellamy makes a deal with an alien intelligence to chase the signal of her mother's soul to a facility light-years away, in the hope she might be resurrected and the two of them reunited." – Chasing the Signal (The Foundry 0.5)

Follow on:

 facebook.com/jfmauld

 @jfitzpatrickmauldin

 @jfitzpatrickmauldin

A PREVIEW OF THE TRANSCENDENCE:

BOOK 2 OF THE FOUNDRY

CHAPTER 1

The fate of humanity was undecided, and I wasn't sure if I could change that. We were here. We were alive. We'd seen progress. And yet, I couldn't shake the feeling deep down in my gut that the rug was about to be pulled out from under us.

Someone was going to screw it all up.

On the hillside beside Perry's bar, I stood watching as twilight on Novae was pushed back by fire, thinking to myself the entire time: *How much longer can we keep this up? When is the other shoe going to drop?*

A wingless shuttle in the shape of an aeronautical lifting body descended from orbit, the brightness of its drive flame lengthening the shadows cast by nearby trees, their large, fan-like leaves dancing along the dappled slopes northeast of the fledgling human colony of Novae. I could only hope this expedition brought us good news and not more disappointment. We'd find out soon enough.

Orange and white fusion exhaust reflected back in the eyes of many a creature, who all took flight in response to the unexpected light and noise, hiding themselves someplace safe, someplace finding prey might be easier. Among them were flocks of the bird-like analogs native to this temperate world, wings spread wide, as well as an assortment of scavenging mammals no larger than wildcats who preferred keeping out of sight.

From the shuttle's belly, landing struts extended, their edges glimmering, making contact with the landing platform. Once firmly on solid ground, the shuttle's engines died, and I was left with only artifacts in my vision, purple spots like upside-down teardrops preventing any chance of stargazing. I tried to rub these blots away with the heels of my palms out of instinct, but that never worked. Not really.

The rumble of the shuttle's engines translated across the landscape to me and was gone, the thump of music from the patio over my shoulder rushing back in to fill the void. Patrons whooped and hollered at its arrival, before returning to their drinking, their talking, their dancing. There were no shortage of momentary distractions tonight at Invictus.

I wondered, who'd gone out? Where did they go? It was likely a set of scientists from the Security and Exploration Arm. Maybe even Mom or Dad. I could use my neural implants to ping the local network and check, but with all the outages eating up our meager bandwidth, too many frivolous queries, I decided not to overburden our systems. I only hoped they'd found something good out there. The better we understood our new world, where the dangers were, what resources lay in wait, the better our chances for survival.

The year was 03 NCE, the third year of the Novae Common Era. We lived in a frontier colony in every sense of the word, hanging off the edge of anything humanity ever thought possible, and yet, here we were. We were surviving. The Isoptera had not killed us at the first Foundry facility, or on our own ship, nor had they the crew of the *Brilliance*—another United Exploration Initiative FICSE Mission ship, whose people lived here with us. The Gene Brokers had not irrevocably altered our DNA, beyond the small modifications on Creatus that had kept us from dying from the silica dust we were breathing in. With a few unlikely friends and the Foundry's unusual brand of assistance, humanity had persisted. We'd traveled to an unknown place, made contact with a fathomless alien intelligence, been hurled across the Milky Way through the Wandering Gate, and found ourselves on a world untouched by the unforgiveable sins of sentient life. A world without war, without crime, without so much of what we left behind on Earth. We could start over in this place. Stay forever. A society of the best and brightest, built on abundance and logic, not scarcity and emotion.

We just had to figure out the abundance part.

Novae had not been our intended destination. The UEI had borne a world-wide project that all of Earth bought into, not just with their minds, but with their pocketbooks. Taxes had been levied in almost every industrialized country to build five massive, fusion-powered starships set to discover the nature of the signal the Foundry sent to us. When we'd left

Earth, everything was in shambles. Climate change had created a vast disparity between the haves and have-nots. Population growth was off the charts, unsustainable. The air was becoming unfit to breathe. Economies were pushed well beyond the breaking point. Our species was desperate. Then a voice from the dark said, *'Hello, humanity. We are the Foundry, come see us soon'*. Something in that signal, a feeling, an impression, told us everything would be okay. That the Foundry would help us survive. This became our mission, the only mission: FICSE, Foundry Intent, Contact and Save Earth.

Five ships set off for five different stars: the *Brilliance, Galileo, Star Stream, Revelation*, and of course, my childhood home, the *Vasco Da Gama*. Three went into the dark and were never heard from again. Two ships, ours and the *Brilliance*, made contact with the Foundry at different facilities. Through this process, we learned that the Foundry itself was dedicated to "Protecting Life." It sought to awaken the Universe's collective consciousness by helping fledgling species like our own survive and thrive. Yet there were rules. We still didn't fully understand what those were. All we knew was that it disabled our ships and after a series of tests, it gave us new ships, better ships. It was never hostile, like the Isoptera or Gene Brokers. but it was not always a friend. We did not know who was in control of it, if anything, or what all its motivations might be, but it helped us survive. We were grateful.

We had kept good on our original mission. We made contact and were still doing what we could to determine the Foundry's intent. As for saving Earth… Novae kind of put that on hold.

"They're back," my wife, Shelly Williams Hughes remarked, sneaking up beside me and giving me a start. I hadn't heard her approach, with all the commotion. "Hope the survey went well."

My lips compressed into a hard line. "Same here. As much as the Foundry has helped us, you'd think…well…"

"You'd think it would have given us a little more than this?" Shelly supplied. "We've been given just enough to get by. Just enough to get started. Access to a few 3D nano printers, a dwindling supply of staple foods, and orbital defense provided by your and Karianna's ships. All things we need, sure, but it still looks like they want us to stand on our own two feet."

"You've been going over Johan's estimates again, haven't you?"

She frowned. "I have. Every month the Foundry is giving us a little less charity. Within five or six months we'll have to be self-sufficient, or people will begin to starve. Think we can retreat back into the Foundry vessels? Is that even an option?"

"I don't think so." I shook my head, considering the idea. "Not unless we're leaving for good. We put down roots. I suppose it wants to see us make use of them."

"Unwritten rules…"

"Certainly not posted ones. Typical Foundry. Hold us accountable to a set of laws and procedures without telling us what they are."

I turned to face her, and saw her body silhouetted by the light of white glow ropes and globes within the open-air bar. It was strange, but despite not being able to see her face in the dark, I knew her expression. Hopeful with a touch of cheer, a half-smile, encouraging. Ever optimistic, just like her father. I reached out and took her hands in mine, placing a kiss on the knuckles of her right hand.

This was my wife. My wife. The love of my life. The woman I had wanted to be with since the first time we doodled pictures in school aboard the *Vasco Da Gama*. No matter where the universe took me, I needed her at my side. She'd been saved from the ills of the Gene Brokers by the likes of the Melcorin, no thanks to me, and I could have kissed the leathery, blue-skinned bastards for it—if they had allowed me.

After getting settled on this world, I had popped the question, using a ring made of junk metal and a piezo electric crystal I'd found in a broken transmitter. Our friend Mary had officiated the quiet ceremony on a hillside to the east of the colony, my parents and a few friends present, and it was done, Shelly in white, her long dress flowing in the wind, me dressed in black, a leather jacket with a crimson, razor-sharp edge blossom pinned dangerously to its right lapel. We'd given our vows, kissed, and tripped over one another's feet as we spun to face our audience, the two of us tumbling onto the dirt in a heap. The blossom had cut me on the arm in the fall, drawing blood, but I'd hardly felt the pain as the purest form of laugher escaped us.

Shelly squeezed my fingers.

"We'll be fine," I sighed, and let go. My attention fell on my right hand, the end of the ivory-and-gold prosthetic arm given to me after the *donation* of my arm to the Foundry. My fingers flexed like flesh but were anything but. Four years of subjective time I'd had this thing, and the matching leg. I wasn't sure if I'd ever get used to it, but at least I wasn't the only freak who'd made a donation. The donation was a part of me now, a reminder of how I'd changed since leaving Earth, of what I'd given up.

The Foundry protects life.

I raised my eyes once more. "FICSE mission folk are tough. We've been through worse. We'll get through this too."

"Funny thing," she started, her tone wistful, hair falling into her eyes, "you dreamed of touching stars, but in the end found yourself digging in the dirt."

"Such is life." I brushed her curls back behind her ear, allowing her eyes to glimmer in the dark. "We all have to do our part. Maybe I can help with the food crisis and cut back a bit."

"You?" She patted my belly. "No. You're already skin and bones. You eat any less and they'll think you're some *moleque* from the *favelas* who snuck onto Novae."

I chuckled. "You've been hanging around Mom, haven't you?"

"Portuguese is a wonderful language."

"You guys want a drink?" an older middle-aged man with bug-like optics asked us, appearing just outside the open-air bar, a pair of glass mason jars in one hand, a jug of sloshing amber liquid in the other. Perry was always an excellent host, but now wasn't the time.

"I'd rather not wake up feeling like my head is in a vice tomorrow morning," Shelly replied before I had the chance.

"Did you say headache?" he asked, shocked. The goggles over his eyes, meant to replace his vision after a failed experiment had taken it, made a whirring noise as they adjusted focus. "A headache? No. No. No. I've got it all worked out now. That Santi-berry business stuff I made last. I'll admit, it was bad. There's a protein in the fruit that caused all that mess. It's fine now. We're using Yellow Rondure. My sweetgums says it's safe, by the way. Tastes just like an apple. I promise, one sip of this, and you'll be transported to the shady groves of red deliciouses back on Earth. No shoddy products at Invictus, not anymore."

"What if I have no idea what an apple tastes like?" I asked, being honest. I was pretty sure I'd eaten an apple aboard the *Vasco Da Gama* at least once, but I had to have been no older than six. Trees didn't travel well through deep space. They needed room to grow and thrive, a place like this, not a garden in a steel box.

Perry's brows crinkled at the edges of his visor. Pretty sure he was narrowing his eyes at me. "Well, I suppose it doesn't matter. Tastes good either way. Come on, let me pour you some."

I raised my hands in objection. "Not today, barkeep. A part of me knows trying this today is a bad idea."

"Bad idea? No, no. A bad idea is being a fish who thinks a hook is a great way to get a lip piercing."

Shelly gave me a withering look, clearly unamused. Perry's jokes hadn't gotten any better with time. "Look, Perry, when the Cultural Center is complete, please don't start up a comedy night. I'd hate to have to boycott you."

"I will have you know that everyone at Invictus loves my jokes!"

"But after how many drinks?" She pointed at the amber jug he carried.

He scowled. "So mean."

What Perry lacked in comedy, he made up for a hundred-fold in other ways. I had known him almost my entire life, and we had become close friends in the past five to six years of subjective time. Acting as a kind of therapist, he had helped me work through much of my mixed feelings over my parents, and been an important part of my crew aboard the *Fidelis*, the ship the Foundry had gifted me.

"Here's a good one," Perry went on, ignoring Shelly's annoyance. "If April showers bring May flowers, what do May flowers bring?"

I rolled my eyes. "What, Perry? What do they bring?"

"Pilgrims!" he said, raising the sloshing jug above his head in exclamation. "Ah! Ah? Come on. It was great! Didn't you get it?"

"No. I don't get it."

Shelly grinned and patted me on the back. "Seasons, love. He's talking about seasons and the start of America."

"Oh. Wait. Like, the *Mayflower*? The ship? Columbus?"

"Yes, like the ship."

"Still don't see how that's supposed to be funny."

"Come on," Perry said, then laughed. "It's great. Pilgrims…"

Across the colony came a thundering boom, and the lights and music of the bar went dead, leaving my ears buzzing in their absence, my vision filled with spots. The fragile network my implants connected with was no longer present, leaving me feeling empty, exposed. I reached for a weapon on my hip that wasn't there.

The crowd of Invictus began to murmur in alarm.

"Shelly?" I whispered, hand searching in her direction. She took hold of my fingers, and I felt my heart calm if only a little. I blinked several times, trying to adjust to the darkness like I had with the bright lights of the shuttle's engines.

"Christ on a cracker," Perry cursed, and something shattered at his feet, the smell of alcohol in the air strong, burning the hairs of my nose. "Damn it. That's a wasted batch. Nothing to do about it now. Did another one of the generators go down? Or did we run out of feculent coal?"

"Hard to say," Shelly replied, her voice calm as ever. "But the cause doesn't matter right now, we need to get everyone inside. Sawtooths like to hang around in the dark. Pretty sure they might like the taste of humans."

A cool wind whipped over the hillside, pulling at my jacket, reminding me that bundles of quills and rows of teeth were hiding in the dark. Were my mechanical augmentations enough to fight back against this apex fauna? I hadn't put them to the test.

Hand lights began to switch on around us, shooting out at every angle, their sharp lights casting heavy shadows, making it somehow both easier and more difficult to see. Some held theirs in their palms, while others clipped them to their chests. Thank the Universe we had these. It was a moonless night, despite Novae having two, and even with a brilliant view of distant galaxies wheeling overhead, our little settlement seemed swallowed by the void.

Perry edged towards his patrons, careful not to trip over broken glass, and began gathering them up. "Come on everyone, come on. Invictus is closed for the night. Let's get you safely back home. No worries, here, we'll get the power situation worked out."

"What about the backups?" someone asked.

"I don't know if I can walk."

A woman sighed. "I've got you."

"This place needs walls," another grumbled. "A hard day's work behind you and can't even get a drink in peace."

"Calm down," Perry assured them. "We'll sort it all out in the morning."

There came a cry in the dark, a shriek like a large bird with an edge like an idling chainsaw. Commanding shouts came from the other side of the bar towards the center of the colony. Security was sweeping the area, which was good, but people could easily be dragged out into the night with little or no way to stop it.

The hairs on the back of my neck stood on end. That sound meant feline forms stalking the dark around us looking for morsels. A pack of nocturnal hunters with iron-hard quills and mouths jointed too many times to ever be mistaken for terrestrial. They were the stuff of nightmares, which didn't answer to sharp words, screams, or the wild waving of the arms like the other animals might, but only to that of a fully jacketed round. Hunters who embraced the dark and loathed any form of light, for which we now had little. Every ecosystem had apex predators, a creature at the top of the food chain, and sawtooths, well, they sat at the top and called Novae home just like us. The trouble was, they were here first, and they knew this place better than we did.

"Everyone calm down, stay together," Shelly said, helping herd the departing crowd. "Let's get indoors. Storage Warehouse 3 is not far away, just down the hill. We'll be safe in there till they get the lights back on. Afterwards everyone can walk home."

"Perry!" a man called from off in the dark, appearing before us a moment later with a wispy, older woman dressed in dirt-covered overalls at his side. He was broad shouldered, dressed in well-worn work clothes, and bore a shoulder-length crop of golden hair as well as a thick, golden beard.

"Lance," Perry said, relieved. "Good to see you."

"Alyssa and I are headed over to work on the generator."

"Okay," he replied, and went to the woman, giving her a tight hug. "Glad you're okay, sweet cheeks."

"I'm fine," she said, kissing him on the lips, having cocked her head to avoid her nose colliding with his goggles. "Though a touch tired of putting out fires. I signed up to save the world, not be a stinkin' pioneer."

The kiss put a bit of steel in Perry's back, standing him upright. It did wonders for your confidence, having someone in your life who loves and believes in you.

"Hey, Lance," I said, reaching out my prosthetic hand in greeting, for which he accepted. "We're going to get these drunken idiots to safety. After that, need any help? I'm at your disposal."

Lance Brittan shook his head. "Nah, we got this. Not sure what the issue is yet, but it's likely we ran out of feculent coal. Great biofuel, sure, easy to get and all, but a pain in the ass to burn right. This will be the last time we make that mistake."

"You're doing great," Shelly assured him. "I've gone over the numbers a hundred times. At a specific temperature, that fuel burns three times as fast. Unfortunately, that temperature can change based on far too many factors. Humidity mostly. Compression too. Our Arm will keep at it. You have my word."

"Abundant fuel. Couldn't be simple."

"Never. And we're working on it. Okay?"

"I know. I know." Lance spun around and raised his voice, shouting at someone I couldn't see in the dark, "Hey! Donaldson! Anyone out there sweeping for those things? It's too dark out there. You tell Chevelle she needs to get your asses organized."

It had taken years for Lance and me to reach a good place. He had been Shelly's other half several times growing up, especially during the period of years she and I hadn't been talking. The son of one of our former pilots, he had lived a life of additional privileges, much like her, and as a result he had turned out to be a bit of a self-centered adult. Time and circumstance had softened his edges. Sure, he could still be an asshole, but he was a good kind of asshole. Most of the time.

We urged the crowd towards the center of the colony, down the main road. I could see armed personnel weaving through rows of buildings made of smooth stone, flashlights mounted at the end of their weapons. Chevelle and Donaldson had roused the minutemen and were hunting sawtooths. If there was one thing we'd gotten good at over the past few years, it was getting our asses in motion during a crisis. You just couldn't live in a crisis all the time.

A few warning shots were fired near the edge of Eighth Street. Colonists shouted in response and redoubled their efforts to keep everyone moving.

"Milo," a voice rang out inside my head. *"Milo."*

I skidded to a halt and closed my eyes.

"Everything okay?" Shelly asked, taking hold of my arm.

I shook my head in response. "Proxy," I whispered, and pointed up to the sky.

Her face blanched. "Oh."

I took a deep breath and opened the connection. My little, all-knowing, orange-striped tuxedo cat needed to talk, and at a time like this, I couldn't imagine it was anything good. Rarely did the Foundry's AI have something positive to say.

"Milo," Proxy reported, images without context appearing in my mind as it spoke, *"I have detected five unknown vessels on course to hit high orbit. I recommend we investigate."*

"A little busy down here," I replied, using thoughts, not words. The trajectories of the arrivals appeared within my mind's eye in wireframe above Novae, a pentagonal formation screaming towards the surface. If this squadron of alien ships did not change course, they would hit the outer atmosphere of Novae in less than an hour.

"I have been keeping track of your situation," Proxy went on. *"And while it might be a bit chaotic on the surface, my assessment is that these contacts are potentially more dangerous than your local wildlife troubles."*

"Who are they? Jevox? Melcorin? One of the others?"

"As I said…" The AI sounded somewhat annoyed for a moment. *"They are unknown. They are of a design with which we are not familiar."*

"Hah. So, the almighty Foundry has no idea what they are?"

"We do not know everything, Milo. And sometimes, even when we do, we do not have ready access to that information."

"Okay. Okay. Fine. Tactical analysis?"

"I have already given it to you. Get into orbit and we will intercept them."

I closed the connection.

"Shit," I growled. "I have to go. Something's headed our way, but I can't leave you down here in the middle of a crisis."

Shelly shook her head. "We'll be fine. On the other hand, if something destroys us from orbit…"

"You could go with me," I offered. "There's no safer place than on my ship. They've got this covered down here."

She leaned in and placed a kiss on my cheek. "Be careful, love."

With a sense of resignation, I let out a long sigh. "You're right. You're right."

I turned to leave, the lights from the crowded group fading over my shoulder, leaving me in the dark. Though I knew my way to the platform by memory, I found myself tripping over rocks and catching my feet.

A growl came from the shadows off to my right, that idling machine shriek, and I took off running. I could see the outline of my shuttle over the trees ahead, its shape blocking out a series of flashing lights. Though I had the mechanical augmentations of my arm and leg, it did not make me much faster.

Something hard slammed against me in the dark, knocking me off balance yet not onto the ground. I twisted around, arms raised, my hand light shining in the direction that it had gone. Gravel shifted on my left, tiny stones crunching, then on my right. An ominous, guttural purr rose a series of needles across my back. I was not prepared to fight a sawtooth. I was unarmed and alone.

From the dark came three bursts of light and crackling booms. A bleeding alien form slid to a halt at my feet, its multi-jointed face and jaw twitching.

"God, I freakin' hate nature," Karianna growled, walking into the glow of my hand light. "You okay?" I raised my shaking hand, pointing the light at her face. The blade of a woman raised her prosthetic hand, metal bracelets jingling, and squinted her eyes. "The hell, dude."

"Sorry," I breathed out, lowering my light. "Thanks."

She shook her head at me. "Whatever." And reached for a pistol tucked in the back of her jeans, tossing it to me.

I caught the weapon and clutched it tight.

"Milo, what did you plan on doing? Karate chopping the damn things?"

"Forgot my gun at home," I replied.

"Good thing I carry a spare."

"Look, I'm a lover, not a fighter."

She barked a laugh, the serious features of her hawkish face exaggerating. "Says the man who has one of the most powerful war machines in existence waiting for him overhead."

"It's a responsibility, not something I was looking for."

"Mmmhmm."

A moment later the two of us were hopping into our respective Swift Shuttles, stripping out of our clothes and submerging ourselves into orbs of clear liquid eight feet across. After the near miss, I was more than grateful for my ship's protection.

As we sank to the bottom of the Star Spheres, a series of tentacle-like umbilicals interfaced with our bodies, providing us with air, with nutrients, with a constant feed of information. Connections sprang to life, and in an instant, we were one with our ships, and the ships were one with us.

Our triangular shuttles ignited their engines and screamed off into the night at a breakneck twenty-five Gs of acceleration, a delta in velocity so great it would turn an unprotected human into a pile of mush. They sliced through the atmosphere like a pair of curved and jagged blades, but Karianna and I felt no discomfort. Our Star Spheres, the machines the Foundry built for us to pilot our ships, were specially designed to protect us from intense G forces, their fluid distributing the pressure such that no one part of our body was overtaxed. This made flying any Foundry-made craft from within a Star Sphere feel as if it were an extension of your own body, not just a machine at your command. The Swift Shuttle was no exception.

"Two minutes for coupling to the Fidelis,*"* I heard Proxy say before the cat appeared beside me.

My body was floating in a field of endless stars, both outside of the shuttle, and not yet within the *Fidelis,* a virtual environment to help me control and contextualize the information given to me. I had three-dimensional, free movement in local space, complete with prismatic visual feedback and streams of data, granted through a mental projection the ship gave me from within the sphere.

I reached down and gave Proxy a scratch behind the ear and the cat began to purr. While it might not be a true feline, and just some weird AI facsimile, this warmed my heart nonetheless.

As the Swift Shuttle broke free of Novae's atmosphere, Prima, the equatorial continent our colony was founded upon, became a shrinking expanse of a few scattered lights, this side of the planet shrouded by night. The *Fidelis* was up ahead, beckoning me, a skyscraper-sized hunk of white and gold the shape of a crystal shard, flat at one end, jagged at the other. North of it, towards the planet's pole ten thousand one hundred and fifteen kilometers away, was Karianna's ship. It was made of the same material as mine, but instead mostly gold and black, and was shaped like a three-dimensional diamond printed on a deck of playing cards.

"You ready to kick some ass?" Karianna asked, her voice echoing into my virtual environment.

"Only if we need to," I replied. "Not every answer comes at the end of a gun barrel."

"You're no fun."

"Let me ask first. Have we gotten executive approval?"

"Who's going to stop us?"

"We live in a democracy, not a dictatorship."

"Fine, fine." She paused for a moment. *"Novae control, this is Karianna Torlen of the Reverie. Requesting orders of engagement for unknown spacecraft headed towards the colony."*

A moment passed. No response came from the surface.

"Don't be a smart ass," I replied.

"Power is out, Mr. Hughes. Looks like we're going to have to use our best judgement."

"Fine. Let's do everything in our power to keep from firing. If they get too close, we'll do what needs doing."

"Much better."

"We don't need to make enemies unless we have to."

Karianna let out an exasperated sigh. *"Ugh. I guess you're right. Not as fun, though."*

"You want to blow things up? We'll go bust some rocks in the asteroid belt later."

"Now you got yourself a date, fly boy."

"Sorry, miss. If you haven't noticed, I'm taken."

"Alright, alright. Stick with your wife, or whatever. Bring her along."

"She doesn't care much for flying."

"Really? Well, that's too bad. Flying is life."

My Swift Shuttle slipped into a port on the belly of the *Fidelis* and locked into place. There was no time to move into my primary Star Sphere near the bow of the ship, nor was there any need. I was aboard my battleship, and I could control it from anywhere within.

The targets were less than two hundred thousand kilometers from our position and screaming towards the surface. I ramped up the main drive and brought the *Fidelis* around, activating the Mercurial Integumentum as I did so, the protective shield of nanobots swarming around me like a second skin.

"Proxy," I said, peering down at the cat that weaved itself between my floating legs, rubbing them with its face. "Have you attempted to make contact with the targets?"

"Yes. No response." It purred against me.

"Do we not understand their language, or are they just being difficult?"

"Hard to say."

"Let's try and scare them off. Power up the Para Lux array. I'm going to get between them and the planet. Karianna, why don't we take a wide formation. You head them off so they can't cut around and go for the colony."

The unidentified ships drew closer, their shapes resolving into something substantial. I got my first glimpse at them and frowned. Each were about as large as an acre of land and were shaped like starfish, their orange and black hulls covered in fractal patterns that reminded me of the inside of sunflower blooms or the outside of pinecones. While they appeared organic at a distance, nothing about the scans that returned supported this idea. Far as I knew, there was nothing truly organic living in the void.

"Any weapons?" I asked Proxy.

"There are high-energy signatures near the center of mass in excess of ten terawatts, but that is all I can see. They are fusion-powered. Not of Foundry make."

"That's reassuring."

"Hardly. If they were of Foundry make, we would know what we are up against. Tactical analysis is much simpler that way. This is an unknown."

A valid point. This was one of the reasons the Foundry recycled all arriving ships when a species visited its facilities, regardless of their technological level. It gave every species who took their assistance an even playing field.

"Almost in position," Karianna said, *"they're still coming."*

"Proxy, keep trying to make contact. Karianna, let's give them a light show."

"Hell yeah."

The Para Lux arrays on both the *Fidelis* and *Reverie* blossomed as we began to cast beams of high-intensity light all around the unknown ships, careful not to cross their paths and slice them in two. The rainbow beams of pure light flashed within our virtual spaces but were hardly visible on the visual spectrum without any atmospheric gases to reflect against.

We got the desired effect. The starfish-like craft broke formation and began to scatter, fusion drives flashing bright. Two turned the opposite direction, slowing themselves to head away from us at a dangerous, fifty G shift, while two angled themselves to miss Novae and head off into the void. The last of them, however, deviated only a little.

"That one's headed for the surface," Karianna said.

I threw the *Fidelis* into a hard burn and moved to intercept. While this ship could travel faster than fifty percent of light speed, it was massive and required considerable effort to turn. The starfish ship shot past us.

"We have to scare it off."

"Fighters?"

"No ancillary pilots on board, just us. I can't control more than about four at a time by myself."

"This isn't a dogfight, Hughes. Throw a damn swarm at them, they won't know the difference."

She had a point. "Okay. Proxy, launch a wing of drone fighters."

As I pivoted the *Fidelis* around to pursue, a half-dozen diamond shaped fighters shot from my belly and rushed towards the unknown ship. I did my best to plot courses that might make them appear as if they had physical pilots.

A few thousand kilometers separated the invader and the surface of Novae. My heart thundered in my chest.

"Get ready to shoot it down," Karianna said.

"No. We wait."

"Do you see how close it is to Novae? I'm serious. We have to kill it. Now—while we can."

"We don't know what it is or what it wants."

"I'm taking it down."

"Wait! Please wait. We can't make more enemies."

Karianna screamed into the open channel, *"Pacifist!"*

"I've been called worse," I mumbled.

Just as the starfish was about to hit the upper atmosphere, the first of our fighters reached it. Without preamble, the unknown ship took a hard turn in response and banked upward, heading off into open space, a trail of blue, ionized gas at its tail.

"They are retreating," Proxy reported. "I would keep an eye on the closest of them, but the rest are accelerating away."

"That was an unnecessary risk," Karianna told me.

I swallowed. She was right, but did attacking someone who showed us no direct threat make any sense either? In the end, no weapons had been used. No overtly aggressive actions taken. They had merely entered our airspace as explorers while keeping their lips sealed.

"They'll come back, ya know?" Karianna ventured when I had not responded.

I shook my head. "Not this time."
"We'll see about that. We'll see."